I0674237

First Life – Volume II

SIGN OF THE GUARDIAN

By

Ryan Logan

ISBN: **0-996739394**

ISBN-13: **978-0-996739399**

FOR

FAYE EMERYL CLINE

CONTENTS

ACKNOWLEDGMENTS

First and foremost, I need to thank my family and friends for your love, support and encouragement to keep going. And as always, thanks to my editor, Sharon Hess. Lastly, thank you to all my readers, who have made it possible for me to write the second book. Your reviews and high praise mean the world to me.

CHAPTER ONE

STRIPPED

The outcry to see color once again had fallen on nature's deaf ears. It was a winter like no other for the Jethian people. A thick blanket of snow and ice had muted the landscape for months. From the earliest times on Polizar, the "people of the mountain," as the flatlanders called them, were a hearty people and long winters were part of their lives. But the cold that had set upon them was different this time: harsher, longer, and crueler than anyone could remember. Spring was late and the winter stores were running low.

A few miles below Jeth, nestled between two mountain peaks, sat a small mining village, Froman, the northernmost watch post of the mountain city. Winter had set in on the village so quickly that for two months the watch post had been cut off entirely from Jeth. Many times the men tried to clear the mountain roads to the south, but the heavy snow and chilling winds were relentless. For every foot they cleared another would take its place and more. And the unnerving echo of cracking tree branches was a constant reminder of how powerless they all really were. All they could do was wait it out and hope for the melt to begin.

At the foot of the mountain range, near the coast of Shorehaven, the weather was cool and quite pleasant; it was colder than years past, but still enjoyable for the tourists. Haydon stiffly walked down the gangplank and stepped onto the dock to the pure sound of the dock master's bell. He closed his eyes and breathed deeply the crisp winter air, relieved to be on land once again. His joints ached from the cramped accommodations.

Even with all his faults, Haydon appreciated beauty in his own way. Not that he recognized that simple things were beautiful to behold, like a dewdrop that clings to a rose petal in the morning light or a low-lying bough sweeping the forest floor in the shade of the evening. But rather, his appreciation encompassed a grander scope of things, the power to create mighty kingdoms and bring them into subjugation. Glancing at the foothills, the exiled ambassador lifted his eyes to the cloud-covered mountain peaks of Jeth, his new home. He inhaled another breath, deeper than before, expanding his lungs until they burned, expelling the last of the musty air from the ship.

Taking in the scene around him, Haydon noticed the Shorehaven docks were loud with merchants and customers negotiating fair prices on trinkets and warm clothing. Most travelers were expecting warmer weather this time of year, but were happy to outfit themselves with more suitable clothing. It was unusual for no one to be clamoring at Haydon's feet, eager to hear his eloquent tongue spin a short welcome speech. He had dozens of them memorized and with a slight adjustment of names and places, could dazzle anyone and everyone with very few words. But with dozens of people more interested in cheap jewelry and warm socks, he found himself feeling lonely. It was a feeling he was not accustomed to, and quickly the loneliness turned to anger. *He took it all from me, my home, my position, everything*, he thought, stepping slowly down the dock.

"Thanks for the coat, mate," a shabby man spouted, slapping Haydon on the shoulder. "Must have cost you a bundle. Maybe I'll see you at the tavern. The first round's on me."

Haydon raised his chin at the man, feigning interest. He shuddered inside thinking about the previous weeks in the dank hull of a merchant ship, shoulder to shoulder with irreverent men with little to no grasp of proper language.

"I almost didn't recognize you, Master," a hooded man said quietly, stepping up to Haydon. He glanced up and down at the already angered Master, his face and hands grimy with dirt and soot. Trying to lighten Haydon's mood, the hooded man continued, "A beard suits you. You look even more distinguished than the last time we met."

"Do not patronize me, Mirone. I have neither the patience nor the time."

"Of course, Master, my apologies. Everything is in order."

"Good," Haydon replied, glancing around again to make sure no one was watching. "First things first. I need a bath."

Mirone glanced at the man wearing Haydon's coat. "You gave

him your coat?"

"I thought it would mask the odor. I was wrong."

"Do you want me to retrieve it for you?" Mirone asked, slyly reaching for his knife.

"Now is not the time to draw attention to ourselves. Besides, you certainly don't expect me to wear it again, do you?"

"No...of course not, Master," Mirone answered with an air of reverence.

"What a waste," Haydon sighed to himself, shaking his head, watching his original Rothlan overcoat disappear into the crowd. "It was one of a kind."

"Let me take that from you," Mirone insisted, raising his hand toward his master's leather satchel. "You packed light for such a long voyage."

"I didn't have the luxury of packing for my trip, now did I?" He stared at his acolyte blankly.

Mirone paused and swallowed hard. He knew he had taken the conversation as far as he could. "Well...you must be exhausted."

He slung Haydon's satchel over his shoulder and began walking toward the pier. "If you will follow me, I've made accommodations for the night. A warm bath, a hot meal and a soft bed await you at the Twin Willows Inn. I spared no expense."

"You mean *I* spared no expense."

"Of course," Mirone agreed. "Get your rest. Tomorrow you will be joining two of the most experienced mountain guides in Jeth. The northern pass is almost impassable and getting worse every day. Soon there will be no way in. But Gerard and Chaterig assured me they could get you as far as Froman Village. You'll have to wait there until spring. There's no way into Jeth."

Mirone led the way through the marketplace, stopping only once to buy a warm cloak for his master to help conceal his identity.

Twin Willows had earned its reputation for opulent accommodations, customer service and the finest dining and amenities for the wealthy and those of prominent status. The front door of the inn was wider than six men and had been skillfully built with thick timbers hewn from ancient thornwood trees. Haydon and Mirone confidently walked through the threshold and were met by the warm pine-scented air from the towering fireplace on the opposite wall. Plush furniture lined the walls accented by dark hardwood end tables with exquisitely carved legs. To the left was a grand wooden staircase twisting up to the balcony overlooking the entire foyer. A few chattering people were standing on the balcony enjoying drinks and the warmer air that collected on the second floor. Haydon could hear the innkeeper boasting to a small group about the fact that everything used to construct the inn was either harvested or mined from the Jethian mountain range. And, of course, the food was grown and harvested in Shorehaven and the surrounding foothills. Even the candles were made from beeswax collected from local hives. It was a story Haydon had heard many times before.

The foyer was busy with a couple dozen patrons all going in different directions. Some were headed back to the wharf for hours of haggling over trinkets, some were off to the hot springs and others were just exploring the many wonderful adventures of Shorehaven.

Mirone spied the front desk and nodded to Haydon to follow him.

"Welcome to Twin Willows, gentlemen," an exuberant man exclaimed, looking up from his ledger. He stood up behind the front desk and straightened his finely tailored tunic, closing the books. It was his typical rehearsed salutation, to greet every patron with a smile and a degree of respect. Twin Willows was, after all, one of the finest inns on the western coast, if not the finest, depending on whom you asked. But as the man darted his eyes from Mirone, who was modestly dressed, to the dirty, bearded man in the cloak, his demeanor changed. "Can I help you?" he asked, looking down his nose at Haydon and Mirone.

"Yes," Mirone shot back, sensing the clerk's arrogance. "I believe you have a suite for my friend here."

The clerk shot Mirone another obligatory smile. "Are you sure you won't consider other accommodations? There's a fine inn near the end of the wharf. Just got new beds about five years ago. They might even have some day-old fish and warm bread. Tell 'em Jink from the Willows sent you. They'll take care of you." He turned from the front desk and sat at the small table, opening his ledger again. He dipped his quill and began writing numbers by the warm light of a candle.

Haydon noticed Mirone's face flush with anger while reaching for the knife at his waist. The Master subtly stepped up to Mirone, brushed the side of his arm with his fingers, and cleared his throat, which did two things: stopped Mirone from making a dire mistake and caught the attention of the clerk once again.

The clerk sighed heavily and deliberately slapped his quill on the table. "Can I help you?" he spouted. He then slammed his book shut. The force of the shutting pages blew out the candle and splattered some of the melted wax on the table, which made him even more impatient.

"Good sir," Haydon began, "if you would simply open your guestbook, you will find that—."

"I have much work to do," Jink interrupted. "If you don't mind, I would like to finish it before the next ship arrives. I'll have many patrons to tend to, customers who can pay for the privilege of staying at the Willows."

Mirone aggressively stepped close to the desk, slamming his fist on the thick stone slab. "This is outrageous! Do you know to whom you are speaking, you pathetic little man?"

Panicked, the clerk shot to his feet and stumbled over his chair, the sound of which echoed in the high-ceilinged foyer. A few patrons on their way to the lower hot springs stopped to see what the commotion was.

Haydon said nothing, only watched the frightened clerk dance around his tipped chair. Mirone had his skills, but diplomacy was not one of them.

"Can I help you, gentlemen?" a deep and distinguished voice asked through the clanking sound of the chair.

"Sir, these…men insist they have a room with us, but obviously they don't." Jink puffed out his chest and brushed off his tunic with the back of his fingers.

"Let's all calm down," the innkeeper said, turning toward Haydon and Mirone. "Now…what seems to be the problem, gentlemen?"

"Your underling here has insulted us twice. I promise there will not be a third time," Mirone seethed, lunging at the clerk, feigning an attack.

The clerk recoiled in fear and tripped over his chair again, which made Mirone smirk.

"Sir," Haydon interrupted, "as I asked your associate, if you simply look in your guestbook, you will find everything is in good order. The name is Mr. Westlyn."

The innkeeper froze. "Mr. Westlyn, you say?" He stared intently into Haydon's eyes for a few seconds and a faint smile crept across his lips. He flipped through the pages of the guestbook, not really reading anything and pointed to a random name. "Ah…yes…Mr. Westlyn, here you are. Our finest suite is ready. If you will follow me, I will personally escort you to your suite. This way."

Haydon turned to Mirone and glanced at the clerk, who was muttering to himself while scraping up the spilt wax. "Be sure everything is in order," Haydon whispered.

"I will take care of everything," Mirone answered respectfully, nodding his head. "Get your rest."

The sturdy steps barely made a sound as the innkeeper and Haydon walked side by side up the twisting staircase, firm as the day it was constructed. As they rounded the balcony, Haydon looked down upon the foyer, watching the privileged go about their petty business completely unaware of the darkness he would eventually unfurl on them and the world.

Together, Haydon and the innkeeper entered a long arching hallway filled with thornwood doors adorned with gilded trim. On each side of every door hung a sconce, which held a glowing candle infused with the essence of pine needles. The aroma was mild, sweet and meant to relax patrons and put them at ease.

"It seems there will be an opening in your staff tomorrow morning, old friend," Haydon said as if he were making light

8

conversation. "Digging is such a pain this time of year."

"I understand, my Master," the innkeeper replied without hesitation. "I hardly recognize you. Even this close you could have walked right past me unnoticed. How long has it been since we last spoke?"

"This is no time for pleasantries, Hutrok."

"No, of course not, Master."

Hutrok walked a few steps in silence and slowed to a near stop in a pool of candlelight. "Is it true? Are you no longer the ambassador? You've been stripped of your position?"

"Word indeed travels quickly in the mountains."

"It does in certain circles. Not everyone knows, but soon they will. Many are uncertain that you can fulfill your promises now. They are saying that you are no match for King Corderian…that you can never take the city now that you are exiled."

"I see," Haydon replied, unfazed by the revelation. "Many, you say?"

"Some, Master," the innkeeper wavered.

"Some? And you, Hutrok, are you also uncertain? Have you entertained the idea that I am less than I say?"

"I am certain, Master. Look around you. This place is mine because of you. I owe you my loyalty."

"I must admit your candor is surprising to me. Most shrink before they can utter such words."

The innkeeper lifted a sconce from the wall and pulled an iron key from his coat pocket. He rattled the key back and forth and opened the door. "Pardon my boldness, Master, but the truth is what you need to hear. The truth will open your eyes. And I would gladly speak it again and again. I at least owe you that."

He held his hand out, letting Haydon enter first. It was a sign of respect.

Haydon stepped through the doorway carefully contemplating Hutrok's words. As he turned around, a rare chuckle escaped his throat. "Well said, Hutrok. It seems my trust in you has been well placed."

Nodding, the innkeeper replied, "Thank you, Master. Will there be anything else?" He placed the sconce back on the wall.

"There is one more thing."

"Yes, what is it?" Hutrok asked, turning back to Haydon, ready to fulfill any of his master's requests.

Haydon glanced to his left and then to his right. They still were alone in the hallway. "I need to get a message to my youngest brother, Thanan," he said quietly. "He is…important to me…to us. Seek out Grimich. You will find him in New Westlyn at the restoration site. He is the foreman there. He will know how to get Thanan the message."

Haydon turned from the door and walked quickly to the desk, passing by a sturdy four-poster bed with a down mattress and silk linens. The suite was spacious and well appointed. It was larger than most homes in the Jethian Mountains.

The beautifully crafted desk sat just below the window, which provided a spectacular view of the Shorehaven coast and the fiery horizon. He opened the drawer, pulled out a piece of parchment, dipped a black feather quill in the inkwell and began writing furiously. Then, with a flourish, Haydon signed the letter with an "H." He then folded the parchment into thirds, taking great care to crease the seams.

"Bring me that candle, Hutrok," the Master commanded. He

took the candle and carefully poured a few drops of melted wax from the well onto the letter and sealed it with his ring. "I'm trusting you to get this to Grimich."

He offered the letter to Hutrok, but he didn't take it.

"What is it? What's wrong?" Haydon queried.

Hutrok pursed his lips, hesitating, not wanting to break the news to his master. "You haven't heard?"

"Heard what, Hutrok?" Haydon asked, growing more impatient by the second.

Hutrok began muttering under his breath. "No, of course you haven't. How could you have? You've been on a ship."

"Tell me now, Hutrok," Haydon demanded, closing the distance between himself and the innkeeper.

"He is not in the city," he replied cryptically.

"You decide now not to speak plainly? What do you mean he is not in the city? And the next words from your tongue better be to the point."

"My apologies, Master. On the same day you were banished from the capital, Thanan too was banished. No one knows why, maybe rebellion. Some say he attacked the king after he exiled you."

Haydon stepped away from his devoted follower and walked to the window. He stared out at the glistening sea, trying to work everything out in his head. Perhaps his influence had worked after all. Maybe Thanan had chosen him over their father.

"Where is he now?" Haydon insisted.

"I don't know. No one knows. There are rumors, but they are just rumors. Some say he may have travelled north, but that's all I know. It's as if he vanished from the face of Polizar."

Haydon withdrew from the innkeeper and turned to the window again, reflecting on his follower's words. He scanned the seemingly endless ocean before him. Towering thunderheads of gold, orange and red had gathered on the horizon. The billowing clouds thrust dramatically upward toward the expansive sky and reflected their array of colors on the glistening sea.

A second later, Haydon caught a glimpse of his reflection in the wavy glass. The glass distorted his face. Having been a virtual prisoner within the dark hulls of six different merchant ships, it was the first time he had seen himself in weeks. He ran his fingers through his wiry black beard. Never before had he had more than a few days' growth. And even though he was hundreds of years old, there still wasn't a single gray hair on his face. His first impulse was to grab a razor and leather strap and shave immediately, but another thought struck him.

"Mirone said that Froman Village has been cut off from Jeth. Is this true?" Haydon asked, still looking at his reflection. He jutted out his jaw and ran his fingers down his scruffy neck trying to discern just how long the hair really was.

"That's correct, Master. The southern road to Jeth is completely impassable and appears it will be that way for months more."

Haydon continued admiring his new look in the reflection. "And how many people are in Froman now?"

"I can't be certain, but this time of year, maybe two hundred, mostly miners who stayed in the mines too long. Why do you ask?" the innkeeper replied, curious by the line of questioning.

It's perfect, Haydon thought. *Two hundred looking for hope…no one to guide them.*

"You know, Hutrok…I think I'm going to keep the beard for a

while," the Master said, changing the subject. He craned his neck back and forth, trying to find fault in his decision, but could find none. "You may go now."

"Yes, Master. I'll be just downstairs if you should need anything."

The innkeeper stepped into the hallway and quietly shut the door behind him, breathing a heavy sigh of relief. It was not an easy thing to deal with the Master alone. One always felt a moment away from death. He glanced left and spotted Mirone casually leaning on the wall fifteen doors down, his face glowing in the candlelight. The assassin had the sole of his foot pressed against the otherwise pristinely painted wall. He scraped his foot down the wall and dropped it to the floor, nodded menacingly at the innkeeper, and then went back to cleaning his thumbnail with his knife, setting Hutrok's nerves even further on edge.

Hutrok shot an uneasy smile at Mirone, then spun quickly in the opposite direction and began walking hastily toward the staircase. Vibrant voices wafting from the foyer beckoned him to walk faster and faster. The long, thick runner dulled his rapid footsteps. And his heart was thumping so hard in his chest he swore he could hear it through their voices. He felt Mirone's stare burning into his skull. He shot a frightened glance over his shoulder, but the hallway was now empty. Mirone had disappeared. The only thing he saw was the subtle flicker of the candle where he had been standing.

As Hutrok neared the foyer balcony he slowed down and composed himself. He exhaled, letting the chills work their way through his body. At the top of the staircase he straightened his posture and descended the stairs wearing his typical gregarious smile and hospitable hands extended outward, welcoming the guests as if nothing had happened.

"Ahh...did you know that those stones were carted all the way from the Bornian River just outside Shorehaven?" the innkeeper announced to a small group of patrons who were warming themselves by the enormous fireplace.

Inside Haydon's suite, the shamed ambassador shed his new cloak and hung it on a coat hook inside the closet. Pivoting around, he took in his opulent surroundings. By his recollection, he had stayed in this particular suite more than 50 times during various summits with Jethian governors and other political figures from the mountain region. He knew every inch of the suite: where the extra pillow was in the linen closet on the third shelf, even where the small chip was in the washroom mirror. But this time was different. He felt haggard, as if his energy were slowly being drained from him. It was a sensation he was not used to.

The bed on the opposite side of the room looked most inviting, but a bath was needed. The smell emanating from his shirt was shockingly pungent. He lowered his nose down to his armpit and recoiled with disgust. Immediately, he tore off the soiled shirt and threw it in the corner, the farthest place from him.

"It should be burned," he said to himself.

There was one thing, however, that he needed to do, something he had to try before bathing or sleeping. It had been plaguing his mind for weeks.

He walked past the bed, gliding his fingers along the silken linens. The expression on his face was focused. He opened a drawer, and taking a pine candle from the nightstand, lit it on a lamp that was hanging on the wall next to his door. He placed the candle in a finely casted borunium silver candlestick on the desk and drew the drapes, darkening the room. One at a time, he moved around the room, snuffing out the lamps and other candles until the only thing lighting the room was the single candle he had taken from his nightstand.

Sitting in the darkness, Haydon let the room around him slip away to the recesses of his mind until there was nothing left but the candle and the slow-moving flame. For many seconds he focused on the flame, taming it with his mind. He could feel the flame resisting his will. The Master peered deeper into the light, trying to bring its primitive power into submission. The flame remained still. Even deeper he delved into the heart of the flame. He slowly raised his hand off the desk, willing the flame to move, but nothing was happening. Just a flutter would satisfy him. For an hour, Haydon sat in silence with his palm out until sweat was dripping from his cheeks and chin. Finally, in a fit of rage, Haydon yelled his father's name and slapped the candlestick with the back of his hand, which snuffed out the candle and sent a spray of melted wax over the desk and onto the floor.

Silhouetted by the faintest light from the edges of the drapes, Haydon lowered his bearded face into his hands, stripped of all he had.

CHAPTER TWO

A COLD WELCOME

The sounds from outside my dark prison are getting louder and louder as time goes by. But now as I think about it, I don't know if the sounds are getting louder or if I've developed a more acute sense of my surroundings. The dull, rhythmic pounding on the walls is still there. My captors may be testing my will, trying to break me in some way, although I have not seen them yet. My body is bound and what little movement I once had is all but gone. No matter how much I thrash at my restraints, they will not yield. My captors will not succeed, for they have never met someone like me. If I have committed some offense, I do not remember it. The bleakness of this prison should be penance enough. It makes me

ponder the things I saw and did so many years ago.

Still following the Goriath captain, Kigron, Thanan observed that the dark fracture they had entered into spilled into a narrow tunnel, which widened into a small room. It was mostly dark except for a small shaft of light that penetrated the darkness like a knife from the outside. Wind whistled past them into the darkness. Hanging on the wall were four iron rings, containing four unlit torches.

Kigron grabbed a torch from the wall and handed it to the Jinian. The metal work was curious to Thanan. The handles were much too large for Jinian hands. They were cone shaped and had ornate carvings of serpents eating each other's tails. The giant then reached into a small leather pouch that he pulled from his pocket. He withdrew his hand from the pouch with what looked like a handful of iridescent sand, which he then sifted through his fingers. He raised his hand above the torch and sprinkled the sand over the top. As the sand fell from his hand, the particles sparked at first, then ignited into a glowing blue flame that radiated throughout the entire room.

Thanan's eyes sparkled with wonder. *Kilian never showed me that*, Thanan thought.

"Come, this way," the giant said, motioning with his torch down a dark tunnel.

"Where are we going?" Thanan asked, still marveling over the immensity of the torch and the unique properties of the sand.

"We are headed to the garrison at Hardrock Quarry," Kigron

whispered, starting to move down the corridor. "We will wait for General Tygrothian there. We are in the king's territory now, so we will have to move quickly and silently. Do you understand?"

The Jinian answered with a nod.

Thanan and Kigron walked swiftly through the winding tunnels. The spy noticed the walls were very smooth to the touch, almost like glass in some areas. He ran his fingers along the cool surface, admiring the skill of such a thing. *Not a scratch*, he thought. He felt the rush of air steadily pushing on his back, surmising the constant flow of fresh air was skillfully being pumped into the caverns. Kigron stopped at every bend, listening for approaching scouts from the king's guard that might be monitoring the tunnels ahead of them. Except for the torchlight, it was completely dark, a foreign landscape for Thanan. Not on the cloudiest night in Jin had he ever seen such blackness.

They entered into what Thanan thought to be a more established area of the caves. The tunnel ceilings were at least twelve feet high, arched at the top, with flickering blue lamps hanging from chains every fifty feet. The glowing lamplight fell off after about ten feet, leaving the rest of the tunnel in darkness.

"Stay close, Jinian," Kigron whispered, peering into the darkness. "It would be a shame to have come so far to be captured now. Here, take this." The giant handed him a double-edged short sword he pulled from a leather sheath in his belt. "If we are discovered, we will have to fight our way out."

Thanan took the sword, admiring its craftsmanship and weight. He gripped the hilt as tightly as he could and wondered what it was made of. It was sturdy and felt like he could slice through a tree in one swing.

"You know how to use that?" the giant asked, eyeing the blade.

Thanan spun the hilt in his hand with ease. "Don't worry about me."

They extinguished their torches and began the long three-day journey to Hardrock Quarry, hiding themselves in side tunnels to avoid the passing patrols. Kigron and Thanan said very little to each other along the way. They couldn't take the chance of being caught. Every once in a while, Kigron would shoot his fist up by his shoulder and freeze, signaling Thanan to stop. Many times they would stand for what seemed like minutes in the dark, listening for any sign of the king's patrols. There were many tense moments when the king's soldiers passed by, but they never detected Thanan and Kigron only a few feet away with swords at the ready.

Thanan and Kigron made it to Hardrock undetected. Upon their arrival at the quarry, four giants dressed in crystal-encrusted armor greeted them with the customary salute of raising their right-fisted hands to their hearts and quickly nodding their heads.

"Welcome back, sir," one of them said respectfully.

"Has the general returned?" Kigron asked.

"No, sir," the soldier replied. "He's been delayed."

Kigron pulled Thanan's hood off his head. "This Jinian is the general's guest. Take him to the barracks and get him a meal. See to it that he is comfortable and safe."

"Yes, sir!" the soldiers said in unison.

Thanan and his escorts arrived at the barracks.

"Wait here until we return. The captain will be here shortly," one of the soldiers said with an oddly gruff voice. Thanan wondered again if he had made the right choice in going with Kigron.

After a short wait, Kigron entered the barracks. "General Tygrothian will not be coming today. In fact, he will not be coming for some time. It seems that while I was gone, the general had some business in Devlin. Come with me and I'll show you to your quarters," he said sternly.

"I've never heard of Devlin. Where is that?" Thanan asked.

"It is military business, not yours. Now get moving, Jinian."

After a short walk, Kigron and Thanan arrived at his new residence. The Jinian peered into his simple tent. A threadbare bed lay in the corner lit by a blue crystal lamp sitting on a wooden crate, which was missing a few slats. At the foot of the bed he saw a hand-carved stone chest.

"You can put your things in there," Kigron said, pointing at the chest.

"For being the general's guest, these quarters are…lavish," Thanan said sarcastically.

"This is a military compound, Jinian, not a palace. You better get used to it; you are going to be here a while."

"Careful, Kigron, you make it sound like I'm a prisoner here," he said with a slight smile.

"Get some sleep now. You're going to need it," the captain replied with an ominous tone. He turned to leave.

"Wait! What do you mean I'm going to need it?"

"Enough, Jinian!" he said sternly. "There is much I have to do before I can sleep."

CHAPTER THREE

DUST AND COAL

"On your feet, Jinian!" a Goriath soldier barked, parting the tent door. "Come with me."

Thanan shot up from his bed, almost forgetting where he was. "Where are we going?" he replied, acclimating to his surroundings.

"I am Arazan. Captain Kigron is expecting you at the armory. Put your shirt on. Let's go."

The garrison was bustling with activity as Thanan and Arazan walked through the main square.

"You are in for a real treat, Jinian," Arazan began as if he were a tour guide.

Thanan walked in wonderment of the immense cavern. *The*

people back home wouldn't believe this, he thought.

The tour guide gestured all around, pointing out the more interesting sections of the quarry. "Hardrock Quarry was once a Zythera Crystal quarry, abandoned long ago. Zythera is the most rare of all the crystals and jewels found in the caverns and in the world. Zythera is precious to our people and very valuable. There are small deposits of undiscovered crystal still hidden in the more remote areas of the caves. The general keeps the miners searching for the few pockets left."

"I felt the walls when I came in. They were smooth, almost like glass in some spots."

"Goriaths are very thorough when it comes to mining. Not one ounce of the valuable crystal is wasted or missed. I wasn't around yet when Hardrock was mined. My great-great grandfather was though. His generation mined and chiseled their way through the rock and rubble until the last remaining bit of crystal dust was collected and the walls were smooth. It's quite remarkable."

They continued walking, all the while Arazan continued talking. "Hardrock is vast and deep with multiple levels that were slowly carved into one side of the cavern wall. We are about a mile under the surface. Originally, Hardrock was a natural cavern that resembled the Crystal City, but was one-fourth the size. Over six thousand of us live in Hardrock, about one thousand being soldiers under the command of General Tygrothian. About a day's walk from here, you'll find Whitehall garrison, another military outpost also under the general's command."

Thanan looked upward, the chiseled tips of the Xavantha crystals looming a thousand feet overhead. The immense crystals transferred much of the sunlight from the outside world to the quarry floor, only the light was softer and had a bluish hue. He was amazed how bright it was.

Thanan scanned the entire cavern. The floor for the most part was flat, with well-worn roads crisscrossing the quarry floor, separating the garrison into small neighborhoods on the north side. The homes were nothing more than tents and crudely constructed shanties with cloth walls. The neighborhoods ran as far as he could see. He noticed various colored flags adorning some of the tents.

"Most of the soldiers and their families live in these neighborhoods, while the civilian population lives on the perimeter of the cavern and on the terraces. Centuries ago, some of the lucky firstcomers made their homes on the ledges overlooking the grandeur of Hardrock. Up there they can see the entire garrison."

Thanan looked up to the highest terrace, wanting to see the view for himself.

At the heart of the garrison was a wide street that ran almost the entire length of the quarry. It was lined with shops bustling with civilians selling food and clothing. The prevailing smell in the quarry was like freshly tilled earth on a summer day, mixed with baked bread just out of the oven.

It surprised Thanan to see fresh vegetables and flowers in the subterranean world. "Do you grow the vegetables here in Hardrock?"

"Yes," the guide replied. "But not the flowers. Some of the more dedicated merchants travel outside a few times a year and bring flowers back. They get bought up quickly, as you can imagine. The general encourages us all to embrace the ways of the Sundwellers."

Also traveling the roads were strange, harnessed beasts pulling wooden carts. The creatures were like nothing Thanan had ever seen back in Jin. They were dark beasts of burden with scarred, scaly hides, driven by their masters' whips. Their hooved feet clacked heavily on the stone streets. Some of the carts overflowed with firewood and coal, their wheels carving ever deeper into the stone, obviously on their way to the blacksmith. Others contained dark soil, headed for the vast garden beds of root vegetables where the Xavantha was the brightest on the southeast side. Some of the soil was destined to go to the dark mushroom farms where Xavantha's light did not reach.

At the opposite side of the garrison, Thanan paused for a moment, noticing four particularly dangerous-looking giants engaged in simulated battle. The way they moved, their agility and speed, was intoxicating to him.

"They are Guardians," Thanan's escort said, pointing to the soldiers. "We are passing their training ground now. They are the elite warriors in our military. Only twelve of the finest soldiers can hold this honored and high rank."

"Guardians," Thanan said under his breath. He craned his neck as he walked by, not wanting to stop watching.

The sharp sound of clashing swords faded away and was replaced by the sounds of hammers and grinding stones, as soldiers busily mended barracks and sharpened weapons.

Thanan stopped again, mesmerized by the giant soldiers. "I've never seen weapons like these before," the Jinian stated.

Upon closer inspection, he saw that the craftsmanship was exceedingly fine. Apparently the Goriaths had become masters in weapon and armor fabrication.

Arazan stopped just outside the armory, turning to Thanan.

"Through the ages our blacksmiths have developed a method of fusing glystian and zil ores with the refined dust of Zythera Crystals. No one else in the world forges weapons and armor like the Goriaths do."

The spy's interest piqued. He loved swords. With the exception of the last three days, he had not held one in more than a year.

They entered the armory, walking down a long row of forges, some glowing red and some dark with new coal. Arazan spoke loudly over the roar of the forges and the high-pitched ringing of heavy hammers.

"The blades of Goriath swords vary in hardness, because of the complicated and lengthy method of forging the blades. The most skilled blacksmiths can take a year to finish only one Zythera blade. There are many kinds of blades in the world, even under the earth, but the Zythera blade is special."

Thanan and Arazan walked under the billows, which towered over two stories high and required four giants to pull the ropes. The giants gritted their teeth, pulling the ropes two by two, powering the forges with oxygen. The heat radiated from the forges, warming the armory to uncomfortable temperatures. Thanan began sweating.

"Don't get too close," Arazan cautioned. "The forges can reach temperatures as hot as the center of the planet, which is how the fusion of Glystian ore and Zythera dust is possible. Over and over the blades are hammered and folded, sometimes tens of thousands of times. With every fold, the crystal dust is added to create one of the strongest substances known to the world."

"It's not polite to be late on your first day of work," Kigron interrupted. "You may go, Arazan."

Arazan nodded. "Yes, sir."

"First day of work?" Thanan replied with a slight smile, ready to get his hands dirty. He quickly imagined himself forging his own sword.

"You should consider it an honor," Kigron said. "No outsider has ever lived or worked among the Goriath before."

"I am going to be an armorist?"

"An armorist?" Kigron balked. "You could not swing the hammer more than three times before you fatigued, but nevertheless it will be up to the master blacksmith to determine what you do here."

Kigron looked Thanan in the eyes. "Listen to me now, Jinian," he said, his tone changing. "This will be what you make of it. Do not waste a moment."

Although Thanan agreed with Kigron's sentiment, he thought it was a strange thing to say to someone he just met. It was like he knew more than what he was saying.

Kigron looked across the shop, the glow of the forges illuminating the dusty air. "That is Purgon, the general's blacksmith. You will report to him every morning and maybe with some luck, you will not be a total loss."

Limping across the gloomy, dusty shop, Purgon made his way to Thanan. He appeared older than any of the giants that Thanan had observed in Hardrock. His face had deep wrinkles like the ruts in a well-traveled road, and his back was horribly hunched. A brown leather eye patch covered one eye and his right arm was noticeably larger than his left, no doubt from decades of hammering in the service of his king and people. He was dressed in tattered clothing, which was covered by a thick leather apron from his chest to knees. The straps over his shoulders resembled suspenders. His feet were bare, calloused, and scarred. Deep pits covered the tops of his feet from slag raining down from the anvil and burning into his skin.

"He is all yours, Purgon," Kigron said, pushing Thanan forward.

The Jinian looked down.

"You have no shoes?" he asked politely.

"I have all I need, pale one," Purgon replied, looking at his feet, wiggling his toes. The curly black hairs on his big toes were odd to say the least.

Thanan picked up a rusty hammer that was lying on top of the anvil in the center of the shop. It was heavier than any hammer he had ever held. *Kigron was right. How could anyone ever swing this?* he thought.

"Well, what will you have me do first?" Thanan asked, rapping the hammer on the anvil.

Without warning, the blunt end of a broom was thrust into Thanan's stomach, causing him to double over and drop the hammer.

"Wait—"

The broom was then brought down on the soft tissue between his shoulder and neck, crushing him to the floor. Thanan lay on his back dazed and confused by the attack and also by the speed in which it happened. His eyes came to focus on the tip of the broom, which was pointed at the bridge of his nose.

"Are you a blacksmith, Jinian?"

"No," Thanan said, holding his stomach, still out of breath.

"This is a military outpost, Jinian. The word you are looking for is 'sir.'"

"No, sir," Thanan shot back.

"Tell me, Jinian…would you dare touch the crown, though you were not the king?"

"No, sir."

"Stand up! If I ever see you touch anything but this broom in this shop," Purgon yelled, throwing the broom at Thanan, "my hammer will find its way to your skull. Do you understand?"

"Yes, sir," Thanan replied, rubbing his neck and shoulder.

"Now get to work!" Purgon scolded.

Looking over the armory, Thanan gripped the broom handle with both hands. It was thick like a boat oar and smooth like a well-used handrail.

"What a mess," Thanan sighed, mumbling to himself. "Don't know why there's a broom in here anyway; it's obviously never been used."

Every morning for weeks, Thanan woke early and walked to the workshop where his giant broom waited against the wall. And every morning, without fail, he bought a warm biscuit from the bakery. The fresh aroma wafted throughout the marketplace, drawing customers in by the dozens, reminding him of his days wandering through Hastentown back in Jin. It was like a little piece of home under the earth.

"Good morning, Purgon," Thanan said respectfully, as he did every day. The aches and pains of sweeping the floor with a broom five times heavier than a Jinian broom had faded. He felt stronger than ever.

Purgon was hard at work forging a Zythera axe, which needed all of his attention. He was always well into a day's work when the

Jinian arrived to begin another grueling day of sweeping.

"Sweep, Jinian!" Purgon shouted gruffly, looking up from the glowing forge.

Many times Thanan had observed the old giant pluck a glowing blade from the forge and pound the malleable metal into the distinctive shape by which all Goriath weapons were known. Over and over again he repeated the process until he could, with confidence, stamp his maker's mark on the weapon.

There were many armorists and blacksmiths at Hardrock, but no other giant could compare to Purgon's skill and perfection. Only Purgon was trusted with forging the Guardians' armor and weapons.

"Don't you ever sleep, Purgon?" Thanan asked, picking up his broom.

"I'll die with a hammer in my hand," Purgon replied as glowing slag rained down from the anvil onto his bare feet.

Thanan went to work. He walked by another blacksmith, who was busy shoveling coal into his forge. For some reason, Thanan hadn't noticed before that every tool, every cart, even the smallest scrap in the shop was always in its place. It was contrary to the uncleanliness of the shop when he first started his sweeping duties.

"I see you have your broom, Jinian," the shoveling blacksmith said condescendingly.

"Why is this place so thick with dust, when everything else is so neat and tidy?" Thanan ran his finger down the length of a metal bar leaning against a post, exposing the shiny surface.

"For some reason Purgon commanded us to stop sweeping nine months ago. It's been hell working in here for months. I developed a cough a few weeks ago too."

Thanan glanced back at the master blacksmith hammering away at the axe head. A hint of a smile crept across Thanan's lips. *The sly old giant knew I was coming*, he thought.

A few days later, outside the shop, the sound of clashing swords and rhythmic chanting caught Thanan's attention again. Every day since he arrived at Hardrock, he watched the Guardians train through the doorway as he swept and reswept the now-dustless floors. Thanan imagined himself in the arena training alongside the Guardians as if he were one of the candidates for the order.

Purgon looked up from his forge and saw his apprentice daydreaming in the doorway. He grumbled under his breath and set his hammer down on the anvil. "Today is your lucky day, Jinian," the hunched blacksmith told Thanan. "Come with me."

"Where are we going, Purgon?" Thanan asked, still watching the Guardians.

"Don't speak; just follow me," Purgon scolded, brushing his hands down his apron.

"Forgive me, Purgon."

Purgon led the way through the armory to a black metal door hidden behind the great billows. The door looked heavy and was arched with riveted reinforcing around the perimeter.

"The finest of Zythera blades are indestructible and in some cases they are legendary, and it all starts here, behind this door," Purgon explained, putting his palm on the cold door, almost lovingly.

A smile crept across Thanan's face as Purgon reached for the broom handle. *Finally,* Thanan thought.

"Hold out your hand, Jinian," Purgon commanded.

Thanan extended his hand as Purgon took the broom and from the shadows grabbed a shovel, placing it in Thanan's empty hand.

"What's this?" Thanan asked disappointedly.

"A shovel, Jinan. Surely you've seen one of these before," Purgon mocked with a rare smile.

"Purgon, you've found your sense of humor!" Thanan said encouragingly. Then he became serious. "What am I going to do with this?"

"Too many years in your palace have made you weak, Jinian. The forges do not just fuel themselves in Hardrock."

Thanan thought about his tireless work in the lumber mills outside New Westlyn and the task of shoveling did not intimidate him at all.

"This is the coal storehouse," Purgon continued. "All the coal for the forges is stored here. You will fill the carts and deliver the coal to every forge throughout the compound. I trust you can do this task without daydreaming about becoming a Guardian," Purgon said, satisfied he had ruined Thanan's day.

Purgon pulled back the heavy latch and pushed the door open. He then grabbed a torch from the wall and lit another hanging inside the storehouse. Warm, dry air rushed past Thanan's face, drying his eyes as he entered the storehouse. Even with the torchlight, the room was dim and towered what seemed to be one hundred feet overhead. At the top was a shaft that emptied into the storeroom. Miners would empty their quarry into the shaft above and the coal would shower down in piles onto the stone floor.

Thanan exhaled heavily, not willing to let Purgon break his will.

Gripping the shovel tightly, which was several pounds heavier than his broom, he began filling the carts with coal. Without breaking for even one moment, he exerted all his energy to the task at hand. His back and shoulders burned. Not once did his thoughts wander to the sound of swords clashing or becoming a Guardian. He wanted to prove to Purgon that he did not belong shoveling coal. He belonged forging weapons. He belonged swinging a sword.

With every shovelful, the Jinian's muscles shook, his lungs stinging with every breath, choking on clouds of coal and zil dust.

The monotonous sound of the shovel being driven into the enormous pile of coal was interrupted every once in a while by the thundering sound of tons of coal raining down from above. Whenever he heard the rumbling coal, he dove out of the way so as to not be buried alive. As he delivered his last full cart of the day, he heard Kigron's voice from across the workshop.

"Jinian! That's enough for today. Put your shovel down and come with me!"

Thanan was exhausted as he and Kigron arrived at the opening of his tent.

"Eat and get your rest, Jinian," Kigron said sternly. "General Tygrothian will be returning tomorrow morning. I am sure he is anxious to meet with you."

Thanan sat on his bed, looking around, concerned. "Kigron...where are the soldiers who are supposed to be posted at my tent?"

"You can be trusted now, can't you?" the captain replied with a slight chuckle.

"Do you have a family, Kigron?" Thanan asked, resting his head on an uncomfortable pillow, changing the subject. "Do you have a wife, a family?"

Kigron turned to the door. "I don't trust you that much, Jinian."

"I will take that as a yes, Kigron."

Kigron shook his head and walked out of the tent.

It was the same thing every evening. Thanan walked to his tent where his meal was waiting on the wooden chest at the foot of his bed. Dry biscuits, a bowl of meat and mushrooms in a thin broth, and a pitcher of warm water was the culinary fare before bed. He always ate alone.

Holding his compass in his hands, Thanan drifted to sleep watching the still blue flame of his lamp.

Thanan was jolted out of a deep sleep by a cold knife blade pressed to his throat. His tent was dark. Someone had put out his lamp. He slowly sat up trying to adjust his eyesight to the darkness.

A voice behind him whispered, "Don't make a sound or it will be your last, Jinian. Stand up…walk outside…slowly."

The Jinian resisted a little, testing the strength of the giant. He judged that he could overpower him in the right circumstances, but given the fact there was a knife pressed at his neck combined with his curiosity to see where he was being taken, he decided to go quietly, without much resistance.

The quarry was silent except for the sound of trickling water that flowed through the sophisticated waterways throughout the caverns. Only a few lamps lit the path leading out of the camp. Xavantha overhead offered very little illumination, only a faint cast of blue lighting up the quarry floor.

"Where are you taking me?" Thanan whispered.

"Silence, Jinian!" hissed a familiar gruff voice. He gripped Thanan's arm tighter.

"All right, all right. Take it easy."

The assailant moved his knife to the Jinian's back so as to not attract any unwanted attention. He silently maneuvered throughout the encampment with ease, almost too easily. Thanan realized that he must be a soldier from the garrison.

"A traitor!" he seethed under his breath. "What were you promised for my capture?"

"You are just as valuable without a tongue," he replied gruffly. "Now shut up."

Realizing that his captor was under strict orders to not kill him, Thanan turned to confront the traitor. He immediately recognized him from the group of soldiers that greeted him and Kigron when they first arrived at Hardrock.

"Treachery," Thanan hissed. "I was content thinking you were one of the king's spies, but a traitor...now things have changed."

The traitor raised his knife in front of Thanan's eyes. "Do not make the mistake of resisting me, Jinian. All you have to do is be breathing when I deliver you to King Grishon. After that, it is up to the king whether you live or die."

Just at that moment when the soldier lowered his knife, Thanan grabbed a lit torch from the wall and swung it wildly at his captor to gain some sort of advantage of the situation. He struck him once on the side of the head and caused the traitor to stumble backward, but he did not fall. Glowing blue sparks rained down over the giant's head. With his knife, he lunged in retaliation, the blade narrowly missing Thanan's ribs. He quickly stabbed again, but

Thanan stepped to the side. The Jinian swung the torch down over the giant's hand, sending the knife sliding across the quarry floor. The giant drove his shoulder into Thanan and crushed him into the wall, the back of his head bouncing against the hard rock. A white light flashed before his eyes and his vision blurred for a moment. He felt warm blood start to trickle through his hair and down the nape of his neck. The traitor held Thanan against the wall suspended inches above the floor with his hands crushing his neck. Over and over he smashed Thanan into the cave wall. The Jinian's vision began closing in on him, like he was looking through a tunnel. He knew he was going to lose consciousness soon. He had to do something.

Thanan dropped the torch, grabbed his captor's shoulders and drove his forehead into the traitor's nose with all his might. They both fell to the ground writhing in pain, blurry eyed and gasping for air.

The giant's nose was clearly broken and bleeding down his face. He wiped his upper lip and nose with the back of his hand, smearing the blood across his cheek. Thanan's sight was still blurry from the many blows to the back of his head. He lay facedown looking up the path as his vision cleared, revealing the giant's knife blade glinting in the torchlight. The bleeding giant noticed his enemy's eyes focus on something up the path. He looked and saw the knife as well. They both scrambled toward the knife, punching and clawing at each other along the way.

Thanan reached the knife first and gripped the handle with all his strength. He rolled to his back as the giant rained blow after blow to Thanan's face and head. In the barrage the giant slowed his attack, seeing the bloody handle of his own knife protruding from his chest, his face in agony. He grasped at the knife, reeling in pain, trying to pull it out and fell to his back motionless, his eyes open and hand still clutching the handle.

Thanan breathed a sigh of relief as he rolled over to get to his feet. His entire face pulsed with his heartbeat. Just then he heard a horrifying howl as a flash of blue light lit up the cave. He snapped his head around to see his abductor on his knees, knife in hand, and ready to strike with a still-flaming arrowhead penetrating through his chest. The traitor slowly fell to his face and ultimately to his death, snuffing the arrow out.

"Are you injured?" Thanan heard Kigron yell through the darkness.

Tremik Tak was still holding his bow with another arrow nocked as he motioned for his men to move in. Two soldiers quickly ran toward Thanan's now-dead captor. They assisted the Jinian to his feet and escorted him out of the tunnel. One of them kicked the traitor, making sure he was dead as they passed by his body.

"Place the traitor in one of the tunnels where the king's patrols will find him," the captain ordered.

Limping into his tent, Thanan sat heavily on the bed. He lit his lamp and looked at Kigron through swollen eyes.

"It seems you have traitors within your ranks," the Jinian managed to mumble. He rubbed his jaw, moving it back and forth to make sure it wasn't broken.

"We suspected we had a traitor among us for some time, but we could not identify who it was until now," Kigron replied in his usual matter-of-fact cadence. "That is why there were no guards posted at your quarters. We had to draw the traitor out."

He dabbed his bleeding face with a wet cloth, his head pounding with every word. "So...I was the bait?"

"It was an unfortunate necessity," Kigron replied. "Besides, you are still alive, Jinian. Be grateful for that. I find that being grateful for what you have is always the best way to look at things. Do you not? We were monitoring your movements throughout the encampment all along. You were never in any true danger."

"It was not you that had a dagger at your throat, Kigron," Thanan mumbled angrily. "Do you see my face? You could have arrived a little earlier."

"We hoped that you and your abductor would lead us to any other soldiers still loyal to the king, but you made sure that did not work."

"Well...next time you should include me in your plan and it might be more successful."

The following morning, Thanan slowly opened his swollen eyes, waking to the typical sounds of the garrison. He had a pounding headache, and deep purple bruises distinctly shaped like giant's fingers encircled his neck. He gingerly touched the back of his head. It was sore and bruised and his hair was matted from the blood. There was a large red stain on his pillow from the wound. Thanan came to the realization that his brief training with Kilian did not prepare him for a knife fight in a dark tunnel with an angry giant who was two feet taller than he was. He decided that after his meeting with General Tygrothian, he would seek the general's approbation to join the soldiers and begin training as a Goriath

Guardian.

Outside the general's tent, Thanan straightened his shirt and stiffened his back. First impressions were everything. He knocked confidently on the post.

"Enter," a stern voice said from inside the general's quarters.

Still sore from the night's events, Thanan tried, but couldn't conceal his limp. He hobbled into the tent as the general rose to his feet. He was taller than the average Goriath giant. His appearance was distinguished and intimidating. A gruesome scar ran from his left eye down his cheek to his chin. *Most likely a battle wound from a Zythera blade,* the Jinian thought.

"It seems you have had an eventful night," the general announced. "My apologies for the unusual methods, but our soldiers are well trained, and it is difficult to identify any dissenters in the ranks."

"Where was he taking me?" Thanan interrupted, still a little foggy about the previous night.

"To the capital, most likely to the king. As you probably know by now, our society is based on, well…capitalism. Most of us used to earn a profit honestly, but as the mines yielded less and less of their precious crystals, the past kings started relying on less reputable methods to satisfy their lustful appetites for wealth. I could no longer in good conscience obey the king's corruptible commands and in time, took all those who would follow me and left Crystal City. Most of the military and their families followed me, along with a few civilians. Even now, after hundreds of years, we still find refugees wandering the caves on their way to join us, those who are brave enough to break away. They leave at great risk. If the king's soldiers find them, they are killed instantly. So now we live as two distinct groups."

"What good could I do the king? What would he want with me? How could he possibly know who I am?" Thanan asked.

"It's simple: ransom," the general said directly. "If we knew you were coming, so did the king. He has ears everywhere. He does not usually take any interest in Jinians, but a prince…well, that is a different thing entirely. You were fortunate that we found you first."

"So you know my father is the king of Jin? And just how did you acquire the knowledge I was traveling through your valley?"

"Young Thanan, I have known you were coming for a long time." The general paused as if he were thinking of a fond memory. "Your journey has just begun here. I knew your father and mother long before you were born. I am much older than I appear. I am one of the two remaining elders from the first generation, the other being Purgon, whom you know already. We, along with twenty others, were blessed with long life when we entered the caverns, but along with this great gift came a horrible curse.

"These crystal-filled caverns gave only a few of us long life. Generations ago, Goriath giants could live to be one hundred and twenty, some longer, but now many are lucky if they reach seventy. We must leave these caves before my worst fears are realized. I have seen thousands of our sons and daughters grow old and die, every generation passing away faster than the one before.

"Your father told me that one day his young son would pass through our land on a great journey. He is a wise man, your father. I consider him a friend and a trusted ally." The general paused again, his countenance changing. "Something awful is coming,

Thanan, something that your father foresaw long ago and will surely come to pass. I can feel it in my bones…a great storm is forming, evil in the west that I fear cannot be stopped."

Thanan knew what storm he was speaking about. Word of Haydon's treachery had already traveled to the far reaches of the planet. Haydon's betrayal haunted Thanan's thoughts.

"Let me help you, General. Let me join your cause and become a soldier, even a Guardian," Thanan said with confidence. "I have learned combat and weapon skills taught to me by my tutor, Kilian, an ancient sentinel. Do you know their kind?"

"I met one…a long time ago, when I was young."

"Then you know of their legendary skill."

"It is not the sentinel's skill that I am doubting," Tygrothian interrupted. "You are young and inexperienced. And your mouth is quicker than your brain, Thanan. Have patience; you are getting ahead of yourself. You overestimate your skills. Look at yourself." The general gestured to Thanan's battered face. "One weak spy did that to you. A Guardian would have heard the spy coming, determined whether he should eliminate the threat or capture him for questioning, then acted, relying only on his Guardian training.

"One cannot simply become a Guardian because he wishes it. To become a Guardian, you must be proved worthy of such an honor and purged of any outside convictions, focused on one singular path and consumed in the perfection of the discipline. Your mind delights in your presumed abilities and is blind to simple truths."

"But, I just—"

"Candidates die, Thanan!" the general said abruptly. "Hundreds of families, spanning generations, have grieved over the death of their candidates. Of the three who were selected last year, two did not return from the final trial and the one who did only lived three days. These were warriors of unparalleled skill and yet they succumbed to hunger and all manner of mortality. You are not up to the task. Go now…ponder the words I have spoken. We will talk again soon."

Thanan began to speak and then closed his mouth, clenching his jaw. He knew arguing with a general was futile and foolish and the last way to get what he wanted most. He nodded his head to the general, turned, and limped out of his quarters.

It was a devastating blow to Thanan, hearing about his inadequacy as a warrior. The general's words penetrated him like a Zythera blade, sharply, painfully. As he walked through the barracks he thought about the long journey that led him to this moment, and now he had been rejected. He felt defeated, yet had triumphed in every aspect of his journey thus far. Self-pity had crept into his young heart, which was contrary to his typical attitude. He thought about his father, his brothers, Kilian. What would they do if they were faced with this? The answer did not come.

For hours, Thanan walked aimlessly through the winding tunnels and found himself in a courtyard full of bustling giants going about their business.

"Make way for the dead!" a giant dressed in red robes announced to the crowd. He held a rusted bell, ringing it as he walked down the road. "Make way for the dead," he continued.

All who were within the courtyard began to kneel and fall to the cave floor with their hands clutched together in obvious reverence as a funeral procession slowly passed by. Thanan was suddenly shaken out of his self-absorbed state of mind. He was left alone, standing among the kneeling giants, looking over their bowed heads, entranced by the scene that was unfolding before his eyes.

Eight Guardian candidates dressed in ceremonial armor along with three Guardians slowly pushed a stone casket down the street. Their heads were bowed in reverence, their eyes never looking up at the kneeling crowd. No sound could be heard except the ringing bell and the creaking metal wheels rolling along the deep grooves that had long been etched into the cave floor.

Dozens of giants followed behind the casket, their heads also bowed like the candidates. The children in the procession held the hands of their weeping mother, who followed the casket the closest.

"What's happened?" Thanan whispered to a bowing spectator.

"We do not speak in the presence of the sacred dead," the old onlooker whispered back. "It is proper to kneel, Jinian."

Thanan looked around the courtyard. He was the only one standing among the kneeling giants. He quickly knelt beside the old giant, embarrassed he had not already done so. The funeral procession passed, the bell still ringing every minute. Thanan helped the kneeling giant to his feet. He leaned against a gnarled walking stick, shaking as he stood, groaning from his aching bones.

"Who deserves such reverence that the Guardians themselves would escort the deceased?" Thanan asked.

"His name was Kongor, a candidate for the Guardian Order,"

the elderly giant said, words wavering. "He was killed while training today. You did not hear?"

"No, I was meeting with the general." Thanan suddenly knew why the general was so adamant in his decision. *He lost a candidate today*, he thought. "How did he die?"

They began walking slowly through the marketplace. Thanan limped almost more than the old giant did.

"Kongor was challenged in the Zythera Circle today. He was killed during the match. He was not the first and will not be the last, though he was one of the finest sword masters I had ever seen. But even the most talented warriors can be bested one way or another."

They came to rest at the waterway, watching the silvery fish darting in the clear water.

"What happened? How did he die?"

"Kongor was indeed a great natural warrior, but he also knew he was great. Arrogance blinds the mind to true learning, Jinian. Remember that. Pride can ultimately lead you to your destruction, as it did for Kongor. His family now bears the weight of his disgrace. Even though outwardly Kongor seemed all that a Guardian should be, he let vanity creep in, and it was the key to his undoing. Even so, we still honor him in death." The elderly giant changed his expression and looked Thanan directly in the eyes. "I feel you would make a powerful Guardian, Jinian."

Thanan stared at the old giant. *What a strange thing to say*, he thought.

"It's been a pleasure, sir. Shall I walk you to your home?"

"Heavens no," the shaking Goriath laughed. "I'll be fine."

"All right, I'll be going now."

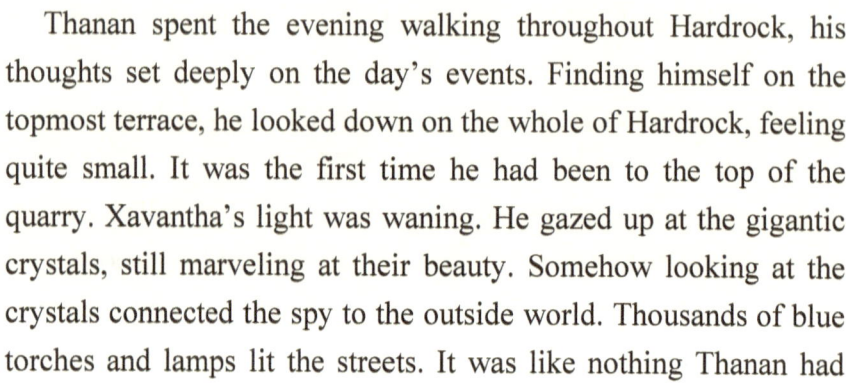

Thanan spent the evening walking throughout Hardrock, his thoughts set deeply on the day's events. Finding himself on the topmost terrace, he looked down on the whole of Hardrock, feeling quite small. It was the first time he had been to the top of the quarry. Xavantha's light was waning. He gazed up at the gigantic crystals, still marveling at their beauty. Somehow looking at the crystals connected the spy to the outside world. Thousands of blue torches and lamps lit the streets. It was like nothing Thanan had ever seen before. Even under the earth, where there was no heavenly expanse, no shining sea, no burning sun to measure days, there were new wonders to experience if you only looked.

He thought about the general, and Kongor's procession. Thanan had changed in some way. He had always worked hard, pleasing others, proving himself in some way. But there was something he had missed in all his service: true sacrifice, a willingness to forget yourself in the service. Things always came very easily to Thanan. Until now, he had never truly understood the value, the commitment to something larger than himself. Kongor and many others were willing to die for something that was bigger than they were. *Can I give my life for this mission?* he thought, looking over the edge into the dimming quarry. The words of Thanan's father suddenly entered his mind with new understanding:

"You must become the enemy. Remember, you are my son and you have great powers that lie deep within you, as do all my sons."

Torchlight glinted in his welling eyes, and a new look of soberness swept over his face. He fell to his knees, overcome with emotion as his mind turned to Haydon, his brother, the betrayer. *How can I become like him?* he thought.

Thanan woke on the cold cave floor overlooking the quarry, his arm hanging over the ledge. Startled, he shot to his feet, heart racing like he had sprinted a mile. He walked to the workshop with an unusual energy in his stride. The distinctive strike of Purgon's hammer pounding the anvil beckoned Thanan to walk even faster.

"A 'good morning' to you, Purgon," Thanan said enthusiastically.

Purgon paused the stroke of his hammer for just a moment. He looked up at the Jinian dismissively. "Hmm…" he muttered, ignoring his Jinian apprentice and continuing with his hammering.

"Cheery as ever, I see. I'll be in the storeroom if you need me."

CHAPTER FOUR

METHINIAN MERCHANTS

Back in Jin, the typical sounds of morning broke on Belenor Harbor. The old wooden docks creaked and expanded as the sun warmed the boards. Extinguishing the mighty lamp, the lighthouse keeper descended the staircase and promptly fell asleep to the sound of arguing sand gulls in the distance. The hungry gulls swarmed above the docks, watching fishermen load barrels of bait into their boats, waiting for the chance to gobble up a squid or fish head that might spill from the barrels.

The harbor bell rang, signaling the arrival of a merchant ship. It was a fine ship, crewed by thirty or more men, busy about their duties opening hatches and securing the rigging from the long voyage. They moved over the ship like well-trained soldiers.

Rich hardwoods with swirling grains trimmed the ship's cabins and railing, contrasting the tar-covered timers of the hull. A painted wooden figurehead in the image of a beautiful woman with long curly hair flowing down to her waist adorned the bow. Jesifaye Moon was the vessel's name, written in white script alongside her bow.

"Welcome back to Belenor, Captain Drun," harbormaster Jonas shouted. He carried with him a thin plank with parchment attached. "What brings you all the way to the capital this time of year?"

"Please, Jonas, we've been friends for ten years now. Call me Samil!" the captain shouted from the helm. "The hull is bursting with rare fruits and trinkets from Methina and other strange lands. I've got something special for you if you get this unloaded early. Need to be gone morning after next."

Samil kicked a small wooden chest at his feet. Something inside clinked as he kicked it. "Mr. Frobrin here will oversee the merchandise. He'll answer any questions you may have." Samil slapped Frobrin on the back.

"Anything for you, Samil! All right, you heard the captain," the harbormaster called to the dockworkers. "Be quick about it."

"Oh, one more thing, Jonas. Where can I find the best tailor in the capital?" The gangplank bowed as Samil walked down to the dock. "I've got a bolt of the finest silk from Netherhaven, from the northernmost outpost," he whispered. "One of the best deals I ever did, if you know what I mean."

Jonas knowingly laughed. "You will want to see Mrs. Brindamin, right on Main Street, in the commerce district of Hastentown. Best dressmaker in all of Jin. She sews all the clothes for the king's family."

"Well, I'll just have to pay a visit to Mrs. Brindamin then. I trust you won't mention this to anyone."

"Of course, Samil." Jonas' eyes darted up to the ship's railing. Looking guilty, he quietly hushed Samil. "Good morning, Jesifaye," Jonas said to the ship's namesake. "You're beautiful as ever, even at this early hour, my dear."

Overlooking the rail, Jesifaye stood, her black curls blowing ever so slightly in the breeze, highlighted by the morning sun. "Please Jonas, too much flattery in the morning. You'll run out of compliments by midday at this rate."

"Never," he replied.

"I see that Samil has you running his errands again. What are you two up to this time?"

Samil, never missing an opportunity to spin a tale, replied, "Just business, dear, nothing to worry about. Jonas was just telling about some pirates he recently dealt with. Sunk the ship just outside the bay, didn't you, Jonas?"

"It was something to see, for sure," Jonas agreed, playing along.

"Uh huh," Jesifaye replied, not appearing fooled.

"There is some breakfast left in the galley. Why don't you go below and eat?"

"No...I think I will take a stroll through Belenor and have breakfast at a café."

"Whatever you like, my dear," Samil replied, smiling at the stunning woman. "Oh, and happy birthday, Jesifaye."

Her fitted dress clung to her youthful physique as she turned away from the rail, walking out of sight.

"Hard to say no to that one," Jonas whispered.

Samil handed Jonas a small leather pouch, coins jingling inside. "You have no idea, my friend. I'll be back before dusk. You and the wife will join us for dinner. I insist. Belenor Blues as usual?"

"Of course. Milda will be so excited to see Jesifaye again."

Small puddles burned off the warming cobblestone streets of Hastentown in the mid morning sun. The township bustled with life. Chattering birds dove in and out of cafés, looking for leftover crumbs from breakfast before roosting in the shadows of the mature broad-leafed trees that lined the streets. The air was warm and sweet, with the faintest hints of sea air and spices. It was a day like any other day in Hastentown with thousands of people walking the streets, busy about their business, shopping for fine linens and culinary delights. The people were quick to say hello and bid their neighbor a fine day as they passed by.

It was a vast land of opportunity for the worldly merchant. Samil loved the Jinian capital, and he relished the chance to strike a deal with the local merchants. His experienced silver tongue, combined with a handsome face and svelte build, made it almost impossible for anyone to resist his negotiations, especially the women. They were potter's clay in his hands when negotiations started.

He had many connections in most every part of the world, but a few. It wasn't just the satisfaction from his merchandise selling throughout the world that kept Samil going; it was the thrill of the hunt, the perfect deal. But this day Samil was on a different errand, saving the deals for tomorrow. It was Jesifaye's birthday, and a dress had to be sewn.

A tinkling bell rung above Samil's head as a heavy wooden door creaked, latching behind him. "Mrs. Brindamin, I presume," the handsome captain announced.

Hunched over a cluttered table at the back of the shop, a lady with curly gray hair looked up from her work. "Yes, can I help you, young man?"

"Did you make all these?" Samil asked. He walked through the shop, passing by mannequins dressed in the finest clothing he had ever seen. He stopped and admired the blue fabric of a particular dress, rubbing it between his thumb and forefinger. He was acquainted with valuables of all kinds, even apparel.

"It does say Brindamin's on the door, does it not?" the woman chided.

Samil smiled slyly at the old woman's spirit. "I have traveled thousands of miles, across oceans and strange lands, and have procured something that I'm sure you have never seen before." He held up the bolt of fabric he was carrying under his arm. It shimmered silver in the sunlight that was pouring in through the windows.

The faintest expression of interest shone on Mrs. Brindamin's face and Samil discerned it.

"Is that what I think it is?" she asked, standing up. She put her needle and thread down on the table, looking around as if she had lost something. She opened a small drawer in the table and pulled out an antique-looking magnifying glass with an ivory handle. "I've had many strangers come here with fake Netherhaven silk before. You should leave now before I discover you are a liar. I know the queen. I can have you arrested if I have the notion to."

"Please, be my guest. Take it. I guarantee it is the real thing. I had two men lose their toes to frostbite to get it. I lost a couple of fingers myself." He held the bolt out for her to inspect.

The old dressmaker hobbled, her rotund hips swaying down the aisle. She spun the magnifying glass in her pudgy hand, ready to disprove the supposed con artist. Samil flashed a handsome smile at her, hoping to soften her demeanor.

"I will not be cheated," she sternly said, snatching the silk from his hand.

"I wouldn't dare cheat someone with your reputation, Mrs. Brindamin. Your skill with needle and thread are known even as far as my island home, Methina."

"I'm far too old for your flattery," she shot back, carefully looking at the silver fabric.

"You know how they make such fabric, don't you?" Samil asked.

She looked up with one giant magnified eye, scowling because of the insinuated ignorance, and then continued her authentication.

"Netherhaven silk is not really silk at all," he continued. "It is spun from molten meteor fragments from the Breminth Crater at the North Pole. I've seen the process with my own eyes, molten strands finer than a spider's web, loomed in secret. It was said that no more fragments existed, but rumors found my ear three years ago that a smaller crater just might exist in the remote glacier region of Netherhaven…ice so thick that the natives couldn't reach it. After six months of chipping away at the glacier, we found it, right where the rumors said it would be."

"Yes…yes…yes, that's a very interesting story, merchant," the woman balked. "I've heard it all."

"It's true, every word. I swear to it." He held up his right hand, his little finger and half of his ring finger missing. "Frostbite."

"Disgusting," she replied, looking through her magnifying glass at the amputated stumps. "We will see. This is the most convincing sample yet, I must admit." She walked over to her table carrying the silvery fabric and sat down. "There is only one true test that can prove the fabric's authenticity though." She raised the fabric in the air and brought her candle underneath, letting the flame lick the frayed edge.

"Wait…what are you doing?" Samil yelled at the woman. He reached for the bolt, but stopped when he realized the fabric was not burning.

The flame swirled over the silvery fabric. Not a hint of charring or scorching could be found on the material.

"I don't believe it," she whispered under her breath. The dressmaker looked up at Samil. "Didn't know it was impervious to flame, did you? You may know many things, merchant, but fabric is my business, and I've waited a long time for Netherhaven silk to pass through my door."

It wasn't often that Samil found himself speechless, so he just smiled at the old woman for a moment, marveling at her cleverness. The captain extended his right hand toward the dressmaker. "I'm Captain Samil Drun."

"Well, captain, it seems this is the real article. I'm Matilda Brindamin, modiste to the queen. Now let's get to the heart of the matter, shall we? What do you want for the whole bolt?"

"Oh, it's not for sale, madam."

Matilda squinted her eyes and narrowed her lips. "Look around, merchant. I am a very busy woman. Don't waste my time. Get to the point."

"I'm looking for someone with the unique skills to sew a dress from this fabric. And since you have never even seen Netherhaven silk, I hardly think you are qualified." Samil wound the fabric around the bolt and turned around, stepping toward the door. "I'll find a dressmaker in New Westlyn. I'm sure I'll find someone there."

"You come into my store and insult me, sir? I make the finest dresses in all of Jin. The queen comes to me and me alone for her gowns. No one in New Westlyn is going to help you. They would relieve you of your fabric and break your legs to boot."

Samil stopped, turning back to Matilda, a sly smile creeping across his lips. "And just what would you give me in exchange for this once-in-a-lifetime opportunity to make a dress from Netherhaven silk?" the silver-tongued merchant asked. "Just think of the stories you can retell to your dressmaking friends, the famous Matilda Brindamin and the Netherhaven gown."

Mrs. Brindamin was tempted in spite of the one-sided offer. She reached out and felt the metallic fabric again, feeling the unique texture between her fingers, knowing her once-in-a-lifetime chance might walk out the door, never to return. "I'm afraid I don't have your gift for storytelling."

"I'll tell you what," Samil continued in his usual flair. "If you can complete the dress and deliver it to Belenor Blues one hour before dusk tonight, I'll let you keep any of the silk that is left. Even the scraps are worth more than your entire shop."

"It would take my entire staff to make such a dress," she replied, exhaling loudly, thinking.

"I am confident you can do it." Samil raised his eyebrows,

waiting for an answer.

"Tabitha!" the dressmaker called.

A few seconds later, a young woman appeared from behind the wall at the back of the shop. In her hands she carried the bodice of a dress and a cloth measuring tape over her shoulders. "Yes, Grandma, what do you need?"

"Gather the entire staff. We have a dress to make."

"Everyone?" Tabitha questioned, looking distressed by the task.

"Yes, everyone. Get moving." The dressmaker turned to Samil. "Now, let's talk about design. What do you have in mind? What's her size?"

"I like this one," he replied, walking past a mannequin clothed in a long dress that was fitted at the waist. The magnificent dress was simple in design yet shouted elegance. Samil thought for a moment and imagined Jesifaye standing on the bow of the ship wearing such a dress.

"You do have an eye for the finer things, Samil. That one we just finished for Princess Liriah."

"I've never seen its equal," the captain said, running his hand down the fabric. "The only way this could be improved is if it were made with Netherhaven silk." He smiled at the dressmaker and handed her the bolt. The fabric gleamed in the sunlight. "So we have a deal then, one dress fit for a princess, delivered tonight."

"Belenor Blues," she agreed, hobbling toward her table, cradling the bolt like a baby.

"Oh, one more thing," he said over the ringing doorbell. "Wrap it in something nice, won't you?" Appearing annoyed by the question, she looked up, gruffly exhaled, but said nothing.

"Of course you will," he concluded, knowing he had overstayed his welcome. He quickly closed the door and headed to New Westlyn for some other business.

Belenor Blues was the pinnacle of opulent dining in Belenor, the restaurant being designed to celebrate the spectacular views of the bay. Nightly, sailboat passengers would travel the coastline to the bay for the opportunity of dining in the famed restaurant.

Each night the wind shifted, blowing in from the sea. Flickering lamps swayed slowly over finely crafted hardwood tables draped in satin linens, setting the tone for the culinary experience.

"It's breathtaking," Jesifaye exclaimed, looking over the bay at the setting sun. "I love Jin this time of year. The sky looks as if it's on fire."

"Good evening, everyone," the waiter said, standing at attention. "I see you already have your drinks. I trust your table is to your liking?"

"Remarkable," Samil replied. "The ambiance, the view, everything I've come to expect from Belenor Blues."

"Thank you, sir. Tonight our own Chef Chantron has prepared something special for you. We will start with sweet sea scallops with just a dusting of salt and pepper, seared to perfection, followed by fala sorbet, a delicate citrus and mint refreshment to cleanse the palette." Everyone at the table smiled, eyes wide in anticipation. "Your main course will truly be a culinary symphony: bacon-wrapped spoonfish, caught just this afternoon…pan seared and finished in our famous stone oven. You'll find just a hint of drinsia from the woodchips in the fire. Your spoonfish will be accompanied by a colorful salad of local greens and citrus supremes."

After finishing what may have been the finest cuisine he had ever eaten, Samil stood from his wooden chair, holding up a glass full of brown ale. He scanned the table, his gaze landing upon Jesifaye. "Many years ago, this beautiful woman changed my life. She saved me when I was at my very lowest, and I owe her everything. Thank you for being my partner in this great adventure. Happy birthday, Jesifaye!" He raised the ale in the air and clanked it against Jonas' glass.

"To Jesifaye!" Jonas announced. Foam sloshed over the rims.

Milda reached under the table and brought out a box wrapped in decorative paper, neatly tied with a brown silk ribbon. "I had this made especially for you," she said, handing the gift over the table. "I hope you like it."

"Oh, what a beautiful box, and the wrapping is perfect. I don't want to open it." She placed the box on the table before her and admired the gift one more time before untying the ribbon. She carefully took each crisp fold and gingerly unwrapped the present, attentive not to wrinkle the paper.

"Come on!" Jonas exclaimed, smiling, running out of patience. "Just tear through it already."

Jesifaye lifted the lid from the box and removed the tissue. Reaching in, she pulled out a silvery slipper, embroidered with white and blue flourishes.

"Beautiful," Jesifaye breathlessly said. "Thank you, Milda, Jonas. They are just perfect."

Samil shot a suspicious look at Jonas. The same color as the dress; this was no coincidence.

"Here, now open my gift." The captain motioned to the headwaiter by waving his hand. From the kitchen walked Tabitha, Matilda's granddaughter.

She walked with her arms outstretched over the stone floor. The stylish box extended well past her left and right shoulders. She wound her way through the tables, taking care not to knock anyone in the head as she passed them by.

"My grandmother wishes she could have delivered this herself, but she cannot walk such distances anymore. She also said to tell you thank you for your business."

"Please tell Mrs. Brindamin that the pleasure was all mine. Oh, and this is for you." He handed the young woman ten gold coins. "That is for the delivery."

"What is this?" Jesifaye asked, standing up, her eyes dancing over the box.

"It's nothing, just a little token of my appreciation," Samil replied, enthralled by her smile. "Go ahead, open it. We don't have all night."

"All right...all right, don't rush me." She lifted the lid and handed it to Jonas.

Tears began to well in her eyes as she stared at the shimmering fabric. The dress was folded neatly in the box, revealing only the neck and bodice. She lifted out the dress by the shoulders, letting the flowing material cascade to the floor.

"Do you like it?" Samil asked, studying her face for an answer.

"There is nothing in the world like it. It's so light, like real silk." She held up the dress and pressed it against her shoulders, modeling it for the group. "Well, how do I look?"

"It looks like a perfect fit. Elegant, suitable for the throne if you ask me," Milda said, picking up the silver slippers. "These will complete the ensemble perfectly."

"Not going to tell anyone, huh, Jonas," Samil said, raising an eyebrow at the harbormaster.

"I can't keep a secret like this from Milda. Have you ever slept on our sofa? I have; it's not comfortable at all."

"That's where you'll be sleeping tonight after a comment like that," Milda said, punching Jonas in the shoulder.

They all laughed at Jonas' exaggerated expression of pain while he rubbed his shoulder.

The night went on and many toasts were made in honor of Jesifaye's birthday. The conversation turned to the many adventures and travels that Samil and Jesifaye had experienced.

"What will you do now that you have been to Netherhaven?" Milda asked, eating her last bite of dessert. "It seems you have done it all. Will you just go back to Methina and run your business or retire on your plantation home?"

"It's true, we are wealthier than I ever imagined, but there is one place that has eluded me all these years," Samil said in a pensive tone.

"Where is that?" Jonas replied, sipping his ale.

"We've all heard the stories about the Crystal City," Samil continued. "It's rumored no Jinian has ever seen the city itself. Sure, they negotiate with merchants outside the entrance, but to have something that their king finds truly valuable is a rare thing. And I believe that I have something that is so rare that the king will have to meet with me."

"Do you mean that you have more Netherhaven silk?" Jonas blurted.

"Shh, keep your voice down," the captain whispered. "Yes, I have more silk, two bolts. There is no way the Goriath king would refuse me. Netherhaven silk is the rarest thing in the world as far as I know."

"I keep telling him that I feel it's a bad idea to journey to the Goriath lair," Jesifaye interrupted. "We have all we could ever need and more, but Samil wants to deal with the best negotiators in the world."

"What do you think the king would trade for the silk?" Milda asked, intrigued by the idea.

"That is part of the adventure, isn't it? Who knows what riches lay within the king's treasury, priceless things that no one has ever seen. Just to see the treasury would be worth the trip." Samil's eyes brightened at the thought. "I must see the Crystal City."

"And just how will you get there?" Jonas asked, finishing his drink.

"Simple really," Samil replied. "I'll find someone who has been there, the giants of Derkshire probably. I'm sure I'll be able to negotiate for the information I need." Jesifaye rolled her eyes at Samil. "She doesn't want to come. She thinks this one is too dangerous."

"There is some truth to all rumors and stories," Jesifaye insisted. "Goriath giants cannot be trusted. The risk is too great. If I lost you, I would have no one left. Besides, it's my birthday. Let's not talk of this anymore tonight."

Walking back to the Jesifaye Moon, the streets and Belenor pier were still and silent. The crashing waves outside the jetty pounded the coastline, yet the sound was peaceful within the bay. Samil and Jesifaye walked down the dock looking across the water. Bobbing lamps lit the decks of hundreds of vessels anchored for the night.

"You go on and get some sleep. I feel like walking some more," Jesifaye said, still gazing at the harbor.

"Are you sure? I could send Mr. Frobrin to keep an eye on you."

"Nonsense," she insisted. "Now go to bed. I will see you at breakfast."

The gangplank creaked as the captain stepped up to the deck. He turned around to see Jesifaye take off her shoes and walk to the end of the dock and sit down, letting her feet hang over the water.

The wind jostled her hair and she brushed it aside with her fingers. She often looked out over the ocean when it was calm and serene, thinking about her parents, wondering if they were watching her now and trying to get a sense of the direction she should go. It was the chance to gain a grasp on the pressing questions on her mind.

Should we go to the land of the giants? she thought, looking into the horizon. It was a question she had been asking herself for months. The decision was hers to make. After all, the vast trading enterprise in Methina was hers. She commanded thirty-six ships and employed more than nine hundred people from her islands, although to the outside observer, Samil ran the business...and Jesifaye was all too happy *not* dealing with merchants.

She trusted Samil with her life and her wealth, but a feeling of doubt always came when thinking about traveling to the Goriath giants. She sighed heavily, the answers not coming to her mind. Placing her hands on the edge of the dock, she felt odd grooves in the wood. She casually traced the design with her forefinger, not looking at the dock, until it finally occurred to her that she was tracing letters in the wood. She squinted her eyes at the weathered word.

"Thanan," she whispered.

Who is Thanan? she thought. A warm feeling began welling in her bosom, as if the answer to her pressing question had come to her in the form of a strange carving on the Belenor dock.

CHAPTER FIVE

A NEW FAMILY

For one and a half years, the Jinian tirelessly shoveled his way through endless piles of coal, fueling the forges at Hardrock, never uttering one word of complaint or disdain. He was now twenty-two and grew stronger and more patient with every day that passed. He also grew to love the gruff old blacksmith and admired his will to keep going unfailingly despite his physical shortcomings and sour disposition.

After a long day's work, Thanan slowly walked home, stopping every once in a while to pick up pebbles and throw them in the waterway that flowed slowly beside the path. Large schools of silvery fish scattered each time a pebble broke the surface. Some of them even tried to eat the pebbles when they hit the surface, but promptly spat them out, realizing the pebbles weren't food.

He paid little attention as he arrived at his tent or at least where his tent was supposed to be. Everything was gone. As he looked around to find some kind of evidence as to what happened, he noticed Kigron approaching. It had been six months since he had seen the captain.

"Kigron, where have you been? Where's my tent? Everything is gone."

"Calm down, Jinian, everything is fine," Kigron interrupted. "Your things have been moved to my family's home, just outside the main square. The general feels that it would do you some good living with a Goriath family now, and I drew the short straw." Kigron smiled at his own humor.

"I knew you had a family," Thanan replied with a smile. "You couldn't keep them a secret forever."

"Yes, you are very bright," Kigron said sarcastically. "Seretha will be expecting us for supper. Move out."

Kigron's home was simple, as were most of the soldiers' homes at Hardrock. Those who did not have families lived in the barracks, but soldiers with families enjoyed a more private life in a more spacious tent provided them by the military. Even though he was the general's son, he did not take advantage. This was significantly different from the main population of Crystal City, where all the homes were painstakingly carved into the rock, affording everyone a spacious cave to live in.

Because of the mobile nature of the military, tents were the home of choice for the residents at Hardrock Quarry, except for the lucky few living on the terraces.

The furnishings, however, ranged widely from the luxurious to a more impoverished décor. It all depended on what each family had the chance or time to take with them when they left the city centuries ago. As for the captain and his family, although they had the means to live a more lavish lifestyle, they chose a simple existence.

"Dadi, Dadi!" three little giants called out as their father entered the tent.

"All right…all right, calm down, you three," Kigron said, smiling as he dragged his son and two daughters across the floor with his ankles.

The children giggled as their enormous father shook them off one by one. The children turned toward the stranger in the doorway.

"Seretha, come meet our guest from Jin."

The sounds of clanging pots and pans in the kitchen stopped abruptly. A tall, slender woman came around the curtain that separated the main living area from the kitchen. She was wearing a worn apron, frayed at the hems, over her dress. She was magnificent to behold, distinguished and plainly beautiful. Long black hair draped over both shoulders, flowing past her hips.

Goriath women's physical appearances were very different from their male counterparts. They were still very tall, averaging six and a half to seven feet, but their build was slender and quite shapely. Their facial features were softer, less prominent.

"So you are the one I have heard so much about," she said, smiling at Thanan. "I've seen you walking through the garrison but never introduced myself. What do we call you?"

"Purgon calls him incompetent," Kigron suggested.

"Oh, be nice, Kigron," she scolded, slapping her husband's arm. "He's our guest now."

"To my family at home, I am 'Seven,'" he said, bowing, his eyes never leaving her gaze. "Kigron calls me 'Jinian,' but my name is Thanan. It's my privilege to finally meet you. Kigron has kept your identity a secret."

"Thanan it is then," she replied, extending both hands to the new family member. "Welcome to your new home."

"Thank you," Thanan humbly said.

"Can you show Thanan to his room?" Seretha asked Kigron. "Supper will be ready shortly. Simo...Tirothia...Tavris, come set the table."

"Coming, Mami," three little voices called back in unison.

The table was set and Thanan sat down to a welcomed home-cooked meal. A basket of warm, crusty bread was passed around the table followed by a large bowl of white fish in a salty broth. The fish had the distinct mineral taste of crystal dust throughout the flaky flesh. It was a flavor that once turned Thanan's stomach, but in time he began to crave it.

The fish were farmed in large underground ponds that existed naturally inside the caves. Sophisticated systems of ponds and waterways stretched from Hardrock to the Crystal City. Hundreds of times, Thanan walked along the cold waterway watching schools of glowing fish lazily meander by. The rolling and spiraling fish reminded Thanan of the silken flags that adorned the great towers of Jin, billowing in the gentle breeze.

The fish gave off a natural luminescence, which made them easy to harvest. Goriath and his followers discovered them long ago when they entered the caves. The silvery fish began to flourish because of the farming techniques introduced by the giants. They grew fat and long. From then on, they had been a staple of the Goriath diet. Thanan was amazed that any life could exist so deep underground without any direct sunlight, yet life thrived in the caverns because of the blue glow of Xavantha.

Seretha passed the bread. "Your room is comfortable, I hope."

"Yes, it's perfect. Thank you," Thanan replied through a mouthful of fish.

The meal was pleasant and the conversation enlightening. Politics, religion, and general everyday life were the conversational fare of the evening.

"It seems I have missed quite a lot while I was away," Kigron began, tearing a biscuit in half. "Tell me, Jinian, how are you faring with Purgon? I see he has not killed you yet."

"Let's just say that nobody knows how to handle a broom or a shovel better than I," Thanan replied.

Seretha laughed.

"He's a good giant, trustworthy. The general could think of no one better to train you."

"Train me? The old giant has barely said a word to me in almost two years."

"That's just his way. He is old, disciplined. He was once a soldier, a captain in fact. He might had even become a general if things had happened differently. His fierce fighting was legendary in the quarry. General Tygrothian and Purgon are the last living giants from the old world. Their skin still shows a hint of the lighter shade of the Sundwellers and their facial features are farer than ours. They are taller too, except that Purgon is hunched from the brutality of the wars. He lost his left kneecap when a Derkshire blade was driven through it, and his left eye was lost because of a stray arrow. Rumor has it that he keeps the kneecap and eyeball in a metal box, next to his cot. In his younger days he would bring them out while telling battle stories.

"One of my favorite stories is when Purgon walked a hundred miles without a kneecap, all the while killing ten more enemies. That one has been told around Goriath dinner tables for centuries. No one knows if it is true or not, but the dried-up old kneecap and eyeball are disgusting."

"When did he become a blacksmith?"

"When Tygrothian was promoted to general, Purgon retired from the military, being too crippled for battle. Purgon's brother, who was a blacksmith at the time, had just died, so Purgon took up the trade of his family. Soon after, he became a master like his brother."

"Your history is very interesting. Why do you live in the caverns instead of the outside?"

Kigron looked at Seretha for an answer.

Seretha poured her new houseguest another cup of water. "It is a long story, Thanan. Are you sure you want to spend your first night talking about such things?"

"I have been here in the caverns for two years now and know very little about your people. I would like to know more. I only know what my tutor taught me in class."

"Kigron is always hesitant to share this story. His family is directly linked to the beginning of the Goriath race. You might hear many versions of how we came to be here, living out our lives in the darkness.

"The Goriath giants' history is an interesting one," Seretha began. "For thousands of years there was only one race of giants, the giants of Derkshire, or as we call them, the Sundwellers. As a rule they were a gentle and peaceful nation that interfered with no one. They were a secluded race of approximately twenty thousand, mostly self-sufficient farmers and fishermen, with no ambitions to aspire to more than what they were, just simple giants."

Kigron interrupted, continuing to tell the story as if he had lived it. "More than a thousand years ago, one giant was not satisfied with merely a simple life tilling the ground and living by the sweat of his own labor."

Goriath Gil was born to an ordinary family of farmers in the heart of the Devlin, a small farming town in the Derkshire province. He grew tired of the life that his father had chosen for him, milling grain for the family business. He started holding secret meetings, ranting about the leaders of the city, their politics and archaic traditions. His rhetoric was enchanting to many who attended his meetings, and soon he gained the confidence of many giants. He then began publicly denouncing the old ways of their society, spouting lies about the true intentions of his new regime, until he had quite a following. He led a bold uprising and was successful in raising a small army against his own city and people.

After many years of war and despair, there was peace for a time. Devlin was left in ruins and the giants began the long process of rebuilding their precious city. Goriath Gil's numbers were dwindling, and in one last futile attempt to overthrow the city, he plotted to assassinate the regent, Hanioth.

Hanioth had recently been appointed leader of the giants because of the failing health of the king and queen. Goriath Gil met with Hanioth many times to convince him to conform to his new way of thinking, but Hanioth honored the traditions of his ancestors. This infuriated Goriath Gil to near madness. The only way to become the king was to remove the obstacle that most stood in his way: Hanioth. After that, the king and the queen would be easy.

Goriath Gil converted to his cause one of the regent's royal cooks, planning to poison Hanioth on the evening of the regent's fiftieth birthday celebration. The whole city would be celebrating not only the regent's birthday, but also the victory over Goriath Gil's insurgency. The regent, as a sign of unity, invited all to attend and even extended his hand of friendship to Goriath Gil and his rebels. Goriath Gil relished the thought of seeing the regent poisoned before his own eyes, so he accepted the generous offer to attend the celebration.

As the festivities commenced, the city was alive with performers and music. Giants throughout the city were singing songs of victory, dancing, and celebrating. Silken streamers waved in the breeze from the rock walls overlooking the square. Food and drink were in abundance.

A grand stage was constructed for the king, queen, the regent, and his wife to be seated along with other heads of government. Goriath Gil and his men were allowed in, but only if they surrendered their weapons to the city guard. They did so willingly because they knew what the true outcome of the celebration would be.

A hush came over the square as the regent tapped on his glass.

Hanioth stood, looking over his people with pride.

"My fellow giants, family, and friends. I stand before you humbled by your devotion to Devlin and our traditions. This celebration marks the time of reuniting with our wayward brothers and remembering those who have fallen, mighty giants who fought bravely and died for their countrymen, families, and lands. Tonight we honor them!"

A loud roar erupted from the crowd.

Goriath Gil stood among the multitude along with a few of his men. With a calm smile on his face, he watched intently while the regent delivered his speech. He took a glass from the waiter who stood next to him. Raising it up, he turned toward Hanioth, relishing in each pointless word. The regent continued proudly, "Please join me in a toast to our brothers." With his glass, he gestured toward Goriath Gil, confident, noble. "May we have continued peace for generations."

The regent raised his glass and drank. He placed his glass down and then raised both hands in celebration.

"To brothers!" the crowd yelled in unison.

Goriath Gil muttered with satisfaction, toasting his men. "To brothers...long live the king." He gulped down the ceremonial drink and then looked at Hanioth and then at the bottom of his own glass with confusion. Goriath Gil's eyes widened with shock, then dilated and rolled to the back of his head. His glass fell from his hand, shattering on the ground. The crowd around Goriath Gil and his men turned and gasped, backing away from the twitching giant. Goriath Gil stood only for a brief moment before the poison ravaged his body, causing him to convulse and collapse to the ground.

Goriath Gil's men turned away from him, intending to flee the scene, when the regent waved his hand.

From the tops of the walls of the square, the entire City Guard revealed themselves with bows drawn. With only a few exceptions, Goriath Gil's army was captured, tried, and sentenced to prison.

Unbeknownst to Goriath Gil, he had been betrayed by one of his own followers, whose guilty conscience got the better of him. The follower had secretly divulged to the regent's guards the details of the deadly plot. It was because of Hanioth's mercy that he ordered the poison that Goriath Gil consumed to not be deadly, but only to paralyze him for a short time.

Later, the remaining insurgents who had escaped capture, led by a young giant named Tygrothian (who was no more than a bitter berry farmer's son), stormed the prison and freed Goriath Gil and many of his soldiers.

Knowing he was defeated and numbering only three hundred, Goriath Gil and his followers vanished from the city, never to return. They traveled to the Crystal Valley, as it was called then, and swiftly destroyed a small clan of wild men who then occupied the caverns. Goriath Gil and his giants began to mine the valuable crystals for which the valley was rightly named.

Over the next few years, Goriath Gil slowly became mad with hatred and greed. He was prone to fits of rage. He proclaimed himself king of the underearth and commanded the worship of crystals and all things precious. He even secretly commanded his inner circle to see to it that the crystals would be ground into an undetectable powder and added to all the food of his followers.

Over time, the population developed a lust for the crystals and soon did not need to be commanded to worship them. It was now their culture, and they passed it from generation to generation. Their lust for all manner of crystals grew deeper, and so the mining went deeper and deeper with generations of avarice passing away with Goriath Gil as their king.

Then Goriath Gil suddenly died, presumably assassinated by poisoning, but the irrevocable damage was done. The actions of just one changed an entire race forever.

"That is an incredible story," Thanan said, realizing he had not taken a bite during the story.

"My father's generation slowly mutated because of the lack of direct sunlight and their gluttonous diet of crystal dust. Goriaths are on average two feet shorter now, and our skin is covered with tiny, pale greenish-blue scales. Some of us, as you know, can disappear, but it's a fading trait. We call ourselves 'Goriath giants' to distinguish us from our sundwelling cousins."

"So General Tygrothian is the reason you are here."

"Yes, it is a weight he bears every day."

"And what about the Sundwellers, the giants of Derkshire? Do you ever see them? Do they know where you are?"

Kigron and Seretha looked at each other with hope in their eyes.

"The general is determined to unite us again."

"Do you really think the general can negotiate a treaty with the Sundwellers?" Seretha asked earnestly. "My mother and father would have given their lives for the reuniting of the two races."

"King Grishon is running the mining crews ragged. It is rumored that the cave slug has enslaved some of his followers who openly opposed him, those who belong to the clans that left with the military centuries ago." Kigron dropped his fist to the table, rattling the dishes. "He holds a grudge against them, because of their names. There must be a treaty with the Sundwellers or war will be upon us for sure. If anyone can accomplish this, my father will. He has rebuilt and maintained a trusting relationship with the king of the Sundwellers for some time now, and a treaty has been the topic of many of their assemblies."

The heated conversation was suddenly doused by a shrill yelp from across the table. A full cup of water flew in the air as Tirothia screamed and danced in a circle as if she had seen a cave ghoul. The cup landed in the center of the platter of fish, spilling its water and one small spiny passenger. A spine-backed cave newt let out a loud croak, glowed red, and scampered out of its water prison, jumping across the table. Seretha leaped back, tipping over her chair as the slimy-skinned visitor jumped to the floor and darted out of the tent.

Kigron was half standing with a knife in his hand, ready to strike like a cornered scaly spitter, when he realized that Tavris was snickering under his breath at the spectacle of the suppertime entertainment.

Tavris or Tav as they called the young giant, even at the tender age of five, had earned a reputation in the housing community as a mischievous trickster, which frustrated Kigron to no end and mortified his mother. This wasn't the first four-legged visitor to have made an appearance at supper, but it was the slimiest.

In addition to his notorious pranks, Tav was also naturally predisposed to archery, which caused Kigron to beam with pride. This was an emotion he tried to conceal from the men. At age four,

Tavris picked off a scurrying greken, a sort of rodent that roamed abandoned hallways, from fifty feet away in a dimly lit tunnel. The arrow was placed perfectly through the scavenger's head, killing it instantly. Even now, a year later, the story is still recounted with ever growing embellishment.

Kigron put down his knife and shouted, "Tav, so help me boy!"

Thanan chuckled under his breath at the captain of the military losing his temper with his young son. Kigron glanced at his guest with one eyebrow raised, not amused.

"Sorry, Kigron," he quickly said, clearing his throat, trying to hide his smile.

"Tav, you will be cleaning up this mess. Do you understand me?"

Stuttering, Tavris replied, "Y-yes, ss-sir."

"All right, girls," Seretha interrupted. "Off to bed."

"Yes, Mami," the girls said together.

The children embraced each of their parents one by one as they left the table.

Tavris paused briefly as he passed Thanan. "Goo-g-good night, sir," Tavris stuttered quickly, hugging Thanan's leg, ignoring his father's command to clean up the mess as he ran off to his room.

Thanan stood, dropping his napkin on the table. "I think I'll retire as well, early day at the shop. Those forges don't fuel themselves."

"Careful, Jinian, you're beginning to sound like Purgon," Kigron laughed.

Thanan turned to Seretha and thanked her for the wonderful meal and retired for the night.

CHAPTER SIX

A NEW TRADITION

Thanan woke to the usual symphony of Hardrock. The distant sound of ringing hammers from the armory was muted by sharp clacking hooves just outside the tent. He plopped both feet on the cold rock floor, rubbing his eyes until they were clear and focused. Inhaling deeply, the sweet smell of flat cakes filled his nostrils, waking him up even more. He sighed heavily thinking of his mission as he began to dress himself for another day of shoveling. There were more questions rather than answers in his mind. He knew there was much more to accomplish in this subterranean world and he wondered if he had made correct decisions thus far. Not for one moment did he doubt his father's direction, but time was passing so quickly.

Thanan stood up from his bed, twisting his neck back and forth, loosening it up. He grabbed a few frags from the crate in the corner for his morning biscuit. Resolved to put full confidence in his father's will, he pushed his questions to the back of his mind, at least for a while.

"Good morning, Jinian," the unusually cheerful Purgon exclaimed as Thanan walked into the shop.

For two and a half years, the gruff old giant never greeted Thanan first before. Usually he was met with a grumble, a dismissive nod of the head, or at best, a "Get to work, Jinian."

"Purgon, do you have a fever?" Thanan asked playfully. "I think the heat from the forge has made you mad. You're smiling. Are you letting me go?"

"Word has made its way from the Whitehall outpost that my great-great grandsons, Agrinoth and Torik, will be two of the next candidates inducted into the Guardian Order. Even your incompetence will not dampen my spirits this morning."

"That's kind of you to say, Purgon."

Purgon held the edge of a sword to the grinding stone. Sparks rained down, dancing on the floor until they were snuffed out.

"Since you're in such good spirits, Purgon, may I try my hand at the forge today? You know, since you're in such a good mood."

The grinding came to a sudden halt and Purgon looked up with his one good eye, examining the Jinian, making him feel uncomfortable. Thanan gulped silently and stared back, his eyes never wavering.

"Hmph," he grumbled to himself, rubbing his chin. "You think you are up to the challenge, do you? I have my doubts."

Thanan looked down at the floor and closed his eyes, a little frustrated, but said nothing. Sweeping and shoveling for so long had begun to take their toll, although he would have happily done so for two more years if necessary.

"But today is a good day, Jinian," he continued, breaking the silence. "Here, take this."

Purgon extended his hand to Thanan. In it was a dusty apron, stiff and crumpled from years of neglect.

"Don't make me regret this," the crippled blacksmith growled.

Thanan, in shock, took the apron and replied, "You won't, Purgon. You won't. You have my word."

The blacksmith studied Thanan's face for a moment and nodded as if he had made the right decision.

"Only a few Goriaths were allowed to use the great forges in the Crystal City, Jinian," Purgon stated, walking his apprentice through the shop. "In fact, there have only been five master blacksmiths in the long Goriath history. I am the last to hold such an honored position. The weapons and armor that a master forges are said to have no equal."

"I have seen the work you have done, Purgon. Not even the masters in my great kingdom can make such weapons."

Purgon paused, looking into the glowing forge, his eyes like fire. "There was one other though, whose skill was legendary; the molten ore seemed to obey his will. He crafted two swords, twins of unparalleled strength."

Thanan put the apron over his head and tied the straps tightly around his waist. The leather straps went around him twice before fitting properly. He stepped up to Purgon's forge. The heat was intense. He stared into the fire, not wanting to make a mistake.

Grabbing the tongs from the wall, he plunged them into the white coal and pulled out a glowing blade, staring at the metal. The vibrant yellow dimmed to orange and then deep red, and finally to black.

"What are you doing, Jinian?" Purgon asked in a tone sounding more like his father than a grumpy blacksmith.

Thanan's heart leaped. He looked at his master, confused. "What do you mean? Did I do it wrong?"

"It seems you have jumped a few steps."

"Sir?"

"You cannot simply pluck another man's work from the forge and begin hammering away. Nor can you use another man's hammer, anvil, or forge."

Thanan looked even more confused. "Why did you bring me here?" The apprentice placed the blade back into the forge and hung the tongs on the wall.

Purgon, suddenly looking even more fatherly, spoke from his heart. "Everything has its way, Thanan. There is an order to all things in the universe, the way the stars move, the setting sun, Xavantha's light. If you leap before your stride is long enough, you will fall. A blacksmith's journey has a beginning. You cannot start anywhere else, but there. Here...take my hammer." He dropped it into Thanan's hand. The Jinian could only slow the weight before it connected solidly to the anvil. It rang through the shop.

Thanan hefted the weight and studied it. He noticed Purgon's maker's mark on the butt of the handle, and it became clear what he needed to do. "Purgon...will you instruct me how to build a forge?"

"Of course," he replied, smiling a rare smile.

On the Fifth Cycle of Zerak, which is to say the summer solstice in Giantish, the entire garrison welcomed the troops from Whitehall for the solstice celebration. It was a joyous time for the Goriaths at Hardrock. Colorful canvas flags representing the clans bobbed up and down as giants poured into the quarry. Purgon welcomed his great-great grandsons with open arms as cheers rose from the multitude and rang throughout the caverns.

The Goriath holiday was a distant echo of the traditions when the two races were one. The holiday was originally spent with family and friends, feasting on the fruits and beasts of the land. It was a grand celebration, full of song, laughter, and the rekindling of friendships.

The giants of Derkshire were simple farmers, and family was central to their faith. They loved the soil and the bounty it brought their people. But the Goriaths in the Crystal City celebrated a diluted version of the holiday. They all would gather in the city square under the glowing Xavantha Crystal, the Light of the God, in the ancient tongue. The giants brought Xavantha tribute and placed it under its radiating light in the hope they would be granted wealth and prosperity. It was a perversion of a beautiful way of life that only benefited the king and his coffers.

However, Tygrothian and his followers, upon leaving the capital city, abandoned the corrupt tradition of the Goriath kings. For centuries, the Fifth Cycle of Zerak was not observed outside of Crystal City.

Giants at Hardrock and Whitehall were now hearkening back to a more simple time in their history, as if the spirits from the past were speaking from the dust, beckoning them from their caves. They owed their rekindled interest in their ancestors' traditions to Tygrothian, who had begun to tell tales of the wonders outside the confines of the caves. His stories had their imaginations reeling as they learned of a time when their blood was more pure.

Many Goriaths had never been outside the Crystal Caves. They never had felt a soft morning breeze briskly caress their cheek, nor had they beheld the expanse of the galaxy-filled sky. Most of them still believed that Xavantha created its own light. The soldiers regularly left the caves for training exercises, but the general population stayed inside, happy in their ignorance.

After many decades of planting the seeds of excitement and interest, the general slowly reintroduced the holiday, bringing his people together to feast and watch their warriors battle in the town square of Hardrock; however, the time had now arrived to bring back the lost celebration to its fullness, outside and under the sun and galaxies.

Excitement filled everyone's heart as they made preparations for the journey to the unfamiliar world outside. They traveled three days to where the long anticipated gathering would take place.

For Thanan, it had been four years since he had seen the sun or smelled the fresh valley air. He paused as he took that first breath, thinking back on the time when he first met his friend Kigron on the crag path. *Things would have gone much differently if he had died falling over that cliff*, he thought.

Thanan looked out over a lush, widespread meadow, which sat

amidst the foothills of the Goriath Valley.

"What is this place, Kigron?" Thanan asked, stepping on the wild grass.

"It is known to be the last encampment of Goriath the First and his dissenters before they entered the caves to begin their subterranean existence."

The family walked together down the green slopes toward the lake. Tavris, Tirothia, and Simo ran for the lake's edge.

"Be careful, you three!" Seretha called out to them. "Tirothia, keep an eye on your brother and sister."

"I will," the girl called back, never taking her eyes off the lake.

"The meadow was named Loriam, after Goriath Gil's first wife," Kigron continued. "It was said that she suffered a horrible wound inflicted by one of the Derkshire archers as Goriath Gil and his men escaped the city wall. They made their way to the valley and stopped in a beautiful meadow because Goriath Gil knew his wife could not make the last climb to the caves. He ordered his physicians to save her life, but to no avail. She died in this blossom-filled meadow and was buried near the lake, bordering the meadow on the north. There is a boulder at the lake's edge that bears her name."

"Things might have turned out differently if she didn't die," Thanan suggested.

"Loriam's death did not change the fact that Goriath Gil was mad. Her death only sped things up a bit. In a fit of rage, he picked up a smooth stone from the meadow floor and bashed it against his unsuspecting physician's head. He died instantly. His other physician, in shock from the attack, attempted to run from Goriath Gil's tent. Goriath Gil tackled him to the ground, his eyes crazed like a wild man. He struck the physician over and over with his fists and finally strangled him. He ordered both their bodies to be hung from the limbs of an old Zinia tree that shadowed the trail leading into Loriam. It was a final warning to any who dared disobey the new king.

"Goriath Gil's hatred for his people deepened even to the point that he detested his own blood. And thus, he ordered his people to eat the dust of the crystal, which changed them forever."

"I think this is the place," Seretha announced, changing the subject. She dropped the blankets and began spreading them over the grass. "The view of the lake is perfect."

The meadow was dotted with trees, offering shade to the first groups of giants that flooded the valley throughout mid-morning. Families were scattered across the countryside cooking their contribution for the feast. All manner of fish dishes and bread would fill the banquet tables along with many varieties of mushrooms, also farmed and cultivated within the darkness of the caves. Those who did not have much to offer to the banquet instead gathered wood for the cooking fires or helped build the arena where the contests would be held.

In the old days, contests of strength were held for entertainment, and bragging rights went to the strongest.

"The general's here!" a voice yelled from across the meadow.

Tygrothian entered the meadow from the west, but he wasn't alone. With him walked ten strangers. Everyone's heads turned as Tygrothian and his companions crossed the meadow together.

Chattering children ran to greet the general and his entourage as whispers rode the wind from camp to camp. The children met them with wondrous eyes as they saw ten beings that were unlike anyone they had ever beheld before. They could not have imagined that the general, who was a mighty giant in stature, was shorter than all the ten. Their skin was tan, but there was something strangely familiar about them. It was their eyes, noble like Tygrothian's.

Thanan was busy helping the giants build the makeshift arena for the games. He noticed the commotion and went to investigate for himself. A large circle of Goriath giants had formed around the general and his guests.

"Everyone," the general said with a smile, "may I introduce our new friends, Prince Ky and Princess Tirin of the Derkshire." Gasps of disbelief and surprise spread quickly through the crowd. "Please make our guests feel welcome."

The giant royalty and the general cut through the crowd slowly, making their way to Tygrothian's table.

"You will do me and my family the honor of joining us for supper at tonight's celebration," Tygrothian insisted.

"The honor is ours," Princess Tirin replied, extending her hand gracefully.

The princess was tall and thin like a willow. Her hips swayed gently as she glided over the meadow. Prince Ky walked beside her, holding her hand gently.

There were four Sundwellers, the bodyguards of the prince and the princess. They showed little emotion as the crowds clamored around the royalty.

Their helmets and breastplates were polished to a mirrored

finish, resembling the colors of the Derkshire Forest at twilight. The armor was ornately etched with leaves and vines. Everything about them seemed to celebrate the bounty of the land, but the other four Sundwellers were different. Thanan observed their demeanor to be more warrior-like than that of the bodyguards, less refined and more menacing. They wore dull, thick armor scarred by many battles of their past. Broad swords hung from their hips. They hefted thick shields, adorned with similar leaves and vines as those on the bodyguards' breastplates, only their shields were unpolished and dented.

"These are our strongest warriors," Princess Tirin said, pointing to the four. "They wish to join with your soldiers in the contests. The giants of Devlin will relish in the stories of the blade and the bow."

"Of course," the general replied. "The celebration will be recounted for generations."

The camps continued to be built well into the late afternoon. As the sky dimmed, the simple tents began to glow and flicker with firelight.

Giants all over the meadow were busy preparing their specialties for the following day's banquets. The aroma of fresh bread and sweet grain cakes swept across the meadow, which overpowered even the strong musky scent of millions of wildflowers that covered the rolling hills of Loriam. The feast would commemorate what the general hoped would be the first of many celebrations for his people.

At the center of Loriam was constructed a rough wooden stadium in the shape of a crescent moon. Benches lined its perimeter six rows high and overlooked the field where the competitions would take place. At the center of the arc rose a tall platform, which held three seats, one for the prince, one for the princess, and one for the general. It was draped in green linens with gold threads woven throughout, and on the trim thereof was sewn in gold the ancient symbol of victory and honor, the symbol of the Guardian Order.

When night fell, the watchman sounded the zortusk horn. An audience one thousand strong gathered all around the arena. When all the seats were filled, families spread blankets and sat along the open end of the meadow.

The general stood from his canopy-covered platform and raised his hands. Blue torchlight pooled around him from above, his eyes focused on his fellow giants. Within a moment the great crowd went silent and looked toward their leader. He was the most respected Goriath among the dissenters who left the great cavern city. When he spoke, it was with great authority, causing one's heart to quake.

"My friends," he gestured to the crowd, "tonight we celebrate as we once did, when our blood ran pure. When the poison of guilt and regret did not stain our garments."

The multitude looked on the general in silence, hanging on his every word.

"Too long did I follow and remain silent. I did not follow blindly, but with my eyes wide open. And now I look through eyes of shame. There are now only two who remember the ways of old, and our memories are emblazoned with regret forever. I have seen generations pass from before my face, each one more regrettable than the one before. Yes, we were mighty in war, but yet we still lusted for more. We were mighty in obtaining riches of all manner, but still coveted that which was not ours. Yes! We were mighty, but we were the mighty arm for a weak spirit. That all changed when we turned our backs to evil and abandoned our weak ways."

Tygrothian paused and looked at Princess Tirin for a moment. He smiled. "Forgive the ramblings of an old soldier. Tonight is for you. Tonight we take our first steps out of the darkness and embrace our future!"

Cheers rose from the crowd, and the general took his seat.

The festivities went long into the night. An enormous bonfire was the centerpiece, which set the stage and offered its light for the night's entertainment. Thanan sat with Kigron and his family throughout the evening and enjoyed a traditional meal of boiled fish and mushrooms with heavy bread. The four warriors from Devlin walked from camp to camp introducing themselves to the Goriath soldiers. When they reached Kigron's camp, they stopped to meet the famed Captain Kigron, General Tygrothian's son. The sundwelling warriors were much friendlier than Thanan had originally thought they would be.

Suddenly, a loud crash broke through the joyous sounds of dining and celebrating giants. Two tents over, Tremik Tak threw over a pile of firewood and cursed as his cooking pot spilled over the fire.

"Where is it?" Tremik growled. The famed archer frantically paced from camp to camp, yelling at whomever dared get in his way. "Where is it?" he yelled again, clutching Digroth by the tunic.

Digroth, in shock from the attack, swung wildly at Tremik and struck his head with his wooden soupspoon. Three warriors from Whitehall saw the commotion and jumped into the fray to protect their fellow Whitehaller, Digroth. The neighboring camp from

Hardrock stormed the group, knocking them all to the ground. Tremik, in a rage, picked up one of the Whitehall soldiers and threw him into a wooden tent post, causing it to splinter and collapse to the ground.

Captain Kigron arrived at the brawl with a look on his face that would scare a rabid Gribon. Just then, Frothian from Whitehall was thrown from the pack and lunged at the captain, hitting him square in the belly with his shoulder. The chanting spectators gasped and instantly went silent. In the frenzy, Frothian did not realize the mistake he had just made. The young soldier looked up at the face of the mighty captain, his eyes as big as boiled eggs. With one quick motion, the unfortunate soldier from Whitehall did not wake until the next morning.

"Tremik!" Kigron commanded. "That's enough!"

Right at that moment, Captain Shimian and his two commanders from Whitehall started breaking up the fight.

"My bow has gone missing, Captain. Digroth was asking many questions about it this morning," Tremik said accusingly.

Digroth wiped the dripping blood from his nose and looked at Shimian and shook his head.

"He's gone mad, I never touched his old bow," he grumbled, spitting blood on the ground.

Tremik shook off the hands that bound him and lunged for Digroth once again, but was stopped short by the thundering command of his captain.

"Tremik, one more step and it's the pit for you! You know I'll do it."

He stopped with a growl and again shook away from his captors, but did not approach Digroth again.

"All this over a missing bow?" Kigron asked dismissively.

"You better tame your animals, Captain," Shimian scolded Kigron.

"It would do you well to remember to whom you speak, Shimian," Kigron shot back, his face blank of expression.

The captain turned to the silent spectators. "Everyone who doesn't want ten days in the pit, get back to your tents at once! Tremik, you're with me!"

Although Shimian showed open disrespect toward his higher-ranking captain, it was just for appearance sake and Kigron knew it. It was all a ploy to regain control over his own rowdy soldiers and it worked. If Shimian was anything, he was loyal, loyal to General Tygrothian and loyal to his senior captain. Shimian was much older than Kigron, but his allegiance to Tygrothian was absolute; because Kigron had his father's blood coursing through his veins, Shimian was undeniably loyal.

"Captain, you know this bow's history," Tremik said, clenching his jaw. "It has been passed down through my family line from the third generation. My eighth great-grandfather, Herozian, crafted it, the first of its kind. You know its invention turned the tide in the Darvinian War until the arrogant Jinians interfered. Many soldiers and their posterity owe their lives to Herozian and those who rained hell from above."

"Do not presume to lecture me, Tremik Tak. You know little of the war. It was your grandfather's generation that left my father on those hills to die like a wounded animal. Do not utter one more word or it will be regrettable what I do to you. Do you understand my meaning?"

Tremik looked down and nodded shamefully. "My apologies,

sir."

"You sought blood among your brothers, and once this tournament is over, the pit will be your home. I'm sure your bow will be found; I just hope it's not by someone from Whitehall. You have done yourself no favors, Tremik."

The captain collected himself. "Now I'm going to forget for the moment that this happened, being that the general would not want his best archer put in chains on the eve of the tournament, would he?"

"No, Captain," he replied. "The tournament will be mine."

The four Devlin warriors looked on with slight smiles, realizing that these soldiers were very much like them, short tempered, but loyal in the end. They felt comfortable in their company.

It was a time like no other in the long Goriath history. Thanan had never seen the Goriaths behave in such a manner as this. So much laughter and unguarded behavior was contrary to the typical Goriath personality. Rows of giants clapped in time, stomping their feet to the music. Some danced through the crowd arm in arm, weaving their way in and out of camps, kicking up their heels along the way. They knocked over a few piles of wood and the occasional boiling pot of stew, but no one seemed to care.

Tavris and his older sister played in the meadow chasing light wisps around a tree trunk. The rising mist from the meadow floor exaggerated the glow emitting from the wisps. Thanan held Simo in his lap, holding her hands and helping her clap to the rhythm. Kigron looked at the Jinian holding his young daughter and a calm expression swept over his face.

"Tav! You and Tirothia stay close," their mother called.

"Yes, M-Mother," Tavris yelled as he snatched a wisp from the air and waved it close to Tirothia's face. She shrieked and giggled as Tavris chased her around a tree.

"I've entered you in the tournament!" Kigron yelled to Thanan over the music, timing it perfectly just as a chain of celebrating giants trampled through their camp.

"What!" The Jinian shouted, with a look of disbelief. He wasn't sure if he heard the captain correctly.

Dancing and singing giants reenacted epic battles from the Darvinian War with plenty of poetic license as the onlooking general just sat there with the slightest of smiles, shaking his head. He had been there on the war torn hills of Darvinshire, bleeding for wickedness in the forgotten age. Applause rang out as the last Darvinian fell to the stage with a loud gasp. Prince Ky and Princess Tirin led the standing ovation, and it swelled as the cast bowed in unison.

CHAPTER SEVEN

LET THE GAMES BEGIN

Cooking pots clanked, echoing over the meadow as the smells of morning swept through the camps. Rubbing his burning eyes only temporarily roused Thanan from his horrible night's sleep. A never-ending cycle of nightmares about stepping out into the arena without a weapon or clothes to speak of had completely worn out the Jinian.

What was Kigron thinking? Thanan wondered, dunking his head in a water basin. He laughed it off, like it couldn't be true.

The zortusk echoed over the field and down the canyon. Prince Ky stood at the banister holding a golden sash high above his head. It was his honor to begin the games. As the zortusk blast ended, he let the sash fall from his hands. It fluttered to the field and settled at the base of the platform. Princess Tirin had brought the ornately embroidered sash from Devlin. Written in green thread among the leaves and vines was the word, "unity." The crowed roared and the games began.

A withered old giant by the name of Kinji limped to the center of the arena. He held a brown wooden box in his hand.

"The first order of business is to determine who will battle in the Contest of the Blade!" he shouted to the eager crowd. "Let all who have the heart of Kizaga step forth and cast your lot!"

The whole presentation was designed to create excitement and anticipation for the onlookers, and Kinji was the best at it.

One by one, five sword-wielding warriors entered the dusty arena accompanied by explosions of cheers from the audience. Clan colors waved in the air to the rhythm of chanting giants.

Only eight could engage in the Contest of the Blade, but with the addition of two giants from Devlin, the rules were changed to allow ten. The first five were chosen by popular vote of Hardrock and Whitehall, and were invited to enter. The invited then would draw the names of the giants they would battle from lots cast by any Goriath who deemed himself a worthy opponent. The first to draw a name was Gyrozian. He walked proudly to Kinji, dropping his hand into the wooden box, drawing out a name. He read the name on the stone silently and gave Kinji a subtle smile of confidence. The warrior handed the stone over and stepped aside.

"Our first match in the sword will be Gyrozian of Whitehall versus Liruth of Hardrock," the old giant announced with delight, revving up the crowd again.

They howled and stomped their feet on the benches. There was a friendly rivalry that existed between Hardrock and Whitehall, and the crowd relished any opportunity to witness them competing against each other.

Although the numbers seemed to favor Hardrock, there was no shortage of pure talent from Whitehall. Some of the most noted Guardians hailed from Whitehall garrison.

Grokan from Hardrock was matched against Koroth, an intimidating looking giant from Devlin. It was an added element of excitement that the Goriaths were not expecting, and they hollered at the top of their lungs. Nimian from Whitehall would battle against Furoth, the other Devlin warrior, who looked nimble and gangly, and stood a foot and a half taller than Nimian: an odd pairing to be sure. Darnak and Shizian, both from Hardrock, would also entertain the audience with their exhibition matches using the blade.

The last soldier to step to the center of the field was no stranger to anyone. Agrinoth from Whitehall, great-grandson of Purgon, walked with confidence toward Kinji. The giants chanted his name as he drew the final opponent from the box. Handing his stone to Kinji, he drew his sword, pointing it toward the crowd. The cheers stopped cold.

"Anyone but me, anyone but me," Thanan whispered to himself.

"Thanan of Jin!" Kinji shouted, holding the stone out for all to see.

Thanan sat there frozen, not wanting to believe what he had just heard. He felt a jolt in his ribs from behind.

"Get out there, Jinian!" Kigron said quietly, pushing him out into the arena.

Seretha looked at Kigron with concern. "What have you done, Kigron?" she asked under her breath.

Thanan walked slowly out into the arena, feeling everyone's eyes upon him. He couldn't help but look down and scan up his legs and torso, just to make sure he was wearing clothes. *I wish I were still dreaming,* he thought.

Silence enveloped the moment until one single clap broke the silence. In all the excitement, not noticing the awkward moment, Tavris clapped proudly for his Jinian houseguest. One by one the giants began to applaud, if for no other reason than to see Agrinoth utterly destroy his clearly weaker opponent. There were a few naysayers in the crowd who expressed their opinions by throwing biscuits and half-eaten wor wren legs into the arena, accompanied with loud booing to make their point well known. The general and his royal guests stood and nodded at Kinji with approval. The matches would stand as drawn.

"The first match," Kinji announced, "will begin at mid hour! But first, the Tournament of the Archers will commence immediately near the lake's edge. Come and cheer for your favorites!"

"Mami, M-mami, may I go w-watch the arch-ch-chers?" Tavris asked excitedly. "P-please!"

"All right, all right," she replied. "Come on, Tirothia, Simo, let's go back to the tent. Let the men have their fun."

The young archer ran toward the lake, bow in hand, quiver slung over his back, imagining he was a hero from the ancient days.

A gentle eastern breeze swept down the valley wall. At the lake's edge, hundreds of giants and their families waited in anticipation for the archers to take the field. As always, there was an abundance of food being passed around.

The tournament was an opportunity for even the novice archer to show his prowess in the high skill of archery. The archers took much pride, for there were many who had descended from great and noble archers.

"Archers," Kinji announced, "enter the field!"

Right on cue, the rhythmic beating of drums drove the spectators wild. One by one, the archers took the field in a single-file line, keeping tempo with the drums. The two Devlin giants stood almost two feet taller than their Goriath counterparts and were much thinner, which made them easy to spot in the long line of archers. Although they were great archers in their own right, the giants of Devlin lacked the immense strength of the Goriath giants and weren't expected to pass the second round of the tournament, because of the great distances that Goriath archers could reach.

The presentation was ceremonious and gave tribute and respect to the art and discipline of archery. Each archer held their bow in their left hand, which was placed over their heart, signifying the sacrifice of life for their people and brothers in arms. Slung over each contestant's shoulder was a leather quiver full of feathered glory, uniquely fletched to represent the archer, his clan, and his lineage.

Tremik Tak led the archers onto the field, his face stern. He clearly had found his lost bow and was ready to humiliate the archers from Whitehall for their supposed prank. The very moment the archers reached the center of the field, the drums ceased with one last ground-shaking beat. The competitors turned in unison away from the lake and lowered their hands from their hearts. The crowd was crazed as Kinji, with his usual flair and showmanship, raised his hands enthusiastically, hushing the crowd.

"It is my esteemed honor and privilege to stand before you fine giants during this, the Fifth Cycle of Zerak. Today we witness greatness, nay...glory! Forty have entered the field and only one will leave victorious! It is with great pride that I now introduce our 'Lady Zinthia,' high judge of the tournament."

The muttering spectators went silent and bowed as Princess Tirin stood from her chair and walked toward Kinji, her hands clasped in front of her. She walked gracefully, her long crimson dress bending flowers as she moved over the field with elegance. Around her neck hung a jewel-encrusted ring, no larger than a Hagron's tail, which would be the prize for the victorious archer. Purgon had crafted it with his usual skill, but the intricate faceting of the stones astonished even him. The brilliance of the jewels refracted the light, resulting in a kaleidoscope of dancing colors on her skin.

Without hesitation, the princess played her part as Lady Zinthia to perfection.

"My new friends, it is surely an honor to serve in such a capacity as this," she pronounced, gracefully moving her hands as she spoke. "May I have the wisdom to judge rightly, that the victory will be just."

The multitude politely applauded the princess.

Kinji hushed the crowd once more. "This contest will be five rounds. Victory goes to the last giant standing. The first round will be three arrows at one hundred fifty paces," he pronounced to the archers and the crowd.

The audience muttered, making private bets among themselves, digging deep into their satchels and throwing frags into the circles. The obvious favorite was Tremik from Hardrock, but Zethrin Uru from Whitehall was a natural and had quite the following as well. The archers all stepped up to the shooting line. The cadence began.

"Archers, make ready," Kinji shouted.

Forty archers pulled arrows from their quivers and the crowd went silent.

Kinji continued, "Draw...aim..."

The creaking sound of bending bows filled everyone's ears.

"Loose!" he shouted.

Forty arrows flew through the air toward their targets, whistling as they spun. The metal-tipped missiles found their targets with dull thuds. The crowd stood and cheered. Tavris cheered alongside his father and raised his bow high in the air in celebration of the first arrow.

Again Kinji called out. "Archers, make ready...draw...aim...loose."

Princess Tirin applauded the Goriath archers' prowess and nodded her head toward the general, suggesting her approval.

Tremik's first two shots were impressive, both within the inner circle. It seemed he would not disappoint the crowd this day. Zethrin matched Tremik's grouping, and only one more arrow would advance them to the second round.

"Archers, make ready...draw..."

Tremik's nostrils flared as he inhaled the moment. His powerful bow bent with the sound of a creaking door, his eyes focused on the very center of the inner circle.

Kinji's voice echoed in his ears, "Aim."

The archer tightened his grip.

"Loose!"

Tremik loosed his arrow, but before it flew, a sharp crack was heard over the quiet field. Six hundred heads turned in unison to watch the arrow's flight, but there were only thirty-nine that found their targets. Looking down the line of archers, Tremik slumped forward onto the field, his face bloody and bow broken. His bow had shattered and flung viciously back into his face with a force and speed that was indescribable. His cheek and jawbone were shattered, as he lay motionless on the meadow.

The spectators jumped to their feet, gasping as Kinji ran to Tremik's side. Tremik's wife ran to her unconscious archer and cradled his battered face, her tears falling, bathing his bloody cheeks.

Kinji knelt down and picked up the shattered bow as if lifting a sleeping infant. Upon closer inspection he discovered suspicious grooves under the grip wrappings. The crowd was becoming nervous as whispers of sabotage began to spread.

Tremik was carried from the field and surgeons began tending to his wounds. General Tygrothian, Princess Tirin, Kigron, Kinji, and Kromag, the general's trusted physician, met privately to decide how to proceed.

"Kromag," the general said, "can Tremik continue?"

"No, sir. Tremik remains unconscious. My surgeons are doing their best to minimize the damage. A fragment of the bow entered his neck, and he's lost a lot of blood. We were lucky. An inch in either direction and he would be gone and you would have a riot on your hands."

"Go tend to him and report back when his condition changes," Tygrothian commanded.

"Sir, it was sabotage. I'm sure of it," Kinji insisted, presenting the bow. "There's no other explanation. The grip was notched, then rewrapped to conceal it from Tremik."

"We understand, Kinji," Kigron interrupted. "General, do we continue with the tournament or begin our investigation and root out this saboteur? Soon there will be cries of retribution."

"No, we will go on with the tournament and report this as a terrible accident," Tygrothian ordered. "We need this criminal to feel as if he has gotten away with it. We will deal with this in secret."

"According to our bylaws, there must be forty," Kinji reminded the council. "Someone must stand in for Tremik or the tournament is forfeited."

"I concur with Kinji," Lady Zinthia stated. "The rules are plain: We must continue with forty. Someone needs to compete in Tremik's place."

"Very well," the general agreed. "Kinji!"

"Yes, sir."

"Present this news to the crowd; let them choose the proxy from Hardrock."

Outside the tent, the masses were becoming discontented. There was money to be made and the sure thing was just dragged from the field, dead for all they knew. Although the Goriaths who followed Tygrothian all those years ago had turned away from the corrupted beliefs of their king, they had riches in their blood in a most literal way.

"My fellow giants," Kinji yelled, walking out to the center of the field, hushing the crowd, "I have just received word that Tremik is awake and stubborn as ever!" Laughter and cheers erupted from the multitude. "But his injuries have left him unable to finish. Therefore, it is up to you, for you now decide who will take his place. So judge wisely."

The crowd went silent and began scanning to see whom they would offer up to take Tremik's place. Nominations were passed around for consideration, some good and some bad.

Kneeling on the ground on the outskirts of the field, Tavris drew circles in the dirt with one of his arrowheads.

Jokingly, a guard from Whitehall pointed toward Tavris. "Why not use the boy? He looks handy with an arrow. Look at the pretty circles he's drawn."

The surrounding Whitehall soldiers burst out in laughter.

"Yes, let the boy take Tremik's place," the crowd said, chuckling loudly.

The laughter made its way through the multitude, catching the ears of a few Hardrock soldiers. They looked at each other, first to join in the laughter, but a moment later they realized that what the ignorant Whitehallers had suggested was brilliant.

"Yes! Let Tavris Gru compete," they began to say.

Tavris' name was passed throughout the crowd until it arrived firmly in Kigron's ear. Hardrock supporters clapped their hands and chanted loudly in unison "Tavris…Tavris…Tavris." Whitehall fans, looking confused at the spectacle, joined in the chant. Kigron's first instinct was to denounce the idea right then and there, but he was a prideful father, and the thought of embarrassing Whitehall after the supposed sabotage was too enticing to pass up.

"I see that look in your eye, Kigron," Thanan said. "This could end badly for you and Tavris."

"You've seen him; he makes my head hurt. But you can't deny

his natural skill with a bow," Kigron replied, relishing the thought.

Kigron looked over the crowd and spotted Shimian and gave him a nod. Shimian knew Kigron approved, and Shimian reciprocated with a loyal nod. This would teach his rabble a much-needed lesson.

"Time is up. Do you have an archer who can stand in the mighty shoes of Tremik?" Kinji howled.

A note was passed to Kinji. He opened it and read the name aloud. "I call the mighty Tavris Gru to come forward! Bring out the boy!"

The crowd cheered in unison, but for very different reasons.

"I hope you know what you're doing," Thanan told Kigron.

"Let them be the key to their own undoing," he replied.

Tavris ran to Kinji, spilling his arrows on the ground. He fumbled for a moment, trying to put them back in the quiver. Kigron winced, closed his eyes, and rubbed his creased brow. Laughter rang out from the Whitehallers. Kinji looked to Lady Zinthia for her approval. She smiled calmly and looked at the general then back at Kinji. Waving her hand in agreement, it was done; Tavris would be the youngest archer to compete in the tournament in giant history.

"We have our archer!" the animated announcer exclaimed. The giants roared with excitement as Tavris stepped to the shooting line alone, bow in hand.

A Hardrock spectator who was standing where Tavris had been drawing his circles noticed that the circles were not circles at all. They were complex mathematical equations illustrating arcs and trajectory. The shocked giant nonchalantly rubbed his foot in the dirt, erasing the evidence.

"Go Tavris!" he shouted.

Kinji placed his hand on Tavris' shoulder. "You have only one arrow, son. This is for Tremik. Make it count."

Kinji stepped back and began his cadence. The giants went quiet and started making their private wagers.

"Fifty frags says the boy misses entirely," a wrinkled old Whitehaller said.

"I'll take that bet," a soldier from Hardrock shot back.

"All he has to do is put the arrow inside the third circle and he advances," Thanan whispered.

"Archer, make ready...draw." Tavris pulled a blue and gold fletched arrow from his quiver and drew his bow. "Aim...loose!" Kinji finished.

The arrow flew, whistling along the way, finding its target with a dull thump. The wiggling shaft came to rest. The crowd was electric. Screams of delight and disappointment were heard over the entire meadow. Tavris had placed his arrow clearly within the second circle. He turned with a smile and raised his bow high in the air. Grumbling Whitehallers threw their lost frags and coins down to the ground in the gambling circles.

"The boy advances to the next round!" Kinji howled.

Twenty archers advanced to the second round: three arrows at two hundred paces.

Many of the remaining twenty competitors were renowned for their skill in archery. Zethrin Uru from Whitehall was the favorite among the loyal Whitehall followers, as well as Tikaga Zik and Lythias Til, nephew of Shimian. Jethor was the front-runner from Hardrock and bore the scar of the Guardian Order. Jarik Kul and the young Tavris Gru were also promising contenders for the prize.

Round two cut the archers by half once again, and to the dismay of many Whitehallers and their gem satchels, Tavris was improving with every arrow.

As expected, the Devlin archers did not make it to the third round. They were met with grand applause as they exited the field. The Goriath archers each shook the hands of the Devlin archers as they walked down the line. The distance of thousands of years between the separated races was closing, and this brought the general and his royal guests some comfort.

In the third round, the pressure of the tournament forced Jarik to overshoot the target completely on his third arrow. Sadly, he did not advance to the forth round with Tavris. The crowd was in awe of the boy who stood in the shadows of the archers beside him.

"Mami-Mami, they're saying Tav's name," Simo said, tugging Seretha's apron. "They're yelling Tavy's name."

Seretha dropped the pan she was washing, snatched up Simo, and ran toward the chanting crowd, looking panicked. She pushed her way to the front of the crowd and found Kigron and Thanan watching the tournament.

"What is going on?" she shouted at Kigron. "Why is Tav out there?"

"Shh…he just edged out Lythias and advanced to round four. There are only five remaining."

"Your final five!" Kinji exclaimed, pointing to the last five archers. "Round four will be two arrows at four hundred paces."

Oohs and ahs rose from the spectators. Lady Zinthia and Prince Ky were astonished by the superior skill of the archers and expressed their approval with a nod to the general.

"Only two will advance to the fifth and final round," Kinji

explained. "The bylaws of the tournament are clear. In the case of a tie, the proxy will not advance."

Zethrin, Tikaga, a surprise to everyone, Jyorian Rul from Whitehall, Jethor the Guardian, and Tavris would stand at the shooting line for round four.

"Be steady, boy!" one giant yelled to Tavris, only motivated by the hundred crystal frags he might lose if the boy wavered now.

Another grabbed his own throat and mimicked choking on a Mankor bone.

"Pay no attention to this rabble," Tavris' father shouted at the hecklers more than to his son. The rowdy giant's mouth shut immediately.

Kinji again began his cadence. "Archers make ready." The five marksmen pulled the first arrow from their quivers. "Draw," the creaking bows flexed in unison. "Aim...loose!" the announcer exclaimed.

In a blink of an eye, the arrows flew out of sight. Four hundred paces away, the judges raised colored flags to signal to the crowd as to which circle the archer hit. At this crucial point in the tournament, only a black, gold, or red flag would be enough to advance them to the final round.

One by one the judges raised their flags. For Zethrin, Tavris, and Tikaga, black flags were lifted. Red flags flew for Jethor and Jyorian, putting them in the fourth and fifth position going into the second arrow.

This was it, the final shot of the fourth round. The archers again stepped up to the line and pulled their arrows from their quivers. Jethor, more a warrior than an archer, showed no emotion as he raised his bow. Tikaga's eyes burned as he wiped the sweat from his dripping brow. Jyorian appeared steady as he nocked his arrow. Tavris was obviously fatigued because of being overbowed, but it was the only way to achieve such great distances. Seretha gripped Kigron's arm, feeling her son's pain. Zethrin was a pillar of stone. He nocked his arrow and drew his bow as if it were his first arrow of the tournament.

"Draw...aim...loose!"

The giants all turned to follow the arrows' paths. Faint thuds reverberated over the meadow. A gold flag was raised for Jethor. It was the best outcome he could hope for. A black flag was raised, this one for Zethrin from Whitehall. The Whitehallers howled with delight and collected their winnings from those who had bet against them. A red flag was raised and Jyorian lifted his bow, embraced Zethrin, and exited the field to a cheering crowd. A fourth flag flew, this one gold. A celebration broke out in the multitude when the gold that flew was meant for Tavris. Because of the bylaws, the only way Tavris would advance was if the final flag were red. His chances were slim, but still he dared to hope. The multitude held their breath, waiting for the last flag to wave.

"It's red! The flag is red!" a crazed giant yelled.

Tikaga's arrow still vibrated, just a hair's width outside the gold circle.

Tikaga lowered his head in disbelief as the whole Hardrock garrison chanted, "Tavris...Tavris...Tavris." It was true; the final two competitors were Zethrin, the great Whitehall archer and the unlikely proxy, Tavris Gru.

"Silence!" Kinji shouted. "Silence, make way for Lady Zinthia."

Once more the princess elegantly floated across the flower-carpeted field. She approached Kinji, Zethrin, and Tav with a graceful smile and turned to the crowd.

"This is the prize," she said lifting the silk ribbon over her head. "To claim the champion's ring the archer must carefully place his arrow within the jeweled ring without disturbing it."

The ring was hung and the fifth round began. The archers pulled reeds from Kinji's hand, and Tavris drew the shortest reed.

"The final round will be a single arrow at four hundred fifty paces. The archer's arrow must hit within the Champion's Ring without disturbing its position. Zethrin will loose the first arrow. Archer…make ready." The master archer nocked his last arrow with one fluid motion. "Draw…aim." The crowd was silent as he drew back his bow. "Loose!" Zethrin loosed his arrow.

Time seemed to stand still as the arrow flew effortlessly and struck the target with a faint thump. The judge ran to the target and without hesitation turned and raised a black flag excitedly, signifying a perfect center shot.

Eruptions of celebration filled the crowd, while sadness crept across the faces of those who had cheered for the unlikely hero of the day. There was no chance that Tavris could place a more perfect arrow. There simply was not enough room for another arrow to fit within the ring. It was the shot of a lifetime and Zethrin did not disappoint. Amidst all the laughter and celebration, Tavris stepped to the line and pulled an arrow from his leather quiver. A sly smile crept across his lips.

"Don't bother, boy. You've lost," a giant from Whitehall mocked, filling his gem satchel with frags.

"Let him shoot," another yelled.

Zethrin raised his hands and quieted the crowd. "I say let the boy have his turn. Go ahead, loose your arrow, son." Tavris raised his bow and took aim. He drew his bow as far as he could. His arms vibrated from the stress.

"What's he doing?" Kigron asked Thanan. "He's aiming too high."

Quiet chuckling began spreading through the crowd.

"The pressure has finally gotten to him!" a soldier shouted.

Tavris loosed his arrow. It sailed high into the air, clearly overshooting the Champion's Ring. He turned and smiled at his father and mother, who were looking quite sober and, frankly, a little worried. Everyone in the crowd was silent, looking at the boy with pity. A moment later, a screech echoed over the meadow. Giants looked at one another for an explanation.

The judge, who stood at the target, ran to retrieve the arrow. One hundred paces past the Champion's Ring, high in a tree, hung the body of a Loriam hen with Tavris' blue and gold fletching protruding from its skull. The wings of the massive bird still twitched erratically as the judge climbed the tree. The judge quickly ran back to report the incredible thing that he saw. As proof, he produced Tavris' arrow and a long green and blue quill pulled from the hen's tail. Looks of disbelief swept over the faces of the Whitehall spectators. Never before had any archer, let alone an unassuming, stuttering boy, so perfectly placed an arrow in a target or beast.

Tears of joy streamed down Seretha's cheeks as Kigron embraced her. Great cheers rang out from both soldiers and civilians alike as Zethrin raised Tavris' hand high in the air in victory. Tavris' grandfather stood with pride and applauded along with the prince and princess. Tavris was carried off the field atop the shoulders of mighty giants, but for this brief moment, in Tavris Gru's innocent mind, he was mightier than them all.

Mid hour came all too soon for Thanan. He walked slowly, hoping against all hope that an energy storm would somehow find its way from the southern skies and destroy the arena.

He passed Purgon along the way. "You look paler than usual, Jinian," the blacksmith said. "Do not distress; it is only an exhibition match, for the crowd. I am sure Agrinoth will take pity on you. For your sake, you better hope he does." Purgon chuckled, slapping the side of his apprentice's shoulder.

"You always give the best motivational speeches, Purgon." Thanan turned and continued to the arena.

The first four matches only served to whip the audience into a frenzy. The giants from Devlin were matched well against the Goriath soldiers. The matches were entertaining and demonstrated the prowess of the Sundwellers and Goriaths alike, although the training and technique leaned in favor of the Goriath.

The crowd reached a fever pitch as Kinji, for the last time, entered the arena. He walked slowly, driving the giants wild with anticipation. Agrinoth was truly loved amongst both Hardrock and Whitehall, and to cheer him on against an oddity such as the Jinian had them foaming at the mouth.

"Now for the moment you've been waiting for!" Kinji announced, shaking his fists in the air. "A battle that will surely be written on the Pyruthian Wall and recounted for generations."

In anticipation of the introduction, the crowd began to make a low growling sound that soon swelled to a full roar. Kinji continued with even more flair than usual.

"May I present for your delectation a giant who needs no introduction…a warrior whose skill with a Zythera blade is like that of Master Kizaga himself. It is my unparalleled privilege to introduce…the Whitehall warrior himself, Agrinoth!"

The wooden benches rocked as the spectators stomped their feet.

Agrinoth stepped from the shadows, not appreciating Kinji's showmanship. His face was serious and focused. Light glinted off the broad Zythera blade he held in his right hand, no doubt forged by his great-great grandfather, Purgon. His massive body was encased in scaled armor that had been hardened by the intense heat of the Hardrock forges.

"And now for the challenger," Kinji heralded, "a stranger from a faraway land, whose stature is shorter than Grimelik's temper…" Grimelik glared at Kinji for a moment and then nodded his head in agreement. He then tore a chunk of flesh from the hen thigh he was ravenously eating.

Laughs exploded from the soldiers, while frags exchanged hands throughout the entire arena. Those from Hardrock who knew Thanan booed the mockery.

Kinji continued, "…The man from Jin with the pale skin…Thanan!"

The roaring crowd stomped their feet and laughed even louder, while the makeshift arena moaned from the stress.

The Jinian stepped out into the arena with as much bravery as he could muster. His armor was ill fitted and far too heavy for his frame, but still he was reasonably agile. His sword was also forged by Purgon, so the blade was hardened Zythera as well.

The two warriors stood at their marks twenty paces apart, staring at each other. Agrinoth adjusted his grip and cracked his neck. The low thunder of drums rumbled as Kinji walked between the combatants.

"Warriors ready!" he announced, pointing to Thanan and Agrinoth.

He raised a gold sash high above his head and dropped it. It gently drifted to the meadow floor and the match began.

Nobody knew what strategy Agrinoth would use to start the fight. Would he slowly work his way to the Jinian, using precise sword blows to disarm his foe, or would he use brute force and quickly overpower the Jinian and thus get to the evening meal sooner rather than later?

Thanan stood, frozen by Agrinoth's intimidating gaze. The great warrior rushed toward Thanan. It only took four long strides to reach the Jinian, and with a swift rise of the knee to Thanan's chest, sent him flying backward, landing awkwardly on his shoulders. The crowd cheered for their beloved Agrinoth. Thanan stood up and faced the giant again. He glanced over at Kigron, who didn't look worried at all, but just waved his hand as if to say, "Go on, get in there."

Just then Thanan heard the pounding footsteps of Agrinoth closing in. He turned just in time to see four scarred knuckles break his nose. A white flash of light temporarily blinded the Jinian as he fell to his back. The metallic taste of blood ran down the back of his throat. Women in the front row winced at the sight. It seemed Agrinoth was content on defeating his opponent without one swing of his sword, which was disappointing to most of the crowd.

"There's no shame in quitting, Jinian," Agrinoth said, looking down at his opponent. "No one will find you a coward. Just drop your sword."

Thanan stuck the tip of his sword in the dirt and pulled himself to his feet. He spat out a mouthful of blood and cleared his head. His sword was heavy. Struggling to lift it, he took a fighting stance once again. Agrinoth shook his head and ran toward the stubborn Jinian. Instead of retreating, Thanan started toward the giant, cutting the distance between them. The two met in the center of the arena with a clash of metal and muscle. Agrinoth's heavy swings rained down on the Jinian. It was all he could do to just deflect the blows, redirecting their energy just out of harm's way.

Thanan was overmatched in every way except one: He was quicker than most Goriaths. Lulling the great warrior in, he feigned to block a mighty overhead strike but stepped aside at the last moment, causing Agrinoth's sword to sink deep into the meadow dirt. The Jinian quickly flicked his sword upward and split open Agrinoth's chin. Gasps of surprise were heard all over the arena as new bets were shouted and wagers made.

Without hesitation, the mighty warrior grabbed the Jinian by his hair and drove his forehead into his already bleeding face and then to his armored knee. Thanan's eyes rolled to the back of his head and his knees buckled underneath him. Thanan was asleep before his face hit the ground. Falling slowly, his hand opened and dropped the sword.

The arena erupted. Chants of Agrinoth were repeated over and over again. So great was the raucousness that the rickety arena collapsed on one side, causing many giants to fall to the ground laughing all the way. Thousands of frags exchanged hands and congratulatory toasts were raised in honor of the swift and brutal victory.

Seretha looked horrified at what Kigron had done to their friend. Agrinoth wiped the blood from his chin and slowly walked away. Kigron ordered two of his soldiers to drag Thanan to the physician's tent for mending.

The crowd dispersed and went back to their tents to make preparations for the champion's banquet. The Jinian was still unconscious when he was laid in the cot next to Tremik. The physician had already stitched Tremik's neck, but his face was swollen because of the fractures he suffered from the sabotaged bow.

"Wha hapned ta hm?" Tremik slurred, looking at the unconscious Jinian.

The physician said only one word as he blotted the Jinian's face. "Agrinoth."

Tremik chuckled under his breath, then winced from the pain.

A grand banquet table was set before the multitude, befitting the royal guests. General Tygrothian sat at the head with Prince Ky at his right and Princess Tirin at his left. Tavris' prize, the Loriam hen, was presented as the centerpiece of the table. Its succulent flesh was garnished with piles of root vegetables, wild mushrooms, and herbs from Loriam Meadow. The vibrant tail feathers hung from torches by way of leather strings, which fluttered in the breeze.

Hundreds of glowing tents revealed the silhouettes of families enjoying each other's company as the chatter of giants filled the air, recounting tales from the day's contests. Every now and then, bursts of laughter would bubble to the surface over all the boisterous conversation, then subside again into low mutterings.

After a few minutes of feasting, the sun-dwelling princess stood and walked to the opposite side of the table. Her entourage appeared almost magically from the tents, ever vigilant in keeping their princess safe. She turned to Tygrothian as if to ask permission to begin. The general smiled, then nodded.

"My dear kinsfolk," she began, firelight twinkling in her eyes. "It has been our honor to have shared in this celebration with all of you. You have honored us with your hospitality and generosity. It is our hope and prayer that one day our two peoples might unite once again. Your great leader Tygrothian has done much in behalf of your people, and he alone has brought us here to this moment. I know that many of you still doubt, but nonetheless you are here. Your loyalty to the general is heartening, and I will have great stories to tell upon returning to Devlin."

She glanced at one of her bodyguards. He stepped forward, holding the silk ribbon with the gem-encrusted ring hanging from it. Sharp flashes of green, white, and blue light reflected as it spun.

"And now for the moment we have waited for."

The enthralled crowd cheered and stomped their feet.

"As your Lady Zinthia, I have one more charge. Zethrin Val," she announced, looking over the audience. "Please step forward and claim your prize."

She held up the jewel-adorned ring for all to see. Zethrin released his wife's hand and walked toward Lady Zinthia.

"Zethrin Val, receive this emblem so you will always remember your day of victory."

He took the ring and held it tight. Giants waved torches in celebration, but Zethrin looked at his prize with a hint of sadness on his face.

"Wait!" he shouted to the cheering giants. "The honor is not mine alone."

The shouts ceased.

"Where is Tavris Gru?" he shouted, scanning the crowd. "Bring the boy out!"

The audience started muttering, looking for the missing archer.

Tavris was busy chasing light wisps with his sisters on the outskirts of the camp, unaware of the ceremony, when he heard his name being called. He ran toward the raucous gathering, clutching his bow. He burst through the crowd and saw Princess Tirin and Zethrin standing before him.

"For undeniable skill with the bow and courage beyond his years, I give the Lady's ring to Tavris Gru, with the Lady's blessing, of course."

She smiled and waved her hand. Seretha cheered for her son and held Kigron's arm tightly. Tygrothian also stood and cheered for his grandson.

The banquet went long into the night. Giants carried on, and for a moment the Goriath giants forgot about their past transgressions and embraced the light.

"Tav, it's time for sleep," Seretha said to her young champion.

"All r-r-right, M-Mami, but I w-want to visit Th-Thanan first."

Seretha looked to Kigron for an answer.

"I'll take him. Come on, son, let's go quickly," the captain said, ushering the boy by the shoulder.

Two guards posted outside the physician's tent greeted the captain and his son. Tavris knelt at the foot of Thanan's cot, staring at his bruised and swollen face.

"How is the Jinian doing?" Kigron asked, looking concerned.

"He'll be fine," the physician replied. "He's been in and out of consciousness for most of the day. Agrinoth sure made an example of him."

"No...regrettably I did." The captain shook his head, mad at himself. Thanan could hear the conversation and attempted to speak, but no words escaped his lips. "Be still, Jinian. You will be home soon enough," the captain whispered. "You will be happy to know that I will be getting an earful when I return to our tent."

"You'll be all r-r-right, Thanan," Tavris said, patting his foot gently.

Kigron turned and walked to Tremik's cot. He was finally sitting up and barely able to speak without sounding like a babbling fool.

"Who did this to me?" he struggled out. "Do you know?"

"I have my suspicions. Don't worry, old friend. It is my belief that another one of the king's spies has foolishly revealed himself to us. The criminal will wish that he were in the pit when this is all over."

Tavris stepped between his father and Tremik, interrupting their conversation.

"Trem-m-ik, I w-w-ant you t-t-to have this," he slowly stammered, holding the prize ring in his hand.

Kigron placed his hand on his son's shoulder, his face softening after the interruption. Tremik's wife wiped a tear from her cheek as she stroked her husband's hair. The injured archer reached for the jeweled ring and plucked it from Tavris' hand.

"Thank you, boy," he managed to mumble, clutching the ring tightly to his chest.

"Tavris, go on and head back to your mother. Go on now," the captain urged his son.

Tavris ran out with all the energy that an eight-year-old Goriath possessed. Kigron looked back to Tremik, his eyes intense and focused.

"Here is the truth, Tremik. We already know the saboteur."

"Tell me and I'll gouge his heart out with my shattered bow," Tremik lashed back, attempting to sit up.

"Easy now, soldier. A plan is already in motion to arrest the criminal tonight," he replied, holding the archer's shoulder down.

"Speak the dirty traitor's name!" the archer demanded.

"One of our own, Joziath Kol. One of our trusted informants has betrayed us. At this point his motives are still unknown, so we do not know if he acted alone, but we will know shortly. Even as I speak, scouts are secretly scouring the borders of Loriam and the lake for any of Joziath's conspirators. I will be joining them shortly. Do not worry. We will get him, and you will have your chance for justice."

Kigron took one last look at Thanan, who was still unconscious and paler than normal, before leaving the tent. "I am sorry, Jinian," he muttered to himself.

Kigron rendezvoused with Shimian and two Guardians at the

lake's edge.

"Tyrix, Jethor. Search the southern shore along the Loriam border, and trust no one," commanded the captain. "King Grishon's spies are among us. Captain Shimian and I will travel the western bank along the forest's edge. Report back to camp before everyone wakes."

Shimian and Kigron set out along the west bank of Lake Loriam, two hours before dawn's first star. A thin layer of mist blanketed the lake's glassy surface. It floated lightly on the gentle breeze, blowing down from the cliffs, cooling the air on the valley floor. The captains walked in silence along the forest edge, scanning for anything that might be out of place. The mist rolled in from the lake, obscuring their vision. Every now and then a fish would jump, breaking the silence and setting their nerves on edge.

Off in the distance, blue torchlight moved across the lake, rising and falling with the small swells. It appeared that someone was in a rowboat coming to shore. Kigron and Shimian picked up their pace to intercept the boat, but the fog was growing more dense by the moment. They watched the torchlight dim then reappear closer to shore. The light finally came to a dead stop and vanished. They halted their pursuit, listening closely for footsteps on the rocky shoreline, but heard nothing but the croaking of blue-throated toads and small waves lapping at the lakeshore.

Suddenly the light reappeared with a rapid series of flashes and then nothing. Then from the darkness of the forest, another torch flashed a similar series of flashes, three flashes, then two, followed by three more.

"They're signaling each other with lanterns," Shimian whispered.

"What are they saying?" Kigron wondered out loud. "The spy must be trying to flee into the forest."

"He must be waiting for the all clear."

The two captains crouched behind tall willow reeds that lined the shore. The dense fog, which earlier hindered their pursuit, now helped conceal their presence from the traitors. It moved in from the shore, engulfing them in a thick camouflage.

They heard steps in the shallow water and a boat being dragged to shore. Without warning, an intense burning on Shimian's forearm caused him to rustle the reeds. He winced and slapped his arm hard, revealing their position. Yellow liquid oozed down his arm. A brown fish spinner the size of a Goriath palm had dropped from its web and sunk its fangs deep into the tissue of Shimian's arm, sending its paralytic venom rushing through his veins.

"Shh," Kigron whispered, frantically looking at Shimian and then back into the fog. "I will have to come back for you."

Shimian slowly fell to the shore, his breathing now shallow and labored. Kigron quickly dragged him from the reeds, removed his cloak and covered Shimian to keep him warm. The captain plunged his knife blade into Shimian's arm, severing the path of the venom from the blood. It would only slow down the ravages of the bite for a short time. Kigron sucked the wound once and spat out a mouthful of sour venom mixed with blood.

"Put pressure on this, brother," Kigron whispered, directing Shimian's hand to the wound.

Heavy footsteps on the shoreline caught Kigron's attention. The spy broke for the forest, bounding up the rocky shore. Kigron jumped to his feet and began his pursuit, leaving Shimian lying on the lake's edge unconscious from the spider's bite. The hooded figure reached the tree line with Kigron trailing behind, just seconds away. The taste of the poison still lingered in his mouth.

The fog closed in and blinded Kigron's vision as the pounding footsteps beckoned him further and further into the thick forest. Kigron reached out, but the spy's flowing cloak remained just out of reach. The trail ran ever deeper into the forest, snaking its way through damp, moss-covered trees. The cloaked figure pulled away from Kigron and vanished from before his face. Kigron continued to pursue in the blackness, the thick fog blocking out any light from the sky.

Then the sound of footsteps was gone. The captain slowed as the trail spilled into an opening in the forest. The spy had disappeared without a trace. Kigron stood in the silence, using all his senses to detect any presence, but there was nothing, only the wind and the fog as his companions in the darkness. A heavy breath of defeat left his lungs. He resigned to return to Shimian when he heard a faint sound behind him, a rustling in the leaves. Turning quickly, he drew his sword and pointed it at the dark trail.

"Show yourself, traitor!" he shouted.

The sharp sound of snapping twigs grew closer. A shadowed figure emerged from the canopied trail into the clearing. At last, the moonlight broke through the eerie fog. A thin mist diffused the moonlight that lit upon his cloak.

"Who's there? Speak your name!" the captain shouted, thrusting his sword at the hooded man.

"Easy, Kigron," the man replied, removing his hood. Kigron lowered his sword, confused by the image before him.

"When I left you, you were unconscious. How did you get here?"

"Don't worry, I was not detected by the spy."

Kigron looked at the forest, then back at the trail. He sheathed his Zythera blade, beginning to walk in the direction of the fleeing spy.

"Come, we still have time to stop them." Kigron started to run. He ran to the end of the clearing, but realized no one was following. He turned back to see an empty clearing.

Mist swirled where the cloaked figure had stood. The temperature plunged and the captain grew cold, his exposed skin stinging as the chilled air blew past it. Kigron scanned the tree line again, to no avail. In a brief moment of disbelief, Kigron wiped the mist from his face and cleared his head. The man had disappeared without a trace.

It was now silent in the forest, as if every sound were vacuumed away. Every muscle in the warrior's body leapt as he sensed the smallest movement behind him. He slowly reached for his hilt and gripped it tightly. The blistering cold metal drew the warmth from his bones. He took one last breath and spun with all his might, drawing his sword. Swinging wildly, he cut through the mist, but missed the dark figure before him. The hooded phantom ducked under the swinging sword and drove his dagger deep into Kigron's chest. The staggering giant stumbled to his knees and looked upon his assassin, the silver moonlight revealing the horror on his face.

"You were my friend," he whispered, holding his heaving chest.

The great captain closed his eyes and fell, his face striking the cold, dew-covered leaves.

"Easy now, Jinian. Calm yourself," the physician insisted. "You have had quite a night haunted by many dark dreams."

Thanan struggled to sit up, breathing heavily, sweat beading on his pale forehead.

"Rest easy; it is almost dawn. Everyone will be headed home today."

"Kigron…where is he? Is he all right?"

"Of course, Jinian. He returned about an hour ago. Had Joziath by the hair and his traitorous hands in chains. I had to sedate Tremik over there when he heard the news." He pointed at Tremik, who was out cold, drooling on the cot.

Thanan breathed a little easier when he heard the news about Kigron, the nightmare still gripping his mind. He put one foot on the ground. He didn't remember his knee being injured in the fight, but it was swollen like his eyes and cheeks. The action of sitting up caused his head to pound, which made him forget about the nightmare.

For the next four days, the giants made their way back to Hardrock and Whitehall. There was a different feeling in the caverns after the celebration. The joyful sounds of giants chattering and reminiscing about the celebration, and looking forward to next year, were heard all over.

Joziath was promptly chained in the bottom of the pit. And when Tremik was strong enough, he would be allowed to pay his saboteur a private visit.

CHAPTER EIGHT

THE CANDIDATE

The spiraling blue galaxy, Falenfel, rose and waned many times over the glimmering walls of Jin. Every now and then Thanan forgot the dim world that enveloped him. He spent many nights remembering the warm summer evenings walking through the great halls of the capital and running through the cobblestone streets of Hastentown. It had now been nine years since the embrace of his own bed held him at night or the sweet taste of fresh fala passed his lips. He longed for the bright sound of the bells as merchant ships entered Belenor Harbor.

He often looked at his paling hands in the flickering lamplight and thought about the boy he had been and the man he was becoming. He now enjoyed the friendship and respect of most of the soldiers and families at Hardrock.

For years, Thanan had pounded raw elements into implements of war. At first, the quality of his craftsmanship left a a lot to be desired. His master was often heard yelling through the shop:

"That sword is not fit to pick my teeth with, Jinian!" Or, "I would hit you with this sword, but I'm afraid it would shatter to dust when it touched your pale skin, Jinian!"

Although Purgon would never admit it, there was pride in his eye when the Jinian's hammer echoed through the caverns. The half-blind master still regularly berated his apprentice, if for no other reason than to express the Jinian's worthiness of his castigation. Thanan was no master, but as more time went on, there were some soldiers whose armor dawned his maker's mark.

"Thanan!" a soldier's voice rose above the hammering. "General Tygrothian has summoned you to his quarters."

The apprentice removed his apron and laid it across the anvil, which he had forged himself, wondering what the general needed of him.

Thanan knocked on the post outside the general's quarters.

"You wanted to see me, sir," Thanan called into the tent. His face was smudged with soot and his hands were black as coal.

"Ah, Thanan. Yes, come in," Tygrothian replied. "There's a water basin in the corner. Clean yourself up if you like."

The blacksmith cupped a handful of the cool water up from the basin. Soot-colored water dribbled through his fingers as he rubbed his face. Then he sat across the rustic table that served as the general's desk.

"How may I serve the general today?" he asked, refreshed.

Tygrothian smiled and let a rare chuckle escape his throat. "Purgon tells me that your skills are improving and that you have, on occasion, expressed your desire to still join the Guardian Order. Is this true?"

"In truth I have not thought about it for months. I have been so busy in the armory. But to answer your question, sir…yes with all my heart, I wish to be a Guardian." He looked intensely at the general. "What is this all about, sir?"

Tygrothian looked above Thanan's shoulder. A strange look swept across his face.

"What is it, sir?"

"What a peculiar sword," the general replied, nodding at the hilt sticking above Thanan's shoulder. "May I see it?"

Thanan reached above his left shoulder, pulling the blade from its sheath.

"Where did you get this?"

"I made it, sir, with the help of Purgon, of course."

The general looked troubled as if he remembered something horrible. "And how did you ever dream this design up? It is quite elegant, Thanan."

"It's funny that you ask, General. That's just how it happened, in a dream." Thanan sheathed the sword. "I woke up one morning with the image of the blade in my mind. I'm forging another one to match. Purgon is letting me keep them. He had a similar look on his face when I first sketched the blade for him."

Tygrothian tapped his gnarled fingers on the table, setting Thanan's nerves on edge. Then he stared into Thanan's eyes for a few silent moments, running his thumb down the length of his scar.

"I would have you tell me why you summoned me here…sir."

"All right, all right, Thanan. Be still. You remind me of your father, not afraid to speak the truth and fearless in the face of your enemy. I loved that about him. Tell me, Thanan, son of Corderian, do you fear darkness?"

Thanan looked strangely at the general. "Like most men, I did when I was young," the Jinian replied, sipping the last of his water.

"Do not mistake my meaning, Thanan, as an infantile fright of apparitions under your bed. An existence of unimaginable despair is at our doorstep. No good...only evil lurking in false paths, to steal away your soul and leave you hollow and of no worth. Goodness has always subdued the purveyors of wickedness in this world, but wickedness has never seen such order before. You know of whom I speak?"

"I do, sir. My brother betrayed us all," he whispered back.

"You have not heard the whole of it, Thanan. High in the shadows of the Jethian Mountains he makes his way, slowly stirring the hearts of men with perfected subtlety. Half-truths and futile promises are his temptations. Most follow him, believing their reward can truly be appointed, but there are some who have knowingly traded their souls for a false portion of power. For them, there is only death."

The great general sighed at the thought. "Your father is most powerful. He sees what we cannot, and leads men to do only good. Of his greatness, I know well. I have seen his might and have felt of his mercy. His promise is prosperity and peace, and this he assuredly gives and gains not. With the sharpness of a Zythera blade, Corderian strikes down all who oppress his people, but not until their choice has been made and their course is immovable.

"Haydon is his father's son and wields his power in a most sinister way. And as time passes, his power comes to fruition. With the patience of a Kol Viper, he lays in wait in dark places, lulling men from the corners of the world with his dulcet tones of freedom and riches. As for them, the ones who succumb to his will, at the end of it all there is only pain and sadness."

"Again, sir," Thanan interrupted, "I would have you tell me why you require an audience with me."

The general's eyes brightened and he chuckled under his breath again. "Just like your father, right to the point, as always. What I require of you is no easy thing, Thanan. Even the mightiest have fallen from lesser challenges. At tomorrow's ceremony, you will be presented as a candidate for the Guardian Order. Two of our High Guardians are retiring and need to be replaced. I expect this will be met with much opposition, but I am sure that I can persuade those who think me mad. I am the general, after all."

CHAPTER NINE

ORIGIN OF ORDER

The great forges of Hardrock were silent, the blacksmith's tools put away for the night. Hardrock was quieter than it had been in some time. The warm subterranean breeze carried with it the lingering scent of tilled soil, boiled fish, and baked biscuits.

Still reeling about the news from General Tygrothian, the Jinian sat across from Kigron with a full stomach, running his finger along the rim of his clay cup, shaking his head in disbelief. A small lamp sat on a table between them, lending its light to the room with a fluttering blue glow.

The sound of clanking pots from the kitchen suddenly stopped and Seretha entered, drying her hands with a tattered towel. "I'm going to bed. You two need anything else?"

Thanan sipped on his warm root tea, thinking about the following morning. "Nothing more for me, Seretha. Good night."

"Good night, Thanan," she replied, turning to Kigron. "Coming to bed, Captain?"

Kigron smiled with his eyes. "Soon, my dear."

"See that you do. Xavantha only sleeps for a few more hours."

"I can't believe I am going to be a candidate, Kigron. Thank you for everything. Your family has done so much for me."

"Stop, Thanan. You have earned this honor. My father did not make this decision in haste. It took him nine years before he felt you were ready. I spoke to him today, and he told me he waited until your heart was no longer set upon it. He did not want your mind to get in the way.

"Words cannot adequately explain what you will go through as a candidate. Guardians are the best of us, trusted councilmen and allies to the general."

"I must know more about the Order, Kigron. Nobody speaks freely about it, how they came to be."

"Well, Thanan," Kigron began, "the history of the Guardian Order is shrouded by intrigue. There are many stories that have been passed down throughout Goriath history pertaining to the origin of the Order.

"Many centuries ago, the long and violent Darvinian War ended with much bloodshed and despair. The Jinian army, led by King Corderian, alongside the Darvinian Kingdom, united against the Goriath army.

"King Goriath III, fearing his wealth would one day run out, sought to conquer the Darvinian Kingdom, and with it, the great abundance of gems and ore that lay deep under her lush beauty. The Darvinian army fought like flame wrocks and beat back the Goriath warriors, holding them at bay and killing hundreds. It wasn't until Tremik Tak's grandfather's bow was introduced to the war that they began to gain ground. From great distances, the sky grew dark with falling arrows, which turned the tide for a short time. Like ravenous corn worjins, the Goriath army consumed everything in their path. All that was above and below the earth was seized in the name of the king, and all who opposed him were slaughtered.

"The weakened Kingdom of Darvin begged for peace, but Goriath III yielded not. In a last attempt to defend the failing kingdom, King Toriniam sent messengers to the shore of the Jinian Realm in hopes of receiving aid from the mighty army of Jin. Without hesitation, Corderian answered Toriniam's plea and led an offensive that left the Goriath army scattered and beaten.

"Goriath and his army retreated to the crystal caverns, and Corderian commanded a thousand soldiers to pursue them. The Goriath army regrouped in the valley below their caves and held the approaching armies at bay from across the river for months before Corderian withdrew his soldiers, letting the Goriaths crawl back to the Crystal City. Thousands died in the defense of their country and thousands more in the name of conquest."

"My father never told me this story," Thanan interrupted.

"This is where everything changed for my father," Kigron stated.

"How do you mean?"

Kigron continued, "Darvinian and Jinian soldiers scoured the battlefield, killing all Goriath survivors who had been fatally injured during the last offensive. It was required of King Corderian to let no fallen soldier suffer needlessly on the battlefield. Mercy was extended to all with a quick death by the tip of a sword.

"The Darvinian hills were dotted with death. No more than two paces separated the dead and dying bodies. For miles you could see the bloodstained fields of grass swirling in the western wind. The usual warm scent of wildflowers on the Darvinian Plateau was subdued by the sickening smell of death that hung heavy on the land. It was the worst battle in generations.

"Off in the distance King Corderian heard a soldier yell, 'I've got another one. This one's a captain!'

"Put a blade in him and be done with it!" another yelled back.

"'Wait, hold your sword! I need to see him for myself,' the king ordered. Corderian ran across the blood-soaked hillside bounding over corpses as if possessed by a vision. He approached the dying captain and knelt gently beside him. The fading Goriath's young face was slashed from cheek to chin and three arrows pierced his torso. Bluish-red blood streamed down his armor. 'Fetch my physician, quickly!' he ordered, gripping the breastplate over the giant's heaving chest. 'What is your name, Goriath? Tell me now!'

"The giant, struggling to breathe, whispered, 'Tygrothian.'

"A calm expression softened the king's face, as if recognizing the giant's name from a distant memory. 'See to it that he lives and take him back to the city,' he ordered the physician and captain. 'It is imperative that he survives.'"

Kigron broke from the story and smiled at Thanan. "Those who witnessed your father's strange behavior thought it an act of pity or mercy, and it was, but it was much more. The greatest plan in the history of the planet was at that very moment set into motion. It was within your city's walls that Corderian's physicians mended my father. Corderian slowly molded and sculpted him from a greed-driven warrior to the great leader and unifying force for good that we all love and follow today."

"I knew that the general and my father knew each other, but I didn't know the depth of their friendship." Thanan shook his head slightly, trying to understand the significance of the events that took place so long ago.

"Tygrothian finally made his way back to Crystal City. He devised a story and recounted it to his king about how he feigned death for two hundred seven days on the Darvinian Plateau, crawling over the hills in the dimming light of the evening and hiding under decomposing Goriath soldiers in the heat of the sun. He claimed he travelled through the wild forests avoiding Jinian scouts, Darvinian soldiers, and ravenous beasts, but that he was finally captured and imprisoned. He spoke of enduring violent torture and other horrible afflictions for another nine months, before escaping.

"My father was welcomed back triumphantly and a celebration was held in his honor. He was declared a hero among his people. A short time later he was made general over the entire army and given great power by the new king. Centuries came and went, all the while Tygrothian bided his time as the loyal Goriath general."

"But when did he start the Order? Was he the first Guardian?"

"Almost two centuries before the general and his loyalists left their beloved Crystal City to live out their lives in Hardrock and Whitehall, he began to subvert the corrupt Goriath king. He had outlived all the Goriaths from the earliest generations, except for a few, and at last the appointed time that had been given him so long ago by Corderian was finally at hand.

"Quietly and without detection he sought out those who would follow him and swear their allegiance to him alone. It took thirty-five years to assemble the first twelve Guardians. They convened in abandoned caves and established a new law, a new way of conducting oneself. Honor and valor took the place of greed and power. The Order was dedicated to the preservation of the old ways, before their Goriath blood was tainted by crystal dust and the lust for all that was not theirs to take.

"My father led an underground campaign, not only convincing more than one-fourth of the Goriath population to join in the revolution, but also the majority of the king's army followed him as well. A small contingent of the king's soldiers felt their loyalty would be better served under the king, their sense of duty motivated more by money than morality. The majority of the civilians in Crystal City stayed because of tradition or fear of retribution by the king or the Xavantha god."

"There is still so much I don't know."

"That is a good thing to know, Thanan. It's late. What you must do now is get some rest."

CHAPTER TEN

THINNING THE RANKS

The tent was long, having just enough room to fit twenty-five cots and a wooden footlocker for each candidate, with dimly lit lamps hanging from each tent post. A narrow aisle separated the two rows of cots. The tent's canvas, having for years housed hundreds of sweaty candidates who had very little time to bathe, smelled musky, stale, and wholly offensive to Thanan's nose. The barracks were nestled within their own private cavern by the name of Krokil Dun, on the outskirts of Hardrock – one of the last deposits of zil ore mined before the entire region was abandoned long ago.

The barracks were noisy with candidates milling around, some aimlessly, making lighthearted talk.

Thanan sat on his cot observing some of the most intimidating Goriaths he had ever seen. They were living and breathing weapons, and they were only going to become more dangerous as time went on.

For an hour Thanan had watched the empty beds on either side of him, all the while folding his clothes neatly, making sure everything was in its proper place, wondering who would finally claim the beds.

"My name is Torik," a voice said from behind Thanan.

The greeting shocked Thanan. He snapped around, looking over his cot at the outstretched hand of one of the youngest candidates he had seen. He was tall like most Goriaths, but his build was leaner, his facial features less prominent, resembling his Devlin cousins. Although he knew that this candidate was strong, as most Goriaths were, Thanan imagined he was incredibly fast as well.

"I'm Thanan," he replied, firmly shaking Torik's hand. It was the first greeting he had received in the barracks. "You're Agrinoth's brother. Purgon talks about you two often."

"No, I'm Agrinoth's more handsome brother."

"I was wondering who would be the first to pick the bunk next to the scary Jinian."

Torik smiled, beginning to organize his belongings. "I just arrived; otherwise, I would have picked it sooner. I'm just happy to be sleeping next to the candidate who probably snores the quietest. It is going to be hard to get any sleep around here as it is."

At that moment, at the tent's entrance, the candidates all began standing, extending their hands, offering congratulations to a candidate who just entered.

"What's that all about?" Thanan asked, trying to see through the commotion.

Torik tilted his head attempting to look around the clamoring candidates. "That would be my brother, Agrinoth. You'll get used to it."

The crowd parted, letting Agrinoth down the aisle. He didn't look pleased with all the attention. The warrior walked through the tent with an intense expression on his face, eyeing each occupied cot. His eyes fell upon the only cot available and then he saw his pale neighbor sitting on the cot next to him.

"Oh...If I only could have a painting of your face right now, brother," Torik said, chuckling. "You might not remember Thanan." He slapped the Jinian's shoulder. "His face looks a little different since you rearranged it a few years ago."

Agrinoth nodded dismissively, which was all he could muster, making it quite clear that he thought the Jinian didn't belong in the barracks. "You better get your act together, Torik," Agrinoth grumbled. "Master Grizak will be here soon."

"You will have to excuse my older brother. He's very serious," Torik said, folding another shirt.

"It would serve you well, Torik, if you took this training a bit more seriously. It might save your life one day."

"Get on your feet!" a voice yelled from across the barracks. A table tumbled down the aisle, lost two legs, and came to rest in front of Thanan's bed.

Each candidate shot up quickly, standing in front of his footlocker. It had finally begun. Thanan's heart raced, not knowing what might come next.

"Your training will be unbearable!" a battle-scarred giant yelled, pacing the stone floor. "Pain will be your constant companion here. Pain will drive you to the brink, and when you lay your pitiful heads down, I pray that pain will sing you piles of greklin dung to sleep. Only when you no longer feel pain, will you truly understand. Make no mistake, the pain will still exist, but it will reside deep within your mind."

Twenty-four Goriath giants stood at attention, not flinching a muscle, eyes looking forward. They formed a literal wall of armor and muscle that only a fool would attempt to breach. There was one weakness, however, a chink in the armor. In the middle of this mighty wall stood the twenty-fifth.

Master Grizak paced the aisle, aggressive and intense. "It looks like I have my work cut out for me on this one, boys," Grizak snarled at Thanan.

The twenty-four showed their discipline by not joining in Grizak's mockery. The pacing soldier stopped in front of Thanan, looking down at the top of his head. "I said, on your feet, Jinian!"

Thanan stood there, his fists clenching at his side. "Yes, sir," he barked.

Torik couldn't help but let a snicker escape his lips.

Grizak stooped, putting his nose right in front of Thanan's. "This must be a mistake. The general's taken one too many blows to his head." A few candidates finally smirked, but quickly regained their composure.

Thanan could smell the fish and bread on the giant's warm breath as saliva sprayed his face. The very air about him was thick and aromatic. He couldn't place the odor exactly, but it was a complex combination of molded biscuits, zortusk swill, and sulfur swamp on a hot afternoon. It was no easy thing for him to stand at attention, motionless, and not have his eyes tear up from the stench.

"I'm making it my personal mission to see to it that you'll break before day's end. Do I make myself clear, Jinian?"

Thanan nodded and swallowed. "Yes, Master Grizak."

Grizak turned from Thanan, a satisfied look on his face. He began pacing the aisle again and kicked the broken table out of his way. It crashed into one of the candidates. He didn't move. Agrinoth slowly glanced at the Jinian with disgust.

"Agrinoth!" the master yelled. "Eyes forward, candidate! Do you have a problem with the Jinian?"

Agrinoth shot his eyes forward. "No, Master Grizak!" he barked back.

"Hmph…too bad," Grizak grumbled. "You all look weak and slow to me. The Black Cavern path will wake you piles of dung."

"Listen up, candidates!" Grizak shouted as he stood at the entrance of an ominous looking tunnel, silhouetted by blue flickering lamplight.

The candidates all stood at attention, wearing no armor, only the clothes and boots that were supplied them by the military. Thanan stared past Grizak into the darkness, focused, thinking only about the task at hand.

"From this moment on, everything you do will be observed by my discerning eye. If I don't think you have what it takes to become a Guardian, you will go home disgraced. Do you understand?"

"Yes, Master Grizak!" the candidates shouted back in unison.

"The Black Cavern path is two miles long. It is treacherous, full of shafts, fissures, and rugged terrain. It was abandoned centuries ago because of the tunnel's instability and unpredictable, hazardous nature. This is why Master Kizaga thought it a fitting place to thin the ranks, and so do I. With any luck, I'll see you all in the morning. If not, rest assured, we will get your body or what's left of it to your family." He looked directly at Thanan.

"When you reach the end of the tunnel, you will climb the ladder and then make your way down to the quarry floor. Look for the lamps. You will know what to do. Once you reach the bottom, it will be an easy one-mile run back to here. Now run!" He turned, backing out of the entrance, making way for the anxious candidates.

The candidates jogged single-file into the mouth of the tunnel, disappearing around the bend, their footsteps fading away.

All of them had heard stories since their infancy told by their fathers, uncles, and grandfathers about the deadly Black Cavern path. They all had the hearts of warriors, still they secretly feared what was to come in the perilous tunnel…all except one, Agrinoth. His eyes showed nothing but the fierceness and focus of Kizaga himself. In his mind, he was already a Guardian, having envisioned himself as such since he was old enough to walk. At a very young age, he was granted permission by Shimian to train with the military. Everybody knew the name Agrinoth and soon some fame followed, which he rejected wholeheartedly, simply not having the time or stomach for it. Nobody doubted that Agrinoth would be in the top three to advance to the final test; he might even go unchallenged in the Zythera Circle.

His younger brother, Torik, followed in his footsteps, but contrary to Agrinoth, he was lighthearted, quick to laugh, and relied heavily on his natural gifts. His devotion to his brother was absolute. Even as focused and gruff as Agrinoth was, jealousy and envy were not in Torik's nature. He wanted Agrinoth to become a Guardian just as much as everyone else did.

Flickering blue torches lined the walls, shining their light down on the candidates as they ran. The Jinian was fast, light-footed, and agile, and for the most part stayed out of harm's way as the candidates jostled for position in the dimly lit tunnel.

A steady headwind pushed against the warriors, drying their eyes. It was warm, stagnant, void of smell, and as they began to sweat, it cooled them. Loose rubble was strewn over the cave floor along with splintered timbers, signs of a cave-in. The fluttering lamplight made it difficult to negotiate the terrain. Shadows looked liked rocks and rocks looked like shadows. Deep ruts were carved into the floor by the ore carts that had once been pulled through the tunnel.

"There's a fissure ahead!" the lead candidate shouted.

One by one they jumped over the fissure. Thanan negotiated the jump perfectly, landing nimbly, springing up to a full run. Amid the pounding boots, a sharp crack was heard, followed by a cry for help.

"Wait!" a candidate yelled from behind the pack.

The leader slowed, as did all the candidates. They turned back to find Zythor, his entire torso leaning into the fissure, legs sprawled on the floor. "Help me get him up! He's slipping!" Zythor shouted.

Suspended from Zythor's hand above the abyss was Gorix, face pained by a broken ankle, forehead bleeding, and barely hanging on.

Without hesitation, Agrinoth jumped, his chest landing on Zythor's slipping legs. "Hurry, get Gorix out of there. We are not going to lose anyone on the first day!"

The candidates retrieved Gorix from the fissure. He knew they had to leave him to limp his way out on his own. He would not ask that they stay behind, nor would anyone.

Thanan was surprised by Agrinoth's actions to save Gorix. He didn't know why he was surprised. He knew very little about Agrinoth, but it seemed contrary to what he did know. Maybe Agrinoth's presumed arrogance was in reality nothing of the kind.

The candidates continued to run as fast as they could through the dim tunnel, jumping over jagged rocks and dark fissures. After getting his legs tied up with two different Goriaths, Thanan knew he was too small to stay in the middle of the pack. He also knew that finishing last was not an option. He couldn't give Master Grizak any reason to throw him out. He peered around Agrinoth and saw a bend in the tunnel about fifty yards away, heading to the right. *That's where I will make my move*, he thought.

Coming up the bend he sidestepped the pack and sprinted by Agrinoth. The candidates thundered around the corner with the Jinian on the outside passing each one. With a perfectly timed shove, a candidate sent Thanan careening into a waist-high boulder. He toppled over the boulder, hitting his thigh hard, and smashed into the far wall. He gritted his teeth as he stood, holding his thigh. The candidates turned the corner, a few of them laughing, leaving him behind. His left thigh felt as if it were on fire, like someone had punched it as hard as they could with armored knuckles.

Thanan started running again, limping at first, then shaking it off. In the distance he saw the trailing candidate's shadow dart to the left and disappear around the corner. Thanan ran faster. Soon he was right behind the pack, working his way to the front.

He shot past Torik, who was still in the middle of the pack, although he probably could have been in the lead. Then he passed Agrinoth, who was fourth from the front. Agrinoth grumbled to himself, watching the Jinian pass.

"That's right Jinian," Torik cheered, knowing his excitement for the Jinian would frustrate Agrinoth to no end. "Get up there!" He accelerated past his older brother and slapped him on the back. "I guess we are going to have to keep up with the Jinian, brother."

Running in fourth place with Torik pacing him all the way, Thanan picked up his pace even more, his thigh throbbing with each pounding stride.

Overhead, thick timbers crossed the tunnel every few feet, reinforcing it from cave-ins. The wood was cracked and dry with a single lamp swinging from every other timber. Thanan saw the front group of three running in and out of the pooling light. He recognized the one who shoved him into the wall. He wanted to push back.

Torik knew Thanan was eyeing the candidate. "His name is Kolrath, Jinan," he shouted. "Don't worry about him. You'll get your chance another day. Best thing for you to do is just beat him." Torik pushed past Thanan. "Try to keep up. This is going to be fun."

Torik and Thanan sprinted ahead and joined the front-runners. They could see the end of the tunnel getting nearer. The five started jostling for position to be the first to reach the wall. Thanan was losing the battle, being edged out by much heavier Goriaths. He dropped back a few steps, still keeping pace, resigning to passing them all on the outside.

At the end of the tunnel, leaning against the back wall, there was a heavy wooden ladder that led up a shaft to the main cavern.

Torik maneuvered his way into second place and was right on Kolrath's heels when he hit the ladder first. Kolrath started climbing, then Torik.

Suddenly something came over Thanan. He couldn't let Kolrath beat him. He sprinted as fast as he could approaching the ladder, bounded on top of a boulder and launched himself toward the last timber, catching it with two hands. He swung underneath, whipping his legs up, releasing his hands. Flying through the air, he reached for the ladder, stretching his arms as far as he could. He caught one of the rungs and held on tightly, his foot accidentally kicking Kolrath in the head. Thanan clamored for a better grip and climbed as fast as he could before Kolrath could think about what happened.

"You'll pay for that, Jinian!" Kolrath growled.

Torik chuckled, not believing what he just had seen.

Thanan emerged from the shaft, not sure where to go from there. He spun around and spotted two swaying lamps a hundred yards away, and sprinted toward the lights, bounding over the uneven rock, never looking back.

Kolrath reached the top, poking his head from the shaft. He saw Thanan running in the distance. The angry candidate climbed out, gritting his teeth and started after Thanan, followed closely by Torik.

Thanan didn't recognize where he was until he reached the lamps. He came to a skidding stop at the edge of a sheer cliff, about fifty feet high, which overlooked the southwest corner of Hardrock. He could see Nikiru field and the Zythera Circle in the middle of it. A knotted rope was tied to each post that the lamps hung from. He quickly turned around, clutching the rope with two hands, and saw Kolrath closing in with Torik following closely behind, barely breathing heavily.

Thanan took his first step backward down the vertical cliff. Hand over hand he descended the rope, his thigh feeling almost dead. He glanced up. Kolrath leaned backward, starting his descent. To Thanan, it looked like Kolrath was running down the wall at full speed. He obviously had done this before. Skipping the last four knots, the Jinian dropped to the ground, his weakened leg buckling underneath his weight. He sprang up and started the last mile back to the entrance of the Black Cavern path.

The final mile was flat and even. Full of adrenaline, Thanan didn't feel his leg anymore, although he knew he would feel it in the morning.

The Jinian led the remaining twenty-three Goriath candidates to the very end until Torik felt it was time to win. He sped passed Kolrath and caught up with Thanan.

"Impressive," Torik said, barely sweating. He paced Thanan a few more strides and bolted to the front, touching the tunnel entrance first. Six minutes later the final candidate touched the wall.

Master Grizak lined the candidates up in front of the tunnel, pacing, scowling, and shaking his head with disapproval. "Do it again," he sneered.

Thanan's dream of becoming one of the Order was now a reality, but the reality was nothing like the dream.

The barracks were quiet. Although they had only run six miles, the terrain in the tunnel had taxed the candidates to their limits, leaving everyone too exhausted to say much, dealing with their own aches and pains. Thanan sat at the edge of his bed pursing his lips, massaging his bruised thigh, too tired to even care about the horrible smell of the barracks. He looked over his shoulder at Agrinoth, who had already fallen asleep.

"He just simply doesn't believe you belong here, Jinian," Torik said quietly. "Many of them don't. They all have their reason. Some don't care because they think you are too weak to make it anyway. Others are afraid of you."

"Afraid of me?"

"Kolrath is afraid, and after tonight so are many more. They don't want to be remembered as the group of candidates that was beaten out by the Jinian. Watch your back."

Thanan looked over the barracks, watching the candidates bunk down for the night. They all looked weary and sore. "And what about you, Torik. Are you afraid of me too?"

Torik smiled at the thought. "The only thing that I'm afraid of is not getting enough sleep, Jinian."

"And what about him?" he replied, gesturing behind himself.

"Who, Agrinoth? He can sleep anywhere."

"No, is he afraid of me?"

"Agrinoth is afraid of nothing. He believes in honoring traditions, and having a Jinian sitting at the council, bearing the mark of a Guardian is insulting to him. There is no room in his heart for someone like you."

"You think he would have saved me in the tunnel as he did Gorix? Or would he have let me fall?"

"He would have saved you as well," he replied, pausing, a smile sweeping across his face. "Only, he would have thought about it first."

Thanan had no sooner fallen asleep, when he was jolted to his feet by the piercing sound of a zortusk horn. He had heard that horn hundreds of times before from a distance, but never like this, so close-up and jarring. It resonated at a wavelength that penetrated the rational mind and brought aggression out in the most self-controlled being. The use of the horn was a tried-and-true method, designed to ignite the senses and force the candidates to control their anger.

Following the zortusk blast, Master Grizak stormed into the barracks, knocking over a chair and kicking two candidates still climbing out of their cots. This was accompanied by a long string of masterfully crafted obscenties that could only be uttered accurately and truly appreciated in Giantish.

"That's right, on your feet, you lazy ingrates," Master Grizak ordered, walking down the dark aisle, observing how slow everyone was. "Anyone want to quit?" He halted, crouching down to Thanan's level, his flaring nostrils just an inch from Thanan's face. "Now's your chance, Jinian. It's only going to get worse from here."

Thanan could see the remains of Grizak's breakfast between his teeth. "No, Master Grizak!" Thanan barked loudly.

Grizak turned about. Walking to the front of the tent, he saw a candidate who wasn't standing at attention properly and hit him in the bare chest with the back of his armored hand. "You will stand at attention or so help me, last night will be like a walk in Krokil Kril. Am I clear, candidate?"

From the front of the tent, Grizak faced the candidates, his hands behind his back. "You all have five minutes. Get your armor on and get to breakfast." He exited the barracks, throwing the canvas door behind him.

The barracks erupted with activity. Candidates were throwing on their underclothes, trousers, and tunics. Leather armor and gauntlets, dotted with metal grommets, were tied onto their shoulders down to their wrists. They wore formfitting breastplates and more grommet-covered leather over their thighs and shins.

Thanan thought they were intimidating enough dressed down, but armored, the candidates looked indestructible and downright frightening.

Thanan dawned his armor with pride. He cinched up the leather straps that held on his breastplate.

"That's the...smallest armor I've ever seen," Torik teased. "Where did you get it?"

"Your great-grandfather."

"I didn't know he works in miniatures."

They both laughed. Agrinoth glared at them. "Let us go, Torik. Master Grizak gave us an order."

Torik slapped Thanan on the back, jolting him forward. "See you out there, Jinian."

Thanan's stomach churned. The Jinian had eaten too fast. Master Grizak had given them three minutes to eat breakfast and report to the field, ready for the first day of hell. The Jinian wasn't used to overeating like a Goriath soldier, gluttonous and fast. Thanan had downed three biscuits, six slices of fried sowbelly, and three eggs with a few seconds left to chug down a cup of water, the thought being that he would need the extra energy for training.

Thanan glanced down the row of armored giants when Grizak turned his back. Thanan could not imagine any force wanting to meet these twenty-three in battle. Although they were only candidates, most of them had spent at least ten years in the military and were approaching the height of their physical strength. Captain

Kigron and Captain Shimian carefully chose them all for their extraordinary skill, strength, and speed.

"Listen up!" Master Grizak shouted. "The obstacle course will test your speed, strength, agility, and endurance. There are five challenges along the five-mile course through Hardrock, and it begins right here. About face!" The candidates spun around in unison. "This is the water run. Right now it looks unassuming, but make no mistake, someone will break an arm today."

Two long waterways ran parallel to each other for a hundred yards. Each one was cut into the rock floor, six feet wide, five feet deep, and filled with water six inches from the top. Bobbing in the water the entire length were four-foot logs, saturated and heavy, just breaking the surface a few inches. The water was thick with them.

Master Grizak stood between the waterways. "Form two lines! You will enter the water when I say so. You will never go under the water to avoid a log. If you do, you will begin again. You must make your way to the other side as fast as you can, pushing the logs out of your way. When you finish, you will then run one mile to the second challenge. Master Thorix here will be waiting to give you instruction. I will be at the third and so on. Do you understand?"

"Yes, Master Grizak!"

"Master Thorix?"

"Yes, sir."

"You may go. Don't let them get away with anything."

The candidates stood single-file in two lines facing the log-filled waterways, flexing, twisting, and loosening up for the challenge. Thanan was third in line and turned to see whom he was lined up against: Kolrath. Thanan knew it was no accident. The angry giant was facing Thanan, trying to intimidate him with hard stares, but the Jinian's stomach was too upset for him to care. He knelt down to tighten his laces.

Torik took a knee behind Thanan, fiddling with his already tightened laces. "Keep an eye out, Jinian," Torik whispered from the side of his mouth. He stood up, continuing to stretch.

Master Grizak gave the command and the first two candidates jumped in. Water washed over the sides. With dull thuds, the heavy logs bobbed up and down, slamming into each other. Thanan watched the candidates, trying to determine the best way to forge the water run.

Thanan and Kolrath lined up at the edge, waiting for Master Grizak to give the go ahead. Despite his churning stomach, Thanan was able to let the sounds of the quarry fade away. He knew Kolrath couldn't do anything to him during this challenge. Just before Grizak let them go, Thanan took three steps back.

"Kolrath, Jinian! Go!" Grizak ordered.

Kolrath jumped in, fighting against the first log, pushing it aside with the back of his forearm. The water came up to his waist.

Thanan ran three quick steps and launched himself in the air, clearing four logs. The water went to his chest. He met the first log with all his strength, pushing it aside. The barkless logs were slimy, algae covered, and immensely heavy, even floating in water. Thanan quickly realized he was vulnerable to head injury because he was shorter than the Goriath candidates.

Kolrath trudged through the water, knocking logs out of the way until he came to a particularly congested area of the waterway. He pushed against the slimy logjam. It didn't budge. Noticing

Thanan pulling further ahead and determined not to let the Jinian win, he began lifting logs. He was strong, gritting his teeth, heaving every log over his head. They splashed behind him as he let them fall.

Seventy-five yards in, Thanan pushed on, his armor weighing him down, tiring him out. Kolrath was gaining on him rapidly. Thanan put his hand on the end of a log just as another log crashed into it, breaking his little finger. He snapped his hand back, shaking it wildly. The finger stuck out at a forty-five degree angle at the second knuckle. He shuddered looking at it. Shaking from the pain, he pulled the finger forward, resetting the bone.

Knowing he couldn't take another broken finger or worse, a broken hand or arm, an idea suddenly occurred to him. He muscled one of the logs in front of him, aiming it lengthwise, and started running. Only twenty yards remained as Thanan used the log as a battering ram, knocking the heavy logs to the side. The last log cleared and he pulled himself out of the water. He had beaten Kolrath by five yards, and the giant pounded the top of one of the logs in anger.

Heavy with water, his boots sloshed and armor dripped as Thanan ran for the next challenge. After a half mile, he started to pull away from Kolrath, when his stomach decided to give up its contents. The Jinian fell to his knees, heaving, eyes watering and bulging from their sockets. His face was flushed and chills ran through his body.

Kolrath ran by the retching Jinian, smirking. Thanan's body shook from the nausea. He pushed up to his feet, two pounds lighter, wiped his mouth and started running.

Slowly he reeled the Goriath candidate in, careful to not expend his energy too soon. The breeze against his wet armor cooled him as he ran through the garrison. In the distance, he saw Kolrath arrive at the second obstacle. A minute and a half later, Thanan arrived, feeling quite well and refreshed.

Master Thorix stood at ease in front of the obstacle. "Keep it up, Jinian. You know what to do. It's all about momentum."

Thanan stood in front of two more parallel trenches, this time only three feet wide and six inches deep, full of sand. A massive granite stone, three feet in diameter and perfectly round, sat in the sand at the head of the trenches.

Placing his palms on the stone, he bent forward, touching his shoulder on the smooth surface. He roared as he pushed. His calf muscles felt as if they would burst from his legs. He thought his achilles tendon was about to snap from the force. The stone moved slowly and made a low grinding sound as it pulverized the sand beneath it. He kept his center of gravity low, pushing faster, keeping the momentum going. Slowing now would be disastrous.

Nothing was slowing Kolrath down. He had the Jinian beat. He easily rolled the sphere through the sand, evenly and steadily. Thanan dug his feet in harder, determined to use every bit of leverage he could muster. He shouted with each shove, which seemed to give him more strength; imaginary or not, it was working. His looked at his little finger while he pushed. It was swollen and stiff, but he didn't feel it anymore. He could see Kolrath forty feet in front of him. It drove him to push harder. The boulder rolled faster and faster as the momentum carried it through the sand. He reached the end with Kolrath only a quarter of a mile ahead.

With every muscle in Thanan's body burning, he took to the quarry floor again, sprinting toward the third challenge.

By the time the Jinian arrived at the rope climb, Kolrath was a third of the way up the cliff. He scanned the wall, trying to figure out which ropes to climb. The cliff rose two hundred feet with dozens of ropes secured to its face, each one a different length. There were many ways to reach the top, but minimizing the number of ropes was the best way.

Thanan gripped a rope above his head and leaped as high as he could, grabbing it with his other hand, starting up the cliff. Even as impressive as Goriaths were at climbing ropes, Thanan was faster. Hand over hand, he climbed up the first rope, never using his legs. The ropes were thick, made for Goriath hands, which made it even easier for Thanan to climb. He stopped a few feet from the top of the rope, looking for the next rope to switch to. Directly to the right, the rope only went up another ten feet before ending. The one on the left, only five, but the second rope on the left continued up another twenty-five feet.

The Jinian pushed off the rock to his right and swung as far as he could to the second rope over, just missing it. He pushed off again, using the momentum of his swing. Letting go with one hand and reaching as far as he could, his fingertips found the rope. He let go of the first rope and continued up the cliff face, closing in on the giant.

Kolrath craned his neck, looking down at the approaching Jinian. Sweat dripped off his forehead. He grumbled to himself as he searched the cliff for a better rope path. Again, Thanan swung to the optimal rope. He was now below Kolrath, one rope over and gaining. From there, only two ropes reached the top, and Kolrath was hanging onto the closest one. The other one was five ropes away, which was too far, when Thanan was so close to catching Kolrath. Just two feet below Kolrath's boots, Thanan decided he couldn't pass him in enough time and get in front of him, so he swung over to Kolrath's rope.

The rope swung violently. Kolrath looked down at the top of the Jinian's head, just below his feet, inching closer. Kolrath knew that once Thanan crested the cliff, the Jinian would easily overtake him in the run. The giant shook the rope, trying to loosen Thanan's grip. Thanan held on as he bashed into the wall over and over, taking the brunt of the force with his shoulder and hip. Kolrath kicked at Thanan's head, trying to force him down the rope, but nothing would deter him. Thanan caught Kolrath's massive boot and threw it aside.

The giant thought about the previous night, how the Jinian had embarrassed him on the ladder by beating him to the top and kicking him in the head. He couldn't tolerate being beaten by a Jinian twice. Bringing his knee up high, he dropped his boot sharply onto Thanan's cheek just as he looked up.

Thanan's vision went blurry then black. He felt the wind rushing by his face. Opening his eyes, he saw the ropes and cliff speeding past him. He stretched out his hand and caught hold of one of the ropes. It burned through his palm as he gripped it tighter and tighter. His momentum came to a sudden stop and his shoulder was yanked from its socket. He yelped along with an audible pop inside his shoulder. The intense pain and loss of strength in his arm caused him to let go of the rope. He fell the remaining fifteen feet to the quarry floor, unconscious, bleeding from his cheek and forehead.

"Welcome back, Jinian," a candidate said as Thanan walked into the barracks.

Thanan nodded questioningly, walking past the candidate, looking over the barracks.

"Jinian," another said, greeting him with a friendly nod as he made his way to his cot.

Arriving at his cot, he met Torik, who was smiling from ear to ear, preparing for bed. Agrinoth glanced up, saying nothing, continuing his own preparations.

"Jinian!" Torik exclaimed, slapping him in the shoulder. "Welcome back. See, Agrinoth, I told you he would come back." Torik turned, facing Shorim. "Pay up, Shorim, fifty frags and not one less. Don't make me count."

"Yeah…yeah," Shorim replied, reaching for his frag pouch.

Thanan sat on his bed, rubbing his shoulder. "I get half, right?"

"You can have the whole thing." Torik felt the weight of the pouch, bouncing it on his palm. He tossed it to Thanan. "I just enjoy taking their money."

"So…what did I miss over the last ten days?"

"Nothing much…except Master Grizak kicking Kolrath's backside all over the barracks."

"He did?"

"He stormed into barracks after the obstacle course and punched Kolrath square in the nose. Grizak told him to get up and he did. He said since he sought to hurt his brother candidate, even if he was a Jinian, he wasn't fit to be a Guardian. Then Kolrath took a swing at Master Grizak. Master Grizak blocked his punch and hip-tossed him to the other side of the tent. Before Kolrath could scramble to his feet, Grizak kicked him in the nose and knocked him out cold. He ordered us to drag his carcass out of here."

"I wish I could have seen that," Thanan replied.

Torik yawned, turning back to his bed. "Get some sleep, Jinian. You have some catching up to do."

After that, there was no time for hatred among the ranks. Sleep was too rare a commodity and no one wanted to face Master Grizak and the disgrace that would follow.

Day after day, Thanan and the Goriath candidates endured the twisting caves and horrible smells of Master Grizak. Although he never would have the immense strength of his Goriath counterparts, Thanan grew stronger with each day that passed. Rolling boulders from one side of the quarry to the other, climbing ropes, pushing carts full of ore through the garrison, and wading through log-infested water were only a few of the strenuous challenges of being a candidate. Thanan also learned how to eat quickly without getting sick, which made him long for Seretha's home-cooked meals and the calming conversation with Kigron at the end of each day. For forty-five days, it was the same routine...until one day when it all changed.

CHAPTER ELEVEN

ZYTHERA CIRCLE

Thanan was jolted awake by the zortusk, followed by the sound of a table crashing to the floor. He shot to his feet, standing at attention as usual. His back was straight and his eyes focused. By Thanan's recollection, Master Grizak had broken at least twenty tables and even more chairs. It had become a sort of joke in the barracks to talk about which the master would kick down the aisle. Torik even went as far as staging the tent entrance to ƒsee if he could predict which furniture Master Grizak would kick. Then Torik took bets on it.

Master Grizak strode down the aisle, hands behind his back, his expression different from days past. "All right, you brutes!" Grizak barked. "Get to the mess hall and then report to Master Kigrorian in the field. He'll take over from there." A devilish smile crept across Grizak's face.

Thanan had heard the name Kigrorian many times throughout the years he had spent among the Goriath giants, yet he had never met the legendary master. He lived a reclusive life on the outskirts of Hardrock. Kigrorian was the high-ranking master of the Zythera blade. He had spent the entirety of his life dedicated to perfecting the discipline that Master Kizaga had developed from the beginning of the Order. It was beautiful, elegant, and efficient.

Not only was he a High Master of the blade, but he was also a High Master in the art of Nikiru, which had been passed down to him from his father. It was a discipline of unarmed combat that combined the grace of the wind wisp and the stealth and deadly speed of the legendary flame wrock. A Guardian was almost as deadly without his blade as with it. Even though Kizaga's method was almost indefensible, it had its flaws; so Tygrothian saw fit to adopt the Nikiru discipline in order to add some grace and subtlety to its already deadly nature. The combination of the two disciplines was a sight to behold: Thanan had watched from afar in his first year with Purgon, how it was passive and graceful one moment, then brutally violent the next.

There were now only twenty. Kigrorian commenced the ceremony of the blade, one by one, calling the twenty by name to come forward and receive their first true Zythera blade and thus fully become candidates of the Guardian Order.

"These few blades are the original Zythera blades fired in the great forges of Crystal City," Master Kigrorian explained. "General Tygrothian procured them over the centuries as the first generations began dying off. The high levels of Zythera dust, glystian, and zil ores in the blades make them unique among Goriath weapons – and much stronger. There were fewer than one hundred ever made with the high concentration, many of them lost in battle in the early wars."

Each hilt bore Purgon's older brother's maker's mark, and Purgon later etched the sign of the Guardian in the blade. On the hilt hung a red sash, which represented blood that was shed by the innocent. It was meant to evoke the responsibility to defend the defenseless and to never let the Goriath atrocities of the past happen again.

Each candidate bowed as they received their sacred sword. There was a noticeable change in their countenances as each one held his Zythera blade, as if a mantle had descended upon them, weighting them with an unseen power and responsibility.

Great warriors throughout the long history of the Guardian Order had wielded these sacred blades while training. As the new candidates each received a blade, the thought crossed their minds that Master Kizaga himself or another legend of the Order had gripped the hilt or run his thumb across the blade before. At the end of the training, the candidates would ceremoniously return the blades to the stone chest, where the blades would stay until the chest was opened again once it was time to begin training a new class of warriors.

It was now the Jinian's turn. Kigrorian raised another blade from the stone chest that lay before him. "Thanan, son of Corderian," the High Master spoke with great authority, "come forward and take your place among the candidates."

The Jinian slowly stepped toward Kigrorian, his eyes focused on the red sash swaying in the breeze. He reached for the blade with some trepidation. Kigrorian noticed the hesitation and didn't release the sword immediately. He looked discerningly into Thanan's eyes, trying to understand the Jinian's uncertainty, and then relinquished the blade saying nothing. The Jinian took his place in line, standing at attention until the last candidate received his Zythera blade.

"From this time forth, the Zythera blade will be at your side," the master ordered, holding his blade high. "Any misuse of this blade will be met with the harshest of consequences." The master's ceremonial gold sash hung from the hilt and symbolized his lifelong dedication to the Order. "A Guardian's sash is a significant emblem of the Order. The three distinct sash colors represent the levels of commitment that one must possess to truly become a Guardian. Although the sash is purely ornamental in its nature and is only used in ceremony, it is nonetheless a vital part of our proud tradition."

A great measure of reverence followed all those who bore the colors. It was common for anyone who passed by a past Guardian or even a candidate to acknowledge their presence with a physical gesture, such as a slow head nod. Or those who were much older and proper would bring one fisted hand and one open palm to their bosom.

One story was passed around in the barracks, however, describing when a sash was used in a less-than-ceremonial way.

Years earlier, one unfortunate candidate was made an example of. Poor Shilian Xil was almost strangled to death with his own sash when he spoke to Kigrorian in a manner that the master deemed not quite appropriate of a Guardian candidate.

The master called him forward and ordered him to take a battle stance before him. He commanded Shilian to advance and with one elegant and effortless movement, he disarmed Shilian, spun behind him, and had the candidate's red sash tightly cinched around his neck until the blood left his brain.

Humiliated and disgraced, Shilian Xil left Hardrock. It was said that he didn't feel the cold stalagmites pierce his chest when he reached the bottom of Kul Lorath.

It was at that moment that Master Kigrorian drew the line for all future candidates. Absolute obedience was essential for leaving behind everything a common Goriath was, in order to make room for a new creature.

"This is the Zythera Circle," Kigrorian explained, dropping the blunt end of his staff to the circle of inlaid stones. "Six months from now this circle will fill your every thought. It will be your first thought in the morning and the last thing you think about before you sleep.

"Seventeen of you will discover within this circle that you are not destined to be a Guardian. But I assure you that you will still find joy in serving your fellow giants in whatever path you will take, whether it be in the military or as a civilian.

"Three of you however, will be found worthy to move on to the final chapter of your candidacy. But before any of that, you must train like you have never trained before."

Thanan stood among giants, listening intently to every word the master was saying, heart beating from his chest. The thought of actually becoming a Guardian struck him greatly. His mind reeled at that possibility. He wanted to look down the line at his fellow candidates. Did they show pride in their eyes as he did, or were they like stone, hiding their happiness behind blank and disciplined eyes? Instead, he focused on Master Kigrorian so as to not miss a word.

"Five days a week you will report to the Nikiru field. On the sixth day you will be in the capable hands of Master Grizak for strength and endurance training. The seventh day, you are free to do as you wish...worship, rest, and ponder the things that you learn here...but you are never to leave Krokil Dun. Am I clear?"

"Yes, Master Kigrorian!" they yelled together.

Kigrorian lifted his staff from the headstone and began pacing, "As it is the sixth day, I am inclined to give you back to Master Grizak, but I am going to give a reprieve. You are dismissed for two days. Remember you are candidates of the Guardian Order, and as such you will adhere to all rules with exactness. You are dismissed."

The candidates broke ranks and departed for the barracks, reveling in the opportunity for more sleep, food, and relaxation.

"Thanan, stay for a moment," Kigrorian called out.

Thanan shot an unusual glance at Torik and then at Agrinoth. Agrinoth wrinkled his upper lip, turned, and kept walking toward the barracks.

Approaching the master, Thanan's heart raced. What did Kigrorian want? "Yes, Master Kigrorian? What can I do for you?" the Jinian asked, standing at attention once more.

"At ease, Thanan. Walk with me."

Thanan and Kigrorian slowly walked through the Nikiru field saying very little at first. Kigrorian walked with a staff, yet showed no signs of a limp or weakness in his legs. At the top of the staff was a smooth stone that had a hole bored into it that fit perfectly over the staff. The round stone was white, had the mark of the Order etched in it, and was unlike any gemstone Thanan had ever seen in the caverns.

"So...Thanan, tell me why you hesitated when receiving the Zythera blade."

Thanan thought for a moment. "I really do not know, sir. Maybe it was a fleeting moment of doubt, maybe something more. I knew that by taking the sword, I could never turn back...that my course would be set."

"Ah...I see. You seem to think that accepting the sword symbolizes a sort of finality, when in reality it is only the beginning of something that is vastly larger than any of us can imagine."

Thanan understood the master's meaning.

"What is troubling you?" Kigrorian asked discerningly.

"I feel as though you may have singled me out among the candidates, sir, spending this time with me."

"Do not worry about such things, Thanan. They all have their weaknesses, and will in turn have their opportunity with me. I want them all to succeed, but there can only be three. I must ensure that every last one of you is prepared. Your bodies be strong enough, I have no doubt, but it's the mind and spirit that concern me most: What a candidate thinks, what drives him to act must be pure."

———◆O◆———

Before Xavantha awoke and the sweet smell of bread and biscuits filled the morning air, the twenty candidates entered the Nikiru field, anxious to begin their training with the Zythera blade. By the light of torches, they lined up in four rows of five, fully armored, holding their swords with the blade flat against their chests. Thanan felt the hilt in his hand, how the grip was worn from centuries of combat training. *Had Kizaga himself held this blade? What incredible things had this blade been part of?* he wondered.

Subtly, he turned his head to see his candidate brothers standing at attention. The only movement he saw was Agrinoth gripping the hilt of his own sword. A hint of a smile shown on Thanan's face, knowing that Agrinoth and he were most likely thinking the same thing.

Master Kigrorian stepped onto the field, slowly spinning his staff with his hands. Like a deadly dance, his graceful footsteps scarcely made a sound as he pivoted from stone to stone. The effortless motion of his hands spinning the staff over his head was mesmerizing to Thanan. Faster and faster, he spun the staff around his back and over his head, the wind whipping and whistling around him until he came to a sudden stop with the white stone only a half inch in front of Grozythian's eyes.

Master Kigrorian slowly lowered the tip of his staff, squinting his eyes, as if looking into Grozythian's soul. The candidate stared back, not flinching a muscle, unfazed by the display. "Candidates, today is the day you will forget who you are," the master said, turning from Grozythian. "Now is the time to become something more, the time to put out of your minds the petty thoughts of jealousy, pride, and hatred.

"These twenty are your brothers. Together, you will learn the ancient arts of the blade and Nikiru. Many of you have been soldiers. Some of you have been blessed with undeniable gifts and can wield a blade even as Kizaga did, but you are shadow of what you will become. The blade and you will be made one when I am through.

"Close your eyes," Kigrorian said calmly, walking among the candidates. "Those who can be taught will clear their minds, stripping every thought of their life before today. For the last forty-five days you have been as animals, crawling over each other in dark tunnels, clawing your way to the top, only to show your brother the bottom of your boot. This is not the way of a Guardian.

"To become a Guardian, you must now put your trust in the brotherhood. Know in your heart that with every swing of the blade, every cut you receive by the hand of one of your brothers, something is learned. And by this acknowledgment, while you bleed in the medic's tent you will think to yourself, 'My brother taught me something today; I should have been faster, parried instead of retreating, lifted my blade higher.' Your failures will become successes. You will be grateful your brother revealed to you a weakness. And conversely, you will never revel in the destruction of your brother. Never let pride enter your mind. It will be your undoing. If you can do these things, a Guardian you shall be. Now let's begin."

Every day began the same, a barrage of mental and physical challenges designed to break a candidate's will and force his mind to submit to a new way of thinking. Thanan endured endless months repeating the same fluid movements until they became second nature, requiring no thought, just reaction. The master's voice echoed in his sleep, "Visualize it one thousand and one times and then do it again."

The Jinian held up to the grueling regimen much easier than anyone anticipated. During the training, he suffered beating after beating and somehow found the strength to get up every time. He became very well acquainted with the physicians, having visited them several times a week for the first five months.

Thanan began to master the ancient techniques one by one, oftentimes leaving Master Kigrorian dumbfounded by what he was witnessing. On occasion, Thanan would see General Tygrothian or Captain Kigron speaking with Master Kigrorian in the distance. He never knew what they were talking about, but caught their eyes looking at him a few times.

Once in a sparring match against Nirkul Gol, Thanan parried an overhead swing, causing the blade to be buried deep into the ground in front of him. Without hesitation he stepped onto the blade and, with incredible force, drove his armored knee into the chin of the hunched giant. Nirkul fell face first in the dirt, unconscious.

All at once the clashing swords stopped and the candidates stared in awe. Agrinoth glanced at the slumped Nirkul and clenched his jaw briefly, not wanting to give any attention to the

Jinian. He yelled at his opponent to raise his blade and began swinging again.

Although they all knew what really had happened, to spare Nirkul any embarrassment when he woke, Nirkul was told that an escaped whiptail boar had blindsided him during the match.

There was no doubt that the Jinian candidate was faster than most Goriaths, but he lacked their immense strength. He made up for this deficit by deflecting the mighty blows of his fellow candidates instead of taking the full force of the swings. This oftentimes put the giants off-balance, and Thanan took full advantage of their instability.

Mastering the Zythera blade was at the heart of becoming a Guardian. The Jinian began reading his opponents' subtle body movements to predict where their strikes would come from, only to react with the minimum blows necessary to subdue his brother. With or without a Zythera blade, there were no wasted movements, no unnecessary methods…only cold efficiency.

Thanan began to understand the stories he had heard as a child in the City of Jin. It was said that the twelve Guardians were as mighty as one hundred well-trained Goriath warriors and deadlier than five hundred Jinian soldiers. Whether it was true or not, the Guardians were feared and revered among the Goriath giants.

Growing up, Thanan heard bedtime stories, told to him by his mother Debethia, about the twelve blue giants traveling throughout the Jinian territories two by two, keeping the peace from the shadows. Their existence outside the caves only resided within whispers on the wind, but it was enough for bandits outside the great city to give pause about their despicable actions; for one never knew when a blue giant might end his misdeeds.

And so, time passed quickly for Thanan of Jin, with each day in the barracks still beginning the same. Grizak, with his fowl morning breath, spouted slurs at the Jinian, which seemed to pour effortlessly off his tongue like the falls of Halitha into Lake Rhinoth, but Thanan always held his temper in check.

Twenty-five Guardian candidates had been whittled down to fourteen. Agrinoth and Torik were the clear frontrunners. The two brothers were different in every way, but they were both destined to be the finest Guardians of their age. It was said around the garrison that Agrinoth possessed the ancient spirit of Master Kizaga himself. He was the embodiment of all that a Goriath Guardian should be. Torik was a natural master. At Kigrorian's request, he often gave instruction inside the Zythera circle. It took very little effort for Torik, but still he remained humble and ready to learn from his master, despite his propensity for frivolity.

Many times, at the end of the day, Master Kigrorian sat in the Nikiru field speaking of the final test with great passion.

"All of your lives you have heard tales about the final test of a Guardian candidate, The Day of the Dark. Your final trial will begin in Krokil Zil and end in Krokil Gronik, on the far side of Whitehall, only a few days' walk from each other. But within those stone doors, you will traverse a world of over one thousand miles of perilous labyrinths, caves, and caverns, pitting three of you against the most brutal terrain and beasts known to the world above or below. You will plunge deep in the earth and see things you thought not possible. Make no mistake, candidates; the journey will test your very core. You will be called upon to use all your cunning, every skill you have learned from me, and still it may not be enough.

"I cannot tell you how to pass this test, for the test is never the same. The underearth is always changing, creating new ways to kill."

Thanan looked around at his candidate brothers, not believing he was still there among the strongest.

"In past trials," the master continued, "candidates completed their journey in six months, some longer, many never. Long ago, Master Kizaga emerged from the darkness in five months thirteen days, carrying the severed head of a flame wrock the last two hundred miles of the journey. There are some here capable of this greatness. There is no way to be fully prepared for the horrors you will face within the darkness. You must rely on your brothers. To go alone would be a dire mistake. It is only after this final and harrowing test that a candidate is truly ready to bear the mark of the Guardian for the rest of his life."

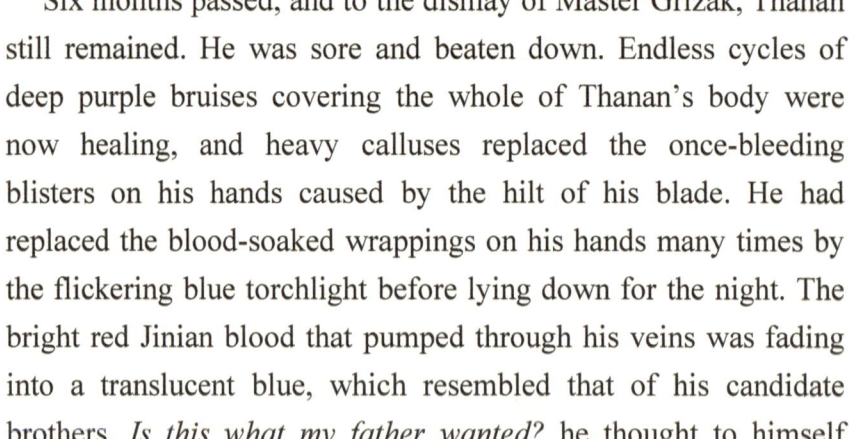

Six months passed, and to the dismay of Master Grizak, Thanan still remained. He was sore and beaten down. Endless cycles of deep purple bruises covering the whole of Thanan's body were now healing, and heavy calluses replaced the once-bleeding blisters on his hands caused by the hilt of his blade. He had replaced the blood-soaked wrappings on his hands many times by the flickering blue torchlight before lying down for the night. The bright red Jinian blood that pumped through his veins was fading into a translucent blue, which resembled that of his candidate brothers. *Is this what my father wanted?* he thought to himself many times. The cuts on his forearms, thighs, and shoulders, which he received by the hands of his fellow candidates, had now scarred over. Each one of them was a lesson learned. He now healed more rapidly and felt less pain as the transformation overtook him.

"The time has come," Master Kigrorian announced from the head of the Zythera Circle. "You have earned the right to enter the circle. This is the only place that you may battle at full strength and speed. There are only two laws within the circle.

"First...competitors shall not leave the circle unless they have yielded the match or they are unconscious or dead. Second...no strikes can be dealt to your opponent while they are on the ground or once they have yielded the match. Breaking this rule will be met with the harshest of penalties. The circle's purpose is to train, not to kill your brother candidates."

Thanan studied the circle as he had done many times before. The Zythera Circle was a circle of inlaid stones at the center of the Nikiru field. There were twelve stones, each one the size of a Goriath's hand and bearing the mark of the Order, and the circle was ten paces in diameter.

The Jinian's heart raced at the thought of being in the circle battling one of his Goriath brothers. Although Thanan knew the true purpose of the Zythera Circle was to continue growing and learning to become a Guardian, he also knew that death did happen on occasion, but it was rare. Many in Hardrock had never heard about someone being killed in the circle. Not because it didn't happen, but because it was not appropriate to speak of the noble dead who fell within the Zythera Circle. They were only sad witnesses to the funeral processions, which passed by every few years.

"Anyone at any time can challenge another candidate to a trial match in the circle," Master Kigrorian instructed from the headstone. "The challenged can refuse, but will spend ten days in the pit for his refusal. If the trial match is accepted and the challenger loses his match, he also will have to spend ten days in the pit, and thus fall behind in his training. This is a way of increasing your rank, but take caution, candidates. You must calculate your risk."

Thanan sensed many of the candidates eyeing him. He felt like a young whiptail destined for the slaughterhouse. He did not make eye contact with any of them, especially Agrinoth. He felt Agrinoth would show no mercy upon him in the circle.

Master Kigrorian lifted a stone box that was nestled between his feet. "The trial matches will begin tomorrow morning when Xavantha shines her first light on the garrison. When you return to the barracks tonight, you will all find a pouch on your bunk containing twenty stones, each one bearing your name in red. Consider wisely whose name you paint on the stone." He held the stone box in front of him showing the lid bearing a hole in it no larger than an egg.

Thanan arrived to find the pouch on his pillow as Master Kigrorian said it would be. He poured a few stones into his hands, feeling their weight. The stones were smooth and flat like river rocks. *One might get ten skips with the perfect throw,* Thanan thought. One on side his name was painted in red and the other was blank. He glanced at the tent's entrance. A flickering blue torch lit the table beneath it. The stone box sat on the table accompanied by a bottle of white ink and a blue quill from a Loriam hen.

The tent was quieter than usual, a sort of reverence filling the room. Thanan studied the other candidates as they sat on their bunks, looking at their own stones in their palms, feeling the glassy texture. He tried to imagine what they were all thinking, what strategies they would implement in the Zythera Circle. The only two who did not open their pouches were Agrinoth and Torik. They prepared for bed as usual and paid little attention to the others.

Heavy footsteps at the back of the barracks caught Thanan's attention. He turned to see Xangroth Kor making his way to the stone box. Soon everyone was watching him slowly stride down the aisle, fist clenched around a blank stone and eyes focused on the box.

It was a serious thing, selecting an opponent for the Zythera Circle, and Thanan could see it in Xangroth's eyes. Some might challenge the strongest first in the off chance they might win the match and advance quickly to the top. Others might challenge the weakest to gain experience in the circle and increase their rank slowly.

Xangroth stepped up to the table and paused for a moment before picking up the quill. A few strokes later he dropped the stone into the hole and faced the candidate onlookers, not making eye contact with anyone so as to not give away his own strategy. No words were said as he walked back to his bunk.

Three more candidates painted names on stones and dropped them into the box. Thanan contemplated making his own challenge, but knew without a doubt he would be in the circle in the morning whether he threw in his own stone or not. So he poured his stones back in the pouch and tried his best to get some sleep.

The usual chatter at breakfast was dampened by anxious thoughts of the circle. Even Torik, with his flamboyant storytelling, was still and contemplative while he ate. Agrinoth seemed the same to Thanan: stern and focused. Nothing seemed to rattle the great warrior, not even the thought of battling a brother at full strength.

Xavantha's light began brightening the Nikiru field as the candidates entered single-file. They gathered around the circle, standing on the stones, wearing heavy armor and armed with Zythera blades. Thanan's armor fit perfectly, having been fitted and forged by Purgon. He subtly rolled his shoulders and twisted his neck, feeling the full range of motion that his armor allowed.

Quietly, Kigrorian made his way to the headstone of the circle, followed by Master Grizak, who was carrying the stone box. Master Kigrorian came to rest on the headstone and lowered the tip of his staff upon the field.

It was silent in the circle as the candidates watched Kigrorian take the box and lift the hinged lid, drawing out the first stone. "So let it be written that Zolgrath has challenged Torik," he read aloud.

From his tunic pocket, Grizak pulled out a small book and wrote as he was commanded with quill and ink. He then took the stone from Kigrorian and dropped it in his pocket. There were many books that contained the history of the Zythera Circle. If one had access, they could retrace every battle, even back to Master Kizaga himself.

The challenge was a surprise to everyone, although they said nothing. Zolgrath had proved himself a formidable swordsman, but his Nikiru skills were lacking, especially when compared to Torik, who had all but mastered the discipline. In Thanan's mind, it was a misjudgment by Zolgrath to make such a challenge at this point.

The trials were never taken lightly among the brothers. Each of them knew it could be the last time one of their fellow candidates might ever hold a Zythera blade, so they did not cheer. They did not hail the victor or jeer the loser. It was a chance to revel in the glory of the battle. It was also an opportunity to behold the magnificence of two warriors – whose prowess with the blade was comparable to the great Guardians of old – as they paired off in an exhibition of skill, speed, and strength.

The two candidates made their way around the circle, embracing the remaining candidates, as was the tradition. The combatants entered the circle and took their places at the center stones, assuming their unique battle stances. Torik did not draw his blade, but rather lowered his center of gravity and readied himself for the swinging onslaught.

The sound of Kigrorian's staff sent Zolgrath leaping across the circle, swinging his blade at Torik's chest. Torik sidestepped the first swing and ducked the second. The entire offensive lasted ten seconds before Torik caught Zolgrath's wrist, twisted it behind his back, and broke his forearm and wrist. The sword flew from his hand and spun in the air. Torik caught the hilt before the blade hit the ground and drove the emblem of the Guardian into the back of

Zolgrath's skull. The challenger fell face first, his forehead striking the center stone. He rolled to his side, unconscious.

Torik took his place at the center stone and bowed respectfully to Master Kigrorian. Agrinoth let a small smile sneak through his stern face as the physicians carried Zolgrath to their tent for mending.

Thanan's stomach churned. He knew his name would be called. He fidgeted in his armor, watching Kigrorian step back up to the headstone and bring out the next stone.

"Let it be written that Xangrothian challenges Thanan," the master announced, looking over the circled candidates.

The temperature in Thanan's face raised ten degrees. His heart began beating against his armored chest. He almost forgot to embrace his brothers in the circle when he was gently nudged by Torik's elbow, reminding him of the proper way.

Xangrothian stood opposite the Jinian, his eyes boring a hole through Thanan's forehead. Thanan didn't give him the satisfaction of glancing away. The Jinian reached for his blade, gripping the hilt, feeling the texture of the wrappings. His hand felt at home on the handle. It was as familiar now as the streets of Hastentown.

The crack of Master Kigrorian's staff jolted Thanan into action. He drew his blade just in time to deflect Xangrothian's swing, deflecting it to the right. He quickly retaliated with own swing, but was stopped short by armored knuckles across his cheekbone.

Torik pursed his lips, restraining himself from shouting out encouraging advice to Thanan, while the rest of the candidates stood motionless looking on.

Looking up from the ground, Thanan saw his opponent nimbly bobbing back and forth, readying himself for the next onslaught. As soon as Thanan was on his knee, Xangrothian closed off the distance, swinging as hard as he could, determined to end the match as soon as possible. The Jinian deflected the giant's first two blows from a kneeling position and fought his way to his feet. Thanan ducked a powerful swing at his throat and continued spinning around, bringing his boot under Xangrothian's chin. The giant bit his tongue and blood began pouring from the corners of his mouth. He spat a mouthful to the ground and breathed heavily from his nose, his nostrils flaring and sweat dripping down his face.

Seeing an opportunity to turn the match to his favor, Thanan launched his own attack. With a lighting-fast step, he closed in, thrusting his Zythera blade at Xangrothian's abdomen, which the giant parried and then brought his foot up into Thanan's chest. To Thanan, it felt as if a panicked draminaton buck had kicked him. He stumbled backward trying to defend himself, his lungs struggling to take in oxygen. The next thing Thanan saw was a flash of metal as Xangrothian's blade cut through the air. The swing was so hard that it pierced Thanan's armor and sliced into his upper ribcage.

Another rap of the staff on the headstone and the match was declared over. Thanan lay in the circle, eyes wide, lungs wanting to expand and ease his suffering. He didn't even feel the bloody gash in his side so strenuous was the kick to his chest. It would take forty-seven stitches to stop the bleeding.

Thanan spent much of his time defending his lowly rank in the circle, only to find himself in the infirmary time and time again. He became very good friends with the general's surgeons. One by one the candidates challenged him, dealing out beating after beating, but to their disbelief, he started winning. Over time, like a skilled frag gambler, he learned the candidate's individual tells with the blade. Methodically, he sent all his challengers to the pit. He had not yet challenged another candidate himself, but the moment had come. There were only three candidates whom he had not fought in the circle, but had observed many times. Tomorrow he would make the formal request to challenge Groziak Zol, who was ranked third, to a trial match in the Zythera Circle.

The remaining nine candidates rarely slept, but when they did, it was restless. They couldn't escape the hellish routine even in their slumber, because their dreams were full of combat scenarios and battle theory. In addition to the lack of rest, they were driven to prepare themselves for the final trial that would test the remaining three to a degree that was unimaginable.

The following morning, Thanan fluttered his fingers nervously as he contemplated the many ways his fight could go. Groziak was fierce, a true force to be reckoned with, but he was all offense and Thanan knew it. He had examined the warrior for weeks and was confident he knew every movement he would make within the circle.

"Let it be written that Thanan of Jin has challenged Groziak Zol in the Zythera Circle!" Master Kigrorian announced from the head of the circle.

The other seven candidates surrounded the circle, standing on the stones. Over the past weeks they all had witnessed raw brutality.

The Jinian had won over the hearts of every candidate with the exception of Agrinoth. The thought had crossed Thanan's mind to challenge him. But truth be told, the mere idea of a trial match in the circle with Agrinoth frightened him greatly, and he knew the fear would cause him to lose.

One by one, the competitors made their way to the seven that surrounded the circle. They paused for a brief moment before each warrior and placed a hand on his shoulder and nodded, as if to say without a word, "Be strong, goodbye, and good luck." Thanan and his opponent both turned to Kigrorian and bowed respectfully to their master.

"Candidates, enter the circle," Kigrorian commanded, pointing to the inner stones.

The tension in the air was palpable as they took their places on the stones. Groziak gripped the hilt and slowly drew his Zythera blade from the sheath, steadying his stance. Thanan also gripped the hilt and took *his* typical stance, which was to not draw his sword until the master gave the sign and the trial began. This method had proved difficult and frustrating for his past opponents because so much could be derived from the initial battle stance one took. The Jinian had become quite adept at remaining unreadable by his fellow candidates.

They respectfully gave each other a nod, their eyes never breaking from each other. Master Kigrorian brought his wooden staff sharply down upon the head stone. Like the lightning-fast strike of a serpent, even as the ring of the stone still hung in the air, Groziak snapped his sword at Thanan's throat. The Jinian, in perfect harmony with Groziak's movement, spun just out of the sword's reach, quickly drawing his own sword as he spun behind Groziak. The move was so perfectly timed and so quick that Groziak didn't realize his Achilles tendon was severed and had rendered his foot limp and lifeless. Not even a wince of pain showed on the giant's face. If not for the pool of blood forming under his foot, no one could tell that he was injured.

Thanan paced back and forth, studying Groziak's face. The realization that his opponent might force him to do the unthinkable struck him with great force. Groziak swung his injured foot high in the air as if to kick Thanan's head, but instead left a swath of warm blood splattered across the Jinian's face, temporarily obscuring his vision. It was an improvised tactic that Thanan was not prepared for, nor had he seen in the circle, and he lost sight of Groziak for the slightest moment. The giant continued his movement by thrusting his blade toward Thanan's chest, but again as if by some premonition, Thanan parried the attack with only a subtle side step and drove his own blade upward through Groziak's bicep. The noble candidate's hand involuntarily sprang open and his Zythera blade fell to the ground. The Jinian withdrew his blade from the giant's arm as fast as he drove it in and turned the blade downward, plunging it deep into the giant's thigh, splitting his femur lengthwise. The Jinian felt the blade grinding the bone as he pulled his sword from Groziak's leg and stepped back. Groziak looked at Thanan, then down at his fallen sword. He stumbled, but did not fall.

A common Goriath would have yielded after the cut to his Achilles tendon, but a candidate of Groziak's skill did not feel pain as he once did. The pain was there, but it resided deep in the recesses of his mind, buried beneath endless hours of mental training. The pain suppression technique proved to be valuable when one had to endure extreme pain, but it could also fool others into thinking a Goriath was all right when in fact they were very close to death.

"Let the sword lie, brother," Thanan pleaded, seeing great drops of blood emerging from Groziak's fingertips.

Nikiru Field was deathly quiet. Nothing could be heard but the distant sound of billows and ringing hammers from the armory. The circle of candidates stood motionless and steadfast, looking on like the mighty statues that guard the coastline of Zun Gorzul.

Groziak looked again at his fallen sword and back to Thanan. His face was pale and he appeared listless as he staggered forward and fell to one knee. The proud Goriath's fingers trembled, reaching for his sword.

Once again, the Jinian took his place at the inner stone, his blade running with Groziak's bluish blood. "Please brother, don't be foolish," he pleaded one more time, to no avail.

Groziak clutched his hilt and slowly rose to his feet. Thanan looked to Master Kigrorian in a silent appeal for mercy, but none came. Those standing in the circle felt an air of uneasiness sweep over them. Might this be the time they witness death in the circle? They hoped not.

The giant fell to his knees again, trembling from weakness. The candidates all sensed the pride of Groziak would cause him to fall. No Guardian wanted to witness the death of his brother, but to intervene was unforgivable and banishment would be his end.

Groziak slowly bent over to lift his sword with his off-hand. He trembled violently, trying to stand upright once again. The pool of blood beneath his feet had now formed tiny streams that flowed between the stones and ran in every direction. One of the streams even had reached Thanan's inner stone.

Thanan's heart was crying out for his prideful brother. "You've lost, Groziak," he pleaded. "Please, withdraw with no shame."

Suddenly, Groziak's countenance changed, as if he were no longer in control of himself. The severe loss of blood had launched Groziak into a crazed state. The giant's eyes were like fire, and his frame began to tremble uncontrollably. He shakily raised his sword and hobbled toward the Jinian, intending to kill him. With no form to his attack, he was no match for Thanan. Thanan knew that the next blow of his sword would surely kill his brother candidate, and an overwhelming sadness filled his mind and body.

He settled into his battle stance with the intent of ending the match. As Groziak limped forward, he raised his sword high in the air in a final burst of life. As his blade reached its pinnacle, the giant's eyes rolled to the back of his head and he limply fell to the Nikiru Field, his pale face splashing in the small puddle of blood at Thanan's feet.

Tradition dictated that Master Kigrorian declare the victor, but Thanan fell to his knees in an attempt to stop the immense bleeding coming from his brother. He pressed his hands on the wounds on Groziak's bicep and thigh. He pleaded for the physician to help him. Kigrorian nodded and the physician ran to Groziak's side. No one had witnessed such compassion from a candidate in the circle before, and it caused all who were present to give pause. Even Agrinoth with his deep-seated hatred for the Jinian wavered because of the scene before him. At that moment, everyone knew without a doubt that Thanan of Jin truly possessed the spirit of a Goriath Guardian, and they quietly stepped aside as he left the bloody circle. His candidate brothers exchanged no words, only knowing glances that they had been beaten by the most unlikely of candidates.

Groziak would recover, but his lofty goal of becoming a Guardian would never be realized. The injury to his Achilles tendon was too much for him to overcome. He would spend his years within the ranks of the White Hall garrison and be hailed as a great warrior, his name bringing honor to his family.

CHAPTER TWELVE

INTO THE DARKNESS

The Day of the Dark had finally arrived. In three days' time, in the remote hall of Krokil Zil, the final test for the Guardian candidates would at last take place.

The exhausted Jinian returned to his adopted home, welcomed with laughter and embrace. Two years had passed since he had laid his head down in the Gru home. He was almost knocked to the floor when Tav, Simo, and Tirothia threw themselves around his neck, waist, and legs, causing him to briefly lose his balance.

"Some Guardian you'll be, stumbling around like a drunken fool," Kigron said, laughing.

Tirothia scrunched her nose. "You look different."

"So do you. You're so big," Thanan replied, smiling.

"That's enough," Seretha scolded softly. "It is so good to have you home again, Thanan. Even for such a short time as this." She embraced him.

"It is good to be here again. Will you all be making the journey to Krokil Zil?" Thanan asked.

"Kigron will be traveling with you, but we will be saying our goodbyes tonight," Seretha answered sadly. "I bet you are hungry."

"You know me too well. I'm famished," the Jinian said, smiling. "Stale biscuits, dried fish, and fatty sowbelly day and night made me long for your home-cooked meals."

"Well…tonight I have made you a special treat, Thanan. A small harvest of white rim mushrooms just came into Hardrock, and when Rolik heard you were going to be our guest tonight, he gave me the lot. So with the extra frags, I bought a whole whiptail sow, and it's been cooking for hours."

Warm, savory air drifted in as Seretha described the meal in glorious detail, and Thanan rubbed his hands together and smiled in anticipation of the feast.

It was so comfortable to be in the Gru home again that it was like Thanan had never left. Loud laughter rang out as the candidate told his amazing tales of the past two years in the barracks and the black cavern and battling in the Nikiru Field. Even though his body and mind had been punished for so long, the burden was, but for a moment, lightened, and the old carefree Jinian showed through ever so briefly. After more than an hour, the conversation seemed to run out though, a heavy air of seriousness falling upon the table. The reality that this might be the last time Seretha and the children might see their adopted Jinian weighed heavily on everyone's minds.

"This is amazing, Seretha," Thanan commented, popping another mushroom in his mouth.

It was true. Seretha had prepared an excellent dinner of smoked sow and mushrooms, flavored with more expensive spices than she usually used. But the comment was really an attempt to break the grim silence that even the children did not break with their usual playful chatter.

"Thank you, Thanan," Seretha said quietly. She said nothing more, so Thanan tried again.

"So, Tav…hunted anything interesting in the back halls lately?"

Tavris, in his haste to begin answering Thanan's question, started speaking, revealing the combination of chewed biscuit and mushrooms in his mouth. Thanan chuckled.

"Please don't speak when your mouth is full, Tav," Seretha scolded.

Tavris swallowed hard, forcing the food down his throat. "Well, I p-p-picked off a hai-hairless ore r-r-rat at sixty f-f-feet in a nar-narrow hallway in the Z-Z-Zoran d-district. Hit it r-r-right in the h-hind end, but I was ai-ai-aiming for the b-back hip. What's a c-c-couple of i-inches?" Tavris laughed, holding his index finger and thumb up in front of his eye with a hair's space between them.

Thanan chuckled again at Tavris's antics and looked over the table at Kigron, who now had a sober look on his face.

Over the years Kigron and his family had been the host to many Guardian candidates on their last night before the darkness. They had been the family with which numerous last meals were shared with candidates who were never seen again.

"I know you all are worried for me," Thanan said breaking the tension. "It will be all right. I am meant to be here."

"It's just that so many times I have said goodbye," Seretha said. "There have been many tests when no candidates emerged from the darkness. I've seen many families waiting at the mouth of the dark cave, ready to receive their beloved warrior in glory, but only despair met them and the journey back to their homes was weighted with wrenching sadness."

Tears welled in Seretha's eyes. "They were left with nothing but a crimson sash hanging on the wall by which to remember their sons."

Kigron knew the fate of so many who had gone before, and this he accepted wholeheartedly as a soldier and as a Goriath giant, but this time was different. The unlikely pale man from Jin had become more like a brother than a friend. He felt a deep respect for Thanan, and he knew that their fates were intertwined. It was a feeling he could not shake.

"Forgive my silence," the captain said quietly.

"Come on Tav, Simo, Tirothia, let's get you off to your beds." Seretha stood and walked over to Thanan and kissed him on his cheek. A slight smile formed on her lips and her eyes welled with tears again, but she fought them back. The physically stunning woman had become more like a mother than a friend to the Jinian during his stay among the Goriath family. It was as if she were saying, without words, goodbye to her own son. It was a night that Thanan would remember with fondness many times in his darkest of days.

Kigron stood, turning to the door. "Get some sleep, Thanan. I will see you in the morning."

"Where are you going at this hour? Do you want me to go with you?" he replied.

"No…just some last minute business before we leave tomorrow. It is nice to have you back, my friend."

Kigron paused at the door and shook his head in disbelief. "A Jinian Guardian. I never would have believed it. We will talk tomorrow. It is a long walk."

"Good night, Kigron."

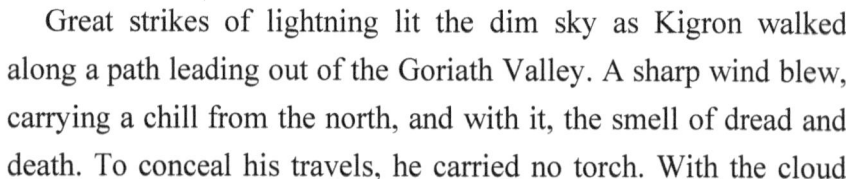

Great strikes of lightning lit the dim sky as Kigron walked along a path leading out of the Goriath Valley. A sharp wind blew, carrying a chill from the north, and with it, the smell of dread and death. To conceal his travels, he carried no torch. With the cloud cover, this made it difficult to see the path before him. He caught quick glimpses of the wet path when the approaching storm saw fit to lend its jagged hand.

Deep groans of thunder echoed from mountain to mountain in the distance. Kigron was uneasy and his pace quickened. Disfigured shadows loomed longer with each strike. As the wind grew, so did Kigron's anxiety. Again, the thunder boomed and with it came screams in the darkness, sounds of horror in the wind.

The air was damp and thick. Large raindrops began falling to the ground, causing a thick mist to rise up to Kigron's waist. He approached a crossroad and stopped as if he were waiting for something. The heart of the storm was almost upon him as the thunder shook the ground, causing the trees to shake and the earth to shudder under his feet. The blinding flashes of light overwhelmed the captain's senses.

He quickly turned around as lightning unveiled the outline of a cloaked man standing behind him. Water streamed heavily from the stranger's hood. Kigron reached for his sword, but stopped short of drawing it, recognizing the man.

"You are late," Kigron said, releasing his grip.

The cloaked man held an unusual sword at his side, but did not speak. The wind caused his cloak to whip behind him. Kigron looked at the sword.

"So the stories are true," he said, gesturing to the blade.

The cloaked figure stood motionless. The storm was upon them now with all its fury. The air was electrified with energy, lightning dancing all around them. Haunting howls from the forest grew closer and closer as the wild wind swirled. Thunder crashed again and again.

Kigron looked down upon the cloaked man. "We have to go now," the captain shouted. "I'll go with you."

Kigron turned away and began to walk, but the cloaked man stood there encircled by lightning, motionless. The captain looked back, concerned.

"It must be now," he yelled. "They are coming."

Horrible screams from the darkness swelled in Kigron's ears. He could barely conceal his fright. He lunged for the cloaked figure's shoulder to pull him onward, but as he reached out, the man pulled a black dagger from his robe and plunged it into Kigron's chest. The mighty captain staggered and fell backwards, splashing on the drenched soil. He gasped for breath with the rain falling upon his face. The cloaked man stepped forward and began to remove the hood from his head. His pale hands slowly pulled back the wet, black cloth as lightning flashed to reveal –

"NO!" Thanan screamed, sitting up in his bed, hands trembling, beads of cold sweat on his face. He breathed heavily, shaking his head, trying to wake from the grip of the nightmare. Heavy footsteps grew louder from the hallway. Kigron rushed to the doorway with torch and sword in hand, ready to strike whatever might have dared invade his home.

"Jinian! Are you all right?" Kigron exclaimed, swinging his torch back and forth attempting to see the threat.

"It was nothing, Kigron," Thanan said, still sweating, chest heaving. "I'll be all right. See you in the morning."

Over the next six days, giants from both Hardrock and Whitehall poured into the high-arching cavern of Krokil Zil. It was a three-day trek to the famous cavern. Families and loved ones carried poles with tattered fabric dyed the colors of their clan. Many chanted songs of bravery and might softly and slowly as they made their way through the dark caverns and twisting tunnels.

Krokil Zil was a hallowed place, filled with the tales of past Guardians' journeys into the deep. Many had taken the dark path toward their destiny, but not all reached the end. Krokil Zil was so named for its once-large deposits of zil ore, which had filled the treasuries of the kings of old. Past clans warred against each other over the precious ore, but those days had long since passed. All that remained was the cavernous opening whose walls revealed the treacherous stories of glory and death painted on her cold arching canvas. Large murals of ravenous beasts with Goriath giants hanging from their jaws loomed overhead. Other images depicted mighty candidates with red sashes standing above the slain beasts of the cave.

One image was especially prominent. At the center of Krokil Zil, at the highest point of the hall, was the grand mural of Master Kizaga himself, holding aloft the head of a rare flame wrock. It had been captured and brought to the cavern from the Fire Canyon within the Great Northern Forest region.

The vast cavern turned deathly silent as the soldiers filed in to witness the momentous occasion. The silence was broken from time to time by a fierce howl or the sounds of sharpened claws trying to make their way through the rusted bars that held them captive.

The painted cavern funneled its way down to a small cave opening, no more than six feet high. A massive round stone, roughly cut, leaned at the cave's entrance, covering it. Etched on its face was the mark of the Guardian Order, which centuries before had been painted crimson but had since faded.

Three large cages stood at the left of the cave opening, the thick and pitted bars scarred by the beasts they held. These terrifying creatures were brought to Krokil Zil for one reason: to kill and devour anything in their path. Their hunger was enhanced by their meager diet of small cave-dwelling rodents, and they were ever so eager to curb that hunger with a meal of Goriath flesh. From a distance, however, Thanan observed one beast that was secured in a curious fashion. Its tail was chained to the thick metal bars and an armored helmet, which muzzled the creature, covered its head and snout.

The cavern floor continued to fill when word came that the three remaining candidates had entered Krokil Zil. A wave of whispers filled the cave, which rose to applause as the candidates cut through the multitude.

The crowd parted as General Tygrothian and his entourage made their way to the mouth of the cave. The soldiers in attendance formed single-file rows and stood at attention throughout the cavern. All eyes were on the general as he looked over his audience.

Krokil Zil was now again silent. Only the sharp shrieks of caged beasts broke the stillness, but no heed was paid to their vicious howls. Thanan stood at attention between his towering candidate brothers, looking over the ocean of giants with awe, his heart pounding.

Kigrorian stepped forward at the behest of Tygrothian. The master's stride was silent and his movement still effortless, even at his advanced age. He had served as the Nikiru High Master for so long, it was hard to imagine anyone else ever filling his graceful shoes. Most supposed that he would suddenly drop dead of old age in the middle of the Nikiru circle, amidst a long, glorious explanation of how to plunge a blade into an enemy but not mortally wound them; or maybe it would happen during a discourse on how one's movements should float gracefully like the sweet jornin tree pollen swept by the warm Loriam wind.

Kigrorian turned to the general and stretched forth his hands. Draped over them were the three candidates' red sashes. "My task is complete. I can do no more. I find these three worthy," Kigrorian said, gesturing to the candidates. "General, receive these sashes." Tygrothian gently took the sashes as he had done so many times before. His eyes lingered a few moments on them. Those who were closest to him noticed his expression was different this time. Having a Jinian as a candidate no doubt was the reason for his hesitation, but in reality it was much deeper. It was fulfilling a promise he had made long ago that was pressing his mind. And now the final stage of his promise was to send his oldest friend's son to an almost certain death in the darkness.

"Great clans of Hardrock and Whitehall! My friends! My family!" the general exclaimed, turning to the multitude. "The time has come so swiftly. Bow your heads before these candidates. Give them your prayers; give them a portion of your will, your strength, and your soul."

Agrinoth stood still, breathing in the moment. He looked up at the great paintings that adorned Krokil Zil. He knew his image was destined to spend eternity on those hallowed walls. Many artists would cast their lot for the honor to paint the great Agrinoth slaying a giant fangrix with his Zythera blade. Agrinoth's gaze fell over the crowd and met his great-great-grandfather's intense eye. An immense sense of honor swelled within Purgon, but only those who knew him well could see the pride in his eye. Thanan perceived the brief moment shared by the grandfather and his mighty grandson. No words were exchanged, but a tender moment was shared by two of the most hardened Goriaths that had ever dwelt in the crystal caverns. Thanan realized he had spent the better part of eight years in the tutelage of Purgon. The old giant was like a father to him. He knew skills he learned, the strength he built within the blacksmith shop would serve him his entire life, and he was grateful that Purgon was part of his incredible journey.

There was very little ceremony for such an important occasion. The true celebration was reserved for the momentous occasion that would take place six months from now, when the candidates would emerge triumphant from the darkness and take their rightful place amongst the great Guardians of old and accept their seat at the council.

The general held up the silken sashes. All knew that the sashes represented the candidates themselves, and they would be displayed proudly outside the general's quarters during the months in the darkness.

The crowd began to chant and clap together in rhythm. The claps echoed throughout the cavern and carried far down the reaching halls. The sound drove the caged beasts to near insanity. They tested the bars once again as they wailed for blood. One chanting soldier from Whitehall felt a creature's fury as its outstretched claws sunk deep into his shoulder, pulling the flesh cleanly from the bone. The fact that the beast had not eaten in many days saved the soldier, as the beast retreated to consume the pale blue flesh instead of subduing his prey and dispatching him. The chanting continued as Tygrothian went before each candidate.

"Agrinoth Jil," the general said, placing his hand on the candidate's shoulder, his back to the onlookers. "May the spirit of Master Kizaga go with you."

"Yes, sir, and you also," he replied in his typical emotionless way. Tygrothian smiled slightly and stepped before Torik.

Torik Jil was quite young, a prodigy in his own right. His mastery of Nikiru came as easily as falling asleep to the sound of the waves that crash on the Nasean coast. His ability to disarm his opponents was unparalleled. It was a rare thing to see Torik draw his sword in the Zythera Circle. To draw a weapon against him was the first step to one's undoing. In fact, more candidates who challenged him ended up being stabbed by their own swords rather than by Torik's blade.

The general spoke briefly to Torik, then moved to Thanan. The multitude's chanting began to soften as their attention turned to the Jinian's and general's interaction. Even though Thanan was generally accepted among the Goriaths at Hardrock, there were many from Whitehall who still viewed Thanan as more of an oddity, a kind of festival freak, rather than as one of them. Tygrothian faced Thanan and placed his ancient hand on the Jinian's shoulder.

"If your father could see you at this moment," he said quietly.

"He probably would not recognize his son," the Jinian replied solemnly.

"Even as the swiftwing is transformed from its lowly existence in the muck in the depths of the sea to its majestic life riding the wind – and is recognized and welcomed by his family as he enters the clouds – so it will be with you, Thanan. It is true, you are but a glimpse of the Jinian you were, but the parts that remain are the best of you. You have passed through the refiner's fire and like the glowing blade is plunged into the black oil and quenched and strengthened, so you too, must plunge into the darkness, only to emerge changed in unimaginable ways." The general raised his hand from Thanan's shoulder then brought it down again abruptly. "So don't get yourself killed in there."

His expression lightened as he turned to face the crowd of onlookers. Thanan realized that maybe that had been the last moment of levity he would experience for a long time, and he considered it a gift, even as fleeting as it was.

The great hall of Krokil Zil turned silent once again. The moment had arrived. It was the moment that everyone didn't want to happen, yet still wished it so. Three soldiers stepped to the massive stone that covered the cave entrance. The grinding echoed overhead as the soldiers slowly heaved the stone away from the cave, the mark of the Guardian glowing as it moved past the torches.

Like a long drawn breath from the deep, the cave opened with a low thundering sound. A chilling breeze rushed over the candidates, causing the hairs on the Jinian's arms to stand on end. No more words were spoken. As the candidates walked into the tunnel, the mad howl of the fangrix was a sobering reminder of the dangers that awaited them in the darkness. In seventy-five days the cave would again be opened. With a single blast of the zortusk horn, the three deranged predators would be released into the cave with no other thought than to hunt and devour anything in their way.

Thanan was the last to enter. With gratitude, he looked back for a moment to gaze upon all those who had played a vital role in his amazing quest. With renewed energy, he turned to the mouth of the cave, took the fiery torch from the wall, and vanished into the darkness. The low mutterings of the multitude faded as the huge stone door slowly sealed them in.

CHAPTER THIRTEEN

FALSE ALARM

Inside the damp cave the three candidates began their journey into the darkness walking single file with Agrinoth leading the way. He was the strongest of the three so he naturally assumed the role as leader, and Thanan and Torik were happy to concede it to him. Walking single file lessened the chances of injury, especially from falling into crevices.

As they walked in the darkness, Thanan remembered Master Kigrorian speaking about how the caverns had an almost sentient way of expressing their treacherous machinations. He would say, "Simply falling into a bottomless pit is almost too easy. There are countless ways the caverns can kill, and they are all concealed by the darkness."

The air was moist, stale and unmoving. Thanan found himself breathing through his mouth to avoid the stagnant odor that prevailed in the cave. It wasn't long before the candidates were mesmerized by the blue torchlight dancing across the pitted walls. Water dripped from the cave ceiling in wildly intricate rhythms, whose symphony soothed their souls and took their minds off their bleak surroundings.

Each of them set out on their journey clothed only with the necessities of survival. They wore leather armor encrusted with tightly fitted Zythera scales on the shoulders and breastplate. Dark cloaks helped conceal the sheen of the scales. Each had a small bedroll, water flask and rations neatly tied together and slung over his back. They would have to hunt to survive.

All candidates received a Zythera blade from Master Kigrorian during their training, but they had to be returned when the training ended. They were allowed to take any weapon of their choosing into the darkness.

Torik carried two daggers and a short Zythera blade, whose edge had not yet tasted blood.

Sheathed on Agrinoth's waist hung a sword worthy of Kizaga himself. It had been mined from an ancient vein of the purest ore centuries before and forged by the scarred hands of his great-great grandfather. It was from a mighty time in Goriath history and bore the scars of many wars.

Thanan carried two unique blades designed and forged by his own hands. Under the tutelage of Purgon, he crafted two swords that resembled the legendary Zythixia. The design had come to the apprentice in a dream, and to the astonishment of Purgon, he had forged the weapons with exactness. Thanan once heard Purgon refer to them as "twin stones". They were perfect in every way except one: The rare green Zythera ore that was used to create Zythixia had long since been mined to extinction. Purgon was one of only two Goriaths still alive who had seen the fabled swords, and he helped Thanan smelt a suitable substitute. The twin swords were smaller than traditional Goriath weapons and fit the Jinian's stature perfectly. They were without flaw or blemish because they had never been drawn in battle.

And so the three candidates walked by torchlight for many days, stopping only to sleep and eat the meager rations they carried on their backs. Every so often they were lucky enough to find a patch of sweet lichen creeping over the cave wall. It thrived where water slowly dripped down the walls. The lichen added some variety to their diet and tasted like it had been dipped in honey.

At the end of a particularly grueling day of marching through the darkness, the three candidates sat around a small campfire, silent except for the occasional grumble.

"I have had enough of these shriveled mushrooms!" Agrinoth growled as he threw his half-eaten mushroom cap into the fire. "I need fresh meat. Even a kopi would do."

Torik smiled at the mighty Agrinoth's whining. "But they're so boney, you wouldn't get three bites." Torik ripped his teeth through a piece of dried fish.

"Well, ten kopi then," Agrinoth gruffly shot back, poking the fire with a femur bone of a lesser fangrix he picked up from the cave floor.

Thanan sat with his back against the damp wall staring at the flickering firelight, mildly amused by their banter. He pulled from his leather satchel his father's compass, the brilliant luster long since dulled. He smiled inside, thinking of his home.

"A juicy slice of fala fruit from the southern slopes of Methina and a cool cup of mineral water from Diloa Springs. That is what I want," Thanan softly interjected.

Torik looked at Agrinoth and smiled, one eyebrow raised. "Forget the kopi; I want what the Jinian is having," he said, laughing at the idea of choosing between two imaginary foods. "And while we are dining in this fine upstanding establishment, can we conclude our meal with a Queensberry pie, topped with rich butter cream and crispy mint leaves? If you want something else, brother, I suggest you get off your giant Goriath backside and catch something."

Thanan chuckled at the sarcasm. Agrinoth showed his appreciation for Torik's mockery by flicking a flaming mushroom from off the tip of his fangrix bone, which landed with a sparking explosion on Torik's lap. Thanan burst into boisterous laughter as the flaming candidate frantically slapped his thighs and lap trying to snuff the flames out. In the midst of the flailing, he kicked the makeshift fire pit, sending the embers rolling in all directions, effectively extinguishing the fire in the many puddles on the cave floor and leaving the three in silent blackness.

"Perfect," Thanan said, breaking the silence. "Now I can't see my pie."

Deep chuckles filled the cave, which quickly swelled into uncontrollable laughter. Thanan located the one smoldering ember left and lit a torch. The blue light illuminated their laughing faces, but Agrinoth's expression turned from joyous to deathly serious.

"What is it? What do you hear?" Thanan asked, quickly drawing one of his blades.

"I do not know yet. If you squealing sows would shut up for a moment and listen." Agrinoth listened intently, pointing his ear down the cave. Torik lit another torch, tipping it into Thanan's flame. They all listened for anything to break the rhythmic sounds of the dripping water. All at once they turned to each other. It was unmistakable.

"Footsteps! Coming this way!" Torik exclaimed in a whisper.

"Strange footsteps. Something is not right. How many days have passed?" Agrinoth whispered, gesturing to Thanan.

"Only forty-one. It's too early. Maybe they made a mistake or the guards were forced to let one in."

"No, this is something else," Agrinoth replied, focusing into the darkness. "I do not recognize this beast, nor do I think it is a Goriath."

The candidates quickly gathered their supplies and began to run. Agrinoth led the way, his huge boots pounding the cave floor. Their splashing feet echoed sharply throughout the caverns. They twisted and turned through the winding tunnels, trying to extend their lead on the mysterious creature that followed them. Each time they came to a fork in the tunnel, they paused to listen for the strange footsteps.

"It's gaining on us!" Torik whispered, breathing heavily.

"What is it?" Thanan anxiously asked.

Usually Goriath candidates were calm and collected in the face of imminent danger, but endless days in dark isolation combined with the anxiety of battling unknown vicious creatures were not the recipe for calmness.

"We were not trained for this," Torik said, peeking around the corner to listen to the now galloping footsteps.

"This is the training, Torik," Agrinoth whispered. "Are you ready?"

Taking his cue from his older brother, he whispered, "I was born for this." He held his torch in front of Thanan's face. "By the way, is there something you could do about your pale skin? You're going to give away our position."

The Jinian smiled.

"Listen!" Agrinoth whispered, whacking Torik on the back with the fangrix bone. "It stopped."

They all went silent. The odd sounding steps were gone. Just the familiar sound of dripping water filled the cave.

"Do you think we lost it?" Torik whispered.

Agrinoth put his ear to the wall. "It is smart, this beast. No, it was almost to us. It still hunts us. I can feel it."

They waited for a few moments, then Thanan lit his torch.

"Let's get moving," Torik said, motioning his head down the cave. "Let's create some distance between this beast an—"

"Be still!" Agrinoth interrupted, holding his hand in the air.

A new sound joined the water droplets. A deep rumbling reverberated off the black rock walls. The echoes faded slowly and started again, but this time the deep resonating sound was much closer. The blue torchlight flickered around the candidates, but only illuminated a small perimeter around them. The creature was careful to stay outside the light so as to not give away its exact position. One more time the vibrations came from the darkness.

Thanan didn't recognize the sound. It reminded him of the purring wildcats that hunted small game in the Jinian hills, but this was much deeper and much more menacing. Thanan noticed Agrinoth and Torik exchange a knowing glance.

"What is it?" Thanan whispered.

Agrinoth slowly drew his blade, its edge glinting in the blue light.

"A Korian fangrix," the warrior seethed, staring into the blackness, realizing that they were in a vulnerable position. "On my word, we run for a more defensible location. One...two..."

At that moment the fangrix let out a howl and leapt into the light, swatting at Agrinoth's sword, knocking it from his hand. With incredible speed, Torik brought a heavy punch down upon the beast's massive head, stunning it just long enough for the three warriors to run.

Their hearts pounded as the fangrix sprinted behind them. The beast screamed as saliva shook from its jowls. The narrow tunnel made an abrupt turn and suddenly widened into a large cavern. The frenzied carnivore, not negotiating the turn, crashed into the wall, letting out a sharp yelp from the pain and continuing its pursuit.

The cavern was covered with towering stalagmites that rose from the floor like a mighty city of stone. The determined candidates poured into the cavern with the fangrix only moments behind.

Agrinoth quickly surveyed his surroundings. "This is where we make our stand!" he commanded.

Thanan and Torik quickly set their torches on the ground to light the entry of the cavern. The candidates hid behind stalagmites, creating a surprise attack for their hunter.

The thundering paws of the fangrix slowed to a walk as it entered the cavern. As its head peeked into the light, Agrinoth discovered why he had not recognized the beast from its footsteps. It had only three legs and was also missing his left ear. The fangrix was sickly, diseased and emitted a low growl from its throat as it limped into the torchlight. It darted its head from side to side as it listened for any hint of the hiding candidates.

Its behavior was very unusual for a fangrix. A Korian fangrix was a true hunter, especially in the darkness. It relied heavily on its keen vision and sensitive hearing, which had evolved after thousands of years hunting in the Crystal Caverns. However, this fangrix, because of its partial deafness, appeared to be disoriented.

As it slowly passed Thanan's stalagmite, it paused and sniffed the air, catching a hint of the Jinian's scent. Thanan held his breath and tried to slow his heart rate. The fangrix's upper lip curled, and the beast suddenly snapped his head to the right and looked directly at Thanan's hiding place as if it actually had seen him through the rock. The beast's coarse mane rose on its neck as it stealthily started to circle the stalagmite.

Thanan's swords were drawn and ready to strike with fury, when from the left side of the torchlight, Torik sprang, swinging his flawless Zythera blade. He yelled as his blade tasted its first flesh, piercing the beast's hindquarters, opening a large gash. The fangrix spun around and roared at Torik, its fangs yellowed and dripping with saliva. It swung its razor-sharp claws at Torik, but the agile Goriath jumped out of the way. It swung again with rapid-fire speed, but Torik evaded each blow.

Just then, Thanan lunged from behind the towering stone. With precision, he opened two more wounds on the animal's emaciated side, breaking its ribs. Spinning on three legs, its head came up to Thanan's chest. The creature wailed wildly, confused and frightened. Its muscles twitched and spasmed violently trying to defend itself.

Now surrounded on two sides, the fangrix seemed so vulnerable. This pitiful beast had wandered the caves for years, burdened with disease, bearing the battle scars of past candidates. It no doubt had taken the lives of many warriors when its strength was great, but now it was just surviving.

In one last exhausting effort, it made a feeble swing at Thanan's throat. Before its claws reached Thanan's jugular, Agrinoth sprang from his hiding place. With one mighty swing, he brought the large leg bone down upon the pitiful creature's head, crushing its skull. The lesser fangrix collapsed to the ground. It moaned and exhaled one last time from its nostrils, sending a small cloud of dust into the air.

The three candidates examined the fangrix's lifeless body. Thanan noticed open sores infesting its wrinkled skin. Its mangy hide was tightly stretched over its skeleton, revealing its ribcage. The right foreleg had been cleanly taken off at the shoulder and had healed nicely, and its eyes were milky white from cataracts.

For a moment Thanan wished he could have fought the beast in its prime, but quickly retracted the thought because this beast most likely would have ripped apart most any candidate who crossed its path.

Torik lit the fire and burned the diseased body in the middle of the cavern. They all watched for a moment to honor the animal that was sacrificed for their training. Agrinoth held up the bone that he had used as a walking stick and that had once belonged to the fierce creature and tossed it in the fire.

Torik quickly reached for the bone to pull it from the flames. "What are you doing, Agrinoth? It's a formidable weapon."

His older brother held his wrist, preventing him from withdrawing the bone from the flames. "The bone is not ours, brother. The creature needs to rest now. It is the right thing to do."

The flames rose high and lit up the darkness. The fire revealed the vastness of the cavern. It was the first time they had seen further than just a few feet. They were fortunate to discover pools of fresh water to quench their thirst and fill their leather flasks. Agrinoth went back for his sword and returned with a satchel full of lichen and cave slugs, a rare delicacy only found in the extreme depths of the caves. They set traps made from twine, catching many kopi.

The warriors dined like kings and recounted their small victory as if they were already Guardians. Torik reenacted the battle swing by swing, his lively shadow dancing on the stalagmite behind him. Thanan enjoyed the spectacle as he slurped down a slug and crunched through a kopi, bone and all. He had become quite accustomed to the Goriath diet. At that moment he truly felt like a Goriath and forgot for a moment his Jinian parentage.

"...And the mighty Agrinoth from Whitehall drew his shining Zythera blade," Torik sang out, mimicking Agrinoth's movement. "The ravaging beast lunged its massive body," Torik's voice pitched up, "...and Agrinoth dropped his blade and screamed like a little girl. Not knowing what to do, he called out for his little brother, The Great Torik, to save the day." Torik drew his blade, raised it majestically in the air, and turned to admire his towering shadow on the wall.

Agrinoth grumbled at Torik's exaggeration but still smirked for a moment. Thanan choked slightly on the slippery slug, trying to conceal his laughter.

Before they drifted to sleep, they all agreed that henceforth the great cavern would be named Krokil Grix, so named for the mighty Korian fangrix that lived and suffered there, and whose blood was spilt on the cavern floor.

CHAPTER FOURTEEN

THE RELEASE

Many uneventful days came and went in the caverns. A numb routine replaced the once alert and tactful regimen the candidates were so careful to implement each day. It was at this time in many candidates' training that they were caught off guard, never knowing which form of death awaited them just around the corner. So monotonous was the trek, that many died from simply not seeing a pit plainly in front of them.

Thanan often drifted back to Jin, being lulled by the blue flickering light, grasping his father's compass. He wondered why the king had given it to him and pondered their last words, before his journey began. He knew he was supposed to be among the

Goriath giants, but he had more questions than answers. He resigned again to put it out of his mind and focus on the task at hand. When this was all over, he would inquire of General Tygrothian. He knew the general had some of the answers.

The Jinian's sight became more acute as each day passed in the blackness. At times he swore, when the torchlight died, he could see the water droplets falling in the distance. He kept his improving sense a secret from Agrinoth and Torik, if for no other reason than to not be the topic of ridicule at day's end. Torik was as adept at the art of Nikiru as he was at the fine art of mockery, so limiting his ammunition was paramount to Thanan.

As the days dragged on, the terrain changed and became more treacherous. Large boulders were scattered along the path as if they had been plucked from the walls and placed in the candidates' way. The Jinian scaled the boulders with ease, bounding over them one by one. He had more energy than his larger counterparts, requiring less sustenance to keep him going.

The last stage of their Guardian training was deprivation: deprivation of food, water, light, and companionship. Even complete isolation would not have prepared them for the horrors of the darkness.

At the top of a particularly large boulder, Thanan slipped down the backside and landed on the stone floor with a loud cracking sound, his torch extinguishing as it hit the floor. The sharp crack caused Torik's face to wince, thinking that Thanan had broken his leg. The two giants scaled the rock quickly and dropped down beside him. They held their torches over the Jinian to discover him lying in a scattered pile of bones.

Thanan, seeing he was facedown in the remains of a fallen candidate, quickly scrambled to his feet and retreated a few steps. He dusted his armor off frantically, slapping his chest and thighs as if he were covered in flame ants. Everyone's hearts were saddened as they took in the horrible scene.

The bones of three Guardian candidates lay strewn on the dry cave floor. One candidate's legs had been crushed under the massive rock that had broken free from the ceiling. Although the crushing rock probably did not kill him, the teeth marks that covered his bones and the bones of the other two giants probably did.

Agrinoth surmised by the distinctive tooth pattern on the bones that a silok was pursuing the three. He walked the gruesome scene, putting the puzzle together. "The ill-timed rock must have broken free, first crushing that candidate and effectively boxing the three of them in."

"They didn't stand a chance," Thanan interjected, imagining the horrible scene.

"In the frenzy of the attack, it did not take long for the silok's venomous teeth to pierce their flesh and paralyze them. They were most likely alive as the beast slowly stripped the flesh from their bones." Agrinoth brought his fisted hand to his chest and bowed his head to honor the fallen candidates.

The bones cried from the dust, and the story they recounted was truly a grim one. Thanan couldn't think of a more horrible way of dying. Still, as they stood there in the tomb of their brothers, they felt pride. For they knew they had died fighting, because not thirty feet away lay the skeleton of their killer. After receiving numerous blows from the swinging blades, the silok finally succumbed to its injuries. The fractured skull and splintered ribs were a fitting end for the beast. The bodies could not be identified, but by the unique design of the Zythera blades, Agrinoth guessed they had been in the caves over two hundred years.

They left the blades as memorials, so that those who followed them would also know what had happened there. The whole scene was a bleak reminder of how many ways one could die in the caves.

Steadily, the winding tunnel sloped downward and the damp floor became dry. The air turned hot, stale, and even more still. Food was scarce, and Agrinoth commanded they begin living on half rations. Twenty-three days passed with the candidates expelling the least amount of energy they could. The strong scent of minerals hung heavily in the air as the candidates made their way through the darkness. The cave walls were covered with dried and brittle fungus, which fell from the wall with the slightest touch. With every step, dust rose from the cave floor.

Thanan grabbed a handful of fungus. "There hasn't been water here for many years." He crushed it and sifted it through his fingers. As he stared at his fingers, the dust cloud drifted to the cave floor. "We should turn back and seek another path. We haven't seen water for ten days."

"We would not survive it. We must press on," Agrinoth answered sternly.

"We should sleep here, conserve our energy, and start again in the morning," Thanan suggested.

"I agree with Thanan. Let's begin again in the morning," Torik said, stopping to prop himself up on the cave wall. He exhaled heavily, stirring up a flurry of dust, which caused him to explode into a fit of coughing. "I've had enough of this tunnel," he choked.

Agrinoth paused for a moment and agreed. "All right, we will rest here and continue first thing tomorrow."

Exhausted, the candidates fell asleep quickly and slept soundly.

"Jinian, wake up!" Torik yelled.

Thanan snapped out of his deep sleep with a sharp pain in his back. He looked up to see Torik's giant foot hovering over his head.

"Thought I was going to have to leave my boot print on your forehead for a moment there."

Agrinoth was sitting on the cave floor, holding his flask, staring pensively at the floor. "My thoughts have been heavy as of late," he said gruffly, swallowing the last of his water. "We have grown weary in body and spirit and thus have become slothful in our duties. We are suffering for our weaknesses. Surely Master Kizaga is looking upon us with sadness."

Torik, appearing very sober, looked up from the hot, dusty floor. Even though he always tried to add levity to the moment, he knew the situation had become dire and respected the group's assumed leader. "What should we do, brother?"

Just then a low thundering sound echoed through the cave. All at once they looked at each other and without words they knew what it was.

"It can't be. Not now," Torik whispered. "We are not ready."

The zortusk horn filled the cavern.

Agrinoth reached down and picked up his satchel. "It seems our decision has been made for us."

At the cave entrance Master Kizaga's image looked down upon the guards in Krokil Zil. They heaved on massive ropes and dragged a cage to the mouth of the cave. The Greater Korian fangrix launched himself at the bars, trying to get at the guards. Its razor claws left shiny scratches in the rusty bars. The beast's shrill screams made the other two creatures uneasy. They tested their cages as well.

"He's real nasty, this one, isn't he?" the guard said, pulling the rope.

"He sure is," another guard replied, thrusting his sword through the bars, poking the beast in the side.

The fangrix batted at the blade furiously, enraged all the more. It hissed, exposing its six-inch fangs. When the cage door was flush with the cave opening, the guards pulled it open and released the wailing creature. For a brief moment, the fangrix looked at the guards in disbelief, creeping toward the opening, and then, like lighting, launched out of the cage into the darkness, its spotted sides and barbed tail streaking as it vanished.

In true Goriath tradition, the guards did not miss this opportunity to make a small wager.

"Ten frags says the Jinian falls to the fangrix, if he's not already dead."

"You're on. I've seen the Jinian fight."

"I want in on that action. Ten says the Jinian falls to that nasty over there," another guard interjected, pointing to the flame wrock in the reinforced wooden cage.

It was a bet that would have to wait six months to settle.

"That's enough!" the head guard barked. "Seal off that cave and get to the next cage."

The guards cautiously pulled the next heavy cage to the door and released a particularly large venomous silok, followed by the rare and most feared of all beasts, the flame wrock; a wingless dragon from the fire canyon.

The candidates quickly gathered their belongings.

"Which way do we go?" Torik asked, rather calmly.

Agrinoth sheathed his blade and replied, "We keep heading down, away from the beasts. We will outrun them. We need to move out now!"

Thanan took two steps, then stopped, looking into the eternal blackness of the tunnel before them. Something didn't feel right. He thought for a moment and remembered something Purgon once told him while they were building Thanan's forge.

"Wait a moment!" he said, grabbing Agrinoth's shoulder.

The giant turned and looked at the Jinian's pale hand on his shoulder. "There is no time for this, Jinian. Our water has run out and now we are being hunted. The only chance we have is to outrun these creatures and get to water. Then we will find a more suitable place to battle."

Thanan nodded in agreement. "What you say, Agrinoth, sounds logical and if we had water I would agree. We do not know what lies ahead, but we do know that there is water behind us. Your grandfather told me a story once. It was a story about when Master Kizaga was in these very caves. When the zortusk horn sounded,

Kizaga's companions' first instinct was to run as well, as do most candidates. They hoped they could outrun the beasts that hunted them and find a more suitable place to stage their attack, but the master convinced them to run toward the oncoming threat."

"You are mad, Jinian!" Agrinoth said dismissively, turning down the tunnel.

"They too thought Kizaga had gone mad, but he believed that if they retreated and tried to outrun the beasts, that they would expend their last breaths in fear, crawling on their bellies like the beasts that hunted them, licking the floor for a taste of water and eating the dust on the cold stones for sustenance that would not come. The master could think of nothing lower."

Agrinoth gritted his teeth with disapproval.

"Make no mistake, brothers," Thanan continued, speaking more like his father than himself. "From the moment we come into this world, we are on a collision course with death. You cannot simply run and hide from it. And at the end of it all, when death finally finds you – whether your tired eyes finally close in the comfort of your own warm bed, your brow caressed by the wrinkled hands of your love, or your eyes behold your enemy as he steals your last breath with your sword still mightily swinging – it is the good that a man does that defines him. The moment you stepped into the darkness, death has hunted you. The fact that these three beasts now hunt us makes little difference. How will you be remembered: dead on your bellies like a dog or dead with your blade in hand? As for me, I choose the latter."

"The Jinian speaks beyond his years, brother. What do you think?" asked Torik.

"I do not believe that we will survive if we go back," Agrinoth replied, gritting his teeth again.

"I understand your hesitation, brother," Thanan continued. "But running away from the enemy is not our way. If anyone has taught me that, you have. There will be three at our heels. There will be no more sleep, only running for our lives. We must seize control of the situation and turn it to our favor. You must trust me, Agrinoth. I'm right about this."

"Master Kizaga was right, Agrinoth," Torik said, trying to convince him. "We need to take these beasts head on with all our fury. Your blade will taste the blood of these creatures! There is glory ahead in the darkness, brother."

Agrinoth groaned under his breath. His mind was waging a war of its own between logic and his underlying jealousy of the Jinian. Although he secretly respected Thanan for his skill and prowess as a warrior, deep within him was welling jealousy. Agrinoth loved his great-great grandfather, but he secretly resented the fact that Purgon loved the Jinian as his own son. And thus the conflict plagued his mind and he hated himself for it. It was beneath a Guardian to feel such a weak emotion as jealousy, for jealousy was akin to hatred; but hearing the Jinian recount a story told to him by his grandfather, especially one that he had not shared with his own grandson, made his blue blood boil.

Although Agrinoth was conflicted, reason always won out in the end. The mighty Agrinoth nodded at Thanan. "All right, Jinian. Lead the way. Keep your pale eyes open for any trace of water."

The winding labyrinths whipped by as they stomped through the darkness. They stopped briefly from time to time, only to catch their breath and listen for any sign of water. For many days they found no water, and the effects were beginning to show, first on Torik. Exhaustion overtook him more easily now and the giant found himself drifting away, only to be brought back as Thanan demanded that he drink a few drops from his flask.

Agrinoth predicted that they could hold on for only five to six more days before their bodies would succumb to dehydration. It occurred to Thanan that he might have to leave his brothers to go in search of water. He proposed his idea, expressing that they would survive longer if they both stayed in their present location, expending less energy, and let him search for water alone.

After a lengthy discussion and much deliberation, the two giants agreed that their best chance of survival was to send the Jinian into the darkness in the small hope that he would bring back lifesaving water.

Thanan emptied all but a few drinks into Torik's flask. He took Agrinoth's flask and slung it over his back. Agrinoth watched as the Jinian disappeared around a dark corner, regretting his own weakness in mind and body.

Thanan paced himself so that he could continue running for long periods of time. The lack of oxygen in his blood and water in his body caused his muscles to cramp often. The sweat on his brow had long since dried, leaving a salty residue on his dusty skin. His lungs burned as he inhaled the hot, dry air. He paused for a moment, moistening his cracked lips with a few drops of warm water from his flask. Water was no longer refreshing. He placed his shaking hand on the cave wall to steady himself as his heart pounded within his chest. Gathering all the strength he had, Thanan continued his quest for water.

Two more days passed with no sleep. Many times the Jinian realized he had been running in some sort of delirium, only to be snapped back to reality, not knowing how long he had been running. He dreamed he saw a great rushing waterfall on the horizon. He ran with haste, but each time he arrived to plunge his hands into the cool water, the waterfall appeared further in the distance. His mind reeled and his spirit fell, as time after time the waterfall fell just out of reach.

His pace now slowed to a staggering walk. He lifted his flask for the last time and four drops of hot water fell on his tongue. He propped himself up on the cave wall with one hand like he had done many times before. Slowly he staggered, dragging his fingers on the tunnel wall. He focused on the uneven texture, how dry and hot it was. He struggled to focus his burning eyes on anything. All he heard were the sounds of his dragging feet and dried fungus dissolving under his hand.

It was in this state of delirium that he realized the cave wall had turned from hot to extremely cold. At first he did not trust his own senses. He pressed his cheek against the cool surface. *What is this?* he thought, tearing off his armor and pressing his chest against the rock. *Can you feel a mirage?* His body temperature slowly decreased, giving his mind some much-needed clarity. He quickly realized that there must be water behind the wall.

Placing his hands on the wall, he walked, trying to identify variations in the rock's surface or some way through. He discovered evidence on the floor, strange scratches as if the rocks had slid over the stone. Upon further inspection, Thanan realized that it was a doorway of some kind that someone had taken great lengths to conceal. The seams between the stones were so tight that no air passed through. He ran his fingers along every seam, but found no weakness or flaw in the construction.

It was obvious to Thanan that whoever had made this wall must have had a long time to do so. The stonework's craftsmanship and precision were impeccable. He determined that there was no way in and resigned to journey on in his search for water.

He knelt down to pick up his sword and armor and discovered that his compass had fallen out onto the cave floor. He picked it up, brushed it off and opened the dull golden lid. He could not believe his eyes. The needle twitched back and forth like it wanted to escape its glassy confinement. It was unmistakable: The compass was pointing at the cold stone door. The Jinian had never seen the compass do anything but point in a southerly direction, which was heading to his home back in Jin.

He placed his father's compass back in his satchel, determined again to find a way through the wall. With sword in hand and a renewed strength, he drove the blade into a seam and chipped the rock. Again he swung his sword into the seam, widening it with every blow. He wailed upon the hard rocks until he had carved out a sizable divot in the wall, but had not yet broken through. He swung until he could swing no more. Dizziness finally overtook Thanan and he fell to the floor unconscious, smashing his cheek on the scattered rubble.

Five days behind Thanan, the mighty Goriath candidates were a pitiful sight. At the verge of death and with not even a single beast slain, Agrinoth and Torik sat in the dark tunnel, completely exhausted and thirsty. They took turns slowly sipping the remaining water, making sure to conserve as much of their strength as possible. They would need to be able to walk when Thanan arrived.

"Do you think the Jinian will find water?" Torik quietly asked, resting his head against the dusty wall.

Agrinoth opened his eyes. "He better, or I'll kill him," he snickered under his breath, delirious from the heat.

"So, it takes a near-death experience for you to say something humorous?"

"Do not tell the Jinian, all right? He will never let me live it down. If anyone can do it, he can. His will to survive is astonishing. That is enough talking, Torik. Save your strength. We need to be alive when he gets here."

"Wait, be quiet for a moment. Do you hear that? Something is coming."

"Yes, I hear it. He made it!"

"No…it's not the Jinian. Not now. Arm yourself, brother! Get to your feet if you can. They are almost here!"

"Swing true and may the spirit of Kizaga be with you."

CHAPTER FIFTEEN

HALLUCINOGENIC HERMIT

Thanan woke in darkness. A dull ache pulsed in his forehead. As he became more aware of his surroundings, he realized there was a cool breeze rushing over his face. He sat up, his nerves on edge. He heard the sound of rushing water echoing off the walls. *This is not the cave I was in before*, he thought, trying to get a grasp on his new situation. He patted the ground around him, trying to locate his swords, but felt nothing but cool, smooth stones. He slowly stood and walked toward the sound. As the cave turned to the right, Thanan's eyes fell upon a scene that even his dreams could not adequately depict.

He stepped to the mouth of the cave to take in the miraculous scene. Off in the distance he saw a large glistening lake with majestic stalagmites breaking its pristine surface. *Another mirage*, he thought. Gigantic stalactites loomed overhead, and in the midst of them hung two glowing Xavantha crystals as if they were ancient gods admiring their creation. They were similar to the Xavantha in Hardrock, but were brighter and the color of wispy white clouds. They cast their light upon the cavern like the evening sun. The air was sweet and heavy. He imagined it might be what the island air was like in Methina. Cool breezes cut through the humid air and rushed up the sloping stone beaches. A great waterfall rained down into the lake, causing a luminescent mist to rise and billow over the surface like a glowing fog that dissipated as it drifted away from the falls.

The cavern was enormous, larger than Hardrock itself. Flowing throughout the cavern walls were large rivers of zil ore and a strange vein of crystals that Thanan thought might be Zythera. He remembered the stories that Purgon had shared with him about the Crystal City, and he imagined that this place might resemble the city when it was young and untouched. As his eyes scanned the shoreline, he was shocked to see plants of all kinds. He had missed them in the grandeur of the entire scene, but all around him bioluminescent plants waved in the breeze. Thanan was dumbfounded and for a moment did not believe his eyes.

"So pale one, you waked up-up?" a deep and strange voice asked from out of view.

Thanan shot around in the direction of the voice, instinctively reaching over his shoulder to draw his blade, but it was not there.

In all the amazement he had failed to notice the flickering fire not more than forty feet away.

"You mights be looking for this-this," the peculiar voice continued.

From over the tall ferns, Thanan's twin swords flew in their sheaths and landed at his feet. He quickly picked up the blades and cautiously walked toward the flickering fire. As he rounded the last luminescent fern, he saw the most curious Goriath giant he had ever laid eyes on. His deeply rutted face lit up behind the firelight, his eyes sparkling with delight at the prospect of some company. He hunched over the fire, stirring a pot of steaming liquid. It smelled delicious to Thanan and made his mouth water.

"Ah, you makes it. Heard you knocking on my backs door so's I came to see who's is coming to dinner."

"Your back door...who are you?" Thanan asked, stepping into the strange giant's camp.

"You's must be hungry-hungry. Sit-sit," he said, stirring the hearty-looking broth in an iron pot. He picked up Thanan's two flasks, now full, and threw them at the Jinian's feet. "You's not like any Goriath I's ever seen-seen," he continued, scratching his long, braided beard. "But you walks like a candidate, and you talks like a candidate...so you musts be a candidate."

"My name is Thanan, son of Corderian, king of Panajin. I am the first of my kind to be honored as a candidate. Again, stranger, I would have you tell me who you are."

The hunched hermit leaned back and bellowed a deep laugh. "Tygrothian musts has lost his minds. I's can see why the generals chose you though-though."

Frustrated by the hermit's evasive answers, Thanan laid down his swords next to his pack and blanket, which had been folded and placed in a neat pile on the ground. He sat down on the largest mushroom he had ever seen. It was comfortable. The velvety cap was plush, like the sofas in Cordero's chamber. It was a welcome comfort that he had not enjoyed for some time.

The odd Goriath and Thanan sat across from each other, sharing a meal. It was the first food that Thanan had eaten in six days. He was weak, but could feel his strength quickly surging back as he ate the flavorful stew full of mushrooms, meat and root vegetables.

Thanan noticed that, off in the distance, the land had been cultivated. He saw many long rows of plants crossing the lush, sloping hills. The vegetation was diverse and prolific. There was also a fenced area, a pen of sorts that held dozens of unusual beasts and ground fowl that Thanan did not recognize.

Observing the peculiar Goriath further, Thanan saw that he was very old and weathered. His clothes had been fashioned from old Goriath armor and animal furs. Corroded armor – alive with small, glowing plants – covered his hunched shoulders. From time to time he would stir the stew, pause for a moment, and then pluck a small mushroom that was growing out of the cracks in his armored shoulder and throw it in the pot. At first Thanan thought it was disgusting that he was eating shoulder mushrooms, but then realized it didn't matter if mushrooms came from the ground or the shoulder of a crazy giant. They tasted the same. Maybe even better.

It was the first time Thanan had seen a Goriath with a beard. The giant had roughly braided it, and still it reached well past his waist. He sipped his stew loudly and belched even louder. It was obvious to Thanan that he had not had the pleasure of anyone's company in a very long time.

"I have two companions about five days' walk down the tunnel. I need to get back to them with water and supplies. I may be already too late. You have been such a gracious host, but I need to ask one more thing of you: May I partake of your supplies and bring them to my companions? I do not have anything to pay you."

The strange hermit looked at Thanan and then toward the lake with a sly smile. "Ah, there's is something you can do for us-us."

"Us?" Thanan asked, darting his eyes around the campsite. "Who else is with you?" He grabbed the hilt of one sword, ready to draw it.

"Oh, she's is Lik-Lik."

Just then, as if it knew its name, a bulgy-eyed yellow lizard scurried from underneath the giant's breastplate and sat upon his left shoulder, bobbing its head up and down in a strange rhythm. One eye stared at the old Goriath and the other eye was fixed on Thanan. Bioluminescent spots lined her back and her tail was like two glorik whips.

The old hermit looked over at his pet, licked her blue dotted back, then fed her something from a small leather sack he pulled from under his clothes.

"She's is my's beauty-beauty," the Goriath said, scratching the lizard's throat.

Thanan chuckled under his breath. *Well that explains a lot*, he thought.

Years of partaking of the psychoactive excretions from the lizard's skin had caused the Goriath to go mad. He did not seem dangerous, but Thanan knew he had to be cautious.

"Well, Lik-Lik, it is a pleasure to meet you—"

"Lik-Lik. Her name's is Lik-Lik," the hermit interrupted.

"That is what I said, Lik-Lik. It is a pleas—"

"No's! Lik-Lik. Her name's is Lik-Lik."

"Lik-Lik?"

"Lik-Lik!"

Thanan sat there puzzled for a moment, trying to avoid the huge staring eye of the lizard. Realizing he had not considered the hermit's speech pattern, he blurted out, "Oh, Lik. Her name is Lik. It is a pleasure to meet you, Lik," the Jinian said patronizingly. "Well, as I said, I cannot pay you, but you will be saving your brothers' lives."

"Take's all you need, but you must returns to do something's for us-us."

"So we are agreed," Thanan replied, slurping down the last of his third bowl of stew.

Thanan fell asleep next to the warm fire and slept more soundly than he had in many days.

He woke to the sweet smell of frying sowbelly and biscuits. As he opened his eyes, the first thing he saw was Lik, staring at him with huge, blinking eyes. She was standing on his chest, one eye on Thanan and the other following every move of the crazy hermit. He sat up and Lik jumped off, climbing a nearby fern frond.

"Ah, you are awake, Jinian. Hurry and eat. Your friends might be dying."

"You are right." Thanan noticed that the old hermit was much more lucid than the night before.

"We have packed your things, lots of food and water in your satchel. Hurry, hurry, eat something and go."

Thanan quickly swallowed six strips of sowbelly and threw as many biscuits into his satchel as would fit. He put his armor on and threw his swords and flasks over his shoulders.

"Lead the way, old timer," the fully energized Jinian said.

The hermit leapt to his feet and ran into the cave where Thanan had awoken the day before. "Lik, come. Let's show our guest out!"

Lik leapt to the ground and scurried to her master, spiraling up his leg and torso and rested on his shoulder, throat bulging. She reminded Thanan of a lookout perched in a crow's nest ready to warn her master of rocks ahead.

Thanan followed closely behind the giant and his overprotective lizard. They came to the dark stone door where the hermit lit two torches, one on the left and one on the right. Then reaching up, he pulled a large wooden lever; the door sliding open with ease.

Thanan looked at the old hermit strangely. "Who are you?" he asked in amazement.

"Quick, on your way," he replied, ignoring the Jinian's question. "You must save your friends. When you return, just knock."

"Thank you. You have my word. We will return and pay our debt." Thanan slipped into the tunnel and sprinted out of sight. A dull thud rumbled through the tunnel as the massive door slid shut.

Thanan ran with a renewed speed, giving no thought to his own safety but only to getting to his candidate brothers before they succumbed to dehydration – or even worse. He easily scaled the large stones that blocked the tunnels. His speed cut one full day off his return trip.

As he approached the final bend of the tunnel, his nostrils were met with the pungent smell of rotting flesh. He slowed to a stop and exhaled a defeated breath, preparing himself for the worst. *I am too late*, he thought, turning the corner. As he entered into the final corridor, the foulness increased. He took his first step; not wanting to discover what he knew in his heart would be the decaying bodies of his candidate brothers on the cave floor.

His foot came down upon something soft and lifeless. Lowering his torch, he discovered the bloody carcass of a sawtooth wulrik that measured about a Jinian's arm from snout to tail. He slowly made his way down the tunnel, stepping over hundreds of rotting sawtooths. Just a few feet more into the tunnel, he finally made out two lifeless shapes lying sprawled on the floor, swords in hand.

"Agrinoth! Torik!" the Jinian shouted, sprinting to their side.

The motionless giants were completely surrounded by piles of stinking vermin, some still on their legs and torso. The two brothers had their daggers and swords drawn, the blades painted with blackened blood, already dried. Some of the bodies had their legs missing and large bites on their necks, and Agrinoth's mouth was covered in tar-colored blood.

"Please be alive. Please be alive," he frantically whispered, opening his flask and pouring the water over Agrinoth's cracked lips. "Agrinoth! Wake up!" Thanan slapped his face, trying to bring him back. "Agrinoth, wake—"

The giant's eyes shot open, and he gasped for air. Thinking he was still under attack, he thrust his dagger at Thanan's chest, but his fist was caught and disarmed with a quick wristlock.

"It's me, Agrinoth. It's Thanan. I came back. Here, drink this." He handed the giant his flask.

Agrinoth's eyes darted around frantically searching for his brother. "Torik," he muttered in a scratchy tone.

Thanan examined Torik's limp body, feeling for a pulse and listening for signs of breathing. He knew Torik's situation was bleak. He had been bitten many times on the arms and legs, and the bites were already swollen and infected. Thanan splashed water on his face to snap him from his feverish sleep. He was pale and sluggish, but the water temporarily staved off the fever.

Torik sleepily looked up at Thanan and managed to whisper, "You made it. I knew you would make it." Then he fell back to sleep.

The three candidates stayed only as long as they had to before moving away from the carcass-filled tunnel. For two days, as Agrinoth and Torik mended, they feasted on biscuits and crispy sowbelly. Thanan told them of his amazing discovery and of the promise that he made to the crazy old hermit in the glowing cavern. Torik, filled with five biscuits and a pound of fried sowbelly, recounted in his typical exaggerated manner the story of the legendary sawtooth invasion, which according to him would be retold for generations. Although he was again in good spirits, his fever was increasing and the festering bites on his legs were getting worse.

"Here's to Thanan," Torik laughed, raising his flask in the air.

They looked to Agrinoth for approval, but his face was stern. He paused for a moment, raised his flask a few inches, and looked at Thanan.

"To Thanan of Jin," the warrior repeated, nodding to his rescuer. The pale candidate lifted his flask and nodded back.

The scent of rotting sawtooths wafted through the caverns like an invisible beacon of death. The fangrix's acute olfactory sense had picked up the putrid scent a few days earlier and caused the ravenous creature to go into a frenzy.

The beast used his keen senses to find many shortcuts through the winding caves, effectively cutting the distance to his prey by half. A Greater Korian Fangrix was five times faster than the average Goriath, and much faster over long distances than the other two beasts; and this one was driven purely by the instinct to feed.

Torik's condition declined as the three candidates made their way to the old hermit's stone door. He hung his arms around their necks as they held most of his massive weight. They sat him on the floor and gave him a flask. Thanan found the deep groove he had futilely chipped into the stone. "This is the door?" Agrinoth asked in disbelief.

"The back door, to be more precise. I couldn't believe it myself," Thanan replied, drawing his sword.

He raised his blade and just before bringing it down, the stone door began shaking and slid open. Agrinoth shook his head, not believing the good fortune that had befallen the pale candidate.

"Someone must be watching over you, Jinian. You are certain about this hermit?"

"We do not have a choice, now do we? We are men and giants of honor."

The rumbling stone door slid to a stop and from the opening popped a lit torch.

CHAPTER SIXTEEN

BROTHER'S LAMENT

"You's alive. Come in, we's been waiting-waiting," a deep and peculiar voice said, cutting through the grinding sound of the door.

They picked Torik up by the feet and shoulders and carried him through the threshold, down the fern-lined path and set him next to the fire. Again, Thanan knelt beside his sickly brother to diagnose his seeping wounds. He blotted the sweat beading on Torik's pale forehead and noticed that Torik's lips were turning translucent white.

"He looks bad," Thanan observed, tearing off another strip of his cloak, soaking it in water. He wrung it out onto Torik's forehead. "The punctures on his arms and legs are turning black, and his fever is spiking to dangerous levels. His tissue is dying."

The shock of the cold water on Torik's forehead caused his body to jump.

"We need medicine. Do you have anything left in your satchel, Agrinoth?"

"Nothing! We used the last of it two days ago," he growled, methodically taking in his surroundings. He rifled through his pack one last time and threw it to the ground in frustration.

"I think I can make an elixir from the plants here, but it will take some time." Thanan looked at the old hermit. "My friend needs our help. Please, take me to your garden. There might be something there that can save him."

"What's are you's waiting for? Come's with us-us." The hermit stood and began walking, willing to do anything for his guests.

"Agrinoth, keep him drinking. I'll return shortly."

The hermit and Thanan bounded down the trail to the garden. Thanan recognized many derivations of medicinal plants that he was familiar with from his botany lessons with Kilian as a youth. He prayed he remembered the proper combinations and ratios to craft the elixir that would stop Torik's infection and fever.

He carefully harvested the lifesaving plants and began the process of mixing the medicine. He pounded the Thysis root to a fine mash and spooned it into a stone bowl that sat amongst the hot coals in the campfire. It sizzled and steamed as he added water to the mix. He squeezed the milky red liquid from the long supple stems of the Locstem into the bowl. Thanan knew Locstem was used in the Jinian military as a painkiller and a fever reducer in the field when medics were not accessible.

The final ingredient of the elixir came from the tender Wyceroptis leaf, but not the whole leaf, only the fragile liquid from its blue veins. Because of its delicate and potent nature, Wyceroptis could only be consumed uncooked and in the exact dosage.

Thanan removed the thickened red mixture from the bowl to cool. Once it had cooled, he added the third ingredient. As he slowly stirred it in, the elixir changed from red to a deep purple. It was the reaction that he hoped for.

"Are you sure this will cure him?" Agrinoth asked, holding Torik's head up.

The pale alchemist tipped the bowl, and the purple medicine poured down the Goriath's throat. "No, but what other choice do we have? I'm confident it won't kill him, though. All we can do now is wait."

They covered their unconscious brother and sat comfortably on mushroom stools around the fire, sharing a meal of biscuits and boiled vegetables, while Agrinoth attempted to discover the true identity of the strange hermit.

"Thank you, stranger, for your hospitality. How long have you lived in this miraculous place?" Agrinoth asked, looking up at Xavantha in wonderment.

The old hermit turned his head and licked his pet. "Ah, we do not remembers how long we's been here-here."

"You were a Guardian candidate, were you not?"

"It was so's long ago. I was the lasts. I was losts. The beast tooks my hand-hand." He pulled up his ragged sleeve and revealed a horribly scarred stump.

The hermit recounted the harrowing tale in his broken speech. He spoke about how the animal bit through his forearm and cracked the bone through, leaving it lifeless and hanging. In the battle, the creature lunged at the hermit, tackling him to the ground. They wrestled, each trying to gain advantage over the other, but even the one-armed candidate was too much for the predator. He drew his dagger and plunged it into the beast's side over and over. The dying creature slumped over and breathed its last breath.

Bleeding and broken, he limped along the dark tunnel without the aid of torchlight, feeling his way along the cold wall, disoriented from his wounds. Loud drops of blood accompanied his staggering footsteps on the wet floor. In his delirium, he thought had died and was tumbling to the underearth for his failure as a candidate, but in reality he had fallen into a deep shaft that plunged into an underground river.

For many days he fell in and out of consciousness, agonizing over the disgrace and dishonor his family would endure. The meandering current cradled him in her cold embrace before spilling the mighty Goriath into the lake. He awoke on the stone shore delirious and alone. He severed his own forearm and crudely tied the skin with a leather strap.

The first few years he rejected his fate, that he had been sentenced to a life of solitude in the underearth. Tirelessly he searched the cavern for a way out, to no avail. Many more years passed surviving on the primitive fowl, small sow-like creatures and fish from the lake. Then the hermit had an idea. He began to till the land. He dredged the lake bottom for soil and to his surprise; the soil was dark, rich and full of seeds from the mountain range. He built walls and fashioned animal pens with fitted stones and filled the pens with wild animals he fattened. But it was his small stone home that he was most proud of.

He lived quite happily in this peculiar world until one day, while fishing for his breakfast; the gods of the underearth caused the cavern to quake. He heard a deep rumble and saw a cloud of dust explode from a distant cave. He bounded up the slope toward the cave-in. As he entered, he discovered that the back wall of the cave had collapsed. With his freedom staring him in the face, he stepped over the rubble and into the tunnel. As he looked back into the cave, to his amazement, sadness set upon him. Years of solitude had changed him. In his mind, he was no longer a Guardian candidate. He loved his life in the glowing cavern. And so he stepped back into the cave and fashioned a stone door, just in case someone might come knocking for dinner.

Thanan and Agrinoth sat astonished as they listened to the tale. He truly was one of the great Goriath candidates. They mused upon what might have been if he had completed his final trial. What stories would have been passed down through the generations about this Guardian?

"Please, we must know your name," Thanan said, examining a green and yellow bioluminescent caterpillar that had crawled onto his arm.

"Ah, you looks hungry. Eat-eat," the old hermit exclaimed, avoiding the question.

Agrinoth shot Thanan a knowing look. "Do you still have your Zythera blade after all these years?" he casually asked the hermit, tearing off a hunk of roasted meat from the bone.

The hermit pointed through the fire toward the stone wall behind Agrinoth. "Ah, we's fished it from's the lake after many years. Still look goods as new-new. I losts it when I fells into the lake."

Agrinoth stood up and walked to the blade. Thanan noticed Agrinoth's face turn pale as he looked upon the sword. He gently picked it up, as if it were a fragile infant. His giant hand cradled the tip of the blade. Tipping the hilt, he looked at the maker's mark. A slight smile crept over his lips.

"I know this blade," he whispered to himself.

"What is it, Agrinoth?"

"I've seen this blade before," he said, turning to the hermit, "in a book, a book that my grandfather keeps in a locked chest in his bedroom."

The old hermit looked up from his mushroom stool.

Agrinoth squinted his eyes. "Is it really you? How can this be? Are you...Zinaka Jil? Tell me please. Is your brother Purgon Jil?"

The raggedy giant looked troubled, as if he were trying to remember where he had hidden something valuable, but had forgotten where it was. His expression suddenly turned from worry to delight, remembering his misplaced memory.

"We's not thought of Purgon's in, well we's do not remember."

"It is you, my great-uncle Zinaka!" Agrinoth let out a great laugh and grabbed up the old hermit.

His exuberance surprised Thanan. The Jinian laughed along with the two jubilant giants. The only one who seemed not to enjoy the moment was Lik. She scurried from her hiding place in Zinaka's beard, as if to chide uncle and nephew in what was to her an unwelcome disturbance, and jumped into a nearby fern frond.

She kept one eye on the old hermit and the other on any food that might fly by.

"That means you have been here for…over five hundred years. My grandfather told me very little of you, because he would not speak of the sacred dead. He did tell me you were one of the fiercest warriors of your time, and that I was very much like you."

"Does my brother still live?" Zinaka asked, with unexpected clarity.

"He does. General Tygrothian and my grandfather are the only ones still living from the old world. They would be overjoyed to know you are still alive."

Although they had never met before and were separated by over five hundred years, it was as if they had known each other their entire lives. They talked until the fire was nothing but glowing embers, sharing stories from the distant past. Agrinoth was mesmerized by Zinaka's storytelling. He hung on every word as if it were precious crystal frags falling from his lips. Thanan began to see some family resemblance as they laughed and ate like gluttons.

Beside the firepit, Torik worsened. His breaths had grown more shallow and labored. Sweat streamed down his pale forehead. The elixir coursed through his veins, but he was losing the battle.

"You must come with us," Agrinoth insisted.

Thanan looked at Agrinoth, amazed at the offer. He knew that the old hermit would die outside the cavern.

"I cannot go back, Agrinoth. This is my home now. I have forgotten my life before this place. Purgon must continue to think that I am dead. You must not tell anyone I am here. Swear to me," Zinaka demanded, looking Agrinoth in the eyes.

"How can I simply ignore your existence? You must come back with us."

"Agrinoth, think for a moment," Thanan interrupted. "We are in the middle of our final test. Torik might not survive his wounds. We cannot bring him along. He would slow us down and he will surely die."

"The pale one is right, Agrinoth. I am an old giant. Look at me; I am not a candidate anymore. I have only one arm and my armor is broken. The leather from my boots now holds the gate shut. I would get everyone killed." Zinaka held one foot in his hand, illustrating his bare feet. He picked at his big toenail and threw it in the fire. "You need to keep on top of toe fungus in this humid climate."

Thanan looked away to conceal his laughter. Agrinoth drove Zinaka's sword into the soft dirt.

"I have had a belly full," he growled, walking down a path toward the lake.

"Do not worry about him, Zinaka. He always sees reason, eventually. So, about this debt we owe you…what task would you have us do?"

"Get some sleep, pale one. You are going to have quite a ride. We will talk tomorrow."

The hunched old hermit grimaced and passed gas as he stood. He waddled toward his small stone home, scratching his backside.

"I am old, Jinian. Sleep well," he grumbled, walking by Thanan.

Thanan shook his head and smiled. It seemed that fireside etiquette had long since left the crotchety Goriath.

"Sleep well, Zinaka."

The exhausted Jinian stood and stoked the fire to keep Torik warm. He walked to a nearby tree and sat by its braided trunk. He leaned his head against the smooth bark, disturbing the tree. The twisting braches above exploded as thousands of glowing wings fluttered from their perches. The display was breathtaking and the light that shown down was that of the brightest wisteryth moon. At that moment, Thanan understood why Zinaka stayed all those years ago. He drifted off to sleep while looking up at the dimming Xavantha.

"Jinian, wake up."

"What is it, Agrinoth?"

"It is Torik," he whispered. "Something is wrong. Hurry!"

Thanan and Agrinoth ran to their brother's side. The convulsing giant thrashed violently. He kicked over the stone pot that hung over the fire, scattering hot embers over the campsite. Thanan grabbed his brother's trembling hand and placed a cool cloth on his forehead.

"Hold him down," Thanan said calmly.

"He is dying, Jinian!" Agrinoth yelled, restraining Torik's legs. "Is there anything you can do?"

Torik's flesh was cold and lifeless. He stared blankly at the cavern ceiling, struggling to fill his lungs. His grip tensed, almost crushing Thanan's hand. The poison had finally overtaken the warrior. The tissue on his legs had completely turned black and smelled of death. He arched his back awkwardly from the intense pain and clenched his jaw until he had broken teeth. After some time, the seizures subsided, leaving the campsite silent once again.

Agrinoth stood and backed away in disbelief. He watched as his brother's breaths became more deliberate and shallow. The Jinian looked up, as if to ask for some heavenly assistance. He noticed the bioluminescent flowers on the cavern roof emitting a most beautiful pale yellow light.

Looking upon his dying Goriath brother with compassion, he whispered, "We are here, brother. It is all right. You do not have to fight anymore. Do you see the stars? They are the great Guardian masters at last out of the darkness. Do you hear them? Go to them, they call for you."

Torik's lifeless hand fell from Thanan's grip, his body now peaceful and still. The Jinian's elixir had failed. He placed his pale hand on his brother's eyes and closed them gently.

Clenching his jaw, Agrinoth paced back and forth looking for an outlet to unleash his anger and sadness. His mind reeled from the agony of his fallen brother, and he struggled to restrain his betraying thoughts that the pale Jinian was somehow to blame.

He drew his sword wildly and with one heavy swing, sliced through a banjin tree as thick as his thigh. He cried aloud, swinging again and again until he fell to his knees, sobbing uncontrollably. Hanging his head low in reverence, he mumbled a Goriath prayer under his breath. It was a prayer that Thanan had heard many times during his stay among the Goriath giants. Thanan had learned to speak the Goriath language many years before. But at that moment, when Agrinoth uttered his prayer, Thanan truly understood the deeper symbolic nature of their tongue, and their language seemed more beautiful than ever.

The next morning, with Zinaka's permission, they used the stones from one of his walls to bury Torik. They picked a serene spot along the lakeshore just at the tree line overlooking the waterfall. The old hermit began lowly humming a tune. It was a song that Thanan did not recognize, but Agrinoth knew it and joined in with his uncle. Their lamentation resonated through the stone cavern as their deep voices harmonized the ancient song. Out of respect for the sacred dead, the rest of the day was spent in silence.

CHAPTER SEVENTEEN

UNWELCOME GUEST

It was all too easy to lose one's sense of time in the glowing cavern. It was unlike any other place, above or below, that Thanan or Agrinoth had ever seen. The entire northern shore was carpeted with vibrant flowers of red and gold that tracked the sky from east to west as if they were following some unknown celestial light. The great Xavantha crystals shone enough light throughout the day to grow crops of all kinds. Great twisted trunks shot up from the ground, spreading their branches as they hit the cavern ceiling. Spectacular explosions of glowing wings moved through the air like clouds of yellow blossoms swirling in the wind over Loriam.

Thousands of peculiar animals found their homes in the trees and grazed in the flowering fields. Most of them were familiar but varied slightly from the creatures seen wandering the caves at Hardrock and Whitehall. There were some animals, however, that were completely strange to Thanan.

The most glaring difference was the bioluminescent nature of almost everything in the cavern. It was a glimpse of a primal time, which had been skillfully tamed by the hand of a giant. What Zinaka had accomplished was truly miraculous. It starkly contrasted the southern side of the lake, where nature had run amuck, choking itself to almost nonexistence.

The time had come for the warriors to repay their debt to Zinaka. The old giant explained that there was only one threat that existed in the glowing cavern. After years of taming the land and increasing his livestock, the old hermit discovered odd footprints in his fields. He tracked the footprints through the jungle and then to the lakeshore. The footprints ended at the water's edge.

Day after day, he spent hours cleaning up half-eaten root vegetables and mending the stone walls that had been knocked down.

Then one day he had an idea. He carefully devised a trap using a rope and the leverage from a nearby banjin tree. He baited the trap with a pile of fresh vegetables that was meant for his own supper.

The glowing fireplace warmed his tired face as he dozed, waking from time to time whenever he heard a noise. He shot out of his deep sleep when he heard the high-pitched squeals, and then he sprang into action. He ran down the flower-lined path, jumped over the stone wall, and entered his vegetable garden. What he saw made him skid to a stop.

There it was, the bane of his existence, swinging high in the twisting banjin tree, a living and breathing version of something he had only seen fossilized at the bottom of the ancient Pools of Tyrixis.

No Goriath had ever seen the legendary beast, but the rocks cried out from the past. Goriath Gil and his followers found evidence of an ancient people, long extinct, who occupied the caverns when they arrived. Ancient writings were scrolled on the cave walls, depicting the creatures emerging from the pools, eyes full of blood lust. Entire villages and clans were lost in a single day. The old ones, in a last attempt to save their people, hunted the creatures to extinction, or so they thought.

The trapped creature was much smaller than Zinaka recalled from the petrified bones, and its speckled scales reminded him of the tasty flinix gill that cruised the brooks and waterways of Hardrock. *No doubt, a distant relative*, he thought, examining the sharpness of his blade.

Immediately his mind went to the dozens of delicious ways he could prepare his surprise catch. Perhaps raw, thinly sliced, garnished with bitter radish and onion. Or maybe roasted, served on a bed of boiled lisxis blooms. He salivated at the culinary possibilities. He raised his blade in the air with the intent of ending the beast.

The ancient creature began wailing and thrashing about, trying to free itself. Terror filled the giant when in the distance, he heard something break the water's surface. Fearing it was the infant creature's mother coming to rescue her young one, he dispatched the beast before it could make another sound. He ran and doused the campfire and extinguished the torches that lined the walkway to his door.

Listening in the darkness, with Zythera blade in hand, he waited behind his stone door, peeking through a small crack at the doorjamb. The ground trembled, but he saw nothing except clouds of scattering bugs and winged things bursting from their homes with every step. In the distance he heard his newly repaired wall tumble to the ground again.

Creeping from his dark doorway, Zinaka walked slowly, concealing himself behind tree and bush in order to catch a glimpse of the living fossil. From the canopy she descended, her long, scaled neck dripping a thick green mixture of water and slime. She sniffed the turned-up soil and half-eaten vegetables, crushing the garden with her clawed feet.

Discovering the severed head of her offspring, she let out a piercing cry. The webbed spines on her back and neck stood erect and glowed red. The slain baby's blood dripped down upon its mother's head. She raised her snout, sniffing the air. The confused mother nuzzled her swinging child, trying to rouse it. A vibrating growl from deep within her throat rose to a full fit of rage.

The mad beast raised her forelegs high in the air and crashed them down upon the tree that held her dangling child. The trunk splintered with a sharp crack and sent branches flying in Zinaka's direction, forcing him to reveal his hiding place.

They both froze, staring at each other for a few seconds. Zinaka slowly tried to conceal his blade behind his back, but a sliver of glinting light caught her eye. The spines on her neck and back glowed red once again. The enraged mother lowered her head and bolted after the fleeing giant, crashing through anything that stood in her way. Zinaka hurdled hedges and bounded over the rock walls surrounding his little home.

Running up the path to his door, he felt the warm breath of the beast on his back. He threw open the door and dove in head first, the beast's teeth just missing his legs. He hid under a heavy table with his sword in his hand. The curious creature peered through the window and sniffed the air. Poking her snout into the doorway, she inhaled a snoutful of floor dust and suddenly sneezed, covering Zinaka and everything in his home with a slimy coat of mucus. She lifted her head, knocking down half of his home effortlessly. The one-armed giant bolted from his hiding place and shot out the back door. Spying him running away, the crazed mother jumped over Zinaka's home, toppling the rest of it to the ground. The earth vibrated under Zinaka's boots with each thunderous step the creature took.

Zinaka made his way to the cave and there he stayed for twenty days until the beast returned to the lake and traveled through the underground spring that led to the open sea. The exhausted hermit walked through his devastated cavern, surveying his scattered livestock. His beautiful garden had been turned into a stone-strewn mud pit and most of the vegetables were inedible. He discovered many fattened sows bitten in half, their carcasses hanging from vines, unsalvageable.

It was every hundred years she returned to her spawning grounds to give birth to a new calf. Fearing that the ancient creature would again start hunting in the caves, Zinaka killed her young every year to prevent the potential threat to his people.

"She will be heres soon, any time now-now," Zinaka said, pointing to the lake. "You's ask us how you cans repay your debt to me? Kills the ancient creature."

Agrinoth scoffed at the idea. "We do not have time for this, Jinian. We must continue our journey through the deep."

"I gave him our word, and I will not break it. You owe your life to your uncle. If he had not rescued me from certain death in the tunnel, your fate would have been as Torik's. You would not have survived another wave of sawtooths. Besides, this is much more than repaying a debt now; it is for all Goriaths. I'm sure that the lake is somehow connected to the waterways in Hardrock. We cannot let this creature discover that."

The Jinian glanced at the cavern ceiling. "And I have a plan that just might work; but first, we are going to need to take this." Thanan quickly grabbed Lik and tossed her into a wooden bucket. She squealed as Thanan covered it with a flat stone, preventing her escape. "We need you sober if this is going to work."

Sheepishly, the old hermit nodded in agreement.

"What is the plan, Jinian?" Agrinoth asked.

"When was the last time you climbed a tree, brother?" Thanan replied, smirking.

"I have lived in a cave my whole life."

"Well, you have missed out."

"What's can I's do?" Zinaka asked.

"How much of that zil have you mined?" Thanan replied, pointing to the large vein of rusty-colored ore behind the hermit's stone home.

"A couple of carts full behinds the house."

"Good, that will do for now. You just keep an eye out for any sign of the ancient beast and make lots of rope. Agrinoth, you're with me."

CHAPTER EIGHTEEN

EXTERMINATION

And so they went to work, plotting the demise of the ancient menace. Zinaka worked tirelessly, soaking shuni vines in the lake and then twisting them together tightly to create rope. It was a method that he had invented in the glowing cavern, and the rope he made was strong and supple. He had not made rope in a long time, so twisting the vines caused the calluses on his old hand to bleed, but the pain didn't detour him from his task. Every once in a while at the end of the day, when they gathered together for a well-earned meal of stew and biscuits, Zinaka longed for a fix. But he never would go back on his word, for he was a Goriath of honor.

At first, when Agrinoth heard Thanan's plan, he thought the Jinian had gone mad, but after witnessing his skill with fire and hammer, he quickly changed his mind.

Thanan dredged the lakebed and brought forth many buckets full of dark soil and clay, which he dumped behind Zinaka's tiny home, forming a mound about ten feet in length, three feet in width, and two feet high. He dug a trench running down the middle of the mound, creating a valley that he would later fill with fuel. After knocking down the south wall of Zinaka's pen, he carefully repurposed the stones by stacking them on the outer edge of the valley, creating a dome over the trench.

Thanan then hammered two tree limbs through the base of the clay and left them in place while the clay and soil hardened. He stacked the final few stones and sealed the backside of the forge. The Jinian had taken Zinaka's small, makeshift forge and quadrupled its size and power.

He then fashioned two billows from thick animal hide and stitched the leather to two large planks of banjin wood. It was quite ingenious, and Agrinoth marveled at the invention. Thanan removed the tree limbs and replaced them with billows. He admired his creation for just a moment and then went back to work.

The first tools that Thanan forged were a heavy hammer and a few hardened chisels, fit for the mightiest of Goriath giants. The implements were crude and heavy, but time was of the essence. His next creation, however, would need all the skill and precision that Purgon had passed to him.

High in the flowering banjin trees, at the roof of the cavern, Agrinoth chipped away at a massive stalactite that loomed over the jungle floor. The sweltering temperature at the cavern ceiling was much hotter than Agrinoth had ever experienced before at the Whitehall garrison, and the humidity made it even worse. He wiped a steady stream of sweat from his brow as he took great care to not cut any of the tightly woven vines that covered the hard stone surface.

The agile giant did well climbing his first tree and after some time, had become quite comfortable in the twisted vines. He made his way around the great stalactite, chiseling, his muscles burning with every swing.

The ringing of the hammer and chisel disturbed the serene atmosphere of the cavern, which seemed to especially drive the tree-dwelling creatures to odd acts of aggression. Every so often, Thanan's ears perked up when he heard a few choice Goriath words echo through the cavern. He would break from his work at the forge to find Agrinoth swinging wildly at a gang of ring-tailed gilix that had stolen his flask. They screamed at the invader as they swung from their long tails just out of reach of the cursing giant. They tossed the flask back and forth, like bullies playing keep-away from a weaker and slower child on the field. But in this case, the weak child was a Goriath giant of unparalleled skill, which made the scene all the funnier. Thanan welcomed the break from the intense heat of the forge.

"Go on, get out of here, before I make a striped belt out of you!" Agrinoth yelled, swinging his hammer and losing his balance. "I have had enough of these vine swingers, Jinian! I would like to see them try this when I am on the ground! I know what I would be having for supper!"

"I think you missed a spot!" Thanan said, pointing to the stalactite.

Agrinoth growled under his breath and went back to chiseling.

Beside Torik's grave, Zinaka sat on a large mushroom amidst the shuni grove, continuing braiding the supple vines into long lengths of rope. The old giant pulled down hundreds of green shuni vines and dragged them to the lakeshore. He threw them in a bog he had dammed from the main body of the lake. Soaking them for a day made them supple and much easier to weave into rope. Tying three vines to a banjin trunk, he began the long process of braiding them into long lengths of rope. It was quite a thing to behold, the old Goriath giant using his teeth and one hand to craft some of the finest rope in all the caves.

Black smoke rose from the far northern corner of the glowing cavern. Thanan recalled all that he had learned from his mentor and friend, Purgon. The intense light from the inferno glowed in Thanan's eyes as he removed the stone crucible from the flames. The boiling ore sizzled as he poured the molten metal into a long cast he had chiseled out of stone. Agrinoth watched the Jinian with awe. It was as if his grandfather were there, creating incredible things from raw elements hewn from rock and refined by fire. The great warrior's path was always clear to him from his earliest memory, and his eyes were fixed on that one single goal, to become a Guardian. So many times he refused his grandfather's tutelage. And watching the Jinian, his warrior heart was softened. He was grateful to know that his grandfather's skill would carry on, even if it were through Jinian blood.

Thanan broke open the cast and out fell a single rod of zil. Its blue sheen was beautiful to him. He ran his thumb over the smooth surface, admiring his creation. Working the billows, he brought the forge back up to the desired temperature. He placed the end of the rod deep in the coals until it glowed red. Sparking slag rained down on the stone floor as he hammered the malleable metal into a spearhead. The forge roared as the billows intensified the heat. The fierce heat singed the blacksmith's cheeks. Over and over he brought the glowing spearhead to the anvil, shaping it so that it would surely penetrate the beast's thick leathern armor.

Many days passed with no sign of the creature. Agrinoth was clearly worried, for he knew that outside this cavern there were three ravenous beasts closing in on their location and thirsting for Goriath blood.

Zinaka always ended each day with a well-prepared meal and good conversation. Aside from Tygrothian and Purgon, he was the only one living who had witnessed the wars early in Goriath history. He often shared stories of war and battle as he stirred the boiling stew, and he relished the particular story of when he met Master Kizaga as a little boy, just before Kizaga died.

"Tomorrow I will finish the net and bury it under the garden," the hermit said, carving a slice of meat from the rack of ribs that he spun slowly over the fire. Greasy drips of fat fell into the flames and hissed as they burned on the embers below. He looked to Agrinoth and continued, raising his chin to the cavern ceiling. "That rock about ready to fall yet?"

Agrinoth wiped his mouth after chugging a mouthful of strong tea that the hermit had brewed in the fireplace of his home. "You sure those vines will hold once I break it free?"

"Do not worry, warrior," Zinaka replied, gnawing on a rib bone. "Banjin vines are tenacious and almost impossible to remove from stone once they set their hooks into their host. The trees are voracious. They have a thirst for stone. I've never seen any other plant like them. They thrive in the caverns by absorbing minerals from the roots as well as the tips of the vines that penetrate the rock. The only things in the glowing cavern that the vines cannot penetrate are Zythera and Xavantha crystals.

"After the gods shook the underearth, I traveled to the southern end of the cavern to assess the damage and found that many of the stalactites had fractured and fallen. The massive rocks swayed silently back and forth, suspended by the banjin vines. I was amazed at the strength of those tiny green fingers. The only way to get those vines to let go is to cut them, and your blades better be sharp, Jinian."

Thanan looked up from the fire, his cheeks singed red from the intense heat of the forge. "Oh, they are," he said confidently, enjoying his last bite of tender meat.

"What about my spear, Jinian? Are you almost done hammering away?" Agrinoth asked.

The soot-covered blacksmith stood and walked over to a nearby banjin tree. From behind the braided trunk, he brought forth a shining spear that only Purgon could truly appreciate and only the mighty Agrinoth could throw.

"I finished it just before supper," he said, hefting the heavy spear into the camp.

Agrinoth's eyes looked with wonder at the metal spear. He shot to his feet, met Thanan halfway, and took the cold shaft in his hands. The giant ran his thumb along the serrated spearhead, cutting his thumb at the slightest touch. He didn't flinch. He only smiled. The bluish tint of his Goriath blood matched the metallic blue surface of the spear.

"Careful, it's sharp. I fashioned the edge after the razor-sharp teeth of the deep-water spironopthys back home in Jin. It takes a lot of skill to bring those nasties in."

"Oh, Jinian," Agrinoth half chuckled under his breath. "It is a work of art. I have never seen a finer spear." He spun the shaft in his hands and thrust it forward into an imaginary foe. "Perfectly balanced too."

"Just make sure you do not miss. You are the only one who can throw this thing and penetrate the beast's armor."

"Do not worry about me, Jinian. The creature will fall and then we can continue on our journey. You just make sure that the rock falls. This beast will kill us all if it breaks free from the net."

"You truly are a peculiar candidate, Jinian," remarked Zinaka as he yawned and walked to his door. "Sleep well, candidates."

Morning came abruptly for Agrinoth and Zinaka. They woke to the clanking sound of Thanan's hammer echoing off the cavern walls. He was busy forging the heavy metal rings that would fasten the rope to the cavern ceiling and stalactite.

The old giant walked to his garden to begin the painstaking process of burying the monstrous net. As he opened the gate, he froze, seeing the familiar signs of the infant creature. Its footprints covered the entire garden, and half-eaten root vegetables were scattered all over. Even though it only happened once every hundred years, it frustrated Zinaka to no end. Stringy green mucus dripped onto the turned-up soil as he picked up a broken vegetable. He threw it to the ground and it landed in a puddle of saliva. His eyes followed the trail of evidence to the lake. Just as before, the footprints led out of the garden and ended at the water's edge.

"It has been here!" Zinaka yelled to Agrinoth.

The sleepy giant stretched one last time, ran to his tools, nimbly climbed the banjin tree, and began chiseling the massive rock once again. For hours he hammered, his muscles aching and his eyes burning from sweat.

Thanan pulled the last ring from the forge and brought his heavy hammer down upon it. As he struck the ring, a mighty crack reverberated throughout the cave. Thanan threw the ring to the ground and ran toward the jungle, where the banjin trees grew tall. Zinaka, who also heard the thunderous crack, ran from his garden, meeting Thanan in the jungle.

"He did it. It broke free," the hermit said excitedly, pointing to the stalactite.

The fractured rock rested neatly, cradled in the vines above Thanan's head, swaying ever so slightly.

"You all right, Agrinoth?" Thanan called out, looking up at the sweaty candidate.

"Zinaka was right!" he shouted down. "The rock broke free, and the vines held the weight!"

Thanan shared in the excitement for just a moment and turned to Zinaka, looking quite serious. "You know what to do, Zinaka. Bait the trap."

They spent the rest of the day making their final preparations. At supper they ate very little, and the typical storytelling and lighthearted conversation were replaced by intense planning. Thanan led the conversation, and both Agrinoth and Zinaka listened and understood the importance of the timing if the plan was to work. They went over every small detail again and again.

"Zinaka, is your net ready? Will the ropes hold?"

"There is no finer rope, Jinian. The net will hold."

"Your job is simple, Agrinoth. Hit it in the heart and be done with it."

"I think we have talked enough, do you not, Jinian?"

"No, you are right. We are ready, brother. May the spirit of Kizaga be with both of you."

They bid each other good luck and walked alone toward their hiding places.

Thanan began the long climb up the twisting trunk of the banjin. He reached the top where the vines branched wildly, and with very little effort, found a comfortable cluster of tightly woven vines and laid down his head. Strangely, he felt like a bird nesting down for the night. He chuckled to himself at the thought. A red-tailed spinik, with its glowing spots, scurried along the vines overhead. It stopped and looked down upon the Jinian invader, sniffing the air with its horned snout and stomping its front foot on the vine as if to chastise him for his intrusion.

"Take it easy," Thanan said, shaking the vine. "I will be gone soon enough."

Beside Thanan lay his twin blades, the hilts pointed toward him, ready for action. He adjusted the blades one more time, then rested his eyes, concentrating on the sounds of the lake in the distance. The rushing waterfall hummed, and everywhere insects of all kinds sang their night songs. It was a beautiful orchestra that accompanied Thanan's dreams each night in the glowing cavern.

Thanan had quite a gift for seeing the beauty in all things, great and small.

Off in the distance, Zinaka walked the perimeter of his turned-up garden. He carefully inspected each rope as he passed, making sure the knots would hold up against the beast. He poured one last bucket of vegetables on the calf's trap and glanced toward the lake.

"Come and get it," he muttered to himself, snapping the tip of a crisp carrot off with his teeth.

He made his way out of the garden, leaned against the garden wall and slipped to his backside, his sword lying in his lap. The giant was weary from his work and drank deeply from his water flask. He groaned from his aching bones as he settled in for the long wait.

On the northern edge of the garden, behind the stone wall, Agrinoth knelt motionless on the cavern floor, his breaths deep and his thoughts clear. His mission was simple: Kill the beast. But as simple as it sounded, it was no easy thing to kill a raging beast intent on biting you in half or crushing you until you are nothing more than a stain on a rock, let alone piercing a moving target in the heart with a fifty-pound spear. He clutched the cold metal shaft in his scarred hands and imagined over and over, his spear flying straight and true, striking his prey, and piercing its heart. It was a skill that Master Kigrorian taught all his candidates, but it was a skill at which Agrinoth truly excelled.

"Visualize it one thousand and one times and then do it again," the master would say, pacing back and forth across the Nikiru field.

For some time, the cavern continued to play its lulling melody as clouds of glowing wings fluttered in and out of the trees.

Suddenly, out of the symphony, a shriek of horror broke its rhythm. A shower of leaves floated and twisted down over the garden as the outstretched branches violently shook. Zinaka peered over the garden wall and saw what he had seen many times before.

The old hermit's trap worked perfectly. Struggling in the ropes, the young beast hung upside down, vegetable greens limply clinging to its sharp teeth. Its shrill screams echoed through the cavern, setting every creature's nerves on edge. Soon the glowing cavern was filled with loud squawks, flapping wings and howling.

Thanan woke from his light slumber and shot from his vine nest, rustling the leaves around him. An explosion of yellow wings burst from the vines, illuminating the area for a brief moment. Quickly, he grabbed his blades and got into position. He clutched the largest vine that held the stalactite and brought his blade to it, ready to cut when Zinaka lit the signal.

Behind the north wall, Agrinoth's eyes remained shut, blocking out the hysterical jungle around him. His body was still and calm even though the wailing babe was in the trap. He even ignored the dozen fluttering thoranipix that had landed on the shaft of his spear, having been attracted by the blue metallic surface.

Off in the distance, the lake's surface stirred with life. Luminescent bugs skipped and danced across the water in turbulent clouds, leaving a glowing ripple behind them. The waterfall's mist hung low on the water as glowing schools of orange-gilled lupik caused the oxygen-rich water to boil under the cascading falls.

At the shore's edge, a giant fish spinner grabbed an unsuspecting fish that Thanan would have envied. The green lighting bolts on its glossy back glowed as it silently wove its paralyzed prey in a cocoon of white luminescent silk.

A spray broke the surface of the lake. Bugs swirled and skipped out of the way of the peculiar breach. Meanwhile, the trapped calf filled the cavern with piercing howls as it pleaded for rescue. Hearing her calf's cries, the mother's spiked back glowed red with anger. Her nostrils exhaled once more with a blast of green mucus. She called back and dove under the water toward the shore.

Zinaka lit his torch and waved it above his head. Thanan sprang into action, hacking away at the banjin vines. Launching itself onto the shore, the enraged creature trumpeted a series of short blasts from the back of her throat, calling to her young.

Hearing its mother, the baby squirmed and twisted, trying to free its legs from the rope. The tree branches swayed violently as the baby answered back with a series of barks, followed by a high-pitched scream.

Sniffing the air frantically, she located her trapped baby. Her throat vibrated with anger, and the sound she made next sent all the creatures in the glowing cavern into frenzy once again. She bore her dripping teeth as she roared and thrashed her head angrily. The great roar penetrated Agrinoth to the very core. The warrior exhaled, slowly opening his eyes and gripping the spear's shaft.

High above the jungle, Thanan sliced through vine after vine, but the stalactite didn't budge. He glanced at the swaying jungle beneath him. Tree branches and leaves were exploding along the trail leading to Zinaka's garden. He noticed the ridges on the mother's back glowing red as she charged up the trail toward her helpless baby. Pounding the cavern floor, she crushed everything in her path; even a few unfortunate ground fowl fell victim to her massive steps. In her fury, she killed Zinaka's animals, biting them in half and tossing their carcasses from her teeth into the twisting vines overhead.

As she approached the garden, Zinaka yelled to Thanan, "Cut, Jinian! Cut with all you have!"

Thanan swung his blades with all his power, severing the tenacious vines from their grip. Suddenly the stalactite fell, but only a few inches before more vines caught the mighty rock again.

The enraged mother leaped into the garden, and spotting her child, bellowed another ear-piercing roar. Her muscular tail whipped, destroying one of the garden walls in its wake. The outer ropes of the net fluttered slightly as the stalactite fell another few inches. Agrinoth knelt, one knee behind the garden wall, armed and ready with his razor-sharp spear. His heart was steady and his breaths calm. The vines above creaked as Thanan's blade worked on a large vine. Large beads of sweat dripped from his brow, stinging his eyes. The heat was intense, but his strength was unyielding.

The creature below ran to her swinging baby. She calmed as their snouts met. A loud snap echoed above, and the stalactite fell. Distracted by her trapped baby, she did not notice the ropes smoking from friction as they flew through the metal rings on the cavern ceiling. At the corners of the garden, soil flew in all directions as the tightly woven net burst out of its hiding place and thrust upward toward the Xavantha.

As the great rock plummeted, a small vine latched onto Thanan's boot, pulling him out of his perch. As he fell, he grasped for anything, but found only empty fistfuls of air. At the last moment, his fingers found a banjin vine, which only slowed his fall and almost ripped his arm out of its socket. He lost his grip and toppled head over heels, crashing through vines, never letting go of his blade. His mind reeled as he fell, grasping for vines as well as his thoughts.

Then in the midst of it all, a warm feeling enveloped his body. He closed his eyes as the wind rushed over his face. Stretching forth his hands as far as he could, the air felt thick and tangible. For the slightest moment, it felt like time had slowed down for Thanan. Suddenly, he was aware of every vine, every tiny insect that rushed by him. Everything went silent. It was as if falling was a choice, something he could control, not an absolute law.

Then, like a crash of thunder, the terrifying situation rushed back. He toppled into a large vine, which threw him sideways like a rag doll. He landed awkwardly on the fractured surface of the stalactite, hitting his face and shoulder on the cold surface with such force that it knocked the Jinian unconscious.

The net surrounded the ancient beast below, but did not lift it. Her scaled legs stuck through the holes in the net, giving her the leverage she needed to fight the ropes. The stubborn banjin vines held fast, still preventing the stalactite from freefalling to the floor. Seeing the net closing in, the beast panicked. She tossed her head back and forth against the net, trying to bite at the ropes.

Agrinoth leaped onto the garden wall and aimed his spear, but the beast's flailing prevented him from a clear shot at her heart. It was his first look at the massive beast. He was taken aback by the sheer size of the creature. Twelve tons, he estimated – larger than any of the beasts he had seen in the caverns. Her armored head was adorned by two horns, one on her forehead and the other on her snout. The horns were boney, unlike like the rest of her scale-covered hide.

She stepped on the ropes on the ground and used her horns to pull the ropes on her head. The net resisted her attempts to break free. Agrinoth looked up to see the floating stalactite swaying from side to side, but did not see the Jinian. *Something is wrong*, he thought, trying to get a better angle on the beast.

"Jinian! The beast is breaking the ropes!" he yelled, knowing the plan was falling apart. "Cut the vines now!"

At that moment, the beast reared up on her hind legs and from the depths of her throat, bellowed what Agrinoth knew in his bones to be a war cry. She crashed her forelegs down upon the dark soil and bolted at Zinaka. She only made it a few steps before the net tangled underneath her feet, causing her to crash to the ground.

Seeing his opportunity, Agrinoth jumped off the wall and sprinted around the beast until they were face to face. He raised the spear and as he brought his arm forward, the crazed beast whipped her tail and smashed it across Agrinoth's chest, sending him over the western wall. The glowing spikes tore through the warrior's leather breastplate. He landed on his back and rolled up to his feet in one fluid motion. Spitting a mouthful of blood to the ground, he gritted his teeth, then called to Thanan again.

"We need that rock to fall now, Jinian!"

Above the fray, Thanan slowly rocked back and forth on the fractured stalactite, struggling to regain consciousness. His vision blurred and focused as he woke to the unfamiliar surroundings. The howls in the distance were muted and distorted as if he were underwater. He shook his head and blinked his eyes, trying to rouse his senses. Crawling across the cold surface, he grasped the rock's edge and looked down upon the furious beast. She snapped her head back and broke one of the ropes. Her terrified calf wailed as she spun and broke another rope in the net.

"She is breaking free, Jinian!" Agrinoth shouted, picking up his spear from the dirt.

Thanan grabbed his blade and cut the first vine he saw. With each vine, the stalactite dropped more and more. The net tightened against the raging creature, causing her to thrash more violently. She bit the net and shook her muscular neck, snapping one of the corner ropes. Seeing his net torn apart, Zinaka jumped over the wall and rushed the massive beast with his Zythera blade, even though the creature stood twenty-five feet high and towered over the giants.

The old hermit swung his blade wildly at the beast's side, but her thick scales deflected each blow. The annoying giant infuriated her all the more and with a quick turn of her head, she snapped her jaws at Zinaka, knocking him to the ground. He rolled head over heels, crashing into the garden wall. The blurry-eyed hermit looked at the beast and then everything went black.

She was just about to free herself completely from the net when Thanan cut a vital vine that sent the hovering stalactite plummeting to the ground. As the rock fell, Thanan ran across the fractured surface and dove out over the edge toward the rearing beast. The net quickly cinched around the ancient creature and hoisted her off the ground. The enormous stone crashed to the jungle floor and shook the cavern with such force that it knocked Agrinoth to the ground.

The beast roared with anger and tore at the ropes with all her strength. The weakened net gave way under her enormous weight, dropping her into the garden. She lowered her armored head and stared at her attacker, free to do as she wished. A blast of green mucus burst from her snout as she emitted a low growl from deep within her throat. Agrinoth knew he was beaten. The ridges on her neck again glowed red as she quickly lunged at the giant.

He dove out of the way and swung the spear, cutting the creature's neck. Pale red blood dripped down her scaly skin. Agrinoth stood his ground, dodging her gnashing teeth. Time after time, she lunged and the skilled warrior sliced the beast's neck. He wielded the Jinian's spear mightily, but he was no match for the creature's speed and sheer strength. She quickly snapped again, knocking Agrinoth to the ground with her horned snout, sending his spear flying from his hands.

The vulnerable warrior lay on his back, ready to accept his fate. There was nothing else he could do. His arms now burned from the immense weight of the spear and his chest heaved from exhaustion. The Jinian's plan had failed. The creature from another time was too much for the candidates.

Agrinoth thought of his people being exterminated over the next few generations as the creature multiplied and spread once again throughout the Crystal Caverns. He saw the terror in the eyes of the giants at Hardrock as they were slaughtered and driven from their homes.

Agrinoth did not close his eyes at the thought of the end. He watched as the salivating beast approached and leaned over him with her teeth dripping and throat vibrating. Her jaws opened and the last sound he heard was her sharp teeth snapping shut, but to Agrinoth's relief, she missed. She was stopped short by something falling on her massive neck.

The incensed beast reared back because of the shock, trying to knock whatever it was off. Unbeknownst to the two giants, when Thanan dove from the falling stalactite, he caught hold of the ropes and made his way over to the garden. Thanan had dropped from the ropes above and landed squarely on the beast's spiny red neck.

The beast thrashed about, whipping Thanan through the air, trying to throw him off. His lost his grip and fell backward, sliding down her neck. He smashed his back against her spines and quickly rolled to his stomach.

Regaining his grasp, he climbed up her neck, grabbing hold of the horn on her forehead. He drew his sword from its sheath and plunged his blade into the only vulnerable place he could think of: the creature's eye. Her horrible scream rang through the cavern. Incensed, she threw her head forward, launching the Jinian's legs over his head. He held tightly onto the sword, which was buried deep in the beast's eye socket. Thanan came down hard, straddling the beast's snout. He cut his cheekbone as his face smashed against her boney forehead. She thrashed her head back and forth, but Thanan gripped the hilt tightly, which twisted the blade even deeper into the bone.

A steady stream of thick blood ran down her snout, soaking Thanan's arms and shoulder. She reared up on her hind legs and roared from the blinding pain, but the pain was nothing compared to the agony of Agrinoth's massive spear protruding from her scaly chest.

The Goriath warrior stood there, his face like stone. Blood dripped from the tears in his leather breastplate.

The beast stumbled backward, entangling herself in the hanging net. The low growl from her throat became breathy and weak and her scaled chest expanded one last time. Never fully hitting the ground again, the beast's hind legs twisted in the garden soil and the ropes creaked as her lifeless body swayed slowly in the net.

Thanan gripped his hilt tightly with both hands and pried his blade from the beast's eye. He climbed down the net and jumped to the ground, landing in front of Agrinoth. Both of them stood there, bruised and bleeding. A slight smile crept over Thanan's lips.

"See, just like I planned, right?" he said, slapping his hand on Agrinoth's shoulder.

"Hmmph," the exhausted warrior grumbled under his breath, feeling the deep cut in his chest.

"I will check on the old giant. Seems he missed all the fun."

Thanan limped over to Zinaka, who had received a nasty head laceration for his trouble. He slapped his bearded cheeks to rouse him, but he did not respond. His heart was strong and his breathing was normal for an old Goriath, so Thanan called Agrinoth over and they carried the smelly giant to his bed in his little stone home.

The two candidates spoke very little as they sat in front of the stone fireplace. The glowing fire crackled and filled the silence. They were exhausted and hungry. The fire began to hiss as fat dripped from the calf meat skewers they both were holding over the flames. The intensity of the preceding events filled their minds with such anxiety that they could not rest, and the meat did not satisfy their hunger. They both knew that their time in the glowing cavern had at last come to an end. Once the unconscious hermit woke up, they would be on their way, journeying again in the darkness.

The morning came and it was time for Agrinoth and Thanan to continue their journey. The departure came with much sadness. The immense cavern was a miraculous place, and they both locked away in the depths of their minds the memories and experiences they had there. Zinaka's secret cavern would never be revealed to the Goriath giants.

After Agrinoth and the old hermit said a brief goodbye, Thanan thanked him for saving them in the tunnel. At the mouth of the cave, Thanan turned back for one last look at the world of glowing things and silently marveled at the scene. He turned away from the light and ducked into the darkness once again.

CHAPTER NINETEEN

THE HUNTED

The candidates stepped into the dry, black tunnel and the stone door sealed behind them. It was strange to Thanan, but the darkness now seemed comforting in a way, like coming home. It wasn't frightening at all. By the light of the torch, they walked single-file toward unknown paths, their satchels and flasks brimming with food and water.

Thanan traveled a little lighter now, because of the loss of one of his twin swords. His sword lay shattered beneath the fractured stalactite. Agrinoth also had to leave a weapon behind. The warrior cringed at the idea of such a mighty spear being reduced to nothing more than a deadly doorstop, all so that Zinaka's crooked door would stay open.

Passing through the dry tunnels, they came upon the bones of hundreds of sawtooths.

"Bad memories here," Agrinoth soberly said, kicking a skeleton from his path.

"Where do you think they all came from?" Thanan asked, holding his torch low, illuminating the bone-strewn floor.

"I do not know, but never have I seen them hunt in such numbers before. They must be starving in these parts. The scent of all these rotting corpses is sure to attract the fangrix, at least. Be ready for an ambush, Jinian. They could be anywhere now. In front, behind, even above."

"I am ready," the Jinian replied, eyes scanning the ceiling.

"I know these creatures. You can never be ready enough." The giant drew his blade and continued walking cautiously, leading the way.

Many days passed with little incident. The narrow caves widened into a long chain of vast glassy caverns, whose walls were smooth and cool to the touch. Every sound echoed wildly off the smooth surfaces, which irritated Agrinoth to no end. Even the smallest sound of a water droplet pierced his nerves. Thanan did not seem to mind the erratic nature of the echoes. His mind naturally tried to make sense of the chaos.

Every once in a while, the drab walls were broken up by beautiful clusters of white hexagonal crystals, which blinked as the torches passed by, like the distant galaxies that hung low over the Great Plains of the Jinian Realm. The two candidates stopped randomly to listen for any unwelcome pursuers. It took many seconds for the echoes to subside, and Agrinoth relished the auditory respite.

From the silence, a deep swelling sound vibrated through the cavern. The echoes disguised the direction from whence they came.

The sparkling crystals appeared as though thousands of eyes were peering from the heavens, like anxious spectators awaiting a battle that was about to take place.

"The fangrix approaches," Agrinoth growled, turning his back to Thanan, drawing his Zythera blade. "Prepare yourself, Jinian. This is not some three-legged, diseased beast that hunts us."

Thanan remembered the Zythera Blade Circle and his numerous beatings and ultimate victories within its stones. The open cavern floor was a definite advantage to the candidates, especially the larger Agrinoth.

Growls rumbled off the glassy cavern walls as the candidates circled back to back, their eyes focused on the blackness. They lit two more torches and threw them all a few feet away, creating a larger perimeter of visibility. Thanan closed his eyes, listening to the erratic echoes encompassing them. The growls intensified and grew louder, but somehow, in all the chaotic sound, Thanan sensed the true direction of the beast.

"Get down!" the Jinian yelled, diving to his left.

From behind them, a streak of brown and gold flew overhead, landing nimbly within the flickering perimeter. Thanan drew his blade as he dove and gracefully rolled into his typical battle stance. The tip of Agrinoth's blade narrowly missed the belly of the beast as it swatted at the giant's head. The creature stood shoulder tall to a Goriath giant, and his chest was as broad as a tree trunk. It stood, teeth bared, silhouetted by the bright torchlight. Agrinoth subtly moved his fingers, signaling Thanan to circle around the crouching fangrix. He stepped slowly to his left, never taking his eyes off the beast. The coarse hair on the fangrix's neck stood and its jowls dripped.

Thanan reached for his dagger and slowly pulled it from its sheath. With a quick flip of his wrist, he threw the dagger. The blade sunk deep in the beast's shoulder, but stopped when it hit bone. The enraged fangrix leaped at Agrinoth with its razor-sharp claws extended. The giant parried the attack and caught the beast's hip with his blade, opening a gash that left it with a slight limp.

Agrinoth stepped toward the beast and raised his sword. As he lifted his arm, a paralyzing pain shot down his shoulder. Agrinoth had not noticed that when the fangrix had lunged at him, its claws had ripped through his shoulder. The sound of his Zythera blade rattling on the floor maddened Agrinoth. It was the second time he had dropped his sword in these caves, and he had had enough. Seeing the giant's hesitation, the fangrix leaped again, its fangs aimed at his throat.

Thanan ran to assist his brother. But before he could swing his sword, Agrinoth spun out of the beast's path and grabbed its thick, furry neck, tackling it to the ground. The sprawling beast gasped for air and clawed at the floor as the furious giant tightened his grip. The fangrix howled as it thrashed back and forth. Thanan looked for any opening to kill the beast, but he knew that one errant swing might hit his Goriath brother. The flailing beast spun sharply, finally throwing the giant off its back. Agrinoth landed heavily on his side and rolled over a torch, singeing his forearm. He stood before the beast, his mouth bleeding, but the blood was not his own; it was fangrix blood. Thanan had not seen this particular look in Agrinoth's eyes before, and it scared even him.

The beast wailed and frantically rubbed the side of its head with its paw. Agrinoth stared at the beast and spat out its bloody ear to the floor.

More determined than ever, the massive beast let out a roar and this time, sprang at Thanan. Its massive head was met with the razor edge of Thanan's blade. Before the fangrix landed, Thanan had cut it three times. The wounded beast crumpled as it hit the cold floor. Thick, red blood trickled down the matted and spotted fur.

Agrinoth wasted no time; he dove on the fangrix, raining heavy blows to the beast's head with his fists. He pulled the dagger from its shoulder and plunged it into its neck, severing its jugular. The mighty predator's head fell limply to the cave floor. The exhausted giant exhaled and lowered his forehead onto the slain fangrix. He pulled the dagger from its throat as he stood up. Walking past Thanan, he dropped the bloody blade into Thanan's hand.

"We will make camp here, Jinian."

"You all right, Agrinoth?" Thanan asked, wiping off his bloody dagger. "How is your shoulder? I think I have something for that in my pack."

"I will be fine. It is just a scratch. That is all," he replied, walking into the darkness.

Thanan understood the mighty giant's meaning, so he let his brother be.

Agrinoth sat on the cave floor, leaning against the wall. For hours he stared blankly at the flickering torchlight casting its abstract shadows on the smooth stone.

Thanan spent some time exploring the jeweled cavern. He pried a milky white crystal from the black wall and held it in front of the torch. The swirling abstractions reminded him of the galaxy-filled sky over the capital. He placed it in his satchel and was about to walk away when something odd caught his eye. On the wall about knee high, he noticed strange scrapes etched into the stone. He ran his fingers along the markings, analyzing them. The lines appeared to be charred, like they had been burned into the stone. He brought his fingers to his nostrils and breathed in a pungent sulfuric smell. His eyes watered from the intense odor. The markings ran about ten feet down the wall and then disappeared around the corner into the darkness.

"How is the shoulder?" Thanan asked, sitting down on the cool floor.

"It will be fine, Jinian," the grumpy giant replied, rotating his shoulder, trying to keep it loose.

"Here, put this on it." Thanan pulled a rolled leaf from his satchel and threw it at Agrinoth. "I made a few of these for our trip."

"What do you want me to do with this?" the giant asked, sniffing the sour-smelling leaf. "I hate medicine. It stings."

"Just unroll the leaf and press it on your shoulder, you big baby. What would the Whitehallers say if they could see their mighty Agrinoth now? 'It stings,'" he scoffed.

"I would rather battle another fangrix than use your Jinian medicine," he replied.

"Speaking of that," Thanan said, changing the subject, "I don't remember Master Kigrorian teaching us the art of biting off fangrix ears."

Agrinoth pressed the slimy leaf to his shoulder and winced from the stinging medicine. Turning to Thanan, he replied, "Remember this, Jinian. There are times when, to defeat a beast, you must become a beast. Now get some sleep. I will take first watch."

Thanan drifted to sleep, understanding more than anyone the words that the giant spoke.

CHAPTER TWENTY

A TRAP

They journeyed long, through endless and treacherous paths, relying only on their finely honed skills, their wits and many tender mercies along the way. The bond of brotherhood grew between the candidates, who passed the monotonous days by recounting memories of their youth. Agrinoth told many stories of growing up in the garrison at Whitehall with Torik, as they trained to become soldiers and were eventually selected as candidates for the Order. Thanan spoke about his beautiful city, the City of the King, where darkness never found her majestic walls. He always imagined his life would be spent within the capital city, busy with the everyday politics and the inner workings of city government.

In the midst of reminiscing, Thanan thought about Haydon, his betrayal of his family, his people and the council. And yet, somewhere deep within the recesses of Thanan's heart was a place for his older brother. His love for him had never diminished. He understood Haydon better than anyone. He too felt the yearning for power when he was young. *Was it all self-serving?* Thanan asked himself many times over the years. He hoped there were moments when Haydon's love was genuine. Even in the throws of his darkest lessons in the museum, Thanan believed there were glimpses when Haydon's evil was stripped away. Those were the times he cherished most with his brother. They were his last fragments of purity, spent away in the darkness trying to convince his unwitting apprentice to join him.

It all seemed a lifetime away to Thanan now, and walking through the darkness into the ready jaws of a beast made him cherish the simpler times as a boy, protected by mighty white walls and royal parentage.

The air grew hot, and the ground beneath their feet trembled more with each day that passed. Ahead in the distance they saw a shaft of light emitting brilliantly from the floor, cutting through the dusty air. The light was intense and starkly contrasted the darkness. They raced down the tunnel, their footsteps echoing in their ears.

The candidates arrived at the light, and Agrinoth was shocked to discover that the beam came from within a deep shaft in the floor. The heated light bent and swayed back and forth as it lit the cave with a brilliant orange glow. Slowly, Agrinoth put his hand into the light. The intense heat singed the hair on his forearm.

"Smells like burnt kopi in here," Thanan said, sniffing the air.

The singed giant grumbled under his breath. Suddenly, deep-rumbling sounds erupted from the molten river below, and the vibration shook the floor more intensely than before.

"Boiling rock from the underearth," the warrior said, brushing his hand on his thigh. "This should not be here. No candidate has ever reported seeing this. The general will need to know."

"Perfect, another way for the caverns to kill us. We better keep moving," Thanan said, stepping around the glowing shaft. He couldn't resist feeling the heat for himself and held his key-scarred palm over the vent. He quickly retracted it and rubbed it on his chest.

As they walked through the volcanic caverns, more and more vents flooded the caves with streams of shimmering orange light. The hot walls were black as soot, and large black crystals encrusted the cavern ceiling.

Breathing the hot air for many days dried Thanan's mouth and cracked his lips. He drank from his flask and poured some over his head, but the stale, warm water gave him no refreshment. With a grimacing face, Agrinoth massaged and rotated his shoulder as he walked. He didn't want to say anything, but Thanan's medicinal concoction had healed it quite nicely.

They maneuvered carefully around the deep shafts, making sure not to get too close to the columns of heat spewing into the tunnels. Out of curiosity, Thanan tied a rope to his torch and lowered it down into the vent. Fifteen feet down, it ignited. He quickly pulled it out and smothered it on the wall. *Only Purgon could truly appreciate this forge of the underearth,* Thanan thought.

"Look! Up ahead!" Agrinoth shouted over the dull hum of the lava flow. "The floor has collapsed!"

Thanan looked down the cave. The floor had fallen into the glowing abyss below. A deep roar swelled from the molten river and sounded like a thousand billows blowing air into the forges at Hardrock.

"Over there, Jinian!" the giant shouted over the inferno. "There is a ledge." Agrinoth pointed along the left wall. "It is our only way around."

Thanan quickly looked around and determined his brother was right. "All right, lead the way!" he said, gulping down another drink of hot water. He glanced at his flask then to the shimmering heat waves. "Wait, we should put our cloaks on and soak them with water." Agrinoth nodded his approval.

Once they had dawned their cloaks and sufficiently soaked them, they jumped over a crack in the cave floor and landed safely on the narrow ledge. Walking side by side, they carefully moved along the lip with their backs against the hot wall. The intense heat waved before their eyes and singed the skin on their cheeks and chin. The cavern wall was uncomfortable to touch it was so hot, but the air only inches from their faces was even hotter.

They moved cautiously along the ledge, shuffling side to side. Thanan's palms began stinging as he clung to the sheer wall. The water on their cloaks was evaporating quickly as they walked over the inferno. Suddenly, the cave shook violently and threw Thanan's shoulders away from the wall. He spun around, frantically grasping for the wall, but his fingertips grazed the stone and pushed him further away from the wall. His arms waved back and forth, trying to regain his balance. He felt the mighty slap of Agrinoth's hand on his back and in one swift swing, his massive hand smashed Thanan against the wall. The skin on his pale cheek split and the blood dried quickly as it ran down the wall.

"You all right, Jinian?" Agrinoth shouted over the roaring river below.

The bleeding candidate winced and nodded his head, indicating he was all right. And so they continued their perilous trapeze act over the river of fire.

"Over there!" Thanan pointed in the distance. "We are almost there." Through the shimmering heat waves, he saw the cave continuing into the darkness. "Agrinoth, your sleeve! You're on fire!"

With no sense of alarm, the giant looked down and calmly snuffed out the flames with his massive palm.

"We need to get out of here," Agrinoth said, steadying himself.

The ledge narrowed, forcing their heels against the wall. Agrinoth pulled out his leather flask and poured it over the front of his cloak and told Thanan to do the same.

"It might buy us some more time," the giant said, turning his eyes from the heated air.

The Jinian's cheeks and chin showed signs of small blisters as the intense heat rushed by. Every breath they took seemingly burned their lips and scorched their lungs. Finally, the ledge widened enough for the two candidates to run. They ran as fast as they could, jumping over small gaps in the ledge, where the fiery river had reclaimed her rock. Thanan looked back and saw parts of the ledge crumbling away and splashing into the bubbling cauldron. There was no turning back now.

There was another quake and the ledge before them broke free and crumbled into the lava. They jumped over the gap, barely making the leap. The lava splashed onto their trailing cloaks, igniting the cloth, but they did not stop. Agrinoth knew that stopping now would surely end their lives. Thanan stripped out of his flaming cloak and threw it away as he sprinted along the ledge. It drifted slowly out into the chasm, where it exploded into flames and was consumed in seconds.

The flames overtook Agrinoth's cloak, but still he flew swiftly along the ledge. One last great leap and they found themselves on solid ground once more. The mighty giant rolled on the cave floor as Thanan poured the last of their water over him, snuffing the flames. They looked back at the fiery scene, in awe of the power of creation and destruction.

"We need to keep moving, Jinian," Agrinoth said calmly, shedding his charred cloak and tossing it into the glowing cauldron.

Agrinoth's face was sooty and blistered, yet he still looked as determined as ever to complete his test. He straightened his satchel, cracked his neck, and began to walk.

"Here, put this on your face." Thanan pulled another rolled leaf from his satchel and threw it at Agrinoth.

He unrolled the leaf and slapped it on his cheek, grumbling and muttering something about Jinian sorcery and smelly leaves, but secretly enjoyed the soothing sensation the medicine delivered. Thanan grinned as he followed the humbled giant once again into the darkness.

For many days the candidates walked easily, traversing the black labyrinth. The temperature was now pleasant and the terrain was flat. Thanan welcomed the reprieve from heat and large boulders in his path. Rumbling cave walls and sudden blasts of steam erupting from the floor became just another part of everyday life. Every so often, they would happen upon a glowing shaft of light that would illuminate the cave and reveal a beautiful array of crystals that adorned the glassy cavern around them. The colors amazed Thanan and all it took was a little light. Small waterfalls fell from high above and cascaded gently over the stone walls. The rushing sound soothed their weary minds and rejuvenated their spirits.

So much beauty in such a hellish place, Thanan thought. He drank deeply and doused his head in the cool water washing down the wall. Dark streaks of soot and dirt ran down his face, his cheeks still stinging in spite of the shocking cold and medicine. He unrolled another large glystenia leaf and applied the medicine to his healing face. It burned for a moment and then became cool.

Agrinoth sat against the wall slowly sipping his water, relishing every drop that crossed his tongue. He leaned his head against the stone and closed his eyes. Thanan noticed the small scar under Agrinoth's chin.

"I remember when I gave you that scar, brother. I was so scared that day."

The Goriath warrior felt his blemished chin. "I forgot about that," he said smiling, thinking about the sunny day in Loriam. "I wanted to humiliate you, make you run back home to your palace, but you surprised me. Torik teased me for weeks about the scar."

"That sounds like him," Thanan replied, smiling.

Agrinoth's expression turned serious.

Thanan knew he was thinking about his brother, Torik. The loss of his brother had taken a steep toll on Agrinoth, but mourning was a luxury that candidates couldn't afford in the final trial.

"I'm sorry that Torik died, Agrinoth. I know you are pained. What a blessing it was to have been in the glowing cavern when it happened, don't you think?"

"Please, Jinian, let's not talk of this. It is not proper to speak of the noble dead."

"I know, but I wanted you to know that he was my friend and his death weighs heavily on me," Thanan said thoughtfully. "I probably would not be here if it were not for him. He always treated me with respect, looked out for me, even in the beginning. I know that I am not of your kind and I could never replace Torik, but it is my hope that you might think of me as your brother, for I consider you mine."

Agrinoth smiled and leaned his head against the wall again, saying nothing.

They had lasted four long days without the comfort of sleep, and the dulcet sounds of trickling water were too much for their weary bodies and minds to resist any longer. And so, against their better judgment, they soundly slept.

After many hours, they woke to a strange sound in the distance. The odd cry cut through the falling water and penetrated Agrinoth's very soul. To Thanan, it sounded like a babe crying in the night, but by the expression on the giant's face, he knew it had to be one of the beasts. The echoes gently carried the cry through the cavern, intensifying and then diminishing as it moved over the odd terrain.

"How far off is it?" the Jinian asked, turning his head, trying to derive the distance himself.

"Too difficult to tell with all this noise," Agrinoth replied, drawing his blade and inspecting its edge. "It could be much closer than we think. These caves play tricks with your mind. Do not underestimate this creature, Jinian. Only one other beast bests the cunning and agility of a silok and that is a flame wrock. Avoid the silok's teeth at all costs. It only takes but a few moments to seize from its venomous bite. And make no mistake: You will be alive when it feasts on your flesh."

"Understood. Eat this. We need to keep our strength up," Thanan replied, tossing a sowbelly-filled biscuit to Agrinoth.

"Our journey is almost at an end, Jinian. I can feel it in my bones." He tore into the biscuit and devoured it in two bites.

They followed the distant cries into the darkness, their torches lighting the way. They wove their way through stalagmite-dotted cavern floors, dodging the glowing shafts that plummeted into the molten river hundreds of feet below. The wailing intensified, beckoning the candidates on. Thanan listened intently to Agrinoth as he described in detail the finer points in battling a silok.

"The siloktrix or silok is an ancient creature, Jinian," the giant began, "believed to have come from the high mountains in the North. It was presumed that they were brought to the crystal caverns long ago by a nomadic tribe. They introduced the creature to rid the caves of a vermin epidemic that had brought a great sickness over the population. They were much smaller then and less agitated. Thousands of years later, they changed, mutated into something different. Their mouths became infested with bacteria from the disease-ridden rodents they consumed, and their bite became deadly. Even the smallest bite causes extreme pain and convulsions, but the pain only lasts a few minutes. Once the paralyzing effect ravages the body, its victim watches in horror as it slowly peels the flesh from his bones."

Thanan shook his head, wondering how deadly the flame wrock must be if it was more dangerous than the silok.

"The beast is close! Be ready!" Agrinoth yelled, picking up the pace.

They stopped outside the mouth of a sizable cavern and hid themselves from view. From the middle of the cavern floor, the veiled beast wailed wildly as if it were challenging the candidates to enter its lair.

"What do you see, Jinian?"

Thanan quickly peeked into the cavern, but only saw a vast labyrinth of heat vents in the floor. Erupting mist obscured his vision, and the heat waves distorted his depth perception.

"I didn't see the beast."

"It is your call."

With a couple of deep breaths, Thanan replied, "I say…this silok will regret ever entering this cavern." He drew his twin blade from his back and his dagger from his belt.

"Remember, stay away from its teeth," Agrinoth stated, holding his Zythera blade.

The two warriors stepped into the unknown cavern. A low rumble moved the stone underneath their feet. The air was hot and humid. The intense heat from the vents in the cavern floor mixed with cooler air that fell from the wet and dripping ceiling, creating a thick mist that smelled of sulfur. Thanan's eyes began to tear from the intense smell, but it did not seem to bother Agrinoth at all. It reminded Thanan of the barracks when he used to lie awake, unable to sleep from the stench of begrimed and snoring Goriath candidates. He tore a swatch of cloth from his tunic and tied it around his head, covering his nose and mouth. Glowing orange light burst from the cave floor through the billowing mist like a thousand sunsets over the Nasean Sea through the morning fog.

With each step the cries grew louder, and the sickening sulfurous smell turned Thanan's stomach as he walked through the dense, steamy eruptions.

"Stench too much for you, Jinian?" Agrinoth mocked. "You are looking more pale than usual."

"Keep your eyes forward, giant. I would not want you to fall to a fiery death."

"Do not worry about me," Agrinoth shot back, looking intently into the dense fog. "We need to surprise this silok."

"What do you have in mind?"

The giant nodded his head and without a word, Thanan knew what the plan was.

"Wait for my signal. Your speed will be crucial, Jinian."

The candidates separated and disappeared into the foggy cavern. Thanan looked back to see if he could catch a glimpse of his companion, but the fog was so thick that he saw nothing but faint shafts of light cutting through. Thanan walked cautiously, making sure to keep the silok's screams to his right. Looking up, he noticed the wispy steam clawing at the black glassy ceiling trying to find a way out. The mirrored rock reflected the shimmering orange light, creating an abstract mosaic of the cavern floor whenever the fog thinned.

Agrinoth deftly moved from stalagmite to stalagmite, concealing himself from the silok's view. Neither candidate had caught a view of the beast, because of the dense mist, but they knew they were closing in.

Sweat poured down Thanan's face and neck. As he moved toward the beast's location, he decided that in order to surprise the beast, he would climb a stalagmite and attack from above. He sheathed his sword and knife and began climbing. The smooth, wet surface was difficult for the Jinian to grasp because of the burns on his hands, but slowly, he made his way up the rock.

Across from Thanan, Agrinoth leaned his back against a massive stone and peered around the edge, staring into the intense light and wafting steam. Then he saw it, about sixty feet away, gnashing its venomous teeth and thrashing its diamond-shaped head. The warrior glanced up and saw Thanan emerge through the dispersing mist. *This silok will never know what hit him*, he thought to himself, readying his blade. He smiled a rare, confident smile. The only obstacle between him and the beast was a glowing heat vent…just a small leap for a giant.

Thanan wiped his brow and looked down through the mist. He pulled the cloth from his nose and mouth, looking focused, ready for anything.

This would be one of the defining moments of Thanan's great quest to become a member of the Guardian Order. He slowly drew his sword from over his shoulder without making a sound. He gripped the top of the rock with his left hand and readied himself for the battle. His heart was pounding, but it was not the heartbeat of panic; it was the strong, steady rhythm of a warrior's heart, ready for battle.

A bellowing war cry cut through the monotonous roar of the cavern. It was the signal Thanan had been waiting for. His muscles tensed as he saw his candidate brother leap through the thick fog, sword in hand and ready to strike. Thanan was about ready to jump from his perch, but at the last moment he saw something in Agrinoth's body language that halted his attack.

Agrinoth stood there, looking at the silok in amazement. The beast hissed with anger but did not attack the giant. Its spiny quills were burned and its back was broken. It just lay there, wailing from the pain.

"It is a trap, Jinian!" the panicked giant yelled, shooting his eyes to the ceiling as if to see something there.

Thanan turned in enough time to see a quick shadow scurry across the ceiling and disappear.

"Get down, Jinian! Take cover!" Agrinoth yelled from below.

Thanan darted his eyes around the cavern but saw nothing. Then he saw something that his mind was not prepared for. From the corner of his eye, he saw glowing sparks falling from the cavern ceiling.

Slowly, a long reptilian-like tail scraped across the volcanic rock, causing a shower of glowing sparks to rain down upon the mesmerized Jinian. Its sparking tail left behind deep, smoldering scratches in the stone. The three flame stones at the tip of its tail glowed like the embers in the hottest forges of Hardrock Quarry. It slowly wound its long tail in front of its face, illuminating the eyes of the monster and the face of an ancient dragon. Its scaly lips quivered, baring its sickly yellow teeth. Black cylindrical stone quills covered the flame wrock's entire body.

Flaring its nostrils, it inhaled deeply, drawing in the hot air and fog. It opened its mouth, exhaling a noxious gas along with a piercing screech that shocked Thanan's ears. The beast's golden eyes glowed as the gas ignited. The brilliant fire passed over its burning tail stones, bursting into a ball of flames. The initial explosion knocked Thanan from the stone and sent him plummeting to the cavern floor. The fire that the creature emitted was a combination of hot flame and a gelatinous substance that stuck to anything that it touched. The fire clung to the stalagmite, burning its way through the stone.

A few drops splashed onto Thanan's armor and began burning through the Zythera-laced leather. He landed on his back, armor smoking, and found himself eye to eye with the angry silok gnashing its teeth just out of reach of his forehead. The Jinian was unable to move for a moment, the wind being knocked from his lungs, but he managed to roll to his side just as Agrinoth's sword pierced the beast's neck, ending its misery.

"Take your armor off, Jinian!" Agrinoth shouted, looking at the cavern ceiling. Thanan quickly ripped off his breastplate, leaving him even more vulnerable to the flame wrock's attack.

High above the candidates, the flame wrock scurried over the stones with ease, its unique stone armor sparking as it scraped the rocky surface. Even in this hellish situation, Thanan admired the beauty of the ancient beast, not only for its sheer maneuverability, but also for its tactical intelligence.

The wingless dragon disappeared from sight, and Agrinoth hesitantly lowered his sword.

"Master Kizaga took one of these wrock's heads?" Thanan asked, snuffing his armor out.

He ran his fingers over the shoulder of his armor. Deep pits pocked the metal grommets that covered the leather and breastplate, while parts of the leather had melted through, offering no more protection.

"Better put that back on now. It is the only thing between you and that burning ooze. Remember, the wrock has two ways of spouting his fire. You have seen the first and most deadly. He needs the intense heat of his tail stones for that. If you see the tail stones glow, just run, Jinian. The second is a ball of exploding flame that will stun you. It is best if you just avoid both."

"Thank you for enlightening me, brother," Thanan replied sarcastically.

"Well you are the one with burned armor, Jinian."

"Do you think he has gone?" Thanan said, changing the subject, adjusting his battered armor.

The giant looked at the dead silok and then up at the ceiling, quite serious. "No, he is still here. This beast is going to enjoy killing us. He is watching us in plain sight. He is a devil, and the devil never kills you quickly. He makes you suffer. It gives him pleasure, but for only a moment."

"How are we going to kill this thing and not get burned up in the process?"

"Keep your eyes toward the ceiling, Jinian. He cannot move without revealing his location. Even in this wet world, he will spark. Look for the sparks and at all costs, do not give him a direct shot. This creature will burn the flesh from your bones."

The giant thought for a moment. "We need to take this beast's flame stones. Take the tip of his tail."

"How do you propose we do that?" Thanan asked, eyes on the cavern ceiling.

Agrinoth looked over the cavern as a rare and slight smile crept across his lips. "Bait," he replied, looking calmly at Thanan.

"Bait?" Thanan asked, with a knowing look on his face. "I don't like where your giant brain is going with this."

"You are the smaller target, Jinian, and faster too."

Thanan stood there with an expression that said, "Your flattery is fooling no one."

"Do not worry. You just draw the wrock over there," Agrinoth said, pointing across the cavern toward two stalagmites that rose dramatically from the steaming floor. "Just get him through those two rocks. He will not know what hit him."

Thanan knew it was a good plan, but looking at the floor and seeing how easily the flame wrock had killed the silok gave him second thoughts. He looked up into the intense eyes of the giant and replied, "Let's do this."

"I always knew you were mad, Jinian. They will immortalize you on the walls of Krokil Zil for this. I promise you."

Thanan recognized the look on Agrinoth's face. He had seen it once before, when he relieved the raging fangrix of one of his ears. The expression bolstered Thanan's confidence in Agrinoth's insane plan.

"May the spirit of Kizaga go with you," Agrinoth said, extending his arm in brotherhood.

Agrinoth watched as the Jinian ran away and disappeared into the foggy air. He listened until he could no longer hear his brother's footsteps and then he turned, making his way toward the twin stalagmites.

Thanan darted from stalagmite to stalagmite, leaping over volcanic vents in an attempt to be as conspicuous as possible. It was a tactic so contrary to all that Master Kigrorian had taught, but to wait for an otherwise invisible foe to emerge from the shadows and burn you to death was no tactic at all. Thanan continued to run, clanking his blade against the stone floor, but nothing seemed to draw the beast from its hiding place.

"Where are you, you monster?" Thanan muttered under his breath, scouring the ceiling.

Losing patience, he slammed his blade into a stalagmite and shouted, "Show yourself, you coward!"

The blow cut a large gash into the stone, which sent rubble rolling across the floor. Thanan took a battle stance and began to circle slowly, scanning the ceiling for the slightest movement. Then from the corner of his eye he saw the smallest glint of a spark. Thanan froze and did not look in the direction of the beast. He slowly grabbed his leather pouch and plucked out a crystal specimen he had collected many days earlier. He held it in his palm and felt its weight. He gripped it tightly and with a quick pivot, threw the crystal into the blackness, striking the flame wrock. The angry beast scurried across the cavern ceiling, sparks raining down.

"There you are," Thanan whispered.

The pale candidate watched in awe as the black dragon released its grip from the ceiling and fell eighty feet, flipping in the air, landing gracefully on the top of a looming stalagmite. Thanan stood there, sword in hand, completely exposed. The flame wrock clutched the stone with its black talons, scarring the rock.

Suddenly its glowing tail stones emerged from behind the stalagmite. An eruption of gelatinous flame spewed from its mouth toward the Jinian. Thanan dove quickly and evaded the molten attack, which boiled and scorched the stone as it oozed over the smooth surface. Another explosion from the dragon's throat came, but this time, a super heated ball of flame ignited the air and knocked Thanan to his back. The heat singed his hair and left his clothes smoking. He rolled with ease to his feet and ran for cover toward the nearest stalagmite. The beast screamed, launching another blast of molten fire at the fleeing candidate. The fire splashed over the rock's surface, shielding Thanan's legs as he dove behind the stone.

The flame wrock jumped from its perch and landed nimbly on the floor, squawking like a bird. It sniffed the air as it walked confidently toward Thanan's hiding place. Amused by its own prowess, the beast gracefully scraped its rock-covered tail against stalagmites as he passed them by, causing great showers of sparks to bounce and skitter across the floor.

Thanan was astonished by the variety of strange vocalizations that the flame wrock emitted from its throat. It was as if it were talking in its own unique language. Thanan imagined the beast sadistically chanting, "Where are you, Guardian? Do not be scared. I don't bite."

Thanan silently crept around the stalagmite as the wrock circled about. He slowly pulled another crystal from his pouch and threw it. The crystal flew off in the distance and shattered on the cave floor with a sharp crash. The flame wrock turned its head, distracted for just a moment. Thanan bolted from his hiding place toward the next large stalagmite. He dove over a large vent, then rolled to his feet into a full sprint. Seeing his prey fleeing, the flame wrock shot after him, leaving a stream of trailing sparks behind. The beast's piercing scream rang in Thanan's ears.

Across the cavern, Agrinoth anxiously waited behind the two stalagmites. His Zythera blade reflected the orange light from the nearby heat shaft. He listened intently for any sign of his candidate brother, yet he heard nothing but the low rumble that was prevalent in the cavern.

"Where are you, Jinian?" the warrior muttered quietly.

The flame wrock closed in on the fleeing candidate. A fireball flew from its mouth, burning the air behind Thanan. He dove to his right, landing nimbly behind a small stalagmite, only waist high. The fireball passed by, but not before it set Thanan's already charred pants aflame. He quickly snuffed the flames out with his palm.

The wrock halted his pursuit and slowly scraped his scaly tail along the cave floor. The orange sparks ignited the stone quills at the tip of its tail. Thanan held his sword at the ready and took three quick breaths to muster all his bravery. The black dragon inhaled deeply and brought the glowing embers to his scaly lips. With unparalleled speed, Thanan sprang from behind the stone and ran toward the inhaling beast. As the noxious gas ignited, the sprinting Jinian slid gracefully under the molten stream, his momentum taking him right through the flame wrock's legs. He raised his sword as he slid underneath the belly of the beast. Sparks fell as the tip of the blade bounced off the creature's stone armor, dealing no damage.

Thanan rose to his feet and looked back at the flame wrock just in time to be knocked head over heels by the beast's nimble tail. A sharp pain shot through Thanan's side as he rolled to his feet and began running toward the distant stalagmites. The flame wrock continued his attack, screeching and spitting fireballs as Thanan scrambled from stalagmite to stalagmite. Thanan ran with all the speed he could, attempting to evade his pursuer by running through thick clouds of mist and snaking his way around large boulders and stalagmites.

Agrinoth looked into the distance and saw explosions of light through the thick fog. It reminded him of the stories his great-great grandfather Purgon had told him about the wars on the Darvinian plains, when the Jinian army launched their fiery attack from the smoke-filled sky. The giant gripped the handle of his sword tightly as the explosions grew closer. He would only have one chance at severing the flame wrock's tail stones, and Thanan's life depended on a precisely timed swing.

The Jinian burst through the swirling fog, eyes wild. "He's coming!" he shouted, holding his sword in one hand and pressing on his broken ribs with his other.

He looked back to see the perfect predator emerge from the billowing fog just in time to dodge another fireball. Thanan ran with all his might and hurdled over the small valley between the stalagmites. He stumbled and fell flat on his face and chest, igniting the pain in his ribs to unimaginable levels. He staggered to his feet and continued to run.

The stone-covered dragon leapt effortlessly through the opening, not noticing Agrinoth hiding with his back against the wall. The beast's trailing tail slithered between the stalagmites, lining up the tail stones perfectly for Agrinoth's swing. He brought his Zythera blade down with a mighty yell. The force of the blow was so powerful that it sent fiery sparks scattering over the cavern floor.

The piercing scream that followed was almost more than the Jinian's acute ears could bear. He fell to the cave floor holding his hands to his ears, consumed by the intense pain. The flame wrock hissed, screamed, and randomly shot a fireball into the air more powerfully than before. It struck a stalactite and broke it free, sending it crashing to the floor.

The cavern shook and the floor cracked from the impact. Agrinoth lost his balance and fell backward through the stalagmite valley. The wailing creature spun wildly around, its lifeless tail stones now hanging by some small piece of connective sinew. Its eyes were now fixed on Agrinoth, its lips wriggling and body shuddering with anger. Agrinoth jumped to his feet and ran at the staring beast.

With a quick blast, a fireball knocked the oncoming giant back against the stalagmite. He crumpled to the floor and rolled to extinguish the flames on his legs and back.

Thanan struggled to his feet, his ribs searing with pain. He brought his sword down upon the side of the beast, but the hardened stone quills deflected the blade with a shower of sparks. The beast quickly snapped his head around to see the Jinian raise his blade again. It was more out of annoyance that the flame wrock raised its hind leg and stepped on Thanan, crushing him to the ground with just enough pressure to subdue the pest that plagued him.

With Thanan firmly underfoot, the wrock again turned its attention to the giant, who was now standing, blade in hand and wearing a most determined expression on his face. Agrinoth gritted his teeth and lunged at the flame wrock. The giant brought his sword down upon the beast with all his fury. He swung over and over again, but the flame wrock's stone armor deflected his blows. The beast opened its mouth and shot out a ball of flame that caught Agrinoth in the shoulder and threw him to the ground. Seeing an opening to finish off the giant, the dragon leaped in the air and landed directly over the smoking and stunned candidate.

Sniffing Agrinoth's hair and armor, the flame wrock seemed more interested in figuring out what form of creature this was that gave him such trouble. Agrinoth froze and just stared into the dragon's eyes. He slowly moved his hand over the hot stone floor, trying to feel for the hilt of his Zythera blade.

Behind the wrock, Thanan struggled to his feet, the pressure from the leaping dragon no doubt fracturing the remaining ribs on his right side. He strained to breathe, his breaths shallow and weak. He cried aloud as he ran toward the black dragon. The shout gave him strength, and the pain subsided as he chopped at the stone armor of the dragon. Sparks flew and danced across the floor with every swing, but this only served as a distraction that gave his brother the smallest of windows to escape from beneath the deadly creature's clutch.

Agrinoth found his sword and plunged it into the beast's neck, the tip somehow finding its way through the stony quills, striking flesh. He withdrew his sword and attempted to stab the beast again, but his blade was stopped short by a deliberate swat of the creature's stone claws. The dragon snapped his head around and shot a fireball at Thanan, but missed as the quick Jinian ducked around the hindquarters, jumping over his swinging tail.

Thanan took one more swing at the flame wrock's tail stones and severed them completely. The creature was incensed. It screamed from the pain, which pierced Thanan's ears, dropping him to his knees again. His sword rattled on the stone floor as he writhed from the pain.

The flame wrock had had enough. The dragon spun with the intent of ending his attacker's life. He shot a small fireball into the Jinian's chest, knocking him to the floor. Lifting his burned cheek up from the hot floor, Thanan looked into the flame wrock's eyes. He could feel the cavern floor beneath him quiver with each step of the beast. Thanan was exhausted. He struggled to breathe, each breath bringing only stabbing pains in his side. He watched the bright sparks fall and dance over the floor as the beast closed in for the kill. Thanan knew by the way the flame wrock moved that the time for play was over. Vocalizing its displeasure, it looked Thanan in the eyes and opened its mouth, bearing its razorlike teeth. Thanan's tired thoughts drifted and his pain left his body. *Father*, he thought, *you were wrong. This mission should not have been mine.* The flame wrock snapped his jaws, and a thunderous crack echoed throughout the cavern. The beast howled as it fell to the cave floor. Thanan looked up at a nearby stalagmite, stunned by what he saw. There he was, standing atop the stone like a god of the underearth, holding a large boulder over his head.

"Come get me, devil!" Agrinoth shouted from above.

The flame wrock shook his head and looked at the still rolling stone that had struck its side. Narrowing its eyes, it snapped its head around and snarled at the giant. With a quick leap, it crashed into Agrinoth, sinking its teeth into the giant's shoulder as they both toppled over the edge of the stalagmite out of view.

Thanan struggled to his feet and limped his way around the massive stone. As he rounded the stalagmite, the battle he witnessed would rival even the battles of Master Kizaga. The stealth and speed of the flame wrock clashed against the brute force of the mighty Goriath giant. The dragon gnashed its teeth and spat fireballs, but time and time again, each attack was defended and met with a heavy Zythera blade across its stony hide. Thick blood ran down its stone quills, leaving an erratic red-stained path on the cavern floor. Thanan slowly pursued the battle, but he could hardly take a breath, let alone run. The flame wrock hissed and screamed as each blow from the giant's blade cut closer and closer to the dragon's jugular.

It was a fight of the ages and the battle would echo in the caverns for generations. A fireball knocked Agrinoth to his back and set his breastplate on fire. Ablaze, he ran toward the flame wrock, his sword red with the blood of the dragon. The flame wrock sprang forward to meet the giant, sparks falling from its quills. Thanan watched in horror as the two collided in the air and fell to the floor, fighting for their lives. Their momentum sent them tumbling uncontrollably across the cave floor, falling into a glowing vent.

"No!" Thanan shouted, running as fast as he could to the hole. He slid to the edge and looked over into the glowing vapor.

The heat was overwhelming. About eight feet down into the shaft, he saw the hands of Agrinoth hanging on a ledge and from his calf, the flame wrock clinging by its teeth. Protruding from its stony neck was Agrinoth's Zythera blade.

"Help me, please," he managed to utter, knowing there was nothing the Jinian could do. It was the irrational pleading of a mighty warrior in the throws of pain. The agony on his face was evident, and Thanan felt helpless.

The flame wrock clawed at the walls to gain some leverage as the intense heat from the vent began to overtake it. It thrashed to escape the heat, and the beast's teeth sawed further through the giant's flesh. As the temperature increased, the dragon's stone hide began to glow like coal in a forge.

Thanan watched, knowing he did not have the strength to lift both the creature and Agrinoth, and it pained him greatly to watch his brother in such agony. Agrinoth did not fault Thanan, for he knew he lacked the strength. Even the mighty Kizaga could not heft the weight of a flame wrock and Agrinoth. He kicked the dragon's snout, trying to free his leg, but the creature would not release. It only bit down harder, trying to preserve its own life. Agrinoth looked into the wrock's eyes and saw the pain it too was experiencing. The sword had severed its jugular, which was weakening the beast's grasp. The mighty flame wrock took one final look at the giant, opened its mouth, and plummeted into the lava.

Thanan lowered his hand, but it was just out of reach. Agrinoth, now without the protection of the flame wrock, took the full brunt of the fire and heat from below. It did not occur to him until that moment that the dragon might be the one keeping him alive. He looked up at Thanan, eyes pleading for relief. His legs burned from the heat. Thanan saw that Agrinoth's leg was broken from the wrock's bite.

"Leave me!" he cried, closing his eyes, his grip on the ledge weakening.

"I won't leave you, brother," Thanan replied, lowering the hilt of his sword. "Take it!" he yelled.

The giant grimaced as he took the hilt with one hand and pulled up with the other. The bottom of his boots started smoldering, the scent of which began penetrating Thanan's nostrils. Thanan held the blade with both hands and pulled with all the strength he had, the blade slowly slicing his palms as he pulled. His ribs burned with each movement, but the pain he felt was nothing compared to the agony of his broken brother. Thanan felt the blade cut deeper into his palms and knew in his heart he could not heft Agrinoth out.

Suddenly, an overwhelming feeling came over the Jinan, a feeling of calm and peace. The thought came clearly to his mind that this giant needed to live. For what purpose, he did not know. A power welled inside him, radiating to his arms and hands. His pain left him, a new strength surging. With one more heave, he pulled the giant out of the furnace, both of them collapsing to the floor. Thanan doused the flames that had overtaken the giant's boots. Agrinoth fell unconscious.

CHAPTER TWENTY-ONE

DESPAIR

The damage to Agrinoth's legs was extensive, and Thanan began the laborious task of mending his brother. It took two agonizing days to drag the giant from the fiery cavern into a cooler, more hospitable area of the dark tunnels.

Thanan set up camp next to a nearby pool that was fed one drop of mineral-filled water at a time. He leaned against a cool stone and stared into the still water and counted the time. The stalactite above dripped one single drop every five minutes and four seconds, and it was the only sound that he could hear. It was a welcome break from the silence, even if it was only a fleeting sound.

Thanan took an inventory of their remaining supplies. It did not take long to exhaust the medicine he had collected in the glowing cavern, but it was enough to stave off the impending infection. The intense heat of the vent had cauterized the bite on the giant's calf, but the bite he sustained in the shoulder now needed immediate attention. He did not have a needle and thread, so he heated his dagger in the flame of the torch.

After two days unconscious, Agrinoth woke to the searing pain of his flesh burning and Thanan found himself lying facedown after being slugged in the jaw by an angry giant.

"You hit like a girl, brother," Thanan said, grimacing, holding his chin.

"Where are we?" the giant grumbled, trying to sit up.

"Whoa. You need to stay still and let me finish cauterizing your wounds. Here, bite on this." Thanan cut a strap of leather from the giant's burned boot and placed it between Agrinoth's teeth. The giant tensed his fists and pounded the cave floor as Thanan carefully seared the oozing bites. The same burning pain that brought him back to consciousness put him to sleep once again.

Thanan sat near the pool, listening to the lonely drip. He winced with each breath and ached when he moved. He removed his armor to examine his ribs, and it was no surprise to discover his entire side was black and deep purple. When he breathed deeply, he could see a few of the fractures under his skin.

Thanan slept soundly in spite of his injuries and woke determined to finish the journey. He wrapped his brother's legs with a thin blanket and began dragging Agrinoth down the cave. Once in a while the sleeping giant woke and groaned some nonsensical words and drifted off again. Thanan labored to breathe, and with each heave came a stabbing pain that sometimes was so excruciating that it made him nauseous.

Moving into a different region of the caverns, water became abundant, and Thanan took every opportunity to get Agrinoth to drink, even if it was only a sip. As he dragged Agrinoth, Thanan heard the occasional squeak of sawtooths scurrying over ledges in front of him. Lighting his torch, he cut down two, then cooked them over the flame. The meat was black, stringy and disgusting, but had enough nutrients to keep the Jinian going.

Nine days had passed since Agrinoth defeated the flame wrock, and the giant's condition declined rapidly. Thanan unwrapped his burned and bitten legs to reveal his worst fear: Infection had set in, and there was no more medicine. The Jinian carefully cleaned the worst of the infected areas with his knife and rewrapped his brother's legs. There was nothing more he could do, only hope he could reach the end of the test before Agrinoth died. According to Thanan's reckoning, they had been in the darkness for two hundred thirty-two days. They were long overdue. *No one will be waiting,* he thought.

He set off again pulling the giant over the unforgiving stone, gritting his teeth with each step. He traveled in complete darkness because he could hold no torch, and felt as if some unseen hand was guiding his steps.

After some time, the tunnels became silent and cool, and Thanan relished the chance to rest his aching body and press his hands on the cold walls. The deep cuts from his own sword were not healing as they should. Over and over he held his hands on the cold wall until the rock warmed and then moved to a new spot. When he rested, he rinsed the blood-soaked rags that wrapped his hands and hung them over rocks to dry while he slept. Day after day he followed the same agonizing routine of dragging Agrinoth's dead weight through the blackness, stopping only to wash his bloody hands and tend to his brother.

"When will this end?" he muttered to himself, wincing with each pull. He scolded himself, remembering to be grateful he was yet alive and that he had the strength to pull his brother.

Many more days passed and to Thanan's surprise, Agrinoth regained consciousness, which bolstered his determination to press on. Although he could not walk, he offered what meager conversation he could, which was only a little better than the lonely drip. The giant held a glowing torch to light the way, and Thanan welcomed the illumination.

He tried to stand the giant up, but Agrinoth had lost all feeling in his feet and lower legs, and fell to the cave floor, frustrated by his enfeebled body. He roared from the pain as he crumpled to the floor.

Thanan cut the leather armor he wore into straps and tied them around Agrinoth's arms, which made it easier for him to pull his immense weight.

Agrinoth's thoughts reeled from the torment of his present situation, his mind clouded by sickness. *There will be no glory for me*, he thought to himself. *It would be better that I die as my brother in these forsaken caverns, than to emerge a beaten Goriath, crippled and scarred for all to pity. And this Jinian who plucked me from the furnace, can he be mightier than I?*

The candidates wore on, speaking less and less until Agrinoth fell unconscious once again.

The darkest of times came upon Thanan as he collapsed to the floor, unable to continue. No water had passed his lips for three days, and his body rejected his mind's desire to continue on. It was at this moment in the darkness, with his head against the cool wall, that he found himself looking at his bloody hands thinking he could not go on. He waited for some other part of his mind to offer a grateful thought, but none came. He closed his eyes and began to sing a song from his childhood, remembering his mother's soft voice as if she were there along side him comforting him with her words.

"Follow in my footprints, all across the sand.
Hear the ocean's roar
And you will understand.
The mighty towers white as pearl and the ocean's foam,
My son, it is your home…

This place, it is yours,
Now come and take my hand.
I'll lead you to the place
You call your land.
To the place you call your land.

The skies so deep you can see them in your dreams,
You can make this your world,
The fair meadows and the streams.
And then you can truly be free…
My son, if you only follow me.

This place, it is yours,
Now come and take my hand.
I'll lead you to the place
You call your land.
To the place you call your land.

Come with me, my little one, so dear.
Feel the gentle breeze.
You are with me, have no fear,
Of the dark dreams that stir your night.
My son, you are home, your strength, your might.

Agrinoth stirred and woke. "Please, Jinian, stop singing," he managed to whisper dryly.

"I didn't think you would wake again," Thanan replied, wiping his tears, grateful for the cloak of darkness.

"If I am going to die, your singing is not what I want to hear when I do." The tone of the giant's voice changed. "You know you have to leave me now."

"That will not happen. Don't ask this of me."

"You lack the strength to carry me any further. I have accepted my fate. You must go and save yourself."

"I just need to rest a bit. Please, say no more. Our journey is at an end. I can feel it," the Jinian insisted.

CHAPTER TWENTY-TWO

BROTHERHOOD

Thanan woke to a familiar smell of fried sowbelly and freshly baked biscuits hanging in the air. He thought he might be dead, but the blackness around him and the deep snoring coming from the smelly giant snapped him to reality.

"Agrinoth, wake up!" he exclaimed, kneeling over the giant. "Wake up!" He shook Agrinoth's shoulder, but could not wake him.

Jumping to his feet, he picked up the leather straps and started again down the tunnel, the smell of breakfast pulling him forward. His muscles were tight, and each step fell with burning pain. The tunnel made a sharp turn to the right and spilled into a room.

Thanan stopped and lit his torch. The flame revealed a large cavern with smooth black walls. Faint paintings of Goriath warriors in battle adorned the ceiling. It resembled Krokil Zil, but was much smaller. On the far wall, shafts of light sliced the darkness. Thanan fell to his knees and covered his face with his palms.

"We're here," he said quietly. "We're here." Then, grabbing Agrinoth's shoulder, the Jinian shouted, "Wake up! We made it!" But the giant did not move. Thanan shook him again, more violently than before.

"Leave me, Jinian. I told you, leave me here," Agrinoth whispered, delirious.

"You don't understand. We are here, we made it. Our journey is done," Thanan replied, overjoyed.

Thanan understood his brother's hesitation. It would be better to have died in the darkness than bear the shame of being pulled from the cave by a weaker Jinian. He knew of the glory that awaited his brother just outside the door, so he encouraged him again to stand.

"You need to stand now and walk out that door, brother." He grabbed Agrinoth, trying to sit him up, his massive weight almost too much for Thanan's weakened state.

"Leave me!" the giant shot back, flopping limply to the floor.

With both hands, Thanan heaved on Agrinoth's charred tunic. "Get on your feet, soldier!" The defiant warrior pulled away once again. Thanan brought his face uncomfortably close to Agrinoth's. "I will drag your crippled backside through that door and there is nothing you can do about it, you weak excuse for a Guardian! I pulled you this far!"

Thanan purposefully brought his fist down upon the giant's shoulder where the flame wrock had bitten him. Agrinoth shot his massive hand upward, grabbing Thanan firmly around the throat and began to squeeze. The Jinian gasped for air, gripping Agrinoth's wrist, trying to pry his hand off. A slight smile crept across his lips.

"That's right," he choked. "I knew I could get you moving, you pile of fangrix dung."

"Do not touch me again, Jinian, or I will kill you."

"You can kill me later, but we need to get through that door, now!" Thanan replied, refocusing the giant to the task at hand.

At last Agrinoth saw the slivers of light around the door. He grumbled and released Thanan's throat. He sat up, took Thanan's hand and pulled himself upright. The painted warriors from the past looked down upon the candidates with approval as they walked across the cavern toward the stone door. Thanan grasped a large hammer that hung from an iron ring and bashed it on the stone three times. He almost collapsed to the ground on the last swing.

Outside the stone door, a multitude had gathered at Krokil Gronik for the anticipated arrival of the three candidates. Their numbers had dwindled because the candidates were overdue by almost three months. The energy that once filled the cavern was gone, and more and more giants left for Hardrock and Whitehall as each day passed. Those who still clung to some hope that the candidates would return set up camps and burned their torches continuously, refusing to leave.

On the far side of the cavern, Kigron walked among the encampments, nodding to the various families as they cooked their morning meals. He hadn't been home in almost four months. He stopped and gathered firewood for an elderly couple who came to celebrate the candidates' arrival. It was at that time that he heard the chilling knocks echo through the cavern. He dropped the firewood and was almost afraid to command the opening in the fear that his Jinian friend would not be there.

Everywhere, giants ran to the door and began chanting.

Over the swelling sound, the captain's voice was heard, "Guards, remove the stone!" The guards heaved on the round stone with all their strength. The door slowly moved, grinding the wall behind it, deepening the ancient grooves. Kigron watched intently for the faintest sign of movement. "Physicians, be ready!" he ordered.

As the light spilled into the cave, loud gasps replaced the rhythmic chanting.

The first to emerge from the darkness was the mighty Agrinoth. He stumbled into the light of a hundred torches without the assistance of Thanan. His burned and bitten legs supported him only a few steps and then he collapsed, but it was enough.

Cheers and chanting broke out all over the hall, but when the light fell on Thanan's pale skin, a hush fell over the crowd. Thanan held his side with his blood-soaked hands and slowly walked through the crowd. He fell to his knees beside his brother, Agrinoth.

"Let it be known among all who now hear my words, that Agrinoth Jil defeated the mighty flame wrock," Thanan asserted. He held up a leather cord and from his palm he dropped the three flame stones from the flame wrock's tail. He placed the stones in his brother's palm and nodded.

The multitude exploded with cheers, and Agrinoth was carried away to the physician's tent to begin mending. As he went away, he looked at Thanan and nodded back.

"Get this candidate to the physician's tent at once!" Kigron commanded, gesturing toward Thanan.

Two soldiers escorted him to the tent where he promptly fell asleep for three full days.

The road to recovery was painful for Thanan, and the extent of his injuries was far more severe than he knew. Aside from all the ribs on his right side being broken, his jaw and nose has also been fractured some time ago. He surmised it was from the fall onto the stalactite in the glowing cavern, but in reality, he was not sure which horrible event was the cause. There were so many. A fractured wrist and ankle also plagued him for a while, and a horrible case of foot rot did not help matters either. Even though his plight was serious, his full recovery was realized fairly quickly.

His own injuries, however, did not matter much to him. As he rapidly regained his strength, he often heard the screams of a mighty giant as his leg was rebroken and set into its proper position or as the physicians' blades cut through Agrinoth's scarred tissue. Kromag, the general's physician, worked tirelessly mending Agrinoth's legs and shoulder, reconstructing the muscles and tendons with unbelievable skill. The damage the flame wrock inflicted upon the giant was extensive, and the physicians were surprised at how fast Agrinoth was healing from the wounds and many surgeries.

"He may even walk again," one physician was heard saying to the general as he made his way through the infirmary.

The agonizing hell that Agrinoth would endure over the next forty-five days made Thanan's injuries seem like a sprained thumb in comparison.

Throughout his excruciating recovery, around his neck, Agrinoth wore the triple stones that Thanan gave him. The stones brought him some unwanted celebrity as the peeking eyes of curious children frequently were shooed away from the infirmary. After all, the flame wrock was a legendary creature, and the only other Guardian candidate to ever kill one was Master Kizaga himself. This elevated Agrinoth's already high warrior status to an unparalleled level, and his recovery was the highest of priorities for the general's physicians. Every so often, Agrinoth would stop the guards from shooing the children and would invite them in. The children delighted in being in the presence of the famed Agrinoth and brought their wooden swords in the hope that he would scroll his name on the dull blades. He had them demonstrate some of their skills and then gave them instruction and sent them on their way. This was contrary to the warrior's character before his experience in the darkness.

In spite of his serious injuries, Agrinoth made a full recovery and went to report for duty, but not before he visited his great-great grandfather, Purgon.

Agrinoth heard the familiar ring of the blacksmith's hammer echo through the streets of Hardrock, and it was his first taste of normal life since he entered the dark cave so long ago. Giants everywhere gawked and gave him a wide berth as he walked by. The fame and glory he once imagined seemed of little importance to him now. He gently acknowledged the spectators and continued on his way. He entered the blacksmith's shop to discover it was Thanan's hammer he heard echoing over the cavern. He was busy hammering a glowing Zythera blade. The pale blacksmith looked up and saw his brother standing in the opening of the tent.

"I heard that you would be released today," Thanan said, plunging the blade into a bucket of oil.

"Where is my grandfather?" he replied, stepping into the tent.

"He left early, believe it or not. Said he might go fishing in the pool at Krokil Zulith. I'm not even sure he knows how to fish, but he said that I had everything firmly in hand here, and left. I'm sure he would welcome your visit."

"The general thought that swinging a hammer might do me some good and acclimate me back into normal life, but it's not helping." He turned and placed the blade back into the forge.

"We are different now, are we not?" the giant asked. "It is as if I am being called away, like I have no place here anymore."

"I feel it too, brother. However, I feel our callings might be quite different; but in the end, I'm sure we will understand the true purpose of these peculiar times we now live. You look well. The ceremony is in two days. Are you ready?"

"I have been waiting my entire life for this moment, but I imagined it much differently. I never thought that my brother would not share in this glory."

"I am truly sorry that Torik is not with you. Purgon was saddened greatly by the news. He is grateful that he still has one grandson left. He visited you many times, but each time you were sleeping. I'm sure he didn't know what to say."

Agrinoth sat on a wooden bench and looked at the glowing blade in the forge. "What is that?" he asked, pointing to the blade.

"I didn't want you to see this yet, but it's your new blade. The flame wrock sleeps with your old one. I figured you might need it for the ceremony. I started it as soon as I could swing a hammer again in the hopes I could finish it in time. Looks like it will be finished tomorrow. I used what was left of the Zythera dust. It wasn't a lot, but it was enough to get the job done. Purgon was keeping some for a rainy day."

"It doesn't rain in the underearth," Agrinoth replied with a rare smile.

"One day you'll thank me for bringing out your sense of humor, Agrinoth. It isn't as strong as the Zythera blades of old. I didn't have years to forge it, but it will do in a pinch. I'd be honored if you used it in the ceremony."

Agrinoth studied its workmanship. "It seems familiar."

"It looks exactly like your old one except for a one thing: My maker's mark will be on the blade. You never know, it might be worth something in a few years when I'm dead."

"If it is anything like the spear you forged, it will be legendary," Agrinoth chuckled.

"That was a piece of work, wasn't it? I wonder what the old hermit is doing right now?"

"Probably sitting down to a seven-course meal and talking to his lizard, happy and content as he can be." They both laughed at the imagined scene. Then they grew serious and quiet, knowing the secrets they must keep. They could never speak of the old hermit and his wondrous world. They had saved his life and in turn prevented the inevitable destruction of the Goriath race. No one would ever know, and they were happy to keep such a secret.

CHAPTER TWENTY-THREE

SACRED SIGN

The day of the ceremony had finally come, and Thanan felt some anxiety as he dressed for the occasion. Staring intently into the mirror over the washbasin, he tied his shoulder-length hair behind his head with a leather strap. He didn't want it getting in the way. The mirror's reflection revealed a body that looked nothing like it did when he began his training. Every inch of his torso, arms and legs rippled with hard muscle. He easily might be the strongest and fastest Jinian to ever walk Polizar, and surely was the deadliest. That knowledge didn't faze him as it might others, because covering his chiseled body were hundreds of painful memories, scars of the underearth, every one of them a lasting lesson. He saw his unparalleled strength and speed as an opportunity to exemplify gratitude, to be humble. There was nothing left to prove. He turned around, craning his neck to see his pale shoulder blade in the mirror. It was the place where he would bear the sign for the rest of his life.

Thanan finished dressing and met Kigron and his family outside their home. Together they walked through the garrison acknowledging the accolades of their growing entourage. Tavris and his sisters loved all the attention. The boy archer held his little sister's hand and his bow in the other, lifting it up and down in time to the rhythm of the chanting. Thanan didn't speak much as he walked through the heart of Hardrock; he only nodded respectfully and shook the occasional hand.

Thousands of soldiers and their families poured into the quarry from the outlying garrisons to celebrate the two new sacred appointments. Whitehall was well represented, and the vast crowd began to chant "Ki-za-ga...Ki-za-ga...Ki-za-ga." Tavris joined in the jubilant chant as he pushed his way to the front row. After all, who would prevent the captain's son from the best view? He looked up at his hero Thanan and chanted the Jinian's name, but no one heard. The thunderous sound reverberated off the quarry walls and rose to an echoing roar. Over and over they repeated the chant until the general stood and stretched out his hands to the crowd, silencing them.

The ceremony was simple and unpretentious, yet grand in its meaning. Picking up a sword with a black sash hanging from its hilt, General Tygrothian raised it over his head.

"I am pleased to present this sword to Agrinoth!"

The crowd began to roar with delight. Agrinoth was the obvious crowd favorite, and the cheering and celebrating continued for a minute and then suddenly stopped when the multitude noticed General Tygrothian standing with the second sword, black sash billowing, outstretched toward the audience. History was about to be made.

The expression on the general's face had changed from joyous to solemn. Although Thanan was generally accepted as a legitimate candidate to the Order, there was a loud gasp in the audience when his name was announced and then silence in the quarry for what seemed to be an eternity for the candidate. Thanan did not know what to do. He stayed seated for a moment and then slowly rose to his feet. A quiet murmur began to make its way through the crowd. The murmuring began to swell and soon there were giants applauding, booing, and yelling. The chaotic sound disrupted the ceremony and the general looked displeased with his people.

It seemed the decision to bestow this sacred position upon a Jinian was accepted by some and still rejected by others, with the Whitehallers proclaiming their opposition the loudest, shouting, "The Jinian has no place in the Order!" and "The Jinian is not worthy of such a position as this!"

Agrinoth looked at his people with contempt. He gripped the handle of his blade tightly, which bore the maker's mark of his brother, Thanan. He ran his finger over the mark and looked at Purgon. They shared the same contemptuous look. It seemed Agrinoth's grandfather had one more lesson to teach him.

"SILENCE!" Agrinoth yelled, pointing the tip of his blade toward the loudest of the dissenters.

The crowd was stunned and a hush came over the cavern.

"His name is Thanan of Jin, Son of Corderian, and he is my brother and your protector."

The crowd stood stunned, some were ashamed and lowered their eyes.

"And you will show the Guardian respect or so help me, you will know the savage nature of my disdain!"

No further words were spoken from the multitude, only uncomfortable glances exchanged by those who had been shamed. For a few moments, the only sound that was heard was that of the trickling waterways snaking through Hardrock, until a single applause came from the front row. Tavris, in his innocent youth, clapped for his hero, which then prompted a smattering of applause from the crowd. Soon, the applause swelled and spread like wildfire through the garrison.

At the command of the general, the two candidates took a knee and bowed before the people whom they now swore to serve and protect.

The general raised a glowing brand and turned to the audience. "These two you see before you will now carry the emblem of Kizaga, the sign of the Guardian!"

He pressed the iron into Agrinoth's hulking shoulder blade. His flesh sizzled and smoked. The Guardian made no expression of pain, only closed his eyes and exhaled through his nose.

It was now Thanan's turn. The general did not waver. He plunged the iron against the Jinian's shoulder blade. Thanan clenched his fist tightly around the hilt of his blade to endure the scorching pain as the smoking brand seared its way through his flesh. The smell of his own burning skin filled his nostrils. He stood with his Guardian brother and together they faced those they swore to protect and serve. The multitude bowed respectfully and the fullness of their responsibility fell upon them like a heavy mantle falling across their shoulders.

CHAPTER TWENTY-FOUR

UNEXPECTED RESCUE

"Time is running short," General Tygrothian began. "King Grishon's greed cannot be quenched, and his reign is at an end."

Captain Kigron, Agrinoth, Thanan, and a few other of the Order were present. They sat across from each other at the general's table in an undisclosed chamber in Hardrock. The secret summons had been delivered to the council that morning, before the general population woke and started about their work. Thanan observed that the seat at the general's left always sat empty. He still had never met all the active Guardians, but had heard many stories of their remarkable deeds throughout the world and their subversive skills within the ranks of the king.

"Word has found my ear," the general continued, "that King Grishon is planning to covertly remove his treasury to a secret location in the Mountains of Jeth, no doubt to join his military force with Haydon. The king has become increasingly brutal and is only taking those that he deems worthy to join with Lord Haydon, leaving the rest of the Goriath population – mostly the old, anyone not considered of pure bloodline, and those impoverished and alone – to fend for themselves."

"My operatives say that Haydon is becoming a powerful force in the Northwest," Kigron added.

"Kigron is correct," the general replied, scanning the council. "Prince Ky's guards also have been monitoring small caravans traveling northward toward the mountains, their carts bursting with gems. That treasure will go far in funding Haydon's cause."

"It is nothing compared to the king's treasury. We cannot allow that amount of wealth to get into Haydon's hands," Kigron interjected.

Agrinoth looked over at Thanan. "It is rumored he is raising a secret army to overthrow the king of Jin. Can this be done, brother?"

It was a difficult thing for Thanan to believe, that anyone, let alone the king's own son, would even conceive of conquering the greatest king who ever lived.

"It would take an enormous army, hundreds of thousands strong, to even have a chance of success. And even then it would be almost impossible. But I know Haydon, and he is nothing if not an extremely convincing politician," Thanan replied.

"Haydon is devilish, devious, and a skilled liar," Tygrothian interrupted. "He is very convincing when it comes to enlisting people in his cause. People who are otherwise good and honest are falling prey to his subtle lies, half-truths, and promises of wealth and prosperity. We cannot allow our wicked king, his army and vast wealth to join forces with Haydon. I am sure that even King Grishon will, in the end, regret his decision to join him."

Even knowing the general's words were true, Thanan was angered slightly to hear them.

In the following months, a plan was devised among the council to intercept the king's secret exodus from the Crystal City.

Much time came and went, all the while Thanan continued to fill his regimented schedule with intense training and crafting weapons that even Purgon didn't turn his nose up at. After a while, life in Hardrock seemed much like the life he once led in Jin, safe behind his city's gleaming walls. He now was respected and loved by most and was met by many happy greetings from the giants in the marketplace on his way to the shop.

"Please, try one of my fresh biscuits, Guardian!" a baker would exclaim, joyfully. "Just out of the oven!"

Or another would yell from across the market, "Guardian, may the spirit of Kizaga go with you!"

It was similar to the respect he was shown as a boy and as a youth, but this time it was not because of his lineage; it had been earned, and he felt some pride as he lived among these simple yet noble giants. They all had their place in society and contributed what they could. Thanan always accepted the gracious offerings of free goods, for it would be an insult to refuse.

Although included in sensitive meetings concerning the welfare of the Goriath giants and military business, Agrinoth and Thanan wondered why they were not sent out on any of the secret assignments the other Guardians were; but they trusted in their general's judgment and always upheld the higher code of the Guardian Order. After all, they were the newest Guardians and their chance would come.

The Guardian Order's purpose was plain to those who understood that the spirit is strong, but the flesh is weak. The Order was the trusted council of twelve that the general had put in place not only to do good and protect all races and creeds throughout the world, but to prevent one giant from ruling his people with a sword rather than reason.

The general knew of his own shortcomings and understood King Corderian's wisdom when he counseled Tygrothian centuries before to secretly create the Order. No mission or law given in Hardrock, Whitehall, or any of the outlying garrisons was enacted without the knowledge and wisdom of the Guardian Order, in council with the general and his two captains. And thus it had been since the inception of the Order.

"There are rumors being reported from the outlying garrisons involving giants starving to death and disease spreading through the Crystal City," Tygrothian said, beginning another council meeting.

"Something must be done, general," Xagrith spouted. "We have waited too long to take action. How many more must die at the hands of this king? I say we move on the capital now and not wait for the king to leave."

The general nodded his head. "What do you say, Kigron? Do

you think it wise to wage war there?"

"Xagrith speaks from his heart today. I too would like to spill the king's blood in the capital, but the cost would be too great. Thousands would die needlessly. No, General, it would not be wise to wage war in the capital. We must see our plan through. If the king wants to leave, let him leave, and we will seize the treasure."

The thought of attacking the capital, his first mission, was exciting to Thanan. He imagined the great Tygrothian entering the majestic hall in the heart of the capital, to take his rightful place and govern the city with honor, reuniting the once-divided people, bringing back prosperity and hope to those who were weak and betrayed. But he also understood the wisdom of separating the soldiers from the citizens.

As the briefing continued, the council heard a scuffle outside the general's quarters.

"I need to see the general," a voice demanded.

"We have orders to not let anyone inside," a guard replied.

"I need to speak with him immediately. Now move aside!"

"What is going on out here?" Captain Kigron shouted, staring down the two guards and Zorithian, who was one of the general's covert operatives in the Crystal City.

The guards held Zorithian by the arms as he struggled to escape. They were not aware of Zorithian's secret status as a spy and supposed he was a merchant, as he was dressed in the typical attire of a baker from the merchant district.

"What I have to tell the general is of great importance, Captain!" the operative exclaimed.

"Do you want us to take care of this problem, sir?" a guard asked, nodding his head and looking down the corridor into the blackness.

"Hmm," the captain grumbled, feigning indecision, concealing the spy's identity from the guards. "Release the baker. I would like to know what is so important that he would disturb the general while he is in council."

Inside the general's tent, Zorithian stood before the small council.

"General, please excuse the interruption," the spy began.

"Nonsense, Zor," Tygrothian replied plainly. "We will always hear what you have to say. Please continue."

"Thank you, sir. Not six days ago in the capital square there was a great commotion. A large group had gathered around the prison to see the spectacle. I broke through the crowd to see what the excitement was all about. There bound in chains were at least six of our spies among a large group of other civilians. I did not see them all, but I know they have the Guardians Grolis and Anax."

The council stirred. No one saw this coming.

"There were even a couple of Jinians in with them. Thieves I think. When I saw our operatives, I left immediately. They don't know who the spies are yet, but they will find out, and when they do, they will uncover our plot to stop the king from moving the treasury."

Xagrith pushed himself from the table. "General, we need to move immediately. They will torture everyone in there. The king will root out our spies. Even if they do not break them and uncover our plot, they will be tortured to death if only because they were suspected."

"Grolis and Anax will not break," Kigron said with confidence.

"But the four others will, Captain. They are just informants like

Zorithian here. They will break, and months of planning will be for nothing."

Everyone around the table was silent, waiting for the general to speak.

"Was Krim among them?" Tygrothian asked, breaking the silence.

"No, sir. His cover is still intact. He will be the one leading the interrogations, I'm sure."

"Do you think Krim can get them out without being detected?"

"No, General. Everyone is being watched, even Krim. The king has already tripled his security. I think it is only a matter of time before they discover who Krim is."

"I agree with Xagrith," Kigron said plainly. "We need to get our people out of there now."

"Although I would very much enjoy storming the prison," Agrinoth chimed in, "we need to think this through."

"Overwhelming force is not the answer here," Tygrothian replied.

"They are not going to simply open the prison doors for us, General," Xagrith shot back.

The brilliant tactician went to work. Everyone could see the general working it out in his mind. "You say there are two Jinian prisoners in with them?"

Thanan's attention piqued even more and he began to stand up.

The spy gulped down a cup of water, breathing heavily. "An older man, a merchant, and a younger woman, his daughter I think. They looked as if they had been beaten and starved for many months, maybe even years before they were brought to the main prison. I never saw them before six days ago. They must have been locked up in the king's private dungeon. He reserves the dungeon for the most grievous of acts. The guards spoke about cheating the king out of some rare frags."

"First of all, are you compromised, Zor?" Tygrothian continued, turning to the spy.

"No sir. My cover remains intact. I am merely a baker on Main Street."

"Your little disturbance outside was not exactly covert, Zor," Kigron added.

"Yes, Captain, I am aware of my unorthodox arrival, but there is no time. There is talk about an execution seven days from now."

"Zor, how many weeks do we have until King Grishon leaves with the treasure?"

"Krim passed word to me that the exodus will be on the Tenth Day of Xolis…five months from now, when the rivers are at their lowest. They won't risk crossing the rivers and losing the treasure in high water."

Nodding his head, the general, in his typical manner, made the decision quickly. "The Jinian prisoners are the key to opening the doors of the prison. The timing will be most crucial. Thanan, you will leave tomorrow and assume the persona of a wealthy merchant from Jin. There is only one thing that will stop the interrogations and get Krim away from the prison: The opportunity to make money. The king will want his best negotiator there. Agrinoth will escort you as far as the Crag Path and wait for your return."

Thanan smiled slightly, admiring the general's genius. "Yes, General."

"Zor."

"Yes, General."

"Can you get the Guardians into the city and close to the prison unnoticed?"

"Yes, General. I believe I can, if they enter from the northeast tunnel. I will need a day, but I can find suitable mining attire for them. I will hide it in a side tunnel a mile outside the city. They can slip in with one of the mining crews. Security will be light in the tunnels because of the interrogations at the prison."

"All right then. Xagrith, you will lead your team into the capital. Krim will clear the guards when he leaves for the treasury."

"How will we get into the prison?"

Tygrothian turned, looking at Thanan. "That is where Thanan comes in. You must be convincing enough to negotiate the release of the Jinians. Can you do this?"

"Yes, General."

"Zorithian, make your way back as fast as you can and get word to Krim. You know what to tell him."

"Yes, sir."

Standing up from his chair, General Tygrothian scanned the room confidently. "Not since the days of Kizaga has there been more noble a council than this. May the master's spirit go with us all. Dismissed."

Xagrith, Jorik, and Syzimian returned to their homes and made ready for the trek to the capital while Kigron and Agrinoth went to work on Thanan's disguise. They commissioned the help of the best tailor in Hardrock to sew the clothing of a wealthy Jinian merchant. Thanan thought it best that the clothing look like it was purchased from the affluent region of Tronis. They were not concerned that Thanan would be recognized by any of the soldiers in Crystal City, because his appearance was drastically different from when he had entered the caves so long ago. His hair was long and almost white. The hue of his skin was pale and bluish. Only those who were closest to him would recognize the Jinian now. With the addition of the perfect disguise, it was impossible to know who he was, except a wealthy traveling merchant who was anxious to deal with the best negotiators in the business, the Goriath giants.

Thanan appeared from the back of the tailor's shop.

"I do not even know who you are, brother," Agrinoth said, looking Thanan over from head to toe. "It was bad enough you were a Jinian in Guardian's clothes, but now you are a Guardian in—," the warrior paused for a moment. "—Well, I do not know what this is."

Kigron laughed at Agrinoth's momentary loss for words.

"I believe what you are trying to say is that I'm one handsome Jinian," Thanan said, looking at his reflection in the tailor's mirror.

"Well, since I only know one Jinian, I will have to take your word for it," Agrinoth shot back.

"All right," Kigron interrupted, with all seriousness. "What is your name, Jinian? What is your business here?"

Without missing a beat, the phony merchant replied, "I am Rolfus Dartmouth. I have traveled very far to do business with your king. Surely he has heard of the great riches in my land, the Havenshore Province of Tronis."

Agrinoth, testing the Jinian further, shot back, "Listen, you pretentious peddler. I could kill you now and take your money."

"Do not pretend you have any power here, you blue rabble," Thanan said calmly, staying in character. He pushed Agrinoth's sword aside with his palm. "What would your king say if he discovered that you killed someone with my wealth and connections, preventing him from gaining all he can? Now take me to your king."

Kigron and Agrinoth stood there in silence for a moment.

"I think he is ready," the captain said, grabbing Thanan's shoulder.

"Let us go, brother. I will escort you through the secret tunnels to the Crag Path."

"Please, call me Rolfus," Thanan replied with pretention.

"He is all yours," the captain said, laughing.

With his satchels filled with jewels and gold and a small dagger hidden in his boot, Thanan followed Agrinoth through the secret caves that would drop them just outside the main entrance to the Goriath city.

The three-day trek was uneventful for the most part, except for Agrinoth's nerves being tested by Thanan's insistence that he stay in character the entire time.

"I know, Agrinoth. How about we tell them I captured you in the valley, while you were indisposed. And now you are my servant?" Agrinoth remained silent, clenching his jaw. "Or, wait a moment," the Jinian continued in his assumed voice. "How about...you were sold to me by a Goriath orphanage when you were young. Your parents abandoned you because you were deaf, dumb, and mute?"

"That is enough, Thanan," Agrinoth finally said, exasperated.

"I am Rolfus Dartmouth and will not tolerate insubordination, Giant!"

"Hmph," Agrinoth grumbled, not able to win.

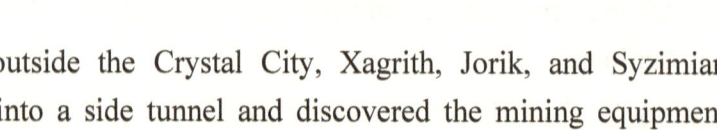

Just outside the Crystal City, Xagrith, Jorik, and Syzimian stepped into a side tunnel and discovered the mining equipment and clothes that Zorithian promised. Their journey through the tunnels had been easy, having to only slip by a few patrols. It seemed that Zorithian was correct about the lightened security.

"Quick, put these on," Xagrith whispered. He threw a pair of dusty trousers with holes in the knees at Jorik.

"Hope they fit," he replied sarcastically, sizing them up against his legs.

Syzimian knelt down and grabbed a pick that was leaning against the wall. "I can't believe they are going to let us walk into the city with these." He swung it with authority through the air.

"Remember, in and out. No mess. That's the plan. We don't kill anyone unless we have to," Xagrith reminded him.

"Everything's a little tight," Jorik interrupted, twisting at the waist and bringing his arms forward, trying to loosen up the clothes. He swung the leather pack over his back and ripped the seams under his armpits. "There…that's better."

With their lanterns lit and picks in hand, they entered the tunnels, hoping to join up with one of the remote crews headed home from a long shift of mining.

On the opposite side of the mountain, Thanan and Agrinoth came to the exit, which was hidden from the main cave. Agrinoth explained that the main entrance to the Crystal City was only a short distance away.

"Remember, be deliberate and calm," Agrinoth reminded Thanan.

The intense morning light poured into the cave. The sun's intensity hurt Thanan's eyes. He tipped his hat to shade his face from the blinding beams. As he stepped outside onto the Crag Path, the warm light enveloped him. Looking up at the galaxy-filled sky, he squinted and filled his lungs with the old world he once knew. Except for his hands and face, he was covered from head to toe in his merchant's disguise. He noticed for a moment that his fingers tingled a bit, like they had fallen asleep, but with the task at hand, he didn't pay much attention.

With another deep breath, he said with a confident smile, "If all goes well, brother, I'll see you soon. Hopefully, we won't be running. And just think: You will then know three Jinians."

"Yes…you and two criminals. It is my lucky day."

The pretend wealthy merchant walked slowly up the Crag Path, truly not knowing what would happen once he reached the cave entrance. He did know one thing, however: He would be met with intimidation, which was a common negotiating tactic for Goriaths. He was at the last bend in the path when he looked down at his perfectly authentic costume. The leather sleeves were shining in the sun and the cloth was unstained. *This is too perfect*, he thought to himself.

He quickly looked around the rocky landscape for a solution. Kneeling down, he grabbed a handful of dirt and rubble from the path and ground it into his clothes, dulling the fabric. Next he removed his hat and thrashed it upon the stone cliff. Finally satisfied that he looked the part, he walked around the bend, revealing himself to the guards in the distance. He did not see them at first, but he knew they were there, camouflaged to look like the rocky backdrop. It was a longtime Goriath tradition to use those who could camouflage themselves best to guard the cave entrance. Kigron had told Thanan that there were only a few Goriaths left who could conceal themselves this way and it was a regressive trait that regrettably even Kigron did not pass to his children.

As the merchant closed in on the cave entrance, from the shadows a voice commanded, "State your name and what your business is here, Jinian!"

"Good giant," the fake merchant said in a perfect Shorehaven accent. "I have traveled many weeks to trade with the greatest negotiators in this land. Will you entertain an offer?"

"I do not do business with Jinians," the voice from the darkness shot back.

"Perhaps I am speaking with the wrong giant. Perhaps I need to speak with a more experienced negotiator," Thanan replied arrogantly.

Then, like an apparition revealing itself, the guard appeared before Thanan, sword in hand. He pointed the tip at the Jinian's nose and walked intimidatingly toward him.

"Perhaps," the guard shot back sarcastically, trying to imitate the merchant, "I should kill you where you stand!"

He grabbed Thanan by the shoulder of his outer coat and feigned stabbing him.

"Such a temper," Thanan said calmly, staring down the tip of the sword. "What will your king say when he finds out you killed someone who can make him quite rich? I would tell you my name, but I feel it would be wasted on someone like yourself."

Thanan reached in his pocket and flipped a gold coin to the guard. "Now go, fetch me someone who understands how to negotiate and quit wasting my time."

It was all the guard could do to restrain himself from stabbing Thanan, but the intrigue of the merchant was too good to resist. The ruse worked.

"Wait here, Jinian." The grumbling guard turned into the dark tunnel. "You two, fetch the negotiator."

As if by magic, two guards appeared against the wall and emerged into the light.

They had been there the entire time and though Thanan never knew for certain, he assumed they might be. "But, sir, he asked to not be disturbed."

"Don't question my orders! Get the negotiator now!"

"Yes, sir," they shot back in unison.

"This will take a while, Jinian," the guard sneered, almost smiling. "Sorry we do not have any chairs."

The two guards glared at Thanan and disappeared into the cave.

Deep in the heart of the mountain, the mining crews straggled into the city, never suspecting three Guardians had infiltrated them. They made small talk with a crew of dusty miners and even promised to get a drink at the local tavern, once they cleaned up.

The dusty Guardians strolled down the street completely undetected. The capital streets were alive with chatter and footsteps. Hundreds of giants walked throughout the city square, busy about their business.

Jorik looked up at the majesty of Xavantha. He had never seen the Crystal City before.

Xagrith noticed Jorik's moment of awe. "You've seen Xavantha a thousand times, brother," he whispered.

Jorik quickly composed himself. "How long do we have to wait?"

"An hour or two. Maybe more. For all we know, Thanan is already dead and Krim has been arrested."

Syzimian sat down on a bench and dusted off his boots, looking indirectly toward the prison. "No, I don't think anything like that has happened. Everything seems quiet. If Krim had been arrested, there would be mayhem right now. And I don't think anyone could kill Thanan; do you?"

"Good point," Xagrith replied, dusting his boots off. "We have a good view of the main gate from here. Let's rest a while and not bring any attention to ourselves." He propped his boot up on his thigh, revealing his big toe where the sole had worn through. "Where did Zor get these clothes?" he asked, quickly putting his boot on the ground.

"Three dead miners, I suppose. Look...I count fifteen guards at the gate."

"Those are just the ones we can see," Xagrith replied, looking through the passersby. "I think we can count on at least ten more in the prison."

Syzimian scanned the north wall. "Something's happening. Two more guards are coming. This could be it."

The three Guardians casually watched as the soldiers approached the main gate. The gate itself was black and pitted, towering twenty feet over their heads. Within the structure of the gate was a smaller door, where everyone entered and exited. The soldiers only exchanged a few words with the prison guard and he promptly unlocked the gate, letting one of the soldiers through.

Moments later, Krim emerged. With the wave of his hand, the gate was locked behind him and the fifteen guards left for their homes, leaving just one guard at the main gate and an unknown number inside.

Xagrith clenched his fist in silent celebration.

"Thanan must have made it. Krim is leaving," Syzimian whispered. "Now we just wait for him to bargain for the Jinians."

Just then a young peddler about the age of thirteen passed by, carrying a basket of rolls from the bakery. "Fresh bread and rolls for sale!" he called out. "Fresh rolls here! Just three flecks for one or one frag for two!" The boy stopped in front of the bench, blocking Xagrith's view.

"Move along, boy. We don't want any of your bread today," Xagrith said, craning his neck around the boy.

"They are fresh from the oven. Are you sure you don't want to try one?" He held a golden brown roll to his nose and sniffed deeply, then offered it to Xagrith.

"Yes, I am sure. Now move on."

The boy stepped sideways, landing in front of Jorik, blocking his view of the prison. "And how about you, sir. Would you like to try one of these special rolls?"

"No, son. Take your basket somewhere else."

"Are you sure? My father just made them. He discovered the *key* to making the softest bread. You might say he *unlocked* the secret to the best bread in the city."

Syzimian, half listening, finally realized what was going on. "I'll take one, boy. Give your father our best."

"That will be four frags."

"Four?" Xagrith spouted. "You just said two."

"This one's heavy, sir. It had to bake a long time."

The Guardian paid the boy and sent him on his way.

Syzimian darted his eyes about, making sure nobody saw the transaction. He tore into the roll and gave half to Jorik. Crumbs rained down on Jorik's lap. He brushed them to the ground. Inside the roll was a key, rusted and pitted.

"It's too small to be the key to the main gate," Xagrith said under his breath.

"It must be the cell key," Syzimian replied, palming the key and pushing it down his trouser pocket.

"How did Zorithian get a key to the prison cells?" Jorik asked.

"Maybe Krim passed it to him somehow."

"Maybe Krim doesn't know about the key at all. Zorithian may be leading us into a trap. The guards could be simply waiting for us to enter the prison and identify our own spies for them."

"That's enough," Xagrith hushed. "We must trust the plan. The general knows what he's doing, and so does Krim. Zor has risked everything for us. Let's not forget that."

Thanan huffed loudly and kicked a small stone down the darkened tunnel. "I'm growing impatient with you giants," the fake merchant lied. "Where is this so-called negotiator? He's kept me waiting for an hour."

"I've had enough of you, Jinian! Shut your mouth."

"Is this how you treat all your guests? Where I come from, we are at least civilized enough to offer a cup of water, a chair to sit in. But…I guess this is what is expected from cave-dwelling folk."

The guard raised his sword and started for Thanan. "I don't care who you are. I'm going to kill you now!"

"What is going on here?" a new voice shouted sharply from the darkness.

The incensed guard halted in his tracks, his blade only inches from Thanan's throat. "This Jinian has insulted me with his quick tongue for the last time. I'm going to cut it out!"

A noble-looking Goriath walked into the sunlight. His red and white tunic and robes were finely appointed. Gold threads were embroidered down the length of the sleeves in the image of a serpent eating a crystal. Thanan was not surprised by the image, for the Goriaths had worshipped many idols throughout their long history.

"Ah…now you look like a Goriath who knows how to do business. Good Giant, perhaps you might entertain a wealthy merchant from Shorehaven?"

"I am Krim, King Grishon's personal advisor and head negotiator," he said calmly, walking around the supposed merchant. "You will have to excuse Grimkil here. He is a little twitchy from all the unpleasantness that our last Jinian merchants caused. And who might you be, sir?"

"I would feel more comfortable without a sword at my throat."

"You will answer my questions, Jinian, or I will let my friend here finish what he started and throw your corpse over the cliff."

"With all due respect…Krim, is it?" Thanan replied,

condescendingly. "You don't want to kill me. Not before your king hears what I have to offer. Now, put your spry hound on a leash and take me to your king."

Krim played his part to perfection. He paused for a moment and commanded Grimkil to release the merchant and follow him into a place where no Jinian, until recently, had gone for hundreds of years: the king's private negotiating chamber.

Entering the cavern, Thanan looked back to see another guard's silhouette appear at the mouth of the cave. Another guard had been there the whole time, hidden in plain sight and waiting to ambush Thanan had the need arisen. The warm light from outside the cave faded and gave way to the cool light of flickering blue torches that hung from their iron rings every few feet. The sound of gold coins clanking in Thanan's satchel echoed in the void tunnel. They walked for some time. Thanan was surprised at the plainness of the walls, but as the tunnel turned to the right, Thanan's surprise turned to awe.

There before him, a city beyond imagination opened to his view. He stepped outside the tunnel, which overlooked the entire Crystal City.

"Quite something, isn't it?" Krim noted.

"I have no words," the merchant replied.

"No time for sightseeing, I'm afraid. We need to go now," the king's advisor urged, pointing down a winding path, spiraling its way down to the cavern floor.

"Are we going down there?"

"Not unless you want to get yourself killed. No, we are headed over there," Krim replied, pointing to the opposite side of the cavern.

Thanan looked over the vastness of the cavern, the bottom of the Xavantha Crystal looming just overhead, illuminating the entire city. Like a sea of organized scorch beetles, tens of thousands of Goriath giants scurried across the cavern floor about their business. Directly across the expansive opening, Thanan saw a brightly lit archway that in his estimation must have stood sixty feet high and twenty-five feet wide.

"We call it the King's Arch," Krim said, interrupting Thanan's thoughts.

As they walked toward the king's chamber, they passed only a few who shot unusual glances at the oddly dressed merchant, but said nothing, nodding respectfully to Krim. Only a small number of Goriaths were allowed on the upper level for obvious security reasons, but Krim seemed to have full reign.

"You must be a very important giant," Thanan said, still taking in the city. "Have we met before?"

"If we had," Krim said, "you never would have known."

"You're that good, huh?"

"In truth, we have met two times before."

"That's not possible," Thanan replied, dumbfounded by the unusual giant's statement.

"No, what is not possible is that I have concealed my identity as a Guardian from King Grishon for twenty-seven years."

"So Krim is not your true name?" Thanan asked quietly, putting the puzzle together in his head. "What is it?"

"I only tell you this now because I will be leaving the Crystal City with you today. My name is Azoth Xor."

Thanan stopped in disbelief and looked into the advisor's eyes, squinting as if trying to see through his disguise. His mind went back to the council chair that sat empty next to the general.

"By your pale expression, I see you have heard of me," Krim continued, looking at the Jinian's face more than his eyes.

Thanan feigned a smile at Krim's double meaning.

"Many think you are dead."

"Oh, I am very much alive, Jinian. In fact, we met in the town square once before, the merchant courtyard, to be more precise, when you first arrived at Hardrock. You looked quite distressed. Do you remember what I told you?"

"Uh…no," Thanan replied, trying to remember.

"I told you that you would make a powerful Guardian. And I was correct."

Thanan's mind reeled. Could it be that the old giant from the courtyard all those years ago was really Azoth Zor?

"I have been the trusted eyes and ears of the general for a long time. Watching in plain sight."

Krim confidently approached the King's Arch as he had done thousands of times before, but this time, escorting a Jinian merchant by the name of Rolfus Dartmouth.

They walked through the arch with an arrogant stride, paying no heed to strange looks from the treasurers who sat behind large stone tables counting the day's take. Negotiations took place at the entrance to the Crystal Caverns, except for rare occasions when the king would personally negotiate in his private chambers with those who offered something exceptional.

As they approached the door of the king's chamber, they encountered two soldiers wearing red armor. It was more ornamental in its design and function than typical armor.

"Just follow my lead," the spy uttered under his breath.

"Kyloraz, Shimioth," he said with confidence, "I am taking this Jinian to the king for a private matter. Open the doors."

"But, sir, he's a Jinian!" Kyloraz replied, moving his Zythera blade in front of the door.

It took only a menacing look from Krim and the guard stepped back, opening the doors.

"Forgive me, sir. It won't happen again," Kyloraz said, lowering his eyes submissively.

The haughty merchant followed Krim closely through the threshold, looking the guards up and down. He arrogantly flipped a gold coin at Kyloraz, saying nothing.

The king's chamber sat amidst the first vein of Zythera crystals discovered in the caverns when Goriath the First entered the caves so long ago. In fact, the chamber itself was chiseled from a single Zythera crystal with the king's throne beautifully rising from the middle of the chamber. Zino, the great city architect, said the gods of the underearth inspired him when he conceived the design. The walls of the chamber glowed a ghostly blue and green. There were beautiful artifacts and art perfectly appointed around the room, no doubt collected throughout the centuries from all over the world. With the obvious quality and quantity of the treasures, Thanan surmised that Goriath kings usually wound up on the upside of most negotiations.

Thanan watched as Krim stepped up to a waist-high pillar of glowing crystal and took from its center a metal mallet, using it to strike the pillar's top; sending out a beautifully harmonic tone that reverberated throughout the chamber, then subsided quickly. Thanan looked around in amazement.

From the back of the chamber, a door opened and out walked a peculiar-looking giant. He was clothed in ornate robes and was shorter than most Jinians. His eyes shifted rapidly around the chamber as if to ascertain the security of the room. The odd giant limped forward and spoke in a high-pitched voice.

"What is it, Krim? Why do you bother the king at this time?"

"Do we really need to do this every time, Fralix?" Krim asked, exasperated.

"Do not be short with me, Krim! I have been here a long time," Fralix shot back.

"Too long, I'd say."

"I will remember you said that, Krim!" the odd giant spat, shaking his finger at Krim's face.

"No, you won't. We will do this all over again tomorrow. Just like we do every day. Now go inform the king that I am here with an opportunity."

"Who do we have here?" Fralix queried, ignoring the king's advisor. "You are a strange-looking giant," he continued, squinting his eyes, examining the visitor.

"Let's not waste anymore of this merchant's time, Fralix. Please get the king so we can begin our business."

"All right, all right!" Fralix shot back. He walked away muttering to himself about impatient giants and something about bath time.

The merchant, containing his laughter, looked at Krim.

"Is he…" Thanan paused for a moment, thinking of the least offensive word for this situation, "…diminished?"

"That was Fralix, the king's uncle. Even with all the king's failings, he doesn't have the heart to let him go. That probably is his only redeeming trait. Fralix was once the best negotiator in the city. He is responsible for acquiring many of the artifacts and treasures you see here. His mind began to cloud a few years ago. He only remembers me because I was here before he started slipping away. And so, every day we do this dance."

"And what of the prisoners? Are they still alive?" Thanan asked quietly.

"Now is not the time. This has to be handled delicately."

The sound of the king's door opening stopped Krim's explanation short. Fralix entered first, followed by King Grishon. The king was portly and slow, swaying as he walked, as if each foot alone couldn't take his weight for too long. No one ever knew if he was smiling because his jowls hung so heavily on his cheeks. His gaudy robes dragged across the crystal floor as he wobbled to his throne. Making himself comfortable, he looked over his chamber and cleared his throat for a few uncomfortable seconds.

"Great King," Fralix began in his unusual voice, "Krim has brought someone who wants to bathe with the king."

"That will be all, Fralix," King Grishon stated, dismissing his uncle with unwavering patience. "Why have you brought a Jinian into my chamber? And a very odd-looking one at that. It seems we have a Jinian infestation as of late...don't you think, Krim? Speak now, or this Jinian will pay dearly. His stink is defiling my chamber."

"Of course, you may do with him as you wish, king, but he claims to be quite wealthy and connected. He may be of interest to you. Maybe help secure those shipping routes for you know who."

"Hmm...what is your name, Jinian?"

"Good King, I am Rolfus Dartmouth from the Havenshore Province of Tronis. Perhaps you have heard of me?"

"I do not care about Jinian merchants. Do you, Krim?"

"Of course not, your majesty," Krim replied, taking Thanan by the arm. "Shall I have him thrown over the edge into the city or over the cliffs into Loriam? I prefer the city. They fall further."

"That is what I love about you, Krim: loyalty," the king chuckled, his jowls jiggling like pudding.

"I am quite well known among businessmen and merchants all along the coastal region from Tronis to Jin. And some of them, shall I say, are less reputable than others." The merchant deliberately adjusted his satchel, causing the coins to jingle. "But if the king hasn't heard of me, I'll take my business elsewhere."

"I never said I had not heard of your dealings. What I said was, I do not care," the king replied, falling prey to Thanan's trap of vanity. "What is it you want, Jinian?"

"Raw zil ore," Rolfus said plainly. "Word has reached my ear of its rarity and unexpected qualities. There is profit to be made in rare ores, especially those that no one has ever seen."

"And what do you have for me that is worth the ore that you seek?" the king replied, appearing interested.

The merchant removed one of the satchels from his shoulder and handed it to Krim. The advisor bounced the satchel in his hands, demonstrating its weight as he carried it to the king.

King Grishon poured a portion of the contents into his palm.

"Is this it? A few gold coins from Jin."

"Not just a few, King. This is only a taste of what I can bring to your table." The merchant opened the second satchel and spilled it on the floor. Hundreds of glimmering gems bounced across the crystal chamber.

The king's eyes brightened for a moment, and then he chuckled.

"Krim...this Jinian is quite a showman, but I am not yet convinced."

"What more could I do to convince you, your majesty?" Rolfus asked, knowing the answer.

"What of these shipping routes? And do not play with me, Jinian."

"Ah, now that will take more than a little zil ore, your majesty," the merchant replied, leading the king.

"Look around you, merchant. I am prepared to make you a wealthy man. What guarantees do I have that you can deliver what you promise?"

"My reputation precedes me. Even you, great King Grishon, said that you have heard of me," Rolfus said confidently, using the king's words.

"Ten percent of my treasury for unchecked access to shipping routes from Tronis to Jin. I truly do not care about your Jinian gold. You can have it back." The king threw the satchel to Rolfus, the coins clanking as it smacked his palm. "Leave the jewels. They go well with my chamber. Let us call it...a deposit."

"No less than twenty percent," the merchant shot back. "And you can keep the gold. I have plenty." Rolfus tossed the satchel onto the floor before the throne.

King Grishon tensed his jaw and his jowls quivered with anger. He glared at Rolfus and tapped his fingers nervously on his throne. The merchant stared back, showing no sense of hesitation.

"And when shall I receive confirmation that your shipping negotiations have succeeded?"

"Six months. Simply name the place and time. I'm sure you and your new associate will be well pleased with my results," Rolfus replied with confidence.

"Fine. Six months from now you will meet me at the Great Divide. Do you know the place I speak of?"

"I know it well, your majesty," the merchant nodded.

"Fifteen percent. No more!" Grishon continued his negotiation with a shout.

"I'm sorry I've wasted your time, your majesty," Rolfus replied, turning away from the king.

"Wait!" Krim announced. "I might know of something that could help us come to an agreement. May I approach, your majesty?" Krim walked to the side of the throne and whispered something in King Grishon's ear. The king, appearing intrigued, pursed his lips, looking more like a fat fish than a Goriath. He nodded his head in agreement.

"How long have you been traveling, merchant?" Krim asked from beside the throne.

"For some time now. I have not been to Tronis in over two hundred days," Rolfus lied.

"And you travel alone? No companions to speak of?"

"I find it's better that way. No one to answer to…no one spending your money."

"Oh, I am not speaking of willing companionship," the king interrupted. "Maybe someone to ease the burden while you travel…fill your lonely nights?"

Thanan's stomach turned at the king's proposal, but he said nothing. He only raised one eyebrow with interest. The king cleared his throat and nodded to Krim.

"Guards!" Krim commanded. "Fetch the Jinian prisoners."

"Jinians?" Rolfus asked. "I had not heard Goriaths were in the slave trade business."

"Slaves! Bah, not enough profit in it," King Grishon balked. "No, these Jinians found themselves on the wrong side of a bad bargain. Please have a seat while we wait." The king moved his fingers ever so slightly, gesturing to Rolfus to sit.

"Fralix! Bring our guest and Krim some refreshment," he barked.

Fralix placed a crystal platter of sweet cakes and dried fruits in the center of the table.

Thanan eyed the food, noticing the quality was better than he normally saw in Hardrock. "Now this is what I expected from the best negotiator in the land."

"Please eat, Rolfus. I have these brought up fresh from the city every day, sometimes twice." King Grishon plucked up a glistening sweet cake with his sausage fingers and tossed it in his mouth. "Mmm…I think I'll have another."

No wonder he looks the way he does, Thanan thought.

As they waited for the arrival of the prisoners, they talked casually about anything but business, which was proper etiquette at this point in any successful Goriath negotiation. Thanan told stories about his glorious adventures in strange lands and flattered King Grishon when he said that it was the great Goriath king that he wanted to do business with the most.

Only the head guard stood at the gate, wide-eyed and ever vigilant. The three Guardians sat on the bench quietly watching the jail for any sign of a trap. All was quiet.

Syzimian glanced around, looking a little worried. "We need to find a way to get closer to the main gate without being suspected of anything."

At that moment, a burst of laughter rang out over the crowd, and Xagrith smiled slyly. "I think it's time we met up with our miner friends and got that drink we were promised, brother…maybe cause a ruckus. Jorik, you stay and keep an eye out for the guards. We can't let that gate shut before Syzimian gets in. Our timing will have to be perfect."

"What do you intend to do?" Jorik asked, still watching the prison gate.

"Let us worry about that. You just make sure that you punch Syzimian hard enough to start the brawl."

Jorik cracked his knuckles, smiling at Syzimian. "Not a problem."

"Just don't hit my nose. It's been broken too many times as it is. Aim for the jaw."

The tavern was obnoxiously loud. Drinking songs and foul arguing filled the Guardians' ears as they approached. The entrance was nothing more than an archway roughly cut in the rock, and the echoing sounds amplified as they entered.

The tunnel was lined with glowing blue torches, flickering violently in a strong breeze coming from the tavern. The tunnel opened into a large room, which still had small veins of zil running through the walls. The ore sparkled and danced in the torchlight.

"Haven't seen you two in here before!" a giant shouted above the loud conversation. "That will be twenty frags each, and leave those with me." The bouncer pointed to their mining picks.

They each paid and handed over the picks. Xagrith and

Syzimian both surveyed the tavern, looking for the mining crew with which they had entered the city. The cavern was electric with activity. They watched both men and women numbing their minds and bodies with strong drinks, making fools of themselves, while the establishment milked them for all they had.

Snaking their way through the drunkenness, they heard boos and cheers from dozens of giants who were gathered around frag-covered tables, betting away their day's wage on the off chance they might win big.

Xagrith lifted his chin in the direction of the cheering mining crew. Syzimian nodded and cut through the crowd.

"Look who made it," an inebriated miner slurred. He held up his drink. It sloshed over the edge onto the floor. "We thought you forgot about us. Everybody…look who's here!" The rowdy miners cheered the Guardians' arrival and placed more bets. "Get these two a drink!"

"Wait, where's your friend? I thought was three of you," another miner slurred from across the table, holding four fingers up.

"I'm afraid we had to part ways. We told our friend that we enjoyed your company so well we decided we wanted to join the red crew. He didn't take it very well, said he'd rather mine with the women than with the red crew."

The miners shouted their distaste for Jorik and raised a toast to the red crew.

For thirty more minutes, Xagrith and Syzimian whipped the miners up against Jorik; then finally Xagrith spotted Jorik at the tavern entrance. He nodded. The appointed time had arrived.

Xagrith pounded his fist against the table, sending frags

bouncing in the air. "We should do something. Make him pay for his insults?"

"Where is this friend of yours?" the miner asked, stumbling over his words.

Xagrith lowered his drink. "Most likely sleeping by now. Why? What do you have in mind?"

"What do you think, boys? Should we show him why you don't mess with the red crew?"

The miners collected their frags and downed the last of their drinks, spilling most of the liquid down their chins and onto their dusty tunics. Xagrith and Syzimian set their drinks down, not having had a single sip.

"All right, let's go!" Xagrith yelled. They all cheered and pushed their way through the crowd toward the entrance. The Guardians collected their picks as they exited.

Outside the tavern, Jorik walked as fast as he could along the northern wall, doing his best to blend into the crowd. He shadowed the approaching guards. They talked amongst themselves, never spotting the tracking Guardian.

Kyloraz and Shimioth reached the gate. "Krim needs the Jinian thieves," Shimioth ordered, rapping his knuckles on the bars. "Hurry up about it. The request comes directly from the king."

"It will be a few minutes. Wait here," the prison guard replied.

Jorik searched the bustling crowd for the rowdy miners. He panicked for a moment when he couldn't find them. He finally made eye contact with Xagrith and gave a subtle gesture with his hand to slow down.

Minutes passed while Xagrith slowly led the miners zigzagging through the streets until he received another signal from Jorik.

"He's over there!" Syzimian shouted, pointing toward the prison gate. "I get the first shot at him!"

The pack of angry miners picked up their pace, attempting to intercept Jorik. They crossed the street in front of the prison just as Kyloraz and Shimioth received the two Jinians into their custody.

Kyloraz shoved the Jinian man in the back. His chains rattled on the stone behind him. "Faster, thief! Keep your head down if you know what's good for you."

Staring his brother down, Syzimian met Jorik in front of the main gate. "Where do think you're going?"

He reached out and grabbed Jorik's shirt, wincing a little. He knew how hard Jorik could hit.

The prison guard looked through the bars, slowly closing the gate. "Move along. Not in front of the prison," he yelled as if this were a regular occurrence.

Just then, Jorik punched Syzimian square in the nose.

"Get him!" Xagrith yelled, slamming into the group of miners, sending them stumbling into the gate, knocking the guard away from the bars. The guard flew back to the gate in an attempt to slam it shut, but was met by Syzimian, who was on the other side of the bars with his boot firmly wedged in the opening.

The guards escorting the Jinians looked back, torn between wanting to break up the brawl or continuing on with their orders.

"It's only drunk miners. Let them beat it out of each other," Shimioth told Kyloraz.

"Get moving, thieves," Kyloraz snarled, shoving the woman in the back.

She stumbled to the ground and hit her knees hard on the stone street.

The melee outside the gate was quickly getting out of hand. Xagrith pretended he was on the miners' side, shouting his anger at Jorik. But with every punch he threw at his Guardian brother, he concealed a quick kick or elbow at the miners. Jorik stayed inside the fray, mostly defending himself from the barrage of weak, flailing punches. The drunken miners were no match for him, and he didn't really want to hurt them if he didn't have to. He made sure the fight stayed right at Syzimian's back so there would be no witnesses to the break-in.

The prison guard clawed at Syzimian's face through the bars, trying to push him away. His fingernails dug into Syzimian's temple and down his cheek. He kicked at his boot, trying to dislodge it from the doorjamb to no avail. Syzimian reached through the gate around the back of the guard's neck, snapping him into the bars. His forehead cracked against the gate. Syzimian tightened his arm around the guard's neck and kept cinching it tighter. The panicked guard gasped for air and tried reaching for his sword, but his arm was awkwardly pinned between the bars and his body. Syzimian looked calm in the face of everything that was going on behind him.

The guard tried to scream, but so tight was Syzimian's grip that no sound escaped his throat. Syzimian felt the guard's hot breath on his face, gasping for one more futile breath. He cinched his arm one more time and the guard went limp. The Guardian dropped him to the ground and slipped through the gate with his pick in hand, shutting the gate behind him. He pulled the prison guard into the shadows by his boots and removed the key ring from the leather strap that was tied to his waist. He lowered his ear onto the still guard, listening for a heartbeat. Satisfied the guard was alive, he crawled to the keyhole and locked the gate. No one saw him enter the prison. He gave Xagrith a nod and returned the key to the sleeping guard.

Once Xagrith knew Syzimian had successfully infiltrated the prison, playtime was over. The two Guardians then began working as a team, not once using the business end of their mining picks. Fifteen seconds later, eight drunken miners lay unconscious in the street. The remaining four fled into the crowd, stumbling over everything in their path.

Xagrith and Jorik walked away, doing their best to blend into the crowd. They walked quite a distance before they turned around and found a suitable vantage point from which to watch the prison gate. Both their faces were bruised, but they had no serious injuries.

Xagrith sat first at the edge of a waterway. "Once Syzimian gets out of there, he is going to break your nose. You know that, don't you?"

"I had to make it look real," Jorik answered, drawing up a handful of cool water. He splashed it on his face. "I'm sure he would have done the same thing."

"Let's just hope that the guard wakes up and thinks he was knocked out in the brawl and nothing more."

"Reporting to his superiors that he was knocked out by some drunken miners through his gate might not be the best thing for his career. I'm sure that he'll keep it to himself."

They watched the red crew one by one regain consciousness and stagger away. Although the Guardians did their best to not hurt the miners, they did sustain a few broken wrists and ribs. One even had his jaw broken by Xagrith's elbow as the Guardian drew back his fist to punch Jorik in the side.

"It's a pity, don't you think, Xagrith?"

"What is?"

"In other circumstances, we might have been friends with a few of them."

In the king's chamber, the grating sound of chains dragging across the crystal floor interrupted the pleasantries. Rolfus turned to see a battered Jinian man enter the chamber, his wrists and ankles bound by heavy chains, but it was what happened next that froze the merchant's gaze. Following only a few steps behind the man, a woman entered the chamber, her torn and soiled dress dragging with her chains. Her head was bowed and her long curly black hair covered her face, except for her bronze cheek and one sea-colored eye. She glanced at Thanan and then looked immediately at the floor. But to Thanan, the fleeting look lasted an eternity, as if past, present, and future existed simultaneously. It was in that moment that he witnessed perfection, bound by chains.

Suddenly, he was all too aware of his own pounding heartbeat and flushing skin. He quickly collected himself and turned to the king, hoping the woman did not recognize him. "What is to happen to these prisoners?" Rolfus asked, doing his best to restrain his disgust.

"I've grown tired of them. Torture only thrills me so much before their cries all sound the same," the king replied, showing no emotion. "Two days from now, when Xavantha is at her brightest, the criminals will be beheaded at a public execution. It is the standard punishment for their particular crime. It's been a while since Jinian blood was spilled under Xavantha."

"Speak your mind, your majesty. What is your offer?"

The chained woman sneaked one more glance at Rolfus, and he could not help but make eye contact with her again.

"It is simple, Jinian," King Grishon chuckled. "Twelve percent of my treasury for unchecked shipping routes and I will throw in the Jinian scum. Surely you can find some use for them. Keep them, sell them, I do not care."

"Twelve percent?" the merchant scoffed. "Did we not settle on fifteen? I thought the king to be a Goriath of his word."

"Fool of a Jinian!" the king snapped, slamming his dimpled forearm and hand on the armrest of his throne. "This is my house. My rules."

"Of course...you are right. Forgive me, your majesty," Thanan replied, collecting himself.

"That is better," the king continued. "As I said, *ten* percent and you choose which criminal goes with you and who stays behind as collateral."

Knowing there could be no further negotiation, Rolfus nodded to the king in agreement.

"You! What's your name?" Rolfus asked, pointing at the bound man.

"Samil Drun," the prisoner shot back, with defiance. "And I will be no one's slave." He spit on the floor in front of Thanan's boots.

Kiloraz shoved Samil from behind, keeping him in line.

"I see...you'd rather have your head roll across the cavern floor? And you! Woman. What's your name?"

"Do not speak to this merchant," Samil commanded the woman.

Raising her chained hands, she pushed the hair from her face, revealing the fullness of her beauty. Thanan's eyes hung upon her lips as they parted to speak. "I am Jesifaye," she spoke defiantly. "My uncle and I set out from Methina many years ago."

Jesifaye's voice enthralled him, and for a brief moment he forgot where he was.

Your uncle, Thanan thought to himself, trying not to smile. *She's not married.* His heart raced at the thought.

"Make your decision, Jinian!" Krim commanded, bringing Rolfus back.

"I'll be taking the woman. She will be of use to me on my long trip back to Tronis."

"No! No!" the woman shouted, grasping for her uncle. "Uncle! No!"

"Krim! Get them out of my chamber!" the king shouted, half standing in his throne. "Remember Jinian, you will get your money and your other slave when you meet me at the Great Divide in Jeth six months from now."

"Come, Jinian," Krim insisted. He grabbed Thanan's arm and ushered him out of the king's chamber.

The prison floor was damp and Syzimian's boots stuck to it with each step, as if it were covered with dark, muddy syrup. He passed many dank cells with nothing more than strewn bones on the floor held together by disintegrating clothing. It was common that some of the more gross offenders were left to die and rot away in their chains, their decomposing bodies oozing into the tunnels and feeding the vermin. Pooling torchlight illuminated the dreary tunnels where still, foul air held the musty odors of moss and rotting flesh. Ignoring the stench, Syzimian crept closely along the rock wall, focusing only on the task at hand.

There were distant cries in the darkness, hopeless and weak whimpers, begging for help. The cries broke the silence from time to time, which set the Guardian's nerves on edge. No guards were posted in the main corridor, but Syzimian knew there could be many guarding the accused spies. He slowly peeked one eye around a corner. All was clear.

His steps were light, even in the muck. The Guardian looked down the length of the tunnel. Sixty feet away, he saw that it intersected another corridor to the left and right. He froze when another sound caught his ear. He saw a flickering light moving closer, brightening the tunnel to the left. Syzimian stepped out of the torch light above him and pressed his back against the cold bars of a cell.

Suddenly, a hand reached through the bars and grabbed his shoulder. "Please," a woman's voice weakly hissed. "Please help me."

The Guardian's heart leapt from his chest. Her voice was raspy, almost nonexistent. His first instinct was to break the woman's arm and stick his mining pick into her head, but as he turned around, the woman's gaunt face came into view. She was old and her balding head was sparsely covered with stringy gray hair, matted from years of filth. The blue skin on her arms, face and hands was covered with sores. And even though she was frail and weak, the woman refused let go of Syzimian's shoulder. The desperation in the woman's eyes touched his heart. But there was no time. He had to continue on.

Syzimian looked toward the growing light in the corridor. Loud steps now accompanied the light. "Release me, woman," he whispered. "A guard is coming."

"Please help me," she managed to say again.

"I will," he replied calmly, removing her hand.

The Guardian quickly reached into his pocket and brought out the cell key. A hint of baked bread still clung to it. Then, as quietly as he could, he unlocked the cell door.

Light flooded the corridor as the prison guard turned the corner with his torch. He saw that the tunnel was empty and quiet. He walked slowly, looking into each cell, not caring what he saw, his senses having been numbed by years of witnessing depravity. Passing by the old woman's cell, he looked in and continued on. The guard paused, a puzzled expression sweeping over his face. The usual whimpering cries for help did not come from the woman as they did each time he passed her cell. The silence was peculiar. He turned back to investigate.

The guard peered into the bleak cell. He stuck his torch through the bars to get a better look. "You...witch! Are you dead?" He slapped the bars with his palm.

The old woman was huddled in the corner on the floor, rocking back and forth. A stained blanket covered her shoulders. She paid no heed to the guard's question, only squinted her eyes in the torchlight and turned away. The guard huffed and lowered the torch, which illuminated two boot prints outside the cell door that were not his. His heart jumped and his eyes grew wide. He reached for his sword, but before his hand fell on the hilt, Syzimian's massive hand reached through the bars and slammed the guard's face into cold metal. A moment later, the stunned guard died when the tip of the Guardian's mining pick penetrated his neck. He dragged the guard's limp body into the cell with the woman.

Syzimian turned to the dying woman. There was no hope left in her sunken eyes. "I will come back for you," he promised. He quietly locked the door and continued down the corridor.

Now armed with the guard's sword in one hand and a pick in the other, the Guardian walked quicker and more brazenly. Time was precious, and he sensed Thanan's negotiations were coming to an end. He came to a sudden stop at an intersection. Hugging the wall, he peeked around the corner. Fifty feet away, he saw four guards seated around a wooden table eating and gambling, speaking in low tones. Their words were rude and crass, which carried down the tunnel like they were whispering in Syzimian's ear.

"Two more hours and I can get some sleep," one of them said, tossing a frag on the table. "Krim's got everyone working long hours, keeping these spies locked up. It almost seems like Krim doesn't want to find out who the traitors really are. I could break them in an hour."

The distinct sounds of shuffling feet and dragging chains caught Syzimian's ear. A guard turned toward the cell across the corridor, throwing a bone at the bars as hard as he could. The sound echoed sharply down through the prison. "Shut up you grek or so help me I'll stick you through these bars. I don't care what Krim thinks!" He feigned drawing his sword and lunged at the bars, mocking and laughing at the prisoners.

"Consider yourself lucky. I have ten more hours with this cave scum," another replied. He tore into the breast of a gini hen and gulped down the last of his drink. "Hurry up with your bet. I have to get to my rounds."

Syzimian was incensed by the treatment of his brothers. How he wanted to explode from his hiding place and end the guards that very moment. His knuckles turned white as he dug his fingers into the slime-covered stone wall. Thinking of the best way to get past the prison guards, he ground his fingers into his palm, letting the dirt and slime drop to the floor. What remained in his grimy palm stirred his heart to even greater anger. Between his giant fingers he pinched a broken fingernail, quick and all, splintered from grasping the stone wall. It obviously belonged to a Jinian woman.

Syzimian picked up his sword and pressed his shoulder against the wall, determined more than ever to rescue the prisoners. His immense weight dislodged a stone. He frantically reached for it, but before he could catch it, it fell to the ground, skittering and bouncing across the corridor. The Guardian hugged the wall even closer, bringing the pick up to his chest.

All four guards sprang from their chairs, turning in unison down the dark corridor.

"What was that?" one of them asked, looking down the hall.

"You stay here," the head guard replied, lifting a torch from the wall. "Keep an eye on the traitors. You two are with me."

The three prison guards crept down the corridor with swords drawn toward the waiting Syzimian. The Guardian knew this had to be fast and efficient. He closed his eyes and breathed silently through his nose, calming himself. It was something he always did in the face of imminent danger. It calmed his heart and helped him focus. He listened to the guards' footsteps coming closer and closer. He firmed his grip on the pick handle and steadied his stance.

As the lead guard came around the corner, Syzimian swung his pick as hard as he could into the guard. The gawking guard dropped his sword and torch, and attempted to pry the cold metal from his chest.

While the bleeding guard still stood, Syzimian followed with an overhand swing with his sword, which struck the second guard between the neck and shoulders, crumpling him to the floor. The third guard sliced through the air frantically, but Syzimian pulled the first guard into the blade's path by the pick handle. The guard sunk his sword into his fellow guard's back, finishing the job that Syzimian started.

Seeing the fight, the fourth guard sprang into action, kicking over his chair. It clanked off the cell bars and came to rest in the center of the floor. He bolted down the corridor, sword drawn and shouting the alarm to anyone who could hear. Syzimian saw the sprinting guard and quickly dispatched the third guard with a precisely placed blade under his armpit. Syzimian spun around, removing the pick and sword from the fallen guards and started into a full sprint toward the fourth guard. The Guardian's movements were jarringly brutal and graceful.

The two giants met each other at full speed, their footsteps echoing down the tunnel. Surely the other prison guards were aware of the Guardian's presence now. Syzimian sidestepped the guard's swing and stuck the mining pick into his thigh, upending him. The guard fell facedown, writhing from the searing pain. His anguish lasted only a second more as Syzimian pushed his sword through his back.

Syzimian looked back and, seeing the dead guards in his wake, knew this was no longer a covert operation.

He sprinted to the first cell, pulling the key from his pocket. Pounding footsteps filled the corridor again. Syzimian opened the first cell and sidestepped to the next. His hands were steady as stone, even after just killing four armed prison guards in less than ten seconds. Peering through the rusted bars, he spotted the Guardian, Anax. Anax rushed to greet Syzimian through the bars. He was dressed in the traditional robes of a Xavantha cleric, which had been his cover for twelve years. Although his robes were torn and covered in filth, there wasn't a mark on him. Krim had obviously protected him from the guards.

They gripped each other's forearms through the bars as Syzimian unlocked the cell door. "Where is Grolis?"

"Three cells down," Anax replied, stepping into the corridor.

Just then eight more guards turned the corner, their torchlight filling the tunnel. "The prisoners are escaping!" the leader called out.

Syzimian handed Anax the key.

"Take this and get everyone out of the cells. Get Grolis first. We're going to need him."

Then Syzimian turned to head off the sprinting guards. Just outside the cellblock, Syzimian met the rushing prison guards with his mining pick, followed shortly by Anax, who was wielding one of the fallen guard's swords. The two Guardians systematically cut down three guards, when suddenly Grolis joined in the fight with nothing more than his fists and a great desire to punish those who took him prisoner. He ducked a wild swing at his neck, spinning behind his attacker. One sharp twist and he broke the guard's neck, and while the dead guard was still standing, Grolis acquired his sword and cut down another rushing guard attempting to stab him in the chest.

The corridor was now filled with prisoners watching the three Guardians make quick work of the prison guards. They all were filthy and smelled horrible.

Syzimian stood in the midst of the dead guards, chest heaving, looking back at the prisoners. "Those who are strong enough, take up a sword and stay close. There could be more guards." He kicked a sword, sending it skidding toward the prisoners.

Grolis extended his arm to Syzimian. "Thank you, brother. I knew someone would come."

"The council leaves no one behind," he replied, nodding.

Lead by Syzimian and Grolis, the prisoners walked through the dark tunnels back toward the main corridor. Many of them had not eaten in days and were significantly weakened from the deprivation. The stronger ones assisted the weak as they slowly trudged through the muck, barefoot. Anax trailed behind with the four spies, informing them that information they possessed was too valuable and that they would be returning to Hardrock.

The prison was now alive with pleas for help. The prisoners began rattling their cells and clanking thin, rusted plates against the bars. The sounds resonated throughout the corridors, inciting even the most violent and vile criminals to reach their hands out for relief. With each cell they passed, their cries fell on deaf ears, except for one. Syzimian stopped, looking into a dark cell. He unlocked the door and extended his hand to the old woman. She limped into the light, revealing her horribly hunched back and despondent eyes. The look of disbelief washed from her face as her trembling fingers took the Guardian's hand. He hoisted her over his shoulder and continued on, determined to get everyone to safety.

After walking for some time, Grolis raised his hand to the group. Syzimian gently put down the old woman. He and Grolis peeked around the last corner, fully expecting the riotous sounds in the prison to have caused the gate guard to raise the alarm. To their surprise, he stood there vigilant as ever, back to the Guardians, making sure no one came or went without his consent.

The two Guardians looked at each other, not believing their fortune. It seemed the battle they were prepared for wasn't going to happen. They nodded to each other and rounded the corner as quietly as they could. Twenty steps seemed like an eternity as they crept closer to the guard. Syzimian gritted his teeth with every squishy step. Grolis was right on Syzimian's heels, the slime oozing between his toes.

They froze as the guard's attention piqued. His head snapped to the right and then the left as if listening to the sounds behind him. He made no attempts to turn around, afraid of what he might see. The guard slowly lowered his hand toward his hilt and shifted his weight slightly.

Without a word, the two Guardians bolted to the gate and tackled the guard before he could draw his sword. They picked him up and slammed him against the wall. The guard's eyes widened when he recognized Syzimian from the brawl outside the prison gate. He struggled as the Guardian searched for the keys.

Syzimian grabbed a handful of the guard's hair. "Where are the keys? They were on your waist. What did you do with them?" He slammed his head into the wall.

Grolis put the tip of his blade under the guard's eye. "The

keys," he growled lowly.

The guard gulped, darting his eyes toward the gate and back at Grolis.

Syzimian walked to the gate with his back against the wall. He quickly glanced at the ground just outside. "He threw them outside the bars."

"Can you reach them?" Grolis asked, still pressing the blade against the guard's eye.

"Yes." Syzimian knelt down and quickly reached with his pick. The point fell in the middle of the metal ring. He dragged the keys back and hid behind the wall next to the gate. The scraping caused a few heads to turn in the street, but no one saw.

Still crouching, Syzimian waved down the corridor. The guard squirmed when he saw thirty prisoners turn the corner. He slapped the sword away, lunging for a rope fifteen feet down the wall. He only made it two steps before Grolis pierced his back with his sword. The guard stumbled, not thinking of anything but sounding the alarm. His lifeless hand at last found the rope as he fell to the floor.

The thunderous prison bells rang only once, but it was enough.

"Everyone outside now!" Syzimian ordered, waving his pick. "Make your way to the mining tunnels! Those with swords fight with everything you have!"

Just outside the king's chamber, Krim and Rolfus waited for the prisoners to exit.

"Follow my lead," Krim whispered to Rolfus. "Kyloraz!

Unchain this woman. She belongs to the merchant now."

"Wait. Let me do it," Rolfus interrupted. He took the key from Kyloraz and brutishly grabbed the woman by the small of her back, bringing her in close with one hand and tangling his fingers in her hair with the other. He brought her long hair to his nose and breathed deeply her scent.

"Don't touch her!" Samil spat, lunging at Rolfus.

Kyloraz hit the angry Jinian in the back of the head with his hilt with just enough force to remind the prisoner who was in control.

"Trust me," Rolfus whispered softly, touching his lips to her ear. "Trust me and we all live."

She darted her eyes and caught the seriousness of Thanan's expression. Something about his eyes was familiar to her, but she couldn't place it. Feigning repulsion by his advances, she pulled her head away, glaring at her new owner. The merchant grabbed her wrists and unlocked the restraints. Her bloody and bruised fingers sickened him. He then knelt down and likewise unlocked her blood-stained ankles.

They all started the long walk back to the cave entrance with Krim leading the way, followed by Jesifaye and Rolfus. Kyloraz, two other guards, and Samil lagged behind because the Jinian's ankles were chained.

"Move, Jinian scum!" a guard demanded time and time again.

"Faster!" another one shouted, shoving Samil in the back.

Rolfus clenched his jaw with every command.

"Remain calm," Krim whispered to Rolfus.

As they approached the tunnel leading to the outside, the distinct tone of the prison bell resonated through the tunnel, putting Kyloraz and the guards on alert. Krim looked worried and stopped

Rolfus and Jesifaye.

"Why have we stopped?" Rolfus asked.

The king's advisor turned and approached the guards. "Let the prisoner have one last moment with the woman," Krim commanded.

"I don't think that is a good idea, sir," Kyloraz replied, tugging on Samil's shoulder. "The alarm has sounded. We need to get the prisoner back!"

"I did not ask you to think, Kyloraz!" Krim shot back, closing the distance between Kyloraz and himself.

Confused by Krim's unusual aggression, Kyloraz instinctively reached for his blade at his waist, but it was not there. He frantically looked down to his side to see an empty sheath. He then saw the tip of his own blade pierce his heart.

The two accompanying guards sprinted for the bell ropes and sounded the alarm. They both turned and ran toward Krim, swinging their swords. As they shot past Samil, the prisoner leaped onto a guard's back, throwing his chains around the giant's thick neck. The choking giant spun, grasping at the chains, and was brought down by Thanan's dagger, which he had pulled from his boot and thrown with precision.

Before Thanan could assist Krim with the last guard, the spy cut down the oncoming soldier with little effort. Krim knelt down and quickly unlocked the prisoner's ankles.

"Follow me!" Krim yelled, spotting more guards coming up the path.

The four sprinted down the torch-lined tunnel toward the cave exit with loud voices shouting behind them.

"Stop them! Krim is a traitor! He killed Kyloraz!" one pursuer screamed.

As they rounded the corner, sunlight filled the cave. The light blinded them momentarily. It was in that moment of blindness that two Goriath guards appeared, as if from another plane. Krim and the first guard clashed in battle, their swords echoing through the cavern. His flowing red robes spun and swirled with each fluid movement.

Thanan pushed Jesifaye and Samil aside, clearing a path to the second guard. He stood there, unarmed, readying himself for the attack. The rushing giant rained down his first blow, but Thanan subtlety stepped to the side, letting the giant's momentum carry him past. Knowing he had to end the battle quickly, Thanan took a posture of weakness, raising his hands in surrender, which drew the giant in. The giant swung at the Guardian's throat, barely missing. He swung again, this time at Thanan's torso. Thanan parried the thrust and, with one foot, buckled the guard's knee. The guard stumbled forward trying to regain his balance. Thanan then plucked a torch from the cave wall and plunged the pointed handle deep into the back of the guard's neck.

Just then, they heard a horrible scream as Krim tossed his foe over the cliff's edge. "Move now!" the spy yelled, looking at the oncoming guards.

Samil, still chained at the wrists, turned to see the approaching guards running with swords drawn.

"Run!" Samil called to Jesifaye. "Run and don't look back!"

"No! I won't leave you!" his loyal insisted.

"Take her now, stranger!" he pleaded with Rolfus.

Thanan grabbed her by the waist and held her back. She sobbed uncontrollably, reaching for her uncle who had taken her in when she was a young girl. She clawed at Thanan's arms as he dragged her toward the mouth of the cave.

The ragged man turned with no concern for his own life and ran toward his fate. He limped heavily, his legs weakened by many beatings. The brave prisoner from Methina did not close his eyes when he sacrificed his body for his loved one. He fiercely looked his captors in the eyes as they savagely cut him to pieces, but not before he slowed them down, ensuring his niece's escape. It was a sacrifice for the one he loved most in the world, the one who gave his life purpose.

Outside the prison, the prisoners exploded from the gate and ran for the north tunnels. Syzimian, Grolis, and Anax took up defensive positions, trailing just behind the escaping prisoners, waiting for the inevitable battle.

"No one gets past us," Syzimian growled. "Is that clear?"

Xagrith and Jorik sprang into action, quickly heading off three soldiers responding to the prison bell, cutting them down before they knew what hit them. The city was in an uproar. People were in the streets jostling for a view of the jailbreak. Everywhere soldiers were pushing through the crowds making their way to the prison. One by one the soldiers came, only to be killed by the retreating Guardians.

"Hurry!" Syzimian shouted, waving his pick in the air.

Suddenly, another alarm sounded. This time the bells came from the King's Arch.

"Back to the king!" one of the soldiers called out. "Protect the king!" The pursuing soldiers stopped battling the Guardians and began running in the opposite direction toward the king.

The five Guardians looked dumbfounded at the retreating soldiers.

They all escaped into the tunnels unscathed, all except one. Half a day from Hardrock, the old woman passed away in her sleep with a full belly and her eyes full of hope.

Thanan, Krim, and Jesifaye ran along the Crag Path with the voices of the angry guards swirling in the wind. As they approached the hidden entrance, they discovered that Agrinoth was missing from his post.

"Krim, take her into the cave. Agrinoth might be in trouble," Thanan commanded.

The renowned spy took her by the hand and ushered her into the cave as Thanan ran unarmed toward the giants' voices. As he rounded the bend, he saw Agrinoth breathing heavily, standing with his back to the valley. Eight dead guards lay strewn over the path with the ninth still sliding off the Guardian's Zythera blade. It seemed that Agrinoth had heard all the commotion and hid himself in an outcropping. By the time the pursuing guards realized they had been ambushed, it was too late. Even outnumbered, the speed and deadly skill of Agrinoth were too much for the heavily armored guards.

"You are late," the warrior said sternly, turning to his Jinian brother.

"Well, we had tea and sweet breads with the king. I thought it would be rude to eat and run," Thanan replied sarcastically.

"And what of the Jinian man?"

"He bravely gave his life to buy us a few extra moments," Thanan replied, realizing the shame of his levity.

"Let us return to Hardrock," Agrinoth said, wiping his blade on a dead guard's shoulder.

Except for a brief introduction of Azoth Zor to Agrinoth, little was said on the trip back to Hardrock, although there were a few uncomfortable moments shared between Thanan and Jesifaye as they tried to steal glances of one another.

A short time before entering the garrison, the weakened woman collapsed to the floor after stubbing her toe on a raised edge of a stone. She fell awkwardly face first, unable to support herself. Her tears bathed the stone beneath her face, and Thanan's heart broke to see it. She trembled, not from any bodily pain, but from her soul crying out for her fallen uncle and the uncertainty of her future.

"Thanan, help her," Agrinoth commanded.

It was the first time she had heard that name spoken aloud. She lifted her eyes to finally see the face of the one whose name she read on the Belenor dock years before, but consumed by despair, she fainted, knocking her head on the stone floor. Even in her weakness, Thanan sensed the strength of Jesifaye. He cradled her in his arms and carried her for the rest of the journey to Hardrock. He carefully laid her in Tirothia's bed, and Seretha began to mend the broken woman.

CHAPTER TWENTY-FIVE

WHIRLWIND

The Tenth Day of Xolis was fast approaching. One month had come and gone and Thanan passed the time hammering zil ore and rare Zythera crystal into fine weapons of war. He especially excelled at fabricating spears, which were modeled from the spear he had forged in the Glowing Cavern; however, these were lighter and easier to wield. Purgon insisted that his apprentice reveal how and where he conceived of such a design, but Thanan never betrayed Zinaka's secret. He simply attributed his design to great tutelage, which flattery only went so far with Purgon.

At the end of each day, Thanan hung up his apron and bid Purgon farewell until the morning. The Guardian wound his way through the marketplace looking for something to catch his eye for supper, but his appetite had waned somewhat over the past few weeks. He often found an excuse to drop in on Kigron, claiming he wanted to talk strategy with the captain, but everyone knew what the true motive was for his visits.

"She is mending quite well," Kigron said, knowing where Thanan's thoughts truly were.

"Who is?" Thanan asked with feigned innocence.

The captain chuckled and poured Thanan another cup of water.

"Since you have not heard a word I have said, I figured you would like to know she is doing well. You know…she asked about you a few times.

"You still have not spoken to her about her time in the Crystal City or her uncle. It might be of comfort to her to speak to someone of her kind. She is all alone in this dark world."

"I wouldn't know what to say," Thanan replied, looking in the direction of the clanking sound of pots coming from the kitchen.

"Go on and talk to her. She is helping Seretha clean up from supper," Kigron replied, waving him out of the room. "Do you want her to know you as Thanan, the Guardian who rescued her, or Thanan, the strange man lurking at her window?"

Thanan sighed heavily. "We already know each other. We met when we were just children. I knew it was her the moment I saw her in the king's chamber, but she didn't recognize me. The truth is, I didn't want her to. I left her to die on a burning ship. I just can't bring myself to speak to her."

"I will never understand Jinians," the captain said, shaking his head. "You were just children. She will understand."

"I wouldn't know what to say."

"All right…this is what you will do. Come by tomorrow and share a meal with my family. Bathe first…you are filthy."

The following day Thanan's mind was anywhere but the armory. He broke four blades and one little finger. Frustrated with his hapless apprentice's performance, Purgon sent him to the infirmary with instructions to splint his finger and have the physician examine his head.

Thanan took two breaths and stepped out of his tent. All cleaned up, finger set and splinted, the nervous Guardian passed by the marketplace looking for a small token to give to Jesifaye. Sometimes, flowers could be found in the marketplace, fresh from Loriam, but this was not one of those times. Not knowing what to buy, Thanan purchased a large bunch of root vegetables and tore off the leafy green stems, bundling them together to form a raggedy green bouquet.

After a few strange looks from Jixon, Thanan handed back the leafless vegetables. "Jix, you can keep these," the Guardian said, fiddling with the crude bouquet.

"Whatever you want, Guardian," Jixon replied, smiling.

Outside Kigron's home, Thanan nervously exhaled and knocked on the wooden post at the tent's entrance. He waited a few moments and knocked again, but still there was no answer.

"Hello! Kigron, are you in there? Seretha? Tav? Anybody home?" Thanan raised his fist, ready to rap on the post one last time, when he heard a voice from behind him.

"Oh, hello," a sweet voice said in a Methinian accent.

Thanan had forgotten how much he enjoyed listening to Jesifaye speak. His heart jumped as he turned to see her. She was carrying a basket bursting with vegetables and bread, but Thanan did not offer to carry it for her. He just stood there, mesmerized by her beauty, her flawless skin glowing in the flickering torchlight.

"The Gru family is not here. They went to the pools for the evening," she continued.

"Of course they did," the Guardian muttered to himself. "Kigron, I'm gonna kill you."

"Are those for me?" Jesifaye asked, looking at the disheveled bouquet.

"Uh...yes," Thanan replied uncomfortably, presenting them to her as if he had just returned from a hunt with the evening meal ready to be cleaned.

"Those are...beautiful," she fibbed, putting her basket down. "I'm sure that Seretha can boil those into something. She is quite a good cook."

"Flowers are hard to come by in Hardrock," he replied, chuckling at her comment.

After a few more uncomfortable moments, they began walking with no destination in mind. For all his skill and adeptness in all manner of politics, public speaking, combat, and survival, when it came to the finer points of interacting with the opposite sex, Thanan was left wanting.

Jesifaye and Thanan wound their way through the marketplace, stopping at the shops that had not yet closed. Many merchants called to the Guardian and freely offered their wares. They spoke very little at first, but as they made their way along the waterway, conversation became a little easier. She recognized quickly that this pale Jinian was nothing like the haughty merchant who negotiated for her freedom. And there was something familiar about him, but she still couldn't place it.

Thanan was all too happy to keep his true identity a secret for the time being. He enthusiastically introduced her to everyone he knew as they strolled the waterways. They paused for a few moments to watch the shimmering schools of fish darting in unison beneath the water's surface. As she took in the beauty of the strange world around her, Thanan stole a few glances at her reflection in the glassy water. To be with a Jinian again, let alone one as beautiful as Jesifaye, made Thanan's spirit soar.

"Good evening to you, brother," a stern voice said from behind.

Thanan and Jesifaye turned to see Agrinoth and Purgon carrying fishing poles and a large basket.

"Agrinoth! Purgon!" Thanan exclaimed with delight. "Off to catch your supper?"

"The old giant thinks he can teach me something about fishing," Agrinoth teased.

"I have forgotten more about fishing than you will ever know, Grandson," the blacksmith shot back. "So...is this who is responsible for your brain turning into pudding today?" Purgon asked, turning his attention to Thanan and Jesifaye.

Jesifaye smiled at the thought.

"Jesifaye, this is Purgon. He is the master blacksmith who taught me all I know. And I'm sure you remember Agrinoth?"

"I am happy to see you are doing well," Agrinoth replied. "Let us go, Grandfather, and leave these two to their evening."

Thanan and Jesifaye continued to walk, content with one another's company. Although they had spoken very little to each other, just a few pleasantries, there was an undeniable force pulling them together. It was an overwhelming feeling of warmth and tenderness. The feeling scared Thanan. His mission was paramount, and a distraction like Jesifaye could undo everything. But the image of Thanan's father and mother strolling through the rose garden flashed across his mind. He remembered as a little boy running in and out of the towering roses and seeing the content expression on his mother's face. It was the same expression that Jesifaye now had. *Is this part of my father's plan?* he wondered, glancing once more at Jesifaye's beauty.

After a couple of hours they found themselves on the top terrace, high above Hardrock, the same place where Thanan had been branded a Guardian. Thanan looked over the vast garrison, with its thousands of glowing torches, Xavantha dimly glowing above, as if it were the first time.

"It's beautiful," Jesifaye said, turning to Thanan. "So…you are a blacksmith? I've met many blacksmiths. You don't look like any I've ever seen."

"Purgon would say differently, but yes I'm a blacksmith," he replied, holding up his splinted finger.

She reached out and gently held his fingers, examining his hand and broken finger. "How did that happen?"

"It's nothing. I've broken every finger except this one." He held up his right index finger and wiggled it. "Actually…I blame you for this one," Thanan answered with a smile.

"My fault?" she scoffed, still holding his hand. "How is it my fault?" Then her expression changed from playful to serious as she turned his hand and looked at his palm.

"What's wrong?" Thanan asked.

"How is it a Jinian blacksmith commands such respect from so many giants?"

Thanan paused for a moment, considering his words carefully, still trying to be funny. "Let's just say that I'm an unusual blacksmith."

"And why did the intense-looking giant call you 'brother?'" she asked, continuing to press Thanan for information. "And why was a blacksmith sent to rescue me? What does a blacksmith know about rescuing someone?"

Thanan opened his mouth to respond, but before he could answer, she continued her barrage of questions.

"When you rescued me, the giant in the robes called you 'Thanan.' Until then, I had only read that name once before, carved into the docks at Belenor Bay. Are you from the Jinian capital? Have you ever been to Belenor?"

Thanan swallowed hard, not knowing what to say.

"When are you going to tell me the truth, Rolfus? I know it's you."

Thanan bowed his head shamefully, exhaling sharply. "When did you figure it out?"

"I was with you when you got that scar on your hand. Don't you remember? The one shaped like a key." She snatched his hand up and ran her fingers over the scar.

Thanan looked at his palm, shaking his head. He was so enamored by Jesifaye that he had forgotten about the scar on his hand. *You showed her your hand, you idiot*, he thought.

"What's your real name? Have you been lying to these giants or did you lie to me all those years ago?"

There was so much Thanan couldn't tell her, but he knew he

owed Jesifaye at least part of the truth.

"I lied to you," he began, looking into her eyes. "My true name is Thanan."

Immediately a weight lifted from his shoulders after the admission.

"I should have told you the truth when we met on the docks all those years ago. And I should have never involved you. I just wanted to share my adventure with someone. I never considered the danger I was putting you in. For years I thought you died on that ship. Many times I rounded the lighthouse and imagined seeing your ship moored to the dock and you standing at the bow just like the night we met. I'm not sure what I would have actually done if I saw you there. Probably would have run away."

"I'm sure I would have seen you lurking behind a water barrel," she interrupted.

"Probably," he chuckled. "I guess I wanted to know you were all right and thank you for saving my life. You were the bravest person I had ever met. That was too much for any 10-year-old to go through and I was selfish to include you in it. I'm sorry."

Jesifaye paused for a moment, mulling over the words that Thanan had just spoken. "I'm not sorry," she replied, to Thanan's surprise.

Then she smiled. "I can't believe it's you, Rolfus...I mean Thanan. You've changed so much. What happened to you?" She reached out her hand and brushed his pale cheek, smiling gently.

Their skin contrasted even more now than it did when they were young.

"But your eyes are the same. What are you doing here? Why do you live here among the Goriath giants?"

"It would take a lifetime to tell that story," Thanan replied, dismissing her questions. "What about you? How did you make it off the Lokarian? The explosion blew the ship apart. No one could have lived through that."

"I almost didn't make it. After I pushed you over the rail I turned around to see the watchman swinging his sword like a madman. I blocked his first few swings, but he was too strong. He knocked the sword from my hands and sliced through my sleeve. I wanted to run, but if I turned my back he would have caught me for sure. He didn't care if he lived or died on that ship; he just wanted me to pay for what we had done. He was howling like a raving beast, mad with hatred. Any rational man would have abandoned his anger in the name of preservation, but the watchman wanted me dead no matter the cost.

He took one last swing as I closed my eyes. The deck under my feet shuddered and I heard a loud crack. My eyes shot open to see the deck had collapsed under his feet and he had fallen through. His chest was scraping over the splintered deck and he clawed at the boards trying not to fall through. He looked so scared. Then the ship shook so hard it knocked me down. I rolled to my feet and started to run toward the railing, but the watchman's cries for help stopped me. I turned and saw only his hands holding the boards. 'Come back,' he said. 'Help me please.' His feet were hanging through the deck just above the flames. He just kept begging me to help him."

"What did you do? Did you help him?" Thanan asked, completely enthralled by the story.

"I tried. I really did. But he was too heavy and the ship was breaking up so quickly. Flames were everywhere. When he realized I couldn't lift him, he tried to pull me in with him, but I broke free. His legs caught fire and he let go of the deck. I still remember the hatred in his eyes, how he stared at me as he fell into the fire. I ran across the deck and dove over the edge before the ship exploded. I tried to find you, but I couldn't see anything through all the flames and smoke on the water. I thought you had died as well. It was two years before my uncle came back to the capital and even longer before he let me set foot on the pier. Each time we sailed into Belenor, I stood at the bow searching the docks for the boy who showed me such fantastic things. My life was never the same after that. What other adventure could compare to a study that opened to other worlds?"

"So we were looking for each other the whole time. But how did you and your uncle find yourselves in a Goriath prison? That has to be an exciting story as well."

"Well, I will make you a bargain," Jesifaye answered, gently moving a few strands of bouncy hair that had fallen over her cheek. "If I tell you another story, you tell me yours. Do we have a deal?"

Thanan nodded in agreement, if for no other reason than to continue to have an excuse to gaze at Jesifaye's perfect bronze face for an extended period of time.

As Jesifaye began her story, the Guardian hung on every word while she painted the beautiful portrait of her life on the Islands of Methina and the adventures she shared with her uncle throughout the world.

Jesifaye was born on Chilipin, the smallest island in the lush island chain of Methina. She was born to merchant parents who lived on the leeward side of Chilipin, whose emerald mountains were fed by rainfall for the majority of the year. The small coastal village where she lived, Lili, was known as the gem of the islands because of the great misty waterfalls that rained down towering cliffs behind the village, which served as a breathtaking backdrop to the merchants' berth on the bay. In the evenings, on rare occasions, the mist glowed emerald green. No one knew why the phenomenon happened, but it was considered good luck to sailors if they witnessed the glowing falls on their way out of the bay, an omen of future prosperity and calm seas.

Lili was a harmonious mixture of the old traditions of the islands combined with the modern industries of trade and shipping. Jesifaye's parents were successful merchants who frequently sailed from island to island, selling fruits, vegetables, and rare spices to eager customers. They sometimes were away from their small island home for so many days that when they sailed into Lili Harbor, their hearts gladdened at the thought of slowing down and spending time nurturing the many orchards on their plantation.

After one particularly fruitful journey to the largest island, Methina, they returned home with their hull heavy with treasure and a womb cradling a new life.

"I'm sure it's a girl," Caryan said, softly rubbing her still-flat tanned stomach. "Bound for greatness, I feel."

"Well, if you are that sure," Zebulon replied, placing his hand on hers as they sat on their porch overlooking the plantation, "What shall her name be?"

"Jesifaye," Caryan said, pausing. "After your sister and grandmother."

"They would be most honored, I'm sure."

It was a profitable year for Zeb and Caryan. Zeb added two

more ships to his fleet, which allowed Caryan to attend to more important matters at home, such as rearing a precocious daughter who was full of wonder.

Five more years of favorable weather and crops followed, which made Zeb and his small family quite wealthy. He added three more ships and even took on a new captain, his brother Samil, who was a skilled sailor and businessman, but had a propensity to operate in the gray.

At the age of six, Jesifaye knew the islands like the back of her hand, having gone with her father on many voyages, buying and selling seasonal goods throughout the Methinian archipelago. The only thing she loved more than the sea was her family – her parents and sometimes her uncle Samil, who was quick to tell a joke and had a tongue shinier than Borunium silver.

Samil soon became Zeb's highest-profiting captain and to reward his brother, Zeb paid him five percent of the entire fleet's profit. This was in addition to his already generous wage.

So great was Samil's gratitude that he proposed his brother and family accompany him on an extended holiday to the affluent coastal village of Windcrest, all expenses paid by Samil, of course.

Windcrest Village sat at the base of the westernmost part of the Jethian Mountains. It took very little to convince Caryan to go, but Zeb, on the other hand, had a vast enterprise to run and convincing him to take a holiday was difficult indeed. But in the end, all it really took was two very sad eyes from a 6-year-old girl and his heart melted.

The well-supplied Jesifaye Sun, which was christened just four years earlier, drifted from its mooring and sailed out of Lili Bay with a small crew and five guests, bound for Windcrest. Zeb,

Caryan, and Jesifaye, along with Samil and his new wife, Violetta, watched their small island shrink into the distance. With some trepidation, Zeb turned and shouted to his brother, "Samil! Take us to Windcrest!"

Holding the metalclad wheel, Samil smiled at his brother, turning with the wind. The main sail went taut and the ship vibrated with approval, cutting through the salty water.

Calm seas and steady winds kept everyone's spirits high as they sailed ever closer to Windcrest. At the end of the eighth day, when the sky was deep red and thousands of stars stared down upon the ocean, they caught their first glance of the Jethian Mountains in the distance. The looming whitecaps glowed red above the low-lying clouds.

Jesifaye ran along the rail shouting at the top of her lungs, "Land ho, land ho! Mom, Dad, Uncle Samil! Land ho!"

Caryan and Zeb laughed at their daughter's exuberance, but their joy stopped abruptly.

"Storm approaching from the south, Captain!" the boatswain shouted.

Just then, as if the boatswain had declared war against the sea, the sails flapped violently, then lost their wind. The air grew warmer, thick, and heavy. An uneasy calmness settled on the water. Across the calm ocean to the south, a towering wall of twisting black clouds and torrential rain loomed over the sparkling water. Brilliant blue and white strikes of lightning struck the ocean, electrifying its surface. It was breathtaking for Jesifaye to see the lightning dance on the water, like bony fingers clawing at an obscure window. She leaned over the railing and saw thousands of swirling glass fish just below the surface, their transparent bodies forming an underwater tornado. She had never seen so many in one place before. They were fleeing from the oncoming storm.

Samil barked out orders to the crew to make ready for the storm. "It will be upon us soon, brother!" Samil shouted over the rumbling thunder.

"Can we outrun it?" Zeb yelled back.

"I'd rather take my chances on the open sea than on the rocks!" Samil shouted, holding the helm tightly.

"Caryan! Violetta!" Zeb called out. "Take Jesifaye below now and brace yourselves!"

Just then, a high swell tipped the ship, sending some of the crew sliding across the deck, grasping for anything to slow their descent. Lightning lit the sky and thunder cracked with the sound of a hundred trees being snapped in half. The crew struggled to reef the main as the ship tossed in the raging waves.

"Furl the jib—" Zeb commanded, holding fast to the rail. "Heave to, Samil! Point her into the waves!"

Samil turned the wheel and brought the Jesifaye Sun's bow into an oncoming wave. The bow rose dramatically out of the water and then slammed down into the trough. The massive timbers groaned from the stress, but the Jesifaye Sun was a sturdy ship.

"Keep her steady!" Zeb shouted over the howling wind. He rubbed the water from his eyes as the stinging spray drove into his cheeks.

Below deck, Jesifaye held on to a rail, watching the raging tempest through a scuttle.

"Get away from there!" Caryan scolded, grabbing Jesifaye's arm. "It's too dangerous!"

Another flash of lightning lit up the sky and shook the ship to its keel. Jesifaye's eyes widened as she saw the mast and the mainsail fall into the water. Caryan placed the lid on the scuttle and pulled her daughter away.

Knowing how dire this was, Jesifaye broke from her mother's grasp with no other thought than to get to her father. As she took her first step up the stairs, the ship shuddered. Jesifaye was knocked to the floor as the massive base of the splintered mainmast punctured through the outer hull, blocking the stairs to the deck. The sea poured in, determined to sink the Jesifaye Sun and kill her namesake. Caryan and Violetta grabbed her up by her arms and retreated to the galley, shutting the door behind them.

"What do we do?" Violetta asked frantically.

"I don't know," Caryan replied, holding her frightened daughter.

"We're trapped!" Violetta yelled, starting to cry.

Above their heads the storm raged on deck. The crew was gone, having been washed overboard and dragged to the bottom of the sea entangled in some of the rigging. In the silhouette of the lightning, Samil held tight to the helm, preventing the ship from capsizing, but the ship was lost, aimlessly tossed by the waves. The weight of the mast, which pierced the ship's side like a god's javelin, caused her to list heavily to port.

Zeb lay on his back, dying, his blood washing over the deck, having sustained a heavy blow to his head by a swinging block. Samil had not seen it happen, being so determined to keep the ship from sinking. Another towering wave crashed over the deck, knocking Samil from his feet. He held on to the wheel and struggled to gain his footing again. The rain drove into his hands and face. He called to his brother, but there was no answer.

The cool seawater rushed into the hull and soon found its way through the galley door. The water quickly rose to the women's waists, and their anxiety rose even quicker. Spices of all varieties bobbed and clanked around them in their glass bottles.

"We at least have to try to escape," Caryan pleaded.

"All right, I'll try," Violetta cried. They opened the galley door and fought the raging current all the way to the stairs. "It's hopeless," Violetta sobbed, her head just above the water.

The ship groaned once more from the stress on the hull. Jesifaye screamed for her mother and clutched her tightly.

"Look at me," Caryan said, distracting her daughter, holding her cheek. "I love you, Jesifaye."

"I love you too, Mama," Jesifaye cried, holding her mother's neck tightly, looking into her green eyes.

"Take a deep breath, baby!" Caryan said, taking in what would be her last breath.

Together, they inhaled deeply and plunged under the water. Caryan guided her daughter to the scuttle and pried the lid from the opening. Jesifaye fought her mother, but Caryan was determined not to lose her only child. She forced Jesifaye through the opening, which was just wide enough to fit her petite shoulders. Jesifaye struggled her way to the surface as the ocean took her mother and Aunt Violetta.

Jesifaye gasped for air as she broke the surface, managing to fill her lungs once before a wave crashed over her head again. She reached for the surface with all her will, groping wildly at the water. Breaking the surface again she took another breath, this time half water. She shouted for her father. Her cries somehow reached Samil's ears, and he gave up the helm. Cutting a lifeboat free, it fell upside down with a great splash. He dove in, narrowly missing the skiff, and climbed onto the bottom of the boat. The waves tossed the boat, knocking him into the water twice, but finally Samil was able to untie a line and throw it to Jesifaye. Skillfully using the line, he righted the lifeboat and pulled Jesifaye in. He unlashed the oars and rowed with all his might away from the unpredictable ship, narrowly dodging the sinking hull.

Samil rowed toward Windcrest, watching the Jesifaye Sun bubble out of sight. Jesifaye sobbed uncontrollably, screaming and reaching for her parents as if to summon them to the surface. Samil's heart was heavy. In one horrible event, he had lost his wife, brother, and sister-in-law. His impulse to end his life then and there was somewhat softened by the whimpering cries of a six-year-old girl who had no one else but him to ease her suffering. And so, in the open sea, he made his commitment to protect and rear the daughter of his brother.

The storm raged on, but the sturdy lifeboat endured the tempest, finally reaching the Windcrest reef before sinking.

"It was there, in Windcrest, that my uncle took me in and our life full of adventure began," Jesifaye concluded, looking over the garrison.

"That was an amazing story," Thanan said, shaking his head with wonder. "I cannot believe you survived."

"That is just the beginning," she replied. "What about your story?"

"Oh? My story? That would not be as exciting as yours."

Thanan glanced up at Xavantha. "It's getting late. Maybe...you can tell me the rest tomorrow, if you like?" Thanan shyly asked, raising an eyebrow.

Thanan and Jesifaye met at the waterway every day for four months, sharing stories of their lives, Thanan being careful not to reveal too much about his true mission. The attraction between the two of them was undeniable, and Thanan feared he had let their relationship develop into something that he could never run from. Thanan knew she would never understand the true nature of his mission, yet there was something still pulling them together like planets caught in each other's gravity.

Thanan and Jesifaye's nightly strolls came to a sudden stop when General Tygrothian summoned all the Guardians to make final preparations for their secret mission. For eight agonizing days, Thanan's mind was splintered between doing his duty and thinking about Jesifaye. Although their time apart was brief, to Thanan those eight days seemed an eternity. He had grown to love the long conversations they shared about their lives, and he struggled to remember what it was like before she came back into his life.

Through their five months together, Thanan found that Jesifaye was so much more than just beautiful. She was gentle and kind, even living the adventurous life she did with her uncle. She was willing to serve those around her and had adopted her uncle's quick wit as well, which she used to no end when recounting the fantastic tales of her life. Thanan was truly enchanted by this Jinian woman from Methina.

CHAPTER TWENTY-SIX

TORN

It was the eve of the mission and at the conclusion of the council, General Tygrothian commanded everyone involved in the mission to retire to their quarters and spend the evening with their families. Thanan, of course, was invited to join Kigron and his family for their evening meal. It had been a few weeks since he had shared a meal with his adopted family, because of his busy schedule as a Guardian. Thanan always considered it an honor and graciously accepted. He knew it would be the last time he would see his Goriath family, and he had grown very close to them throughout the time he had lived among the giants.

His stomach fluttered thinking about seeing Jesifaye again. It had only been eight days, yet it felt like weeks. It was a feeling that he hated. *A Guardian is supposed to control every emotion*, he thought as he walked to the Gru home.

Seretha prepared a farewell feast that only a Goriath giant could truly appreciate. They all sat around a modest, cloth-covered table adorned with a savory assortment of Goriath cuisine. Sautéed mushrooms in a fish broth gravy slowly dripped down over a mound of freshly caught fish. The buttery smell of warm biscuits floated through the air and made Thanan salivate, but the one thing that the Jinian had not experienced before was the ground cave snails, stuffed in their shells with herbs and minced mushrooms. After the truly disgusting things he had to ingest while on his journey through the darkness, the snails seemed like a delicacy by comparison.

"Oh, I've missed this," Thanan said, smiling at the beautiful cook.

Knowing it would be the last time he would sit down with Jesifaye and Kigron's family, he was unusually nervous and shot an uneasy smile at Jesifaye.

"Why don't we eat like this all the time?" Simo asked, reaching for a biscuit.

Seretha rapped her knuckles.

"Remember, guests first," her mother scolded lovingly. "It is not every day that we have a Guardian at our table. Go ahead, Thanan."

The Guardian grabbed a fluffy biscuit from the bowl. "Thank you. These smell delicious."

"I do not remember the last time that I got the first biscuit," Kigron said, half serious.

"Well, you're just a captain and he is a Guardian," Tirothia said innocently, in her high-pitched voice.

She picked up her fork and mimicked wielding a sword. Simo quickly picked up her spoon and clashed it against her sister's fork. Everyone laughed and Kigron took the second biscuit.

During supper, Tavris proudly shared his adventures in the back caves, picking off kopi with his friends and delighting in ridding the cavern of sawtooth vermin.

For the most part, Jesifaye was silent during the meal, only offering an occasional laugh at Tav's antics. She too loved her adopted family. Thanan caught her more than once staring at him with a pensive look, and he sensed there was something pressing her mind.

After the meal, Kigron shared more stories of the old world with one particular story intriguing Thanan. He told of a master blacksmith who created twin swords for King Goriath III. To honor the king on the fiftieth anniversary of his coronation, the king's wife, seven years prior, had commissioned in secret that the blacksmith forge two Zythera blades from the purest zil ore and Zythera crystals ever mined from the caves. The rare green Zythera crystals had been passed down from king to king and she thought it a fitting use of the gems.

The blacksmith labored seven long years creating the two masterpieces and, when he was finished, had forged the two strongest blades known to the world. They were given the name Zythixia, that is to say Twin Stones in the ancient tongue of the giants, named for the two mighty monoliths beneath Xavantha in the Crystal City. Once they were completed, the blacksmith was mysteriously killed in an accident in his workshop. Rumors spread that he was murdered to ensure that no greater swords would ever be forged.

"I've heard of these swords. Purgon has spoken about them a few times, but never in detail. Where are they now?" Thanan asked.

"No one really knows. Some believe they were buried with King Goriath III, but I believe they are locked away in the king's treasury and will be in close proximity to King Grishon under heavy guard. Most believe that they never existed at all, that they are just a legend."

Kigron paused for a moment and finished his drink. "The hour is late, my friend. Go and rest. Our mission begins tomorrow, before dawn."

On his way out, Thanan passed by Tavris' room. By the light of a dimly lit candle, the boy lay on his back with his bow in hand, pretending to shoot some imaginary beast above his head.

"Is that a fangrix or a silok?" the Guardian whispered, peeking his head in.

"It is a flame w-wr-wrock, and I hit him bet-t-ween the eyes," the boy said with excitement, loosing another imaginary arrow at the beast.

"I'm afraid your arrows won't work on that creature, even if the arrows do come from the mighty Tavris."

"I can k-k-kill it," he replied with confidence.

"You could, could you?" Thanan stepped in and sat on the floor beside Tavris' bed. He pulled from his pack a small pouch. "I wanted to give you this. I won't be needing it anymore."

The scratched up, old compass his father had given him fell from the pouch into his palm. The boy's eyes lit up as he sat up in bed.

Just outside the room, Jesifaye quietly stood and listened. She smiled at the unexpected meekness of her love, and it was at that moment that she finally resigned herself to what she had known all along. At the top of the cavern, overlooking a thousand flickering torches, she would at last express her deepest feelings.

"This compass saved my and Agrinoth's lives in the caves. My father gave it to me when I began my long journey, and now it's yours, if you want it."

"Th-thank you, sir," Tavris replied with reverence in his voice. He grasped the compass and opened the gold lid. "Does it still work?"

"It survived the fire of the flame wrock. I don't think anything can break it. You will take care of it, won't you?"

"Y-yes, sir."

"I know you will. I'm leaving tomorrow and won't be returning. Maybe one day we will see each other again. Tell your sisters goodbye for me and give them these crystals I found in the deepest of the caves." He poured out the colorful gems.

"All r-r-right," he replied, looking at the compass, his active mind already in another place.

Thanan chuckled to himself and stood up.

"You should go to sleep now. I'm sure your mother will be checking on you shortly. You know how she feels about weapons in your bed."

He turned to see Jesifaye softly smiling at him. "Oh…how long have you been there?" he asked, standing up.

"You're the Guardian. You tell me," she replied walking down the hall, beckoning Thanan to follow.

Thanan and Jesifaye walked as they had done so many times before, but a feeling of sadness loomed heavy. They walked slower than usual as if trying to put off the inevitable. Overlooking the garrison, Jesifaye felt safe to tell Thanan anything, and she held nothing back.

"I know you can't tell me everything, Thanan," she began, "…why you are truly here and to what end. I don't expect you to." Thanan smiled and gently took her hand. "But if I were your wife," she continued, "there would be no need for secrets. I could share your burden. I have seen the world, explored it. I could help you."

"I'm leaving before the garrison wakes. What you ask is impossible," Thanan replied, torn between his duty and his unexpected upheaval of emotion. He looked at her petite hand and felt the subtle texture of her skin.

"Kigron could marry us outside the caverns, and I could go with you," she replied, pressing his hand to her cheek.

"Please don't tempt me," he whispered. "You must return to Methina and tell no one of this place. I have revealed things to you…details of our mission that I should not have. What I have to do, you could not bear to see. Nor do I wish that you think less of me."

"There is nothing for me there," she softly replied, drawing Thanan's lips close.

"Please don't," Thanan replied, fighting his own words.

"Why do you forbid me?" She sighed, lowering her head, defeated.

"Because I will not have the strength to leave," he whispered, pressing his lips to her forehead. "And I must leave."

His fingers tangled in her hair and he breathed deeply. Thanan's heart pounded in his chest and his face flushed. Tears ran down Jesifaye's bronze cheeks. She nodded her head trying to convince herself this was the right decision.

Those were the last words they spoke to each other within the depths of the Goriath world.

Thanan's heart was heavy as he lay alone in bed. Sleep finally found him just moments before being rousted by Kigron's firm grip on his shoulder.

CHAPTER TWENTY-SEVEN

TRUTHS REVEALED

After six months of precise planning and preparation, they were ready to embark on their mission to seize the great wealth of the king and bring it back to the Crystal City, preventing a tyrant, his enormous treasure, and his army from joining Lord Haydon. They took great measures to ensure the complete secrecy of the mission, thus the small number involved in the planning. The general couldn't risk any information making its way back to the Goriath king.

Syzimian, Anax, Jorik, and Xagrith were covertly sent ahead three months before to the place where the trap would be set. They worked tirelessly falling trees across well-traveled paths, creating rockslides over the roads leading out of the Goriath Valley, making them all impassable, save one: the gateway to Evergreen.

The gateway was a narrow canyon that wound its way northward and spilled into Evergreen, the Realm of Lady Etheryl...the Angel of Evergreen.

The canyon had only one entry and one escape. Azoth had brought with him intelligence that the king, in his arrogance, would be traveling with only a small contingent of his most trusted soldiers. All this to ensure his safety and not draw any unwanted attention to his actions. Hundreds of the king's soldiers and civilians had already joined with Haydon in the Jethian Mountains, and the king's treasury would be his last grand gesture of loyalty.

Armed to the teeth with bows and Zythera blades, General Tygrothian, Kigron, the spy Azoth Zor, the great archer Tremik, Agrinoth, and Thanan set out before dawn, beginning their secret mission to relieve the king of his vast wealth and to stop him from joining his forces with Lord Haydon.

The small band of warriors embarked on their journey three days behind the exodus to conceal their presence from the king's trailing scouts. As Thanan stepped out from the same crevice in the mountain that he had entered so long ago, he realized that it was the last time he would ever see utter darkness again. The thought struck him hard and saddened him, for he had made darkness his home for so long. He learned much about himself there: how to control his fear, how to trust another with his life.

He breathed a deep breath of sweetly scented valley air and felt a rush of energy course through his frame. His eyes squinted, beholding the green, lush valley below. He saw Loriam in the distance, her flowered fields gently sloping to the lakeshore. There was peaceful silence throughout the valley, which comforted the Jinian's soul.

As his eyes acclimated, he glanced down and noticed his hands were pale, almost sickly, and changed shades of greenish blue as he moved them in front of his face. "My hands and face feel very strange. What's happening to me?" he yelled.

Kigron laughed, "The same thing that happened to our ancient ancestors, although I did not expect it to happen this fast or at all for that matter."

General Tygrothian looked concerned. "We knew something would happen, Guardian, but we did not know how your kind would react to the constant exposure to the crystals. You may experience some unforeseen side effects as your body acclimates to unfiltered sunlight again."

"Unforeseen side effects?" Thanan replied.

"I think we should stick him back in the cave. I do not think I can bear to look upon his paleness without squinting my eyes," Agrinoth stated, only half joking.

Tremik and Azoth laughed at the mockery.

"What should I do?" Thanan asked, fluttering his fingers in front of his eyes.

"Embrace the change, Thanan. Only time will bring about the true gifts you've been given. Focus on the task at hand," the general said sternly.

Agrinoth tightened his belt, looking out over the valley with determination. He pulled the hood of his cloak over his head. "We must speedily find our quarry and rendezvous with our brothers," he announced in his usual dry cadence.

They covertly scaled the Crag Path, avoiding detection of the king's guards at the Crystal Cave entrance. Upon reaching the valley, they ran with haste, following the winding river for one day, stopping only for water. As they ran it seemed as though the earth was shifting below Thanan's feet, and his eyes began to blur. *What is this?* he thought to himself. What have the caves done to me? He paused for a moment, pressing his hand against a tree trunk to collect himself.

"Are you all right, Guardian?" the general shouted. Thanan shook his head and his sight cleared.

After many miles, the small band turned northward into the wild, traveling unkempt paths overrun with dense vines, which prevented most of the sunlight from penetrating to the path before them. The dark shade comforted the Jinian. For hours they forged ahead through the wild thickets, hacking and slashing as they went; with each swing of the blade, they gained on the king and his small army.

Thanan's sword seemed to become lighter as he cut his way through the dense growth. With every swing he grew faster and stronger, and suddenly a wave of nausea dropped him to his knees, his strength gone. Thanan feared Agrinoth might have been correct, even in his jest, that he should stay behind in the cave.

"I fear I've compromised the mission, General," he said, eyes watering, retching the morning meal.

"It will pass, Thanan. Just keep moving." Agrinoth helped him to his feet, looking worried for his sickly brother. Thanan thanked him with a nod and went back to swinging his blade through the brush.

Kigron led the group most of the way, while Agrinoth trailed behind to ensure that they were protected from anyone who dared follow them. Thanan did not envy the unfortunate scout who might stumble upon their location. The mighty Guardian would surely cut down the unsuspecting giant before he knew what he had discovered.

Their journey continued north for a day until they were within striking distance of the suspected trailing scouts of King Grishon. General Tygrothian was very familiar with the king's military tactics, so he knew the king would leave behind scouts to identify any potential threat to his exodus. Although the king and his military had grown fat from their affluence, they were still Goriath soldiers armed with Zythera blades, bows, and deadly training.

Suddenly, an intense burning swept through Thanan's hands and face, like they were set afire, but there was no flame. He poured cool water over his face and clenched his fists over and over to alleviate the pain. The burning continued for a brief time and then subsided. *This is getting tiresome*, he thought.

General Tygrothian looked over the forest with discerning eyes and spotted a secluded cluster of trees below a rise in the land. "We will set up camp over there," he commanded. "The trees will conceal our presence from any scouts who might wander too close. Keep the fire low."

After setting up their modest camp, they all sat around the fire, staring into the flames. The forest was alive with all manner of creatures that did not seem to mind the intrusion, so they shared their symphony of peaceful sounds. Azoth added to the melody by humming a haunting song of his own.

Thanan admired Azoth's ability to sing in harmony with the forest orchestra. "What song is that?" he asked prodding at the fire with a crooked stick.

"It's an old song from the Zor clan. Some say you can trace the melody all the way back to Derkshire," Azoth replied. His face became peaceful as he stared into the orange flames of the fire.

"What is it Azoth? You look a thousand miles away."

"This is how we once were, taming the earth, living under the colored sky. It's what we were born to do, what our ancestors held most dear."

"It will be again, brother," Kigron said encouragingly, tossing a biscuit to Azoth.

Sipping on river water from their flasks, they ate an easy meal of cured sowbelly, biscuits and wild bitter berries, which flourished in the most shaded and damp parts of the forest.

Thanan noticed Agrinoth rubbing his calf, revealing his horribly scarred skin. "Still hurts?" He gestured toward Agrinoth's leg with a stick.

"Only when I walk…or stand…or eat," he replied, half smiling. Everyone chuckled at Agrinoth's rare attempt at humor.

"Serves you right, letting that dragon chew on you like that," Tremik interjected. "If it were me, that beast would never have come within thirty steps."

"That is only because all it would have seen is your old fleeing backside," the achy Guardian shot back.

Thanan laughed at the banter.

"Kigron, tell me more about Zythixia." Thanan drew his sword, looking at it with fondness.

"They may be with the king, maybe not. I do not know if the

twin stones truly exist, Thanan. They were made for childhood stories," the captain replied, looking at his father.

Tygrothian poked the fire with his own stick and looked at Thanan and then at Azoth. "The blades were forged when I was still in the service of King Goriath III. His real name was Jorithian. He was the third son of Goriath II. It was the way back then to assume the name of Goriath, to carry on the traditions of the throne. He was a good king, compared to his father. He was the only king determined not to take his people into war, until his wife, Kirithel, commissioned the twin blades be forged with the green Zythera crystals. Only one small vein of green Zythera was ever found, and its properties were unique. Grik Jil was the name of the blacksmith who forged Zythixia."

Agrinoth was about to tear a hunk of sowbelly off with his teeth, but stopped, his interest piqued. It was a name he knew well.

"Yes, Agrinoth, he was Purgon's older brother, your uncle. He was one of three brothers from the Jil clan who made the first trek to the caverns. Purgon's youngest brother, Zinaka was a candidate to the Order, a mighty warrior who sadly died in the darkness."

Thanan and Agrinoth shot a knowing glance at each other.

"Grik, however was a brilliant blacksmith when we lived in the sun, but when he began experimenting with Zythera crystals," the general paused, "the weapons that followed emboldened future kings in their conquest for wealth and power. The blades could not be broken, and the armor: almost impenetrable."

"You never told me this," Kigron interrupted.

"I have lived longer than any giant should. I have committed many sins, and whether by commission or by omission, they are the same to me, my son. I saw many atrocities and did nothing when I was young. I killed in the name of the king and conquest."

Everyone in the circle was quiet. The fire popped and sparks floated up, then died. The mighty leader and father they knew and loved was nothing like the description of his younger self.

"That was long ago, General," Agrinoth stated, nodding his head respectfully at Tygrothian, dismissing the story.

"I do not tell you this for pity's sake," he replied, looking sorrowful. "Zythixia was conceived in secret for a dark purpose. It is something I wish with all my heart did not happen, but it did. And twenty lifetimes of penance cannot make up for it."

They listened intently deep into the night while the general spoke of Goriath history that only he regretfully carried.

Jorithian and Kirithel began to fight between themselves only a few years after he took the throne and changed his name to Goriath III, as was the tradition. Jorithian was for the most part a peaceful king who only wanted to delve deeper into the mountain, rather than stealing, plundering, and murdering. The Goriath giants loved him but began to express freely their discontent with prior laws that they thought somewhat oppressive; they hoped Jorithian might hear their pleas. Jorithian embraced the freedom of expression in the hope that he could more easily transform the society into a republic, with capitalism being the driving force of their economy rather than a monarchy. He hoped that he could reestablish trade and other profitable ventures with the Sundwellers and create allies, like the Jinians.

Jorithian's wife, Kirithel, liked the old ways and saw his new way of ruling as a weakness; she appealed to him many times privately, to no avail. Soon her petitions became public and confidence in the king's ability to rule came into doubt, but Kirithel was a patient woman. She conspired with two giants, loyal to her and the old way of governing.

In secret, Grik Jil worked for seven long years forging Zythixia. Many even thought that he must have summoned the help of some sort of earthen god that could meld the minerals of the underearth in unnatural ways. When the anniversary celebration was over and the king and queen lay in their chamber, Jorithian opened the metal box one more time to admire the kingly blades before he slept. He died before his head hit the pillow. Before the king's body could be examined, the queen ordered the corpse be burned in the city square under the Xavantha crystal in a great ceremony.

The queen seized the throne, convincing everyone that Grik had cursed the swords. She seduced her captain, the second conspirator, with the promise of her devoted love, wealth, and position, and he regrettably killed Grik to ensure the secrecy of the dark plot. Her lust for wealth and power drove her to delve deeper into the rock as well as go to war against Darvinshire. It was there that she sent her captain to the front lines to be slaughtered. It was a war to conceal a coup.

Before the Goriath army was defeated and driven back into the crystal caves by the Jinian army, the queen died. Against the foreman's wishes, the queen had demanded that the excavation continue in a weakened mineshaft. The mine collapsed, entombing her in the crystals she loved. Her faithful captain returned a hero and was made general.

"Please forgive an old fool, Agrinoth."

The Guardian looked at Tygrothian for a moment and then at the fire. "I do not know this general of whom you speak."

Everyone nodded in agreement. The Tygrothian that they all knew and loved had spent many lifetimes in the service of the Goriath kings, and his tainted past was a distant memory.

"But what of Zythixia? How did Jorithian die?" Kigron asked, baffled by the new information.

"Ever since King Goriath the First conspired to kill the regent so long ago, poison has been the weapon of choice for assassinations. There has always been a certain...elegance to a good poisoning. Don't you think, Thanan?" Tygrothian asked.

Kigron glanced at the Jinian strangely, then back at his father. The question seemed out of place.

"The green crystals in Zythixia are unlike any crystals ever found in the mines. There is a strange power in them, and in the hands of the right person...now that power would be something to see. No king after Jorithian ever wielded the swords out of fear of being cursed or killed, so they were hidden in the treasury. I am sure King Grishon will have them close by, a kingly gift for a dark lord," Tygrothian explained.

Breaking camp in the morning, they started toward the gateway to Evergreen, walking silently through the forest in a staggered formation to prevent them from being attacked all at once. The forest was quiet and shafts of light broke through the branches, dappling the earth with warm light. Thanan looked upward and spotted a small flock of birds twisting and turning through the tightly woven branches. Red bitter berries contrasted the green and yellow foliage around them. In the distance they could see the jagged canyon walls of the gateway.

"We are close," Tygrothian whispered, motioning to everyone to take cover.

Agrinoth climbed to the top of a bluff for a better view of the soldiers. He returned with a sober expression on his face and even more sobering news.

"What did you see, Guardian?" Azoth asked. "Is Grishon in the canyon?"

"Yes, the king's carriage is in the canyon, but he is accompanied by his entire army...five hundred at least."

"It seems that your intelligence was wrong, Azoth," Tygrothian stated.

Azoth was pained by his inaccuracy. It was something to which he was not accustomed.

"The king must know we are coming," Kigron added.

Their hearts sank after hearing the report. Three hundred and fifty battle-ready giants led the king's march toward Haydon's secret rendezvous, with one hundred or more trailing behind. Surrounding the king's carriage was his royal guard, the elite members of the royal army.

"This can't be the end of our mission," Thanan stated. "We are too close to go back now."

The small group was overwhelmingly outnumbered and there was nothing they could do but bravely go to their deaths.

"Thanan speaks the truth. No, we will not retreat. We will not fail our people," General Tygrothian said proudly. "We will press forward and join our brothers and find victory on the battlefield.

We still have a few tricks left."

Suddenly the forest became eerily silent, and Kigron had just enough time to draw his Zythera blade when they heard a whisper in the air. Thanan quickly turned to see General Tygrothian fall to the earth, revealing an arrow shaft protruding from his side. Agrinoth and Tremik drew their bows and took cover behind a closely spaced group of trinia trees that filled the forest before the gateway, while Kigron and Azoth dragged the general behind a jagged boulder. Kigron quickly snapped the shaft and threw it to the ground.

"A scout!" the captain shouted, pressing on the bleeding wound. "You are going to be fine, Father. I must leave you now." Kigron took his father's hand and pressed it against the wound.

"Go…I will stay with him," Azoth assured him.

Kigron bolted for the trees and disappeared into the thick brush as Thanan took cover behind a nearby tree and peered around, drawing his bow. At first he didn't see anything, but as he focused his eyes, they began to burn. He closed his eyes and shook his head. *Not now*, he thought, blinking his eyes heavily. Just then, another arrow flew, narrowly missing the Jinian's cheek. The arrow crashed into the brush behind him, which brought him back to the moment.

Determined to kill the assassin, he looked again around the tree and perceived the faintest shift of light sixty paces away amongst the brush. It seemed as though the leaves moved, but there was no breeze. He indicated to Agrinoth and Tremik that he saw something, and the giants acknowledged Thanan's signal with a nod.

The Jinian looked over to where Kigron and Azoth had dragged the general, but Kigron was no longer there. Tygrothian was sitting with his back against the boulder holding his side, blood running between his fingers. With one hand Azoth grasped the general's shoulder, holding him up against the rock. With the other, he drew his sword, ready to kill anyone who threatened his general.

Suddenly, another arrow rushed by Thanan's head, missing his shoulder by inches, sticking into a tree behind him. Without thinking, he quickly loosed an arrow blindly back from where the scout's arrow had originated. The scout fell from his hiding place to his knees, Thanan's arrow protruding from his shoulder. Just as the scout started to retreat he was struck in the ribs by one of Tremik's arrows, causing him to stumble to the ground. The heavily armored scout managed to scramble to his feet once again. He turned to run, but stumbled only two steps before he was jolted by Kigron's cold Zythera blade piercing his stomach. It seemed that in all the excitement, Kigron had slowly and stealthily closed in on the scout without detection.

As the scout's wide eyes met Kigron's, the captain whispered, "This is for my father."

The scout closed his eyes, slipped off Kigron's sword, and slumped to the ground. The captain took the scout's quiver and ran for his father.

They all gathered around the general as Kigron and Azoth helped him to his feet.

"We must fall back to the caves and bring more men," Kigron pleaded, holding his father up.

"This is our only chance. The king will be gone by the time we return," Agrinoth insisted, looking around the rock for more signs of the enemy.

The general, obviously weakened, replied, "Agrinoth is right. There is not enough time. You must continue on without me."

"You will not make it back on your own," Kigron pleaded, pulling out one of the scout's arrows from its quiver. He sniffed the arrowhead and turned up his nose, repulsed by the odor. "Tipped with anthepitis," he growled, throwing the arrow to the ground in disgust. "Coward!"

The general nodded knowingly at Thanan and continued, "You must not fail. Now go! I will be all right. Azoth will get me back to Hardrock."

Kigron gripped his father's cloak tightly as if to say, "I will not leave you," knowing there was nothing he truly could do. It was an unspoken goodbye from father to son, general to captain, both bound by duty.

"Hear me now, each of you," the general commanded. "In secret, I ordered Captain Shimian from the Whitehall outpost to set out one day behind us on a training exercise with his battalion. The battalion is following the path that we made for them. They are ignorant as to why they are coming, but they will know shortly. I am truly sorry for the deception, but it was necessary. We couldn't afford to be detected by the king's spies. Captain Shimian is the only one who knows the true purpose."

Kigron glanced briefly at Thanan. It was an expression of sadness. Then, the expression turned to determination. "We know what to do. Move out!" he barked.

They left General Tygrothian and Azoth Zor vulnerable, hiding behind the boulder.

CHAPTER TWENTY-EIGHT

TWIN STONES

Captain Kigron, Tremik, Thanan, and Agrinoth secretly pursued the king and his giants into the narrow canyon, growing ever closer to their appointed position.

"We know one thing," the captain announced. "We need to hold off the king's guards until Captain Shimian's battalion can join the battle."

Arriving at the entrance of the canyon, The cliffs rose dramatically toward the galaxy-filled sky. No vegetation grew there. It was as if the forest that stood at its doorstep was afraid to cross its threshold. One by one they began to climb the cliffs where the Guardians had concealed thick ropes among the shadowed canyon walls.

To see a Goriath giant climb a rope was almost indescribable. Kigron and Agrinoth hefted their massive weight hand over hand, as if gravity did not apply to them. Tremik trailed behind, out of sight. They reached the top of the canyon and ran along the ledge, concealing themselves behind large boulders that lined the ridge, until they overtook the trailing guards. The trio paralleled the king's carriage and his numerous carts of treasure and jewels for another five miles, and then it began.

As the king's leading soldiers slowly marched past the waiting rockslide, Tremik signaled the Guardian, Anaz, who had gone before, by firing an arrow into the chest of the king's closest bodyguard, dropping him where he stood riding on the edge of the carriage. By the flight of the arrow, they supposed the attack came from the direction of the tree line.

"We're under attack!" the king's general called out. "Protect the king and the treasure!"

The first rockslide was triggered, and all the soldiers could do was helplessly watch as the granite boulders crashed down the cliff walls. The sea of rocks swept over them, engulfing at least seventy-five giants and successfully separating the king from the majority of his protectors. The six Guardians and their captain sent a wave of arrows down into the canyon, striking many of the bodyguards who had taken defensive positions around the king's carriage. Tremik sent a steady wave of perfectly placed arrows, dropping many soldiers where they stood.

Another rockslide was triggered; this time behind the king's carriage and the dozens of carts full of treasure, killing many and cutting off the trailing guards from the king. About two hundred and fifty of the king's guards still remained. They began launching arrows blindly in the direction of the Guardians but struck far from their marks. The small band had the definite strategic advantage of being in an elevated position, and they exploited that advantage with perfection.

"Protect the king!" the king's captain screamed from behind the rockslide. "Get back to the king!"

Some of the soldiers began the long climb up the towering rockslide to defend their king and the treasure. Others took cover from the falling arrows in the deep crevices of the cliff walls. Some even abandoned the king and fled through the gateway, no doubt to join up with their brothers in the Jethian Kingdom. The king's captain spotted the deserters fleeing northward.

"Shoot those cowards!" he ordered, ducking a Guardian's arrow.

In the confusion of the falling rocks and flying arrows, the king's army could not detect that only a small group of eight caused all the mayhem. They supposed that the Sundwellers, under orders from Prince Ky, sought to steal the treasure and take some sort of vengeance upon their Goriath ancestors.

A few of the soldiers discovered the hidden ropes and started climbing under cover-fire provided by their skilled bowmen. Agrinoth ran to the ropes and began cutting, but the king's archers rained arrows at him, forcing him to retreat behind the ledge, out of sight. One by one, the Guardians flung their arrows at the climbing soldiers, causing them to fall to the canyon floor.

Thanan looked at the opposite ridge and noticed the soldiers were approaching the top of the ledge. He shouted across the canyon, "The ropes! Quick, the ropes!"

They turned and saw the king's guards crest the ledge. The Jinian quickly loosed an arrow at the leader, sending him two hundred feet to his death. The falling soldier took three with him. Syzimian and Jorik drew their swords and rushed the oncoming soldiers, engaging them in battle, cutting them down with ease.

Thanan turned his attention to the king's carriage, which was stranded between the rockslides. He started down a rope and was almost to the bottom when an arrow grazed his cheek. Knowing he was in the archer's sights, he dropped fifteen feet to the canyon floor and rolled to his feet, drawing his Zythera blade in one fluid motion as he stood. He took four quick steps and cut through the archer's wooden bow and exposed neck with one swift swing. Turning to the king, Thanan ran toward the carriage.

"Kill that Jinian!" the king ordered from his window, jowls wagging.

Without slowing down, Thanan met the first bodyguard one hundred feet from the carriage. Before the oncoming soldier could lift his sword, Thanan flung his own blade with a smooth upward swing, then followed with a quick flurry, slicing the soldier's thigh and torso. Thanan's attack was so fast it appeared as if the bodyguard was standing still. He was already on to his next attack when the lifeless soldier fell to the ground. The Guardian continued dispatching the king's personal guards one by one, with little effort. The last bodyguard stepped from the carriage and drew his sword with a smirk on his face. He was larger than the others, no doubt the king's closest and most skilled protector. He rushed toward Thanan with a mighty overhead swing. The Guardian skillfully stepped to the side and sliced through the back of the rushing guard's leg. He roared in pain but did not fall. He lunged again, this time at Thanan's stomach. The Jinian nimbly parried the attack and thrust his sword into the giant's chest. Thanan glanced to his right and saw another archer draw his bow. Quickly grabbing the bodyguard's shoulders, he spun; and with a dull thud, the arrow struck the back of the guard. Thanan reached the carriage before the king's guard fell to his knees, slumping to the ground.

The pale Guardian climbed into the carriage, not surprised to discover the king cowering on the floor with a jeweled dagger in his hand. Thanan calmly sat on a cushioned bench and bounced his backside on it a few times, admiring how comfortable it was.

"Guards!" the king shouted.

"Shhh...sh...sh..." Thanan said, holding his finger to his lips. "Where's Zythixia?" Thanan leaned on his sword as if he were having a conversation with a friend.

"I do not know what you are talking about, Jinian," the king replied, still cowering.

Thanan ran his fingers along the silken cushion, creating more anxiety for his prisoner.

"This is a real nice place you have here, King. Where are you going with all this treasure? Where are your people- the old ones and the children? Did you leave them all behind to die?"

Sweat was pouring down the king's face and puddling in the folds of his neck. He eyed his dagger.

"You would do well to stay on the floor, like the cave slug you are," Thanan stated.

Grishon seethed, but said nothing.

"Do you know who I am?"

The king stared at his captor, his mind trying to make sense of what he was seeing. Then his eyes widened and his skin paled.

"The merchant," he muttered under his breath.

"Very good, King. And by the way, I won't be coming to our rendezvous at the Great Divide."

"We burned the Jinian's body in the City Square and danced on his ashes. Too bad we did not have a chance to listen to the woman squeal like a sow. She was pretty, for a Jinian. I could see why you wanted her." The king wetted his lips with his devilish tongue.

"Shut your filthy mouth!" Thanan shouted, kicking King Grishon's pudgy face. It was all the Guardian could do to not kill the king right then and there, but that was not the plan and he restrained himself.

"You are a ghost and do not even know it!" Grishon growled, lips and nose bleeding on the carriage floorboards. "So you are this Jinian Tygrothian has taken such an interest in. Soon this will all be Lord Haydon's. And you will suffer grievously for what you have done."

"You call him Lord Haydon?" Thanan scoffed. "What is he lord of? A few rabble in the mountains... your pathetic army?"

Just then, a soldier rushed into the carriage and promptly met Thanan's blade. He crumpled to the inlaid wooden floor.

"You should leave now, Jinian," the king pleaded, trying to reason with his captor. "You are outnumbered. You cannot kill all my soldiers. Leave me now and I will spare your life."

"That is a very generous offer, King," Thanan replied, mocking the king's assumed majesty by bowing his head slightly. "I'm going to ask you one more time. Where are the twin swords?" The king was silent and looked nervous. "Zythixia!" the Guardian yelled, pointing the tip of his blade in front of the king's bleeding nose.

King Grishon slowly sat up, his arms shaking to support his weight. He darted his eyes to the floor of the carriage.

"Stand up!" Thanan demanded.

Thanan quickly moved to the floor of the carriage and found a hidden compartment under the floorboards. Opening the trap door, he found a long metal box inside. He pulled the box from the hold and examined its ornate lid. The outer edge was inlaid with rare crystals and jewels. Its design was uniquely early Goriath and etched in the center of the lid, the phrase, "Goriath My Love" in elegant scroll. As he ran his fingers down the length of the cold surface, the Jinian's pale hands started to burn and shift color again.

The craftsmanship of the box was only eclipsed by what Thanan found inside.

He opened the box to reveal the legendary weapons; blades crossed and beckoning him to pick them up. The Jinian may have been only the fourth person to ever touch Zythixia, and he considered it an honor to be in their presence. As he reached for the twin blades, a sudden wave of weakness ran through his body and his eyes began to blur. The sounds of fighting soldiers grew loud and were distorted, then faded off into the distance. He could hear Kigron yelling from afar to his men so clearly, as if he were in the carriage next to him.

"Take cover!" Kigron screamed.

His commands grew louder and louder and then became almost muted. Thanan swore that he heard Captain Shimian ordering his battalion to move faster, but that couldn't be; he was still so far away.

In Thanan's delirium, the king saw his advantage and lunged for the swords, but Thanan stopped him short by tackling him and pinning his thick wrist to the floor as the king struggled to stab him with his jeweled dagger. The king pawed at Thanan's face and finally grasped the Jinian's throat.

"Your hands are not worthy to touch Zythixia!" the king screeched, his eyes wide with blood lust.

Thanan struck the king in the head with the hilt of his sword, knocking him unconscious. He placed the king's dagger in his belt and looked over at the swords.

The twin stones pulsed waves of green energy from the blades. Thanan squinted his eyes and shook his head in disbelief. Can this really be happening? *Would anyone else see this, or is this my imagination?* he asked himself. The force of the energy seemed to pull his hands toward the swords, almost uncontrollably. The power became intoxicating as his hands drew closer. Thanan was so overcome by his desire to hold the them that he had forgotten where he was and that his Guardian brothers were fighting for their lives just outside the carriage.

The sounds around the Jinian were confused and loud, swelling then subsiding. He grabbed the first sword and all at once the noise stopped. The silence was jarring. He reached for the second sword and held it in his hand, feeling the weight and studying the craftsmanship. Energy radiated through his hands then into his arms. Thanan felt a familiar warm power rush over him, similar to the power in the King's Tower in Jin, except the power was within him, not around him.

Just then, Thanan's surroundings came back to focus, but with more clarity than before. A hand reached into the carriage and grabbed his foot, yanking him out of the door, his forehead bouncing off the ground. The stunned Guardian turned over and brought his new sword down on the soldier's forearm, cleanly removing it from his body. The Jinian sprang to his feet and followed with a second blow with his opposite hand; the blade slicing through the giant's crystal breast plating.

Thanan looked up at the ridge to see Kigron and Agrinoth cutting many soldiers down with their swords.

"Fall back to the trees!" Kigron commanded, waving his hand.

From behind a boulder, Tremik loosed an arrow, cutting one of the ropes that held many climbing soldiers, sending their bodies hurtling toward the canyon floor. The great archer continued to offer cover as Kigron and the Guardians made their way toward the tree line.

Thanan ran to the canyon wall and began to climb toward soldiers who were headed for Kigron and Agrinoth. The first soldier he encountered didn't notice him behind, until he felt the Jinian's hand on his heel and the rush of the wind on his back as he fell one hundred feet to the rocks below.

Thanan continued up the rope with ease toward the next unfortunate soldier, who looked down to see the king's dagger plunge deep into his thigh. He let go with one hand to grab his leg, screaming in agony. He then let go of his leg, drawing his sword, swinging wildly at Thanan's head. The Jinian quickly ducked the soldier's swing and sliced his forearm, causing him to drop his sword. The giant tried to hold on but fell from the rope, groping at Thanan's armor as he dropped to his death.

Thanan met three more soldiers on the rope, quickly introducing them to the canyon floor. He reached the top of the ledge and joined Kigron and Agrinoth. The Guardians and the captain ran on opposite sides of the canyon toward the forest.

Kigron looked at the sky while he ran. "We need to hold them off for just a little while longer," the captain shouted. "We need to lead them right into the path of Shimian's battalion."

After running for some time, they all dove over the edge into the safe arms of the towering trees branches that lined the gateway and scurried their way to the ground. Seventy-five heavily armored soldiers trailed behind them, intent on killing the assassins. They found cover behind the wide trinia trees and took aim at their oncoming enemy.

Eight arrows flew and eight of the king's soldiers fell. They reloaded and one by one the soldiers were stopped by their precision archery. They continued to fall back deeper into the forest, stopping every fifty lengths to take cover and let more arrows fly at their pursuing foe. More and more soldiers climbed over the rockslides to rejoin the fight in the forest.

The galaxy-filled sky shifted from the brilliant blue and gold of midday to the fiery red of dusk, darkening the everything. Traversing the dense forest was becoming more difficult without the aid of torchlight. They could see the torches of King Grishon's army growing closer by the moment. The eight had exhausted all of their arrows. The air was quiet now and cool. Torches dotted the forest floor as soldiers methodically searched for any sign of their attackers.

The captain and the Guardians concealed themselves under leaves and behind brush, hoping their pursuers would pass them by in the darkness. Tremik had disappeared. No one had seen him for several hours. Kigron supposed he had fallen to an archer's arrow, and it saddened him greatly. The soldiers were close enough for Thanan to hear their footsteps. He closed his eyes and held his breath. With each break of a twig under the soldiers' feet, the Guardians grew more nervous that they would be discovered.

"Over here, I found one!" a scout called out to his captain.

Swords began clashing in the dimly lit forest. Agrinoth broke from his cover and rushed to assist his fellow Guardian. In his haste, another soldier discovered Kigron's location, and a second battle ensued.

"I'm coming, Kigron!" Thanan yelled. He drew his twin blades and ran ahead of Kigron to intercept the approaching attackers. The cloaked Jinian met the first soldier from his side at a full sprint. He swung his sword through the giant's thigh and continued toward the next attacker. As he met each one of them in battle, he left them lifeless on the forest floor.

Kigron took cover behind a particularly gnarled trinia tree and watched in awe as the cloaked silhouette of his Jinian friend singlehandedly killed fifteen Goriath warriors within a minute. It was a truly masterful exhibition of grace and brutality. During the skirmish he saw something unusual. With every clash of Thanan's swords, he noticed that a green flash lit up the immediate area, when the flash should be blue.

Kigron surveyed the scene. The king's soldiers were becoming too numerous. "Thanan, fall back deeper into the forest." As they retreated together, they could hear Agrinoth and the Guardians fighting in the distance. Flashes of blue light exploded in the darkened woods as their swords clashed.

Agrinoth's skill in battle could only be compared to Master Kizaga himself. Every movement was precise as he maneuvered among the enemy, sometimes cutting them down two at a time.

To witness five Guardians fighting together as a unit brought fear to those who opposed them. As the oncoming soldiers fell by the sword, so did many also fall from broken necks and fractured spines. Most of the king's army had never seen a Guardian in action, let alone met one on the battlefield. So skillful were the Guardians that they wasted no movement. Every swing of the Zythera blade fell with a purpose and each pivot of the foot was a deadly dance. It made onlooking soldiers tremble with fear at the thought of joining in the fray.

Away from the battle, a few soldiers slipped by Kigron and Thanan, and they found themselves surrounded. They stood back to back, ready to fight to the death.

"Well, what do we have here, boys?" a cocky guard mocked, while ten others circled and laughed. He looked Kigron up and down, recognizing a captain's armor. "I think we've found their captain. He's the traitor general's son."

"You!" another soldier commanded. "You are the smallest Goriath I've ever seen. Were your parents some sort of freaks? What's your name?"

"Do not speak," Kigron whispered.

Thanan pulled the hood from his head, revealing his pale face and long hair.

"It's the Jinian scum the general warned us about. He stole the legend blades from the king's carriage. The general wants him alive. He wants to cut off his head and stick it on a spike himself. You can kill the captain."

They laughed again.

"Drop your weapons," the soldier ordered.

"The general warned you?" Thanan said, smiling slightly. "He warned you about a weak Jinian? Why do you think he did that? Oh, I remember," he continued, mockingly. "I left your king unconscious in his carriage lying in a puddle of his own urine."

"You took Zythixia? Why would you do that?" Kigron whispered. "You're going to get us killed! Shut your mouth."

"Now's not the time," Thanan replied, speaking from the side of his mouth. He slowly raised his hands submissively. "All right, all right. We'll go quietly." He drew the twin stones from behind his back, appearing as if he were going to toss them at the soldier's feet. His hands began burning as they neared the hilts. "Are you ready for this, Kigron?"

"I hope you know what you are doing."

Twenty-five soldiers now surrounded them. The pale Guardian took one step toward the loudest of the king's soldiers as Kigron drew his sword and looked up for what he believed to be his last sight of the glorious galaxy-filled sky. Then a puzzled expression came over the captain's face.

The commanding soldier followed the captain's gaze toward the sky. "Look at the sky! Take cover!" a soldier warned his men.

Suddenly, like an answer to Kigron's prayer, hundreds of flaming blue arrows fell from above, striking soldiers all around the captain and Thanan. One arrow narrowly missed Kigron's boot, igniting the leaves on the ground.

"They're here! The battalion is here!" Kigron yelled.

Thanan looked up again to see another glowing cloud of blue arrows raining down upon them.

"Shimian doesn't know we are here. We have to run!" Thanan shouted, ducking a flaming arrow. "Come this way!"

All around them, arrows fell, creating havoc among the king's soldiers. Screams of horror echoed throughout the forest as arrows found their targets. The intense heat of the arrowheads set afire all that they came in contact with, causing the flaming soldiers to run frantically until they succumbed to the pain and were finally consumed by the fire.

In all the chaos, Agrinoth witnessed Syzimian mortally wounded by oncoming soldiers, but not before he cut down five more of them and bravely fell with many arrows sticking from his torso.

Agrinoth and the remaining three Guardians retreated deeper into the forest toward the battalion and disappeared into the torch-filled forest. Kigron and Thanan also ran toward Shimian's army, but were cut off by a wave of fiery arrows, which forced them to alter their course away from the chaos. They fought their way through dozens of disoriented soldiers as they dodged the glowing blue streaks that were falling from above.

Making their way through the dense forest, the sound of fighting and clanking swords faded into the distance. They finally found themselves alone and exhausted.

"This way," Thanan directed. "It looks safe over there."

They sat against a tree to catch their breath for a moment. Suddenly, Thanan felt weak and dizzy and collapsed to the ground.

After some time, the Jinian awoke to the sound of Kigron's voice. "Good, you are not dead," he said, with a smirk on his face. "You had me worried."

Thanan rubbed his eyes. "What happened?"

"Throughout the night you spoke of secrets and darkness, mostly gibberish, though. So, you did take Zythixia, I see. The legend is true." The captain held one of the twin blades in his hands and ran his thumb along the sharp green edge.

Thanan's attention was turned when he heard a distant voice calling for the captain.

"We must go," Kigron said anxiously, starting toward the searching voice. "I must get back to my father. He may be dying."

The Guardian did not follow.

"Did you hear me, Thanan? We need to get back."

"I'm not going back," he answered plainly, pulling the hood over his head, darkening his face.

"This is no time for games. Turn around and come with me."

Trying to steel himself, Thanan's eyes began to well up, afraid of what he must now do...and began walking away.

"Where are you going, Thanan? Halt! That's an order."

Thanan stopped, slumping his shoulders. "Forgive me, my friend. It is no mistake that we find ourselves here, alone." He exhaled heavily, steadying himself. Reluctantly, Thanan lowered his hand to his waist. He slyly pulled King Grishon's knife from his belt, concealing it within his palm.

"Believe me, there is no pleasure in what I now do," Thanan said soberly, his voice shaking. A tear fell off his lash. "I'm sorry...my friend."

"I have heard enough of your veiled speaking, Guardian. Face me now and return with me at once!" Kigron ordered, grabbing Thanan's shoulder from behind.

Thanan spun around and plunged the king's dagger deep into his friend's chest. Kigron fell to his back gasping for breath, his eyes wide with shock. He swung his sword weakly in a futile attempt to defend himself, but as Thanan approached, he easily knocked it from his hand. He knelt beside his captain as he struggled to realize what was happening. Kigron gasped, grimacing from the pain.

"It has to be this way. Please forgive me," Thanan said, cradling the captain's head.

Kigron looked up at the morning sky, then slowly closed his eyes as his body went limp. A chill ran through Thanan's frame as his nightmares had come to pass. He gently lowered his friend's head, looking toward a large boulder as if he had seen it before. Pounding footsteps in the forest came to a sudden stop. From the corner of Thanan's eye, he saw the soldier's muddy boots standing at the edge of the clearing. The moment of his betrayal had finally come. The Guardian took one last look at his friend, turned to the standing soldier and slowly pulled the blade from Kigron's chest. "You were not supposed to see this," Thanan said, holding the bloody dagger. A maniacal expression swept across Thanan's face as he slowly stepped toward the witness.

The unwitting Whitehall soldier was frozen and couldn't speak. What he had just witnessed was beyond belief. A Jinian Guardian had just murdered his captain. Even though the person in front of him was only a Jinian, the soldier knew he was no match for the Guardian. Thanan's reputation had already grown into legendary proportions. But he had to try. He felt duty-bound to do so. The soldier launched himself at the approaching Guardian. He swung his sword as hard as he could, but Thanan deflected each swing and disarmed him quickly. It took only two punches and a skull-cracking blow to the head with the hilt of Zythixia to knock the soldier out.

With his witness unconscious, time was now more critical than ever. Quickly, he ran to Kigron and grabbing his limp hands, began dragging him toward the large boulder, when he heard a familiar voice exclaim, "What have you done, Thanan?"

In the fray of things, Thanan had not heard more footsteps approaching. The Jinian quickly snapped his head to see Agrinoth standing not thirty feet away with his sword drawn, looking down at the unconscious soldier. He was out of breath, and the expression on his face was one of surprise and confusion, which quickly turned to intense anger as he put the pieces of the puzzle together in his head. Thanan knew that expression all too well. *Of all the giants to witness this horrible thing, it had to be you,* Thanan thought.

"Stand up," the mighty Guardian growled.

Agrinoth gripped his sword tightly and started to walk closer. Thanan's worst fear had come to pass. He didn't fear battling another flame wrock in the heart of the underearth or being eaten alive by a ravenous silok; rather, there was only one thing he feared: fighting Agrinoth. Thanan slowly rose to his feet and turned to face his greatest fear in battle. Agrinoth paced back and forth like a leashed ridgeback grimalkin, ready for the horns to sound.

"I don't want to fight you, brother," Thanan said, trying to calm the warrior. "Please trust me. There are things at work here that are greater than the two of us."

Agrinoth's mind reeled with confusion. He wanted to trust his Jinian brother. He knew Thanan to be an honest man, trustworthy to the end; but the evidence was right there, lying lifeless in the leaves.

"I cannot just let you go," Agrinoth growled. "Do not make me do this. Come peacefully and I will see to it that you receive a fair trial. The general will hear your case and judge fairly."

Thanan had witnessed how vicious the Guardian could be, but never had he seen Agrinoth behave this way before. He was unusually agitated and distressed.

The Jinian paced opposite the giant, matching his movements. Thanan drew the twin stones from over his shoulders, the green blades glinting in a shaft of light that had pierced the smoky air. Agrinoth suddenly stopped. Thanan saw fear in his brother's eyes when he looked at the swords. It was the first time he had seen fear on the Guardian's face.

Agrinoth was afraid, but it was not the swords he feared; it was the thought that Thanan might force him to do the unimaginable.

"We both can go our separate ways right now," Thanan insisted, staring at him.

"Drop your swords now!" Agrinoth commanded. Agrinoth started to circle to his right, and Thanan matched his movements again.

It became deathly quiet in the forest. With every step the giant took, Thanan's senses grew more acute. Agrinoth was smart. He stood across from a highly skilled Guardian who was wielding one of the most deadly weapons in the world. He knew a battle with the blade would end with one of them certainly dead, but the responsibility of a Guardian was to ensure justice would prevail, no matter the circumstance. Knowing that Thanan would not yield, Agrinoth lowered his sword and dropped it to the ground. He clenched his fists until his knuckles were white. Thanan, reciprocating, tossed his twin blades to the ground.

Everything around them seemed to fade away, as if all life on Polizar had hushed to watch their battle. Thanan noticed Agrinoth's weight shift ever so slightly to his back foot and for a brief moment he loosened his fists. It was in this small moment that the Jinian began his attack. He closed the distance between them in two quick steps and swung at the giant's head with his armored knuckles, which the giant blocked. He then threw a sharp uppercut, which caught the giant's chin. It was the second time the Jinian had cut Agrinoth's chin, and the warrior growled out loud as the blood dripped down his neck.

Agrinoth was on his heels now, deflecting the Jinian's powerful swings and kicks. Thanan's speed was unparalleled among the Guardians, and Agrinoth struggled with the seemingly endless barrage. The giant at last found an opening, blocking a heavy swing to his cheek. In an instant, Thanan was on his back, eyes blurry and bleeding from his forehead. He scrambled to his feet before Agrinoth could capitalize on the opportunity. Back and forth they exchanged offensives, to no avail.

The two Nikiru masters circled one another, looking for a small flaw in the other's defense. Their chests heaved for air. Agrinoth glanced at his captain lying on the ground. The anger in his eyes turned to rage. He flew at Thanan, his thundering steps echoing in Thanan's ears. For a moment, Thanan thought he had gained a small advantage when he ducked a wild swing and punched Agrinoth squarely in the nose, crushing it.

Agrinoth groaned from the pain and quickly was on the attack again. He defended his way close enough to grab Thanan around the chest. The giant picked him up and threw him to the ground. Thanan felt all the bones flex inside his body as he bounced and rolled to a stop.

His hand fell upon one of his swords. Desperate, he gripped it, staggering to his feet, hoping to hold Agrinoth at bay until his head cleared. The giant stopped his attack.

"I don't want to kill you!" the Jinian yelled, picking up his second blade. He gripped his swords tightly, shaking his head, still fuzzy from the throw.

"No, Jinian, you cannot kill me!" Agrinoth seethed, looking at Thanan with confusion in his eyes. His brother's dishonor was too much to take.

Thanan's heart sank. It had been quite some time since his Goriath brother had called him "Jinian," and he saw all the hatred from the past fill his brother's heart and magnify his anger.

In the distance, they heard voices in the forest coming their way.

"Over here!" Agrinoth yelled, not taking his eyes off the assumed murderer. Agrinoth ran for his own blade. It angered him even more that the Jinian had forged it for him.

Thanan realized he needed to end the battle quickly. He heard the voices growing nearer. It was the Guardians; Anax and Xagrith. They had heard the fighting and came to investigate.

Agrinoth's skill and strength were almost too much to contend with. With every swing, he grew more powerful and began to force Thanan back. Thanan stumbled backward over a tree root and fell awkwardly against the trunk. He looked up to see Agrinoth's sword falling upon him. Thanan raised his own sword to block the powerful swing, but the strength of the blow sent one of the twin blades spinning through the air, landing on the forest floor behind the tree.

"You've lost, Jinian. Put your blade down!"

Thanan looked into his brother's eyes. Agrinoth knew he would never give up. It was not in the Jinian's nature. It was the trait that had saved them both in the darkness. The giant quickly recoiled and swung wildly at Thanan's remaining sword. At the very last moment, the Jinian ducked and Agrinoth's sword sank deep into the tree.

It was at this time that Thanan saw his opening and knew he had Agrinoth beaten. He was about to plunge his blade into Agrinoth's stomach, but stayed his hand instead. He could not take his brother's life. He lowered his shoulders and dropped his sword. The green blade rolled in the leaves.

With a few heaves on the hilt, Agrinoth managed to dislodge his sword from the scarred tree. It took all his restraint not to take the Jinian's head, but his desire for justice was stronger than his desire to kill him. In one last burst of anger Agrinoth leaned over Thanan, clutched him by his shoulder and punched him in the jaw as hard as he could. Thanan's head twisted violently and snapped back.

"You were my brother!" he growled through bleeding lips.

Thanan raised his pale, trembling hand in a weak attempt to block Agrinoth's final swing, but without warning, the Jinian felt a rush of power course through his body and erupt from his open palm. The glowing pulse lifted Agrinoth high in the air and threw him twenty feet away, snapping tree branches with his back as he flew. He landed firmly on his back with a deep thud. Burning leaves slowly drifted through the air, lighting on the ground. The giant groaned from the impact, his white-hot armor smoldering from the heat of the blast.

Confused, Thanan stared at his hand, still glowing slightly from the energy that had just passed through it. "What?" he said out loud.

He heard the Guardians approaching, picked up the twin swords and started to run from the scene.

Anax and Xagrith entered the clearing. Agrinoth lay on his back, still moaning and smoldering from the blast.

"Stop him," the dazed Guardian managed to say.

"Over there, it's Thanan!" Xagrith shouted, spotting the fleeing Jinian running through the forest.

Thanan limped slightly as he ran from Agrinoth's brutal assault. But even a limping Jinian's speed was too much for the Guardians. They quickly lost sight of him in the dense forest and halted their pursuit.

CHAPTER TWENTY-NINE

ALONE

After running for what seemed like hours, Thanan came upon a rock formation jutting from the earth and hid himself within a crevice. He was exhausted and drank deeply from his flask, catching his breath. In the shadows, he collapsed to his knees trying to grasp the gravity of what he had just done. He quickly made the decision to wait throughout the night before continuing his journey toward Evergreen in the morning. He was sure by then the search parties would have given up hunting for him and begin transporting the king's treasure back to the Crystal City to disburse it among the impoverished Goriaths who had been left behind.

Morning light crept across the forest floor, warming the ground, drying up the dew. Thanan's bones ached. He twisted his neck back and forth, forcing his muscles to loosen up. He had only slept an hour. Many times throughout the night, Shimian's patrols had passed by, unaware of his presence only an arm's length away.

Thanan realized that he was not safe, hidden in the crevice, and quietly slipped away; avoiding the last of the patrols that were still scouring the forest. He found a more suitable hiding place to stay a few days until the forest became safe to travel once more.

Thanan walked through the devastated gateway toward Evergreen. The king's soldiers lay heaped in piles, still smoldering from the fiery arrows that fell upon them. Thanan covered his mouth and nose with his hood as he walked through the scavenger-picked carcasses. The smell was almost unbearable. Thanan kicked one of the vultures that squawked over the last remaining scraps that had not burned. The charred frame of the king's carriage stood as a tragic monument of a race separated by hatred and greed.

Among the rubble, Thanan discovered a small fragment of the box that had held Zythixia for so long. A wave of sadness rushed over him as he brushed the soot from the surface to faintly reveal the words, "My Love." As he gently held it in his hand, it disintegrated to dust and fell through his fingers.

The canyon was desolate. Captain Shimian and his battalion defeated King Grishon's army with little resistance. Thanan estimated from the number of burned corpses that a third of the king's army fled out of the canyon into Evergreen to seek refuge in the mountains with Haydon.

Thanan looked up as he exited the canyon. A towering tree was carved out of stone on each side of the canyon wall, marking the southern entrance into the Realm of Evergreen. He stood in awe of the astonishing detail of the leaves and branches that formed the archway that stretched outward over the canyon floor. The branches tapered toward the center and were held together by a sunburst-shaped keystone. No one knew who made the archway, but it was rumored to have been created before most of the galaxies in the sky began to appear.

As Thanan passed under the arch, he thought to himself, *My father, in his infinite wisdom, put me on a path that collided with a world beyond belief, but it all was a charade. I am now a wanted man. No, I am a hunted man. Agrinoth has now lost two brothers. It is a loss that he must reconcile. In the end I hope we can speak again as brothers and put his heart at ease.*

The vast Evergreen forest now stood between Thanan and his mission. After thousands of years, many had forgotten the mysterious Lady of Evergreen. Some presumed she was simply a legend. Some believed that she was still there, secretly living a life of solitude away from all that threatened her realm. However, Thanan recalled his lessons with Kilian- his teachings about her power over nature; being able to create life from the invisible elements around her. That she was old and wise.

And so, Thanan of Jin entered her realm, alone.

My prison of blackness does not bother me much anymore. I am

comfortable in my solitude. The droning sounds that engulf me are now my comforting companions. As I think about my time in the caves, my experiences in the darkness, they showed me that absolute darkness is not the absence of light, but rather the absence of hope. My brother, Agrinoth, taught me that.

Ryan Logan is the author of the *First Life* fantasy series. He lives in the foothills outside Sacramento, California with his wife, five children, three rats and one cat.